T0130530

ALSO BY KATE WENNER

*Shamba Letu*

KATE WENNER

# Setting Fires

Scribner

NEW YORK  LONDON  TORONTO  SYDNEY  SINGAPORE

SCRIBNER
1230 Avenue of the Americas
New York, NY 10020

SCRIBNER and design are trademarks of Macmillan Library Reference USA, Inc.,
used under license by Simon & Schuster, the publisher of this work.

Designed by Brooke Koven
Text set in Adobe Janson

Manufactured in the United States of America

1   3   5   7   9   10   8   6   4   2

Library of Congress Cataloging-in-Publication Data
Wenner, Kate.
Setting fires/Kate Wenner.
p. cm.
1. Jewish families—Fiction. 2. Fires and fire prevention—Fiction.
3. Anti-Semitism—Fiction. 4. Arson—Fiction. I. Title.

PS3573.E55 S48 2000
813'.54—dc21
99–089602

ISBN 978-1-4767-9074-9

*For Gil, Jake, and Sophie,*
*who bring endless love and laughter into my life*

Self-deceit is a strong fort.
It will last a lifetime.
Self-truth is a lightning bolt lost as I grasp it.
And the fires that it grasps can raze my house.

You ask me to yearn after truth, Lord,
But who would choose to be whipped with fire?

Unless in the burning there can be great light,
Unless the lightning that strikes terror
Lights enough to show the boundaries
Where terror ends,
And at the limits, still enduring and alive,
Shows me myself
And a hope no longer blind.

—Mahzor for Rosh Hashanah and Yom Kippur,
A PRAYER BOOK FOR THE DAYS OF AWE

# Setting Fires

One

# 1

Two fires taught me lessons about my life, two fires separated by nearly six decades. The second fire was mine, but the first was my father's, and it happened in 1931, when he was fourteen years old.

My father, Abraham David Fishman, was a short boy with large dark eyes, a Buster Brown haircut, skinny arms, and bowlegs. He was the youngest of four children living in a dreary, two-room apartment on Flatbush Avenue in Brooklyn. Abie's father was long dead. Abie's mother was a walnut-faced woman with the shape of a fireplug, who pursued her small family's survival with brutal tenacity. It had taken Minnie Fishman—an immigrant from Russia—three decades in America to reach the pinnacle of all her hopes: her own dry goods shop stocked with everything from bolts of fabric to ladies' undergarments.

There had been other fires in Minnie Fishman's stores, but they were a dim and mostly forgotten part of young Abie's experience. The fire that changed his life, the one that became indelible, took place on Christmas Eve, a night of plummeting temperatures before a dusting snow.

As usual, Abie was helping his mother and sister in the store. Even though they were Jews (by birth, if not by practice), Christmas was an important season for the Fishmans, a time to sell to the Italian immigrants who had moved into the neighborhood. Because of the holiday they had been busy sorting and organizing merchandise until midnight. As they prepared to lock up, Minnie ordered Abie to bring in the empty cardboard boxes he had stacked in the alley that morning. Abie didn't understand why his sister, Fanny, older by five years, was pulling the paper stuffing from the boxes and spreading it across the floor. Or why Fanny and Minnie were whispering. Or why they ran out to hush him up when he whistled a John Philip Sousa march as he cranked up the awning.

At home, two short blocks away, Abie and Fanny were hurried into bed. Their mother pretended she had been sleeping when the police came pounding at the door. Terrible news: Her dry goods shop was blazing. The Fishmans ran back up the street they had just come down. Abie saw the yellow-orange flames flicking through the broken windows. The new snow touched his eyelids.

Minnie Fishman wailed in despair, holding her head between her hands and rocking it back and forth as if to deny the awful thing that was happening to her. The Irish policemen nodded in sympathy. The poor Widow Fishman. To think of such bad luck at Christmastime.

Minnie Fishman was an expert at self-induced fainting. She crumpled right on the spot, and the policemen shooed everyone away so they could minister to the fallen widow. Unnoticed, my father stepped back into the protective shadows of the night. He felt the heat, and when he smelled the oddly familiar stench of burning cotton, the scrim of childhood lifted. At fourteen, Abie Fishman was now old enough to see clearly. As the flames grew and destroyed all of Minnie Fishman's unsold and insured merchandise, the drama that formed my father's character, the story of his life, began.

My fire happened fifty-six years later. At that time I did not know about his fire. I'm sure that in a way he didn't really know about it either. My father had dedicated himself to leaving his past behind. He had been a poor boy, and now he was a wealthy man. Doggedly he had used his wits and his will, tackled life's adversities, and won. He had gained the trust and admiration of other wealthy men who turned their money over to him so he could double and triple its value in real estate investments. He protected their profits with clever foresight and a rigorous manipulation of the federal tax codes. He did not break laws, but he found the gray areas where interpretation could be argued. My father knew he was smart, and he relished his intelligence. Sometimes he would muse proudly about how we peripatetic Jews had developed our splendid brain pool by constantly having to pull up stakes and move on with nothing but the cargo between our ears. At other times, in a less sanguine mood, when a cranky antagonism overcame him, Abe Fishman would explain that the reason he had resolutely turned his back on his Jewish roots was because the words "Jew" and "poor" were synonymous to him.

The date of my fire was October 4, 1987. When I got the call, I was working in my eighth-story office, the back half of a converted loft in the Tribeca section of downtown New York. From that perch, where I had a sliver of a view of the Hudson River, I ran my own small documentary production company, which had won a respectable number of awards for programs that investigated injustices done to women and children. That was my niche.

I could never manage to eat much before the sun went down, so during the daylight hours caffeine kept me going. The phone call came at eleven-thirty in the morning, about the time I had finished my third cup of coffee. A neighbor who lived a quarter of a mile down the road from our country home, a small farmhouse in the town of Brookford, Connecticut, had spotted smoke pouring from our chimney. Maybe it was only something wrong with the furnace, but to be on the safe side she had summoned the fire department.

I telephoned the house, hoping to talk with the firemen as soon as they arrived, but each time I dialed, the phone was busy. I called the operator. She put me on hold while she checked the line. I stared at the second hand on my watch as I waited for her return. In a minute and forty-two seconds she was back. Our phone line had shorted out. I might want to call the local fire department to have them go over and take a look. Just a precaution, she assured me. Better to feel secure.

Panicked, I called my husband, Josh. At eleven-thirty in the morning he'd be holed up in his cubby in a corner of the newsroom of *The New York Times* poring over the pile of photographs that were under consideration for the next edition of the newspaper. Josh's job was to select the pictures of the politicians, heroes, and criminals that illustrated *The Times* each morning. He would have preferred to be the one taking the photographs, but the truth was his temperament was more suited to coping with the frenetic pace of the newsroom than it was to being out on the streets of the city battling other newspaper photographers for the best shot.

"The house in the country might be on fire," I said quickly, getting in the crucial information before he could bark at me for calling.

"Annie, I've got to get into the front page meeting."

"Josh, did you hear me?"

My second line was ringing. I put Josh on hold while I picked it up. It was our neighbor, confirming that indeed there was a fire. At that very moment our beloved country house, the place that had depleted our small savings nine years back, the run-down Colonial we had joyfully restored to its original simplicity, the peaceful retreat where we had brought our children when they were newborn babies—our home and refuge from New York City life—was burning out of control.

Three hours later (an hour for Josh to meet his photo deadlines and two hours for us to drive northeast at a terrifying speed) Josh and I fell silent as we rode up the last hill to our house. I had been biting my cuticles raw for the last hour of the drive, and now I dropped my smarting hand over Josh's as he shifted into a lower gear. He did not look away from the road, but he opened his long fingers to enclose mine.

Pickup trucks lined the road in front of our house. They belonged to the local men who coped with town emergencies—the men who manned the town ambulance, drove snowplows and salt trucks through frigid winter nights, put out fires. These men would come at any time of day or night to pull a neighbor's car out of a snowbank or to ferry a child with a broken arm thirty miles to the nearest hospital, accepting only a handshake for thanks. We always sent our donations to the volunteer fire department, the ambulance service, the town recreation committee. We enjoyed the contact we had with these men, all Brookford year-round residents, but we generally saw them only when we needed some help with electricity or plumbing, or when we went into town to do errands. Even though they had certainly fought for our house with the same ready courage they would have used to protect their own homes, we were not at all prepared for the sudden intimacy of having them move through our bedrooms with hoses.

From a hundred yards off, we still saw no signs of a fire, but as we closed in, the blackened and broken windows looked like hollow eyes. Exploded sofas, scorched chairs, soaked mattresses, burnt sheets and blankets, were strewn across the vibrant green lawn, and the white clapboard siding showed black plumes where the smoke had seeped from within.

The fire had been extinguished, but a handful of firemen had remained behind to be sure no hidden cinder reignited the flames. It had rained briefly, and the rising smoke, driven back down by the mist, became a film of soot that covered the lawn, the house, everything. We stepped across the moat of broken glass and up to a kitchen door that was no more. The town fire marshal, Norman Jukes, and a man who introduced himself as "Eddie Shank, the fellow the insurance company sent to help you out," dropped back to let us go on alone—the bereaved making our first inspection of the ravaged corpse.

The house was a dark cave. Water dripped from the ceiling, down charred walls, forming obsidian pools on the floor. The smells were powerful—acrid smoke, melted plastic, burned wool. As we stepped ahead I remembered once traveling down deep into a coal mine and the feeling of sinking into earth, falling farther and farther away from light and breathable air. That's what it felt like now as I stepped into my blackened home. My eyes were watery with shock, not tears. My throat constricted around a filament of breath. I started to shiver uncontrollably. Josh took my hand and held it hard.

The fire had been halted just short of the kitchen that formed the south end of our house. Cooking was one of our favorite family activities each weekend. Josh made pie crusts and fresh pasta with our two children; I made soups and stews, since I was only good at cooking things in which the careful measurement of ingredients didn't matter. Now the kitchen looked like the inside of an abandoned backwoods shack that had been left neglected for years. The pine cabinets were blistered and cracked. Threads of soot hung from the ceiling. The floor was piled with sodden bedclothes that had been pulled off the mattresses as they were carried out to the lawn.

The children's playroom was directly above the kitchen. It was the only other room the flames had spared. Josh and I stopped at the top of the stairs to stare at the strange scene that looked like a fairy tale in which toys had been granted a few minutes of life and then frozen in midaction. The intense heat had stretched Barbie's plastic arms, which seemed to reach out for love. He-Man's bulbous muscles had bubbled up and then collapsed to flab. The Fisher-Price tape recorder had cracked open and disgorged a spaghetti of brown tape.

Then I saw the wall covered with our children's drawings. At the center were the self-portraits they had drawn the previous Saturday afternoon. Eli and Hannah had stretched out on the playroom floor on long sheets of white butcher paper while Josh and I traced around their small bodies with red markers. Kneeling above their outlines, they industriously crayoned in the details of their imagined selves. Seven-year-old Eli, who was lanky like Josh and had his unruly black hair, had turned himself into an astronaut. Nine-year-old Hannah had made herself into an Olympic gymnast, complete with a red-white-and-blue leotard and a gold medal hanging around her neck. Hannah took after me in looks and temperament. We were wiry, small-boned, with frizzy, straw-colored hair, and we were both edgy by nature.

Josh and I walked up to these two life-sized portraits. Ragged black tributaries ran through them where the built-up heat within the walls had seared the paper. It was a terrifying vision of what could have happened to our children had we been sleeping in the house when the fire broke out. I pressed my hand across my mouth to keep myself from moaning.

"You were lucky, Mrs. Waldmas." The insurance man came up behind me and slid his arm around my shaking shoulders. "I've gone into houses where the children were lying dead in their beds." I quickly pulled away from him. I had never met Eddie Shank or seen his pockmarked face before.

Beyond the playroom, the section of the house that had contained our bedrooms was a gaping hole. The remaining, singed ends of the thick eighteenth-century beams were like amputated stumps. We lifted our eyes to the wide opening in the roof above. Soft rain drifted in and wet our faces. We peered down three stories to the mounds of burned debris collected in the basement. The fire marshal, joining our slogging inspection, pointed his flashlight into the darkness below. "There was a short in your basement wiring. Should always have the wiring checked in an old house. That's the thing, isn't it? Electricity's a force of nature."

"The trouble is, people don't like to think they're sleeping in a tinderbox," Eddie Shank chimed in. He was wearing a blue satin baseball cap, which he pushed back. One of his front teeth had a gold cap, and he ran the tip of his tongue over it.

Norman Jukes went on, "City folks buy themselves a nice place to escape to in the country and never imagine it can bring them troubles. By the time I'm on the scene, sorry to say, it's too late to take the necessary precautions."

I folded my arms and pulled them in tight against my ribs. My muscles ached from cold and lack of breath. The gray afternoon was still wet, both inside and outside our blackened house, and I had not stopped shivering. I would have liked to lean into Josh, to find comfort against his long body, but Josh was standing at a calculated distance. I suppose he knew instinctively that this wasn't a moment to reveal too much of ourselves.

"Was that what caused Shelly's fire? Was his fire electrical, too?" Josh asked. Shelly Weiss owned a small sandwich shop and bakery, the Brookford Café, one of the few businesses our small town could support. Just over two weeks back, in a fire that raged before dawn, Shelly's place had burned to its cement foundation.

"Still lookin' into that," Jukes said. "That one's still under investigation." It was clear he deemed it professionally inappropriate to offer anything more.

"I see," Josh said. "Shelly had a fire, we had a fire."

I studied my husband. Shelly Weiss was the only Jewish merchant in Brookford, and as far as we knew, we were one of the only Jewish families. Was Josh looking for a connection?

Norman Jukes must have realized what Josh was thinking. "Come on down to the basement, Mr. Waldmas," Jukes suggested. "I'll show you where the copper wires fused from the electrical short. It's pretty straightforward once you see it."

I followed behind the three of them as they set out on their mission. They climbed over rubble that had fallen when the floors above collapsed, then bent their necks to get a view of what remained of the basement ceiling, where the scorched electrical wires were still tacked in place.

There it was, the evidence of our neglect. Two frayed ends hung down from the spot where the copper wires had melted through the insulation. Norman Jukes showed Josh how they had fused into small, hard lumps. The only thing that could cause that sort of copper fusion, he explained, was the extreme heat of a short circuit—the same powerful heat that would ignite a fire.

"See how the short burned the basement ceiling right above it?" Jukes pointed to where the basement stairs had been. "Stairwell makes a natural draw, like a chimney. Sucks the fire right up through the house, where there's plenty of fuel to keep it going. Once the heat blows out the windows, the oxygen comes in and the fire builds fast. Bad luck the short wasn't down there further." He tipped his head back toward the garage door. "Wouldn't have had such a natural draw the way it did with the stairs right here. That's the way it is with fires. Luck always has its part, good or bad."

I watched as the three men shook their heads, commiserating for a moment over the powerful combination of nature and bad luck. As the afternoon waned and grew colder, our future felt colder, too. I could see ahead to an exhausting project of insurance negotiations, cleaning, reconstruction. For a moment we were all silent in the dripping cold of the basement. The only sound I registered was my own teeth chattering, like a relentless windup toy.

In spite of our shock and disorientation, we were obliged to discuss the insurance claim procedures with Eddie Shank. "I'm the adjuster assigned to your calamity," he told us now. "From here on in, you work with me." He instructed us on how we were to "secure" our house before leaving "the premises." Any vandalism or further damage that occurred because we failed to take the correct precautions could invalidate our policy. Once he received the fire marshal's written report, he would contact us and inform us of our next steps.

"That's it?" I asked. "We just wait?"

"You don't give us some sort of check here to get us started?" Josh asked.

Eddie Shank smiled. "You watch too much TV."

It was dark and well into the evening by the time, with the help of a couple of the volunteer firemen, we had boarded over the broken windows and doors with plywood we purchased from the local lumberyard. Our fingers were numb and our faces black when we finally climbed back into our car and set out for New York. I thought about Hannah and Eli, who would be getting ready for bed about then. That morning I had hastily arranged to have the college student who picked them up from school most afternoons stay with them until we got back. I had instructed her to say nothing about the fire. Now I wondered how I would tell them what had happened to our house, to their bedrooms, their toys, their drawings.

We drove on into the cheerless night without even a crescent moon to light our way. Cold and fear had stiffened every muscle in my body, and I pulled the children's blankets from the backseat and wrapped up in them, drawing myself into a tight ball, my knees to my chest. I was still in a state of shock, and for many miles I couldn't think or talk. Josh was silent, too.

Eventually, as the heat in the car warmed me, I settled into the mental work of trying to put the day's events into some kind of perspective. I tried to make myself focus on the thought that however horrible it was, we had seen the worst of it. We had already begun to make things better—boarded up the house, begun our dealings with the insurance adjuster. I reasoned that was the best way to see it, a thousand small steps we would have to take to get back to where we started. In time the frightening images would fade from mind. Though the fire had caused enormous damage to our home, we were all safe. That was the truly important thing. But with that thought fear came back—what if we'd been there when the flames broke out? And then another fear—what if we *hadn't* seen the worst of it? What if there was more to this fire than we knew at this point? Finally I couldn't keep silent anymore about the question that was sitting like a bear between us.

"Do you believe it could really be possible?"

"What, Annie?"

"Arson. That somebody actually set that fire."

Josh scowled. Even the question made him angry.

I pressed on. "Not just arson—anti-Semitic arson. That's why you were questioning Jukes, wasn't it?"

"Two fires in two weeks, both Jewish property—the coincidence is pretty hard to miss."

"But here in Connecticut? It's unthinkable."

"Unthinkable? You thought it. I thought it. Clearly Jukes thought about it, too. He was awfully eager to show me that short."

"But there *was* a short."

"Yes, that's what it looked like."

"That wasn't enough for you."

"Annie, I don't know anything about electricity and fire. All I know is that it's a pretty weird coincidence."

"But I love it in Brookford. Nothing like this could happen there."

Josh kept his eyes fixed on the dark highway ahead. He was tense, irritable. "We'll take things one step at a time."

"But it's our home. I don't want to leave it," I protested against what Josh was choosing to leave unsaid.

Nine years ago we had come upon our beloved, quiet town, set among dairy farms and apple and peach orchards, completely by accident. Our Volkswagen Bug broke down on Route 84, and we had to be towed off the highway by a wrecker. We ended up spending the night at a local bed-and-breakfast while we waited for a part to be trucked in the next day. In the morning, wandering around the village green, we noticed a bulletin board with a small card offering a "fixer-upper" on the outskirts of town for an unbelievably low price. With nothing else to do while we waited for our car, we phoned the broker and were driven out to see the place. The house had been abandoned for several years, and the owner was willing to accept almost any offer we could manage. We called our bank in New York, asked them to transfer our savings into our checking account, and wrote out a check on the spot. It was an impulsive move, but I was pregnant with Hannah, and impulsivity fit our frame of mind. Later we learned that a small group of wealthy Boston Brahmin families owned land on the eastern end of town, but they kept to themselves around their large private lake down a long dirt road, and we never met any of them. Eventually we did meet a few other young New York couples who, like us, had stumbled onto adjacent towns and fallen in love with the isolation of this distant corner of northeastern Connecticut. As the years went by and our lives in New York got ever more harried making a living and taking care of our growing children, the house in Brookford became our treasured escape.

The night closed in around us. I studied Josh's grim, soot-smudged face, and decided not to point out that he was driving too fast. I was sure he was still thinking about the possibility of an arson motivated by anti-Semitism. Though Josh was resolutely secular, he was deeply convinced of the vulnerability of all Jews, a worldview inherited from his father, Józef Isaiah Waldmaski of Lódz, Poland.

Józef had been a photojournalist in Poland during the 1930s as the Nazis rose to power and encouraged Polish Catholics to give free rein to their long-standing anti-Semitism. The Catholics were particularly resentful because Jews were leaving their shtetls and crowding the Polish cities. Józef's passion was taking portraits of these forward-thinking Jews, who were willing to tackle the twentieth century and were making important contributions in the arts, academia, medicine, and music. His photographs appeared weekly in the Lódz newspaper *Lodzher togblat,* until one night an angry mob of Catholics who hated the Jewish advances that Józef's photographs celebrated broke into his shop, stole his treasured photographs, and made them into a bonfire in the street. Six months later, depressed and bitter, Józef booked passage to America, where he became Joseph Waldmas and made an adequate living taking wedding photographs. When Hitler invaded Poland in 1939, the sister and mother Józef had left behind were rounded up and eventually joined the three million Polish Jews annihilated by the Nazis. Józef's message to his own children reflected his personal experience: There would have been no Hitler if there had been no willing accomplices; Jews must never let down their guard in a Gentile world.

"Josh, can I tell you something? The weekend when I drove into town and saw Shelly's café burned to the ground, the first thing that popped into my head was the fact that Shelly's Jewish, and that we're Jewish, too. I didn't tell you because I figured it was silly paranoia. It's not like I've ever felt the slightest bit of prejudice against us in Brookford. I'm sure people know we're Jewish, but I doubt it really matters to them."

"Of course it matters to them."

"But no one here is going to set fire to a house because the owners are Jewish."

"Why not?"

"Josh, sometimes you're such a New York Jew, seeing anti-Semitism lurking behind every bush."

"Weren't you the one who brought it up?"

"Then what if we find out it's true?"

Josh glanced over at me, and then turned back to the road. I knew he was sparing me the full force of his pessimism. We had already been through enough for one day.

"Josh?"

"We'd have to leave."

"I don't want to leave."

"You'd stay there knowing someone tried to burn your house down because you're Jewish?"

"Then I don't want to find out it's true," I answered petulantly. "I really don't want to know."

# 2

October was destined to be a month of bad news. Less than two weeks after our fire, I had an unsettling phone call from my father in California. My father and I were very close, and we talked almost daily. I knew his moods almost as well as I knew Josh's. After I hung up, I had a hunch he wasn't telling either himself or me the whole truth when he described the "minor medical procedure" scheduled for the following week. He said it had something to do with a pill he had taken that may have irritated his stomach lining and caused a small polyp that the doctors would have to remove. He announced that he was going off to his ski house in Mammoth for the weekend. "I'll be damned if I'll hang around L.A. all weekend waiting for them to jab me with their knives."

My father had been a single man for nearly thirty years, ever since my parents separated when I was twelve. There had been a hundred girlfriends, but none, as my father liked to say, was a "keeper." I was his oldest daughter. I knew about my father the kinds of things a wife knows about a husband—when his irritability was fear, and when a second phone call that same day to check on an idea for Eli's birthday present was the most he could manage in the way of a direct request for help.

"So what is this procedure exactly?" I asked.

"I don't know. They say it's no big deal, so I believe them."

"You sound a little worried."

"Naw." I could see him, three thousand miles away, pushing his hand through the air to put me off. I picked up a photograph from my desk. My father was carrying nine-month-old Eli in a backpack. They were both grinning.

"I can't wait to test out my new skis. Can you believe they've already got a foot of snow in October?"

"So we'll talk on Monday then."

"Monday, Tuesday—sometime next week when things quiet down."

"Maybe we'll talk on the weekend," I suggested.

"If you need me, you'll call me," he said, and abruptly hung up.

With a little hair dye at the temples, my father appeared to be a man of fifty-five and often lied about his age to his lady friends. But only a month before this suspicious phone call, my sister, my two brothers, and I had organized a grand family affair to celebrate his seventieth birthday.

Generally my siblings and I depended on our father to bring us all together, particularly since our mother had opted out of the maternal role shortly after their divorce, and had tended, ever since, to keep a protective distance from the family. Without our father's prodding I'm not sure my siblings and I would have gone out of the way to see much of one another. It wasn't only that we had settled in four different cities and were busy with our own lives. It was also that we had inherited some of both our parents' skittishness about intimacy. It took three months of phone calls to agree to hold my father's seventieth birthday party in Minneapolis, equal traveling distance for each of us.

Tony was the oldest in the family, and lived in San Diego near Sally and his three children. I came next, and Tony and I were the only ones who had produced grandchildren so far. Tony was a tough case himself; he had our father's short stature and brusque, prove-it-to-me demeanor. Professionally Tony had followed in Abe's footsteps and was bent on making himself rich as a real estate developer. My other brother, Charles, two years younger than me, was quite different from his older brother. Charles was strikingly good-looking, though it didn't mean much to him, and he was soft-spoken and innately gentle. Charles majored in forestry in college, and now worked for the Bureau of Land Management monitoring logging on public lands. He had married two years ago, and he and his wife, Sissy, lived in Washington, D.C., where Sissy worked as a public school teacher. My sister, Ellen, the youngest in the family, was the most distant from the rest of us, and the most private about her life. Ellen ran a center for women students at the University of Colorado. She was a solitary soul, a jogger, a hiker, and a cross-country skier. She had Charles's good looks, but she was still single at thirty-six, since she seemed to share our mother's view that for women marriage led to misery.

We rented rooms at the Minneapolis Hyatt and took the hotel's small private dining room for the birthday dinner. Though there were only the four of us and our families, we dressed to the nines to please Abe, a man who was not easy to impress. Ellen had tracked down a string quartet from the Minneapolis Conservatory of Music to play a baroque rendition of "Happy Birthday," and we all chipped in on a beautiful silver picture frame because the surprise and highlight of the celebration was to be a photo shoot in which all of Abe Fishman's progeny would gather around him. Though he wasn't convinced that any one of us truly loved him, we were his pride and purpose in this latter stage of his life.

On the night of his party we gave Abe the silver frame and told him to show up in the lobby the following morning at 8 A.M. Tony pulled up in a rented van, and we piled in and drove across the river to the factory district of St. Paul. We had gotten spruced up for the photographs, and my father had dressed up, too. Clearly he had pried the basic information out of one of us. While he liked the intention of a surprise, he was deeply uncomfortable whenever he did not know exactly what was coming.

We rode up a clanging service elevator and stepped into a loft equipped with tiers of professional lights, rolls of colored backdrops, a female assistant dressed in black spandex, a makeup artist, and a hairdresser. The photographer we had hired generally did advertising shoots, and we had asked him to treat my father as one of his best clients. A linen cloth had been spread over a long table. There were pitchers of fresh orange juice, platters of bagels and lox, and an iced magnum of champagne. My father's eyes widened, and then he smiled.

Abe Fishman liked fine things, discreet signs of wealth, things done "right." He had schooled himself in California wines, European holidays, and the likes and dislikes of wealthy women who wore small jewels. As he calmly watched the flurry of activity, he looked supremely natty. He was a small man, tight-muscled, compact, and always tan. He favored leather vests, freshly pressed open-collared shirts, and immaculately creased slacks. He never wore suits, and he never wore a tie. He carried a thin wallet in the breast pocket of his vest, and in it there were always five crisp one-hundred-dollar bills. He was a man who paid his own way and generally picked up the tab, no matter who his guest or what the occasion. My father did not wish to be beholden to anyone. He habitually summed up any new situation and placed himself in charge of it, scanning the scene for whatever he needed to master, new information to store, mechanical or financial things he could study, dissect, command. My father had a speedy mind. He could do *The New York Times* crossword puzzle in the time it took an ordinary mortal to tie his shoes. He had two favorite pieces of personal wisdom of which he reminded us constantly: "Fortune favors the prepared mind," and "Every crisis is an opportunity." He had both sayings printed and inserted into Chinese fortune cookies, and he kept a glass bowl of the cookies on his living room coffee table for unsuspecting guests.

It was quite a trick to get five squirming grandchildren to stay still long enough to please the photographer, who was used to dealing with professional models and inanimate bowls of vegetable soup. In the end it was that very lack of control that made the photograph so wonderful. Before each flash of the strobe, one grandchild or another would wrap an arm or leg around some parent or aunt or uncle, taking possession or getting ballast, indifferent to the perfectly balanced family fresco the photographer envisioned.

And there stood Abe Fishman, the pint-sized patriarch, at the very center of it all, delighted to have all this life around him. He knew we were not perfect, that we had our marital difficulties, and that we harbored doubts about him and about each other. He didn't point out our faults or demand that we be different. He never had. He had confidence that we would work out the difficulties of our lives in due time. He wished for our happiness, that we be good parents, that we do better at living peaceful lives than he had done. Abe Fishman worked hard for his outward appearance of calm, but he knew—and we knew—that inside, where his blood pulsed, he was a relentlessly driven man. He had enough self-knowledge to recognize that such drive and whatever was behind it weren't necessarily good for health or marriage. He had his mantra for us, "Be happy, be yourselves." The truth was that we had all inherited some of his relentless drive.

The family photograph was in my mind's eye as I dialed my father's internist and longtime friend, Max Greenberg. My father invested Max's money in successful real estate ventures; Max took care of my father's insides. Max came to the phone right away, leaving a patient waiting in his examining room. I told him about my conversations with my father and my fear that the little "polyp" he described was something more serious than he was letting on. Max was relieved to get my call and to allow me to persuade him to break his promise of secrecy to my father. I was the old-est daughter, after all, and Abe had no wife; under the circumstances my father's request to keep the information a secret from me was simply not reasonable.

As I suspected, Max Greenberg was concerned about cancer. My father had come in complaining about stomach pains and difficulty swal-lowing. Max had ordered a preliminary endoscopy, which revealed suspi-cious lesions in the lower esophagus. They biopsied the tissue, but the results were inconclusive. To know for sure Max had insisted on a second, deeper endoscopy to discover whether there might be a stomach tumor. By Monday, when my father returned from his weekend skiing, he would be told definitively whether what they found was benign or malignant. If it turned out to be malignant, a surgeon would cut open my father's stom-ach on Tuesday morning at dawn.

"I'm sorry, Annie," Max said. He had known me since I was a teenager. "It's a damned lousy situation."

I got on the phone right away to my three siblings to tell them what I had learned, and for the rest of the evening the phone calls flew across the country as the four of us discussed what we should do. Each one of us commented that it was lucky we'd had the birthday party and taken the photograph. We puzzled over the questions that faced us: Would he be more comfortable imagining we didn't know? Should we fly to him imme-diately? Why hadn't he told us the truth?

My father professed himself to be ruthlessly truthful. Though he was "creative" in business and tax matters, he never cheated. In fact, it some-times appeared that good and evil were polarized in his mind with almost religious fervor. According to his personal ethic, he was a man to be trusted, a man who rigorously resisted the ever-present temptation to pocket that extra little bit of uncounted profit that was routine in real estate. If real estate was his vocation, this was his avocation: to prove he was a moral man.

On Sunday night I telephoned my father to say I was flying out to Los Angeles the next day to be there in case it turned out he had to have the operation on Tuesday.

"What operation?"

"To take your—" I paused, then decided to use his word, "polyp," instead of my word, "tumor." "To take your polyp out."

"You mean the test?"

"Pop, Max says it's an operation."

"You spoke to Max? He took your call?"

"People care about you, Pop. I care about you. Anyway, I'm coming. I spoke to Ellen. She's coming out, too."

"Ellen?"

"Sure, Pop. She wants to be with you, same as me."

On the flight from New York to California I listened to the Jupiter Symphony on my headset and cried. As promised, Max Greenberg had called that morning with the test results. The tumor was malignant. The flight attendant passed by several times, checking to see if I was all right. I suppose flight attendants are used to people crying on airplanes on their way to sickness, death, funerals. The problem was I had let myself be tricked by my father's youthful appearance into imagining he was immortal. Sometimes, sensing the fragility of my denial, I would force myself to contemplate the idea of his death, but it was beyond my comprehension, impossible.

Perhaps one reason my feelings for my father were so intense was because of my mother's deep antipathy to being depended on by anybody. When the last of us went off to college, she marked it as the day of her emancipation and commemorated it each year by sending Mother's Day cards to all four of us, a joke I didn't think was funny. Once we were all gone, she moved into a small cottage overlooking the ocean in Laguna Beach and spent her days painting the seascape until she achieved a measure of fame as a local watercolorist. She was happy at last, now that her days weren't complicated by demands. Her visits to her children and grandchildren came in short, semiannual bursts. She could take just so much human interaction before she had to return to the isolation of her life, like a Peruvian Indian who lives at high altitudes in the Andes, and can stay for only short visits at sea level before the oxygen-rich air begins to kill him. My mother used her answering machine to screen all her calls, on the pretext that she was engrossed in her painting. The truth was that she needed to prepare herself to talk with people. The only way to get in touch with her was to leave a message and wait for a call back. Dutifully, I had telephoned to tell her about my father's malignant tumor. My parents hadn't lived together for twenty-eight years—it had probably been a dozen years since they had seen each other or spoken—but, still, I felt she would want to know this news that would deeply affect the children and grandchildren they shared. Following the prescribed drill, I left a message on her phone machine and was taken by surprise when she returned my call within minutes. She wanted to know all the details, but I barely knew much myself.

"He never smoked or anything," she said.

"Mom, it's stomach cancer, not lung cancer."

"He always had a nervous stomach."

"Ellen and I are going to L.A. to be with him."

"Good, good. I wish I could be there myself."

"We'll let you know how it goes."

"I guess I shouldn't call him."

"Not right now."

"Let me know if I can help in any way."

"Sure, Mom."

When I hung up I had to talk myself down from the call, as always. It was easy to get tricked into thinking she really would go out of her way to help in some way. I suppose she wanted to believe that herself. But I knew that the moment she hung up, any such impulse would disappear.

I suppose my determination to be a different kind of mother from my own was what had made me glum on Monday when I had to say good-bye to Hannah and Eli and tell them I was uncertain when I would return.

"Can't Grandma take care of him?" Eli asked.

"Honey, you know they haven't lived together in years."

"But Grandpa's sick," Eli protested, knowing, as he always seemed to, the essential right and wrong of things.

"And that's why I have to go take care of him," I said, skirting the issue.

Hannah folded her arms. "Why can't Aunt Ellen go stay with him? She doesn't have kids she's supposed to take care of."

"Honey, I'm not going only because he needs someone to stay with him. I want to be there with him. He's my father and I love him."

"More than us?" she demanded, her frizzy hair backlit by the low sun as she stood on the sidewalk watching Josh put my suitcase into a cab.

"You know that's a silly question."

Her eyes filled, and I pulled her to me. We held tight, two bony bodies, until Eli pried us apart for a hug of his own. I climbed into the taxi, and Josh drew the children close to him. As they waved good-bye, I pressed my face to the window, watching even after I couldn't see them anymore.

My father was waiting at the same United Airlines gate where he had awaited my arrival a hundred times over the years. He kissed me and took my backpack, and we walked the long blue-and-yellow-tiled corridor to the baggage claim. We had made this walk each time I returned from some adventure or from college, or, as now, when I visited him from my own home three thousand miles away. Usually he was the one checking me for changes, but now I studied him and saw that he was already much thinner than he had been in Minneapolis a month ago.

"Hard to eat with this damned thing irritating my stomach," he said when he caught me examining him.

I wondered how to let him know I knew about his cancer. Of his four children, I was the one to whom he was most likely to confide his worries. After all, I was the one who had always mediated family matters when our mother was no longer interested. Many times I had maneuvered my proud and defensive father back onto speaking terms with one of his children as we all battled our way out of adolescence to adulthood.

My father and I were side by side with our eyes fixed on other people's luggage going round the carousel.

"So, how are you feeling about tomorrow?"

He cocked his head the way he did when he presented business options to investors.

"Two possibilities. I'm going to live or I'm going to die. We'll find out."

It was a relief to me that this first bit of truth emerged so simply. Later, when I looked back on those early days, I saw the way truth has its own geology. It's like a pool of black oil that flows to an open pocket formed in layers of rock. It lies there for a while, spreading slowly, seeking a new crack to seep through. Then it penetrates farther, to another layer of rock that holds and keeps it until a new fissure is found. And then it moves again.

My father drove us north on the San Diego Freeway in his silver Porsche, a prized possession. He liked control, and he liked driving. He was never, ever at ease as a passenger in anyone's car.

"I called Josh after you left, to check your flight time. He told me he's considering hiring a private fire investigator to look at your house." My father knew our initial worries about arson.

"He's not completely confident in the fire marshal's report," I said casually, not wanting to give away my irritation at Josh's ploy of trying to enlist my father on his side of the argument we'd been having. To me, the fear of anti-Semitism seemed a bit ridiculous in the light of day. Brookford was an idyllic New England village, not some backwater Mississippi town. My concern was getting the insurance settlement resolved as quickly as possible so we could start rebuilding.

"Second opinions are always good," my father advised. "It'll cost you a couple of hours, maybe a couple of hundred dollars, but you'll get some peace of mind."

"Everyone has assured us that the town fire marshal knows his stuff. They say electrical fires are pretty common in these old New England houses. We were foolish not to redo all the wiring when we remodeled the kitchen. Unfortunately, it didn't occur to us at the time."

"You ought to rule out arson," my father persisted in the bossy tone that always succeeded in putting me on edge.

"It's been ruled out by the fire marshal."

"You don't want to let something slide because it might be upsetting."

"I'm an adult, Pop. I can handle this."

We drove on in an irritated silence until I said, "By the way, I called Mom to tell her about your operation."

He looked away from the road to me. "Why the hell did you do that?"

"I thought she'd want to know."

"Why?"

"Maybe because she's our mother—maybe because she used to be married to you—"

"I don't want to hear this," he said, turning back to the highway.

Ellen arranged for someone to step in for her and run the women's center for the week, and she arrived in Los Angeles later that evening. That night the three of us sat out on my father's patio at the top of Beverly Glen within a stone's throw of the winding ribbon of Mulholland Drive. We lay on wooden chaises, and the air was clear and warm as we looked out at the jeweled Los Angeles landscape. We had turned off the patio lights so we could see the stars, and the darkness let us talk.

We spoke of small subjects and big ones, putting aside for the night the strains in our relationships. Ellen and Abe had always been ill at ease with each other because Ellen had chosen to side with our mother's view of why the marriage didn't work, blaming my father for his obsession with work and money. I had taken our father's view of things, that my mother's self-centeredness had made it impossible to be married to her. Those allegiances had defined the terrain of our family life. Perhaps because he lived the closest to our mother, Tony tended to line up with Ellen. Charles, who lived on the East Coast, generally lined up with me. Ellen often patronized what she regarded as my boring choice of a middle-class family life, husband and two children, though I knew she envied it as well. Even though she had sided with our mother, she was jealous about the inevitable result—that our father trusted me more.

The upsetting news of his cancer diagnosis had pushed aside these old tensions, at least for now. We laughed at my father's corny jokes and dreadful puns, and we ate chocolate ice cream straight from the Häagen-Dazs container, passing a silver spoon back and forth. At midnight we still weren't sleepy. Why sleep when time was newly precious? My father put his hands behind his head and talked about his life, his pride in his children and grandchildren, his business successes, his ability even at seventy to ski from the moment the lift opened until it stopped in the afternoon. He wanted to build an addition onto his ski house so all of us could come at the same time. He had loved the reunion in Minneapolis.

"I've been considering letting that young fellow I took in deal with more of the day-to-day business. He's a Brooklyn boy, like your old man here, a real *Yiddishe kopf*. Of course I'll still keep a tight rein on things, but the point is I won't have to go in so often. I've put that off too long. At last, I'll have some real time to myself."

"That sounds good," I said encouragingly, but I was struck by the plaintive sound of what he'd said. He rarely spoke of his regrets.

Around one in the morning, knowing we had to leave for the hospital at seven, I suggested we get some sleep. At the sliding glass door, my father put his arms around us. "I'm glad you kids came out, though you really didn't need to disrupt your lives." He hugged us a little harder than usual. "You two are really something, traveling all this way for me."

Over the next months there were a number of specific moments when one detail would predict what lay ahead. The moment would stand out so starkly that it commanded both attention and an internal process of adjustment to the change. The first of those moments was watching my father wheeled away on a gurney, the metal sides pulled up as if he were a baby in a crib. I held his hand until we got to the chrome-plated swinging doors, the gleaming portal to the miracles of medical science. This was where we would have to leave him, to trust him to the efficient orderlies in pale green hospital garb. But we were our father's daughters—we trusted no one.

He had been telling us jokes and making us laugh while we waited in the prep room for his turn to go. When they came to wheel him out, he still commanded authority, instructing the orderlies about the angle they needed to get the gurney through the narrow door. But out in the hall, when the orderlies lowered the head of the gurney and my father lay flat, his arms already pierced with needles, he tightened his lips and went silent. I loved him in that shocking moment, when I saw him vulnerable as never before. I thought of a photograph he had taped to his dressing mirror: He is a young boy standing on the beach at Coney Island. His blue jeans are rolled above his knees, the sleeves of his shirt are rolled above his elbows. One arm is bent behind his back, his fingers gripping the other arm, which hangs down beside him. He's smiling, an easy, contented smile. His hair is combed over his forehead, touching down between his bushy eyebrows. His eyes burn as bright as embers.

We waited for hours in the family room at the hospital. I paced, read back issues of *People*, traded uninformed predictions with Ellen. The tension of waiting put Ellen and me right back into our old relationship, cautious of each other, distant. I noticed that even though she was wearing sneakers, blue jeans, and a T-shirt like me, she managed to look put together and beautiful. She was tall and had our mother's high cheek-bones, smooth auburn hair, casually erect posture. I am short, frizzy-haired, a sloucher; jeans and a T-shirt make me look like a sloppy teenager. I wondered if my sloppiness would somehow affect my father's fate, give the message to the powers that be that I didn't care enough. I scoured my mind for ways I could tip the balance back. I could promise to temper my awful habit of sarcasm. I could promise never to argue with Josh or be short-tempered with my children. But who was I making these promises to? With whom was I striking my bargain?

I watched Ellen flip the pages of her magazine and felt lonely. I calculated the time it was in New York, almost the end of Hannah and Eli's school day. Bonnie, their baby-sitter from Barnard College, would be standing in the huddle of adults waiting on the sidewalk for the children to be dismissed from P.S. 87. I let my mind alight on that moment, the anticipation I felt when I was the one waiting for the glass door to swing open. Even when I was tired or irritable, as soon as Hannah and Eli ran out and jumped on me for their hugs, I always felt restored, and I knew that no matter what kind of mother my own mother had been, it was past history and my own family was steeped in love. I'd walk home with my children up Amsterdam Avenue, past the Hispanic men camped out playing cards in front of bodegas, listening to salsa on small radios, as Hannah and Eli interrupted each other, overflowing with the indignities and triumphs of their day.

I tapped Ellen on the shoulder to tell her I was going to find a pay phone to call Josh. I wanted to ask him how things had gone that morning getting the kids out of the house and to school. And I was curious about whether he had reached Eddie Shank, the insurance adjuster. We had finally received his letter outlining the steps we had to take to pursue our claim. I had decided to ask Josh about whether he had done anything further about hiring an independent fire investigator. Though I had put my father off, his comment about letting upsetting things slide had stuck. Not that he couldn't be a master of denial himself. When my father didn't want to look at something, he could be as impenetrable as a Brink's truck.

As I waited for Josh to pick up, I checked myself in the dark reflection of the glass booth to see if I really looked as unattractive as I felt next to

Ellen. In the early morning as we hurried to leave for the hospital, I had clipped my hair back into a barrette. With my hair pulled away from my face like that, I looked like a fledgling sparrow. I unsnapped the barrette and flicked my hair free so the thick mass of it would hide me.

When Josh didn't answer, I left a message on his voice mail. "Waiting sucks."

It was four interminable hours before the surgeon appeared at the waiting room door. I saw him before he saw us; I saw him recompose his expression into cheerfulness.

He settled on the arm of the couch to give us his report, using the back of his prescription pad to take us through the steps of the procedure he had completed. He had peeled a "golf-ball-sized tumor" away from the posterior wall of "the stomach." (Did he mean my father's stomach or some lonely organ lying at his mercy on a chrome table?) He had detached the tumor from the lower esophagus, where it had lodged and was growing through. I imagined he was recalling the details of the surgical report he had dictated as he informed us that 65 percent of my father's stomach had been discarded. With the golf ball metaphor and the number 65, I had the nasty thought that this surgeon with his bronze tan was taking us blow by blow through the holes of a golf game. The surgeon said that, happily, he had been able to reattach the esophagus, which meant my father could continue to eat like a human, but, unhappily, the cancer might have already entered the nearby nodes. The nodes were "the body's subway stations." The cancerous cells could hop on a subway car, travel through the lymph system to any destination they chose, and then hop off again and multiply. Chemotherapy and radiation could help all that, the surgeon assured us as he concluded his presentation. He tucked his prescription pad back into his pocket and put a hand on each of our shoulders. "Your father is a lucky man to have two such beautiful daughters." Once he'd swung back through the doors that had delivered him, I replayed the first face I'd seen—his irritation that this one wasn't a winner, the almost imperceptible nod as he reminded himself that even a surgeon as great as he could do only so much if people came to him too late. Later on, when my father dubbed this coldhearted man "Dr. God," I understood his anger.

In the ICU Ellen and I stood on opposite sides of the gurney where our father lay with tubes going into his mouth and nose. His face was drawn in pain. His lips were as cracked as the dry earth I had once seen at the Dead Sea. At the sound of my voice, his eyes fluttered open momentarily. Around him clicking and sighing machines breathed on behalf of weary, cut-up bodies, including his own. Too many patients were crowded together, too many gurneys parked at scattered angles, leaving no room for privacy or pride.

I took a piece of ice from the pitcher beside his bed, and, asking his permission when he couldn't possibly answer, I put the ice to his lips and rubbed it there until a drop of water formed. I used my index finger to guide the drop through his parched lips. The corners of his mouth turned up slightly in relief. Was he relieved because I had met his need or because when he couldn't speak, I had heard him?

I knew that for my father's sake I must not show any sign of fear, though the sight of him so tubed up and utterly helpless was shocking. I didn't need to be upbeat—he would not ask that—but he did need to know that things were being managed. If he couldn't control the world, the next best person for the job would be a direct inheritor of his DNA.

I put my lips close to his ear. "I love you, Pop. You're doing fine." In my imagination I heard him ask the critical question—did it work out? Am I going to live? I took his hand from under the sheet and brought it to my cheek, once again seeing the young boy in the Coney Island photograph, the hopeful boy who had doggedly survived to become my father.

When he closed his eyes to sleep, I told Ellen I wanted to try to reach Josh again. She had already made the calls to our mother and two brothers. I left Ellen to watch over Abe in the ICU and went looking for a pay phone. By now Josh and the children would be home.

Hannah picked up on the first ring. Had she been standing guard for my call?

"It's Mommy!" she screamed like the town crier.

Eli came running, and I had to listen while they fought over the receiver. Josh picked up on another extension.

"How is he?"

"He's resting now," I said obliquely, knowing by the silence that either Hannah or Eli had won and was listening in. "The operation's over. It will be a few days before we know anything more."

"Are you coming home?" Eli asked.

"In a few days, honey. Grandpa sends you a big kiss. He wants you to make a drawing for his hospital room."

"I'll draw him and me on top of Mammoth Mountain."

"He'd like that. Ask Daddy to put it in the mail so Grandpa can get it right away. Now let me speak to Hannah. And remember how much I love you."

"As much as the number of drops of water in the ocean?"

"Even more than that."

Hannah took the phone and said, "I want to talk to Grandpa."

"He can't talk yet. But he asked me to tell you that he loved the poem you sent him about his birthday party. He put it in a frame. It's right on his desk."

"Did you tell him I'm going to be a poet when I grow up?"

"I certainly did, and he said he's sure you'll do it."

"I'm going to dedicate my first book to Grandpa since he always liked my poetry."

"Can I tell him that too when he wakes up?"

"Tell him it's not just because he's sick. I really mean it."

"I need to talk to Daddy now, Hannah. I'll talk to you tomorrow."

"You said you'd come home tomorrow."

"Hannah, you know I didn't."

She hung up the receiver without saying good-bye to make sure I knew she didn't like my answer.

"She sure knows how to push my buttons," I said to Josh.

"She'll survive."

"It doesn't look good for my father."

"What did they say?"

"We're waiting to get the report, but the doctor said the tumor had grown through the stomach wall. If it's in the nodes, it'll be in the liver in a matter of time."

"Does he know?"

"Not yet. I don't look forward to his reaction."

"Your father's a realist, Annie."

"This may be a little too real, even for him."

For two days he was in and out of consciousness, but every time he opened his eyes either Ellen or I was at his side. Sometimes the nurses sent us out of the ICU while they took advantage of his sleep to wash him and check his dressings; it would be a betrayal of his trust if they inadvertently let his daughters see his genitals while he was sleeping. Once, when he was awake but still kept mute by the plastic tubes, a nurse came in and asked me to step outside so she could check him. I got as far as the door when I felt a powerful yank on my mind, like a cane hooked around an actor's neck in a silent-movie comedy. My father had sent his thoughts directly into my cerebral cortex. Instantly I turned back. Unable to speak, he was asking—no, demanding—that I stay. "Pop, they want me to leave while they wash you. I'll be right outside the door. I won't go anywhere. Is that okay?" His eyes dropped as if he were considering whether this was good enough. Then he nodded, and I left to stand out in the hallway and take in yet another stunning moment.

Ellen and I monitored our father's stay in the ICU of St. Catherine Hospital like marines on watch, taking turns sleeping, exchanging information at the door to the ICU as we traded off. Between courageous efforts to smile for our benefit, he would grit his teeth in pain. When enough tubing was removed so that he could try to talk again, he complained in a small, hoarse voice that the nurses yelled in his ears. The nurses took no offense at this. They knew about the rage of powerful men robbed of their dignity. My father, a short man, once poor, was probably among the worst of them.

At last he was transferred from the ICU to a private room on the oncology floor, a determinedly cheery, sun-drenched place with yellow walls and pin-striped curtains. The windows faced the smooth, azure Pacific Ocean, where the horizon faded to a milky blue. Cortés and Balboa had once regarded that horizon, imagining their future. When my father looked out now, did he imagine his own future—whatever and wherever it would be?

As planned, my brothers both arrived in Los Angeles to join the hospital room vigil as we waited for the tissue evaluation in the pathology report that would decide my father's fate. Five thousand times a day Abe Fishman demanded to know when his damned doctor would show up with the results. We were learning that waiting and cancer are synonymous. The challenge was learning how to wait and still make your lungs breathe in and out.

As he regained his strength, my father grew more agitated. We hadn't pulled the curtain to the right position. There were too many flowers, not enough ice cubes in his pitcher, too much noise in the hall. The juice beside his bed smelled sour. The television was at an angle where sunlight coming through the window cast infuriating patches of opaque gray. Abe Fishman pointed imperiously in one direction and another and sneered at our failures to anticipate his needs.

Dr. Samuel Hopkins, aka Dr. God, wore civilian clothes when he arrived at last for the bedside session. He sat and bent one narrow knee over the other so that his Armani slacks crept up his leg and revealed the garters that held up his black socks. He nodded at his patient's improving appearance, the confirmation that he, the talented surgeon, had done a splendid job. Then he wove his fingers around his bent knee and asked a question certain to tick my father off. "Tell me, Mr. Fishman, have they been treating you right?"

"That's not the point," my father informed him, undaunted by the humbling, flowered hospital garb that he was required to wear. "How come it takes so goddamn long for your people to check out a few cells under a microscope? This isn't nuclear physics, for God's sake."

"I'm only a lowly surgeon here, Mr. Fishman. You'll have to take that up with the nuns who run the place. Myself, I've never had the courage to question them." He smiled at my father, waiting for appreciation of his attempt at humor.

"I'm assuming you're here to talk about the pathology report," my father replied, turning the hospital room into his own executive office.

"Yes, Mr. Fishman. I've gone over the results."

"Give it to me straight."

Dr. Hopkins looked back toward the four of us leaning against the walls, waiting silently.

"They're my children. They can handle this."

Hopkins accepted this statement of his patient's wishes. "Mr. Fishman, as you know, the tumor in your stomach was malignant. We were able to get most of it out, but unfortunately some of the tumor was so deeply embedded in the stomach lining that we were unable to remove it all. In addition, we saw clear evidence that the cancerous cells had spread to adjoining lymph nodes. The pathology report shows that the cancerous cells are relatively undifferentiated, which tells us they are quite young. Given the extensive growth and the large size of your tumor, this indicates a type of cancer that is extremely aggressive. It's impossible to know how long you've had this cancer, but it's certain that it's growing fast. The oncologist will come by later today to discuss your options for treatment. As your surgeon I advise you to elect the most aggressive course of radiation. Unfortunately, we don't have much luck with stomach cancers. The problem is where they're situated, right there at the center of things. Untreated, you might have six months to a year. If you're very lucky, maybe two."

I don't know which one of us in the room gasped. I know it was not my father. His face closed down, slowly but surely, a door shutting on an uninvited stranger.

Hopkins pushed back. "We should be able to get you out of here by next Friday. It all depends on when we can get you eating solid foods. You've still got a good-sized stomach in there. Your job is to get it working like the old one. I'll come by tomorrow morning to check on you." Hopkins turned and left, not looking any of us in the eye.

My father lifted his hand and waved us out of the room. We filed out, saying nothing, and walked on down the hall, no destination. Ellen was already sobbing. Perhaps the distance she had kept between herself and her father had dawned on her with full force.

My older brother, Tony, shook his head. "That doctor is an asshole."

Charles was more philosophical. "I guess when you're seventy you stand a chance of getting dealt out of the game."

"We shouldn't leave him alone too long," I said. No one answered, so without waiting for their agreement, I turned back.

My father was staring out the window when I came to his door. I asked if I could come in, and he didn't answer. I went in anyway and sat down in the chair the surgeon had pulled up to the bed. Since my father still did not look my way, I was free to study him. The skin of his cheeks, which only weeks before had been taut and tan from racing his bike and skiing, was now withered and yellow. A stubble of gray around his chin gave him the appearance of a tired Chinese elder, and his hair, pressed up by the pillow, made a little plume above his head. He seemed profoundly sad. He was up against the facts.

I stared at him and thought, Well, here he is, my father, and he's going to die. I had slipped through a door into a room where new knowledge was kept. I couldn't even recall what room I'd left behind, what blissful ignorance. My father, this man before me, with eyes that would not blink, tendons making columns around his long neck, bony legs draped with hospital sheets, bare toes sticking out—this was my father, who would soon die and be no more. I sat as motionless as he. What could we do?

"Pop, this is a time when you've got to be a fighter."

"I'm tired," he confessed.

"Tomorrow you won't be so tired."

He shrugged. It was completely unlike my father to shrug. He always knew what he thought, wanted, was prepared to do. He would count off the steps of a well-thought-out plan, raising his thumb first and then his fingers one by one, laying out the concrete elements of a strategy carefully conceived to achieve his goal. Fortune favors the prepared mind. Fortune favors. I leaned forward and tried to hug him, but at that moment my father wasn't accepting any hugs.

That afternoon I went to Robinson's Department Store to buy him an electric shaver. His accustomed brush, blade, and shaving cream were too much for him to manage, and he was weary of being ministered to by nurses. A soft-rock station was piped in overhead as I moved along the swimsuit racks to men's toiletries. Carly Simon sang, "You've got a friend." The tears spilled out of my eyes with no warning, as if someone had tilted a pitcher of water down my cheeks. What a stupid, dumb song, I told myself, my tears unstoppable.

Ellen was discouraged by our father's withdrawal. She said it was so unlike him that it felt like the first sign of death. I suggested she give him twenty-four hours. "He needs some time to hit bottom, but he'll be back." At ten the next morning he called us all into his hospital room for a family meeting. He was sitting up in bed, his hair neatly combed, his face clean shaven, his chest bare with his IVs and feeding tube sticking out of him as if he wanted to show us that there was nothing to be afraid of in cancer. Here was his flesh, as strong and good as ever. Some repair was needed. That was all.

"There are two possibilities," he announced. "Either this thing is going to beat me or it won't. But I'll be damned if I'm going to sit here counting the tiles in the ceiling. I'm back in. I'm going to fight. And it's because of you guys. You're what makes me want to fight." His eyes drifted to the family portrait from his seventieth birthday, which we had placed on a table in his closest line of sight. "I didn't ask any of you to come out here. God knows, I did my damnedest to keep you away. I told myself it was because I didn't want to worry you. The truth is I was afraid to find out you didn't care. I know it sounds ridiculous. But that's me. That's my problem." He spread his hands in a gesture of apology.

"Fighting sounds good to me." Charles nodded. "I've got a suggestion."

"What's that?" Abe Fishman asked his youngest son, the child least like him.

"We approach it the way you taught us to approach any problem. First we get information. Then we consider our options. We'll find the top experts in the country. We'll use our minds. We'll use our wills. Isn't that the Fishman way?"

We decided to go meet the experts as soon as Abe was well enough to travel, but I needed to do a little of my own research before heading back to my family in New York. On the way to the airport I stopped in on my father's new oncologist, Dr. Michael Armadas. There is a handoff in cancer treatment—from the internist who makes the diagnosis, to the surgeon, who takes the first, radical steps, to the oncologist, who oversees the highly uncertain efforts of containment. It was easy to see which aspect of his personality had drawn each of my father's doctors to his specialty, or perhaps how the experience of it had shaped him.

Dr. Armadas and I were the same age—forty—but it was clear that seeing so much dying at close range had made him older. His shoulders were rounded forward from his hours of bending toward patients who could only whisper. In the hospital I had noticed that he always made some sort of physical contact with my father, a touch on the shoulder, a handshake, but his eyes stayed focused at a middle distance, as if he were already preparing for loss.

Dr. Armadas looked kindly at me across his desk in the tiny office sandwiched between his examining rooms. Though he had seen me a number of times in the hospital dressed in jeans and a T-shirt, I decided to wear a dress for this visit to his office. I wanted to present myself as the sort of person he could be frank with, even though the way I sat with my arms wrapped around the backpack I used for a purse must have let him know that I was not ready to be an orphan.

He rubbed his temples with his thumb and forefinger, taking a moment to draw his attention away from his waiting patients. Then he opened his palm against the stubble of beard that had grown in the long hours since he'd rested last. "How are you doing with all this?" he asked.

"Okay, I guess."

"You two are very close, aren't you?"

I nodded. I was afraid if I answered this question out loud, I'd cry.

"I'd like to keep him in the hospital for a little while longer. If he decides to opt for radiation, I want to get some weight back on him before we start."

"I'm sure once my father makes his rounds of the cancer gurus, he'll make his decision quickly. He likes to get all his information first."

Michael Armadas smiled and nodded. "Yes, I've gotten that impression of your dad."

"I like information, too," I said. "I guess I'm my father's daughter."

Of course he knew why I had come. He glanced toward his windows, where the blinds were drawn, then looked back to me. "I wish there were more I could tell you. I can give you the percentages, but they don't help much. It's not a good situation any way you look at it. Perhaps this is the best way to say it to you. In the last year I've had six patients with stomach cancer. Today not one of them is living."

I nodded maturely as my insides turned to cement.

"That doesn't mean we won't try our damnedest to save your father. We'll do absolutely everything we can. There are miracles."

When I could speak again, I said, "I'm not going to tell my father this yet."

"He'll let us know when he wants to have more information. It's always like that."

I didn't say anything to my three siblings about this conversation, either. Perhaps they also had their private consultations with Dr. Armadas and were sparing me. Of all the information we gathered over the next few weeks, that brief encounter with Michael Armadas was what prepared me best for the months that lay ahead.

# 3

On the last Wednesday in October, on a stunning fall day, Josh took a day off work and we drove up to Brookford. We had arranged for the private fire investigator to come midweek so we could make the trip while Hannah and Eli were busy in school. We didn't want to bring them with us. Even though by now we had told them in general terms about the fire, we saw no reason to subject them to the sight of their burned home.

A dark blue Ford pulled up to the front of our boarded-up house. The driver who stepped out and surveyed the sorry scene was Ken Mott, a retired industrial security expert with a specialty in arson. We had hired him to answer our nagging fears that our fire had not been an accident.

Mott's long face was disconcertingly narrow, as if it had been squeezed in at the sides. He stuck his large hand out toward Josh to shake, then flipped open the trunk of his car, pulled out an orange jumpsuit, unfurled it, then zipped himself into it in a single motion from crotch to throat.

"Soot," he explained.

For Josh and me, soot, its stubborn stains and acrid smell, had become a constant in our lives. We had carried it away from Brookford in our noses, in the weave of our clothes, in the few items we had salvaged and brought to our New York apartment in black plastic garbage bags. Like car oil, soot took days of repeated washing before it finally left your cuticles, and months or years, I supposed, before it left your mind.

Mott took out a large flashlight and slammed the trunk shut. "Tell me what makes you think arson's a possibility here." Mott was beginning his investigation, and his first step was to evaluate us.

"It's not so much that we believe arson's a possibility," Josh said. "It's more that we want to rule it out. The town fire marshal determined that it was electrical."

"But you doubt him."

"No, I wouldn't say that."

"Well, what *would* you say, Mr. Waldmas?"

I flinched at the tone this stranger was taking with my husband, but Josh apparently did not take offense. "There were two fires within two weeks of each other—ours and a business in town. The owner of the business is Jewish, and so are we. It's probably only an unfortunate coincidence, but it was enough to worry us. We felt it was better to be absolutely sure. That's why I called you."

"I see," Mott said and stepped toward the house. "Generally I work these things from the furthest point of the fire back to the point of origin."

"So we start in the attic?" Josh asked, keeping apace.

"That's correct, Mr. Waldmas." Mott pushed ahead through the gate, the only thing still white enough to catch the light of the low-angled, late autumn sun.

As I busied myself in the rooms below, scouting for anything more that could be saved, I listened to the voices that came through what was left of the ceiling. They were discussing the chemistry of fire, techniques of house construction, the types of building materials used in different eras. These were subjects on which Josh could match details with the most experienced men, and I sensed Mott becoming less peremptory as he grew impressed with Josh's knowledge.

Though Josh loved photographic images, he also loved what he could touch with his hands. He knew wood and loved to work with it. He could mix stains that looked as if Rembrandt had taken a hand in bringing golden light into the color. Josh had lovingly applied linseed oil to our Shaker cabinets with a cloth soft enough for a baby's skin, weekend upon weekend of work. Any nineteenth-century Shaker carpenter would have appreciated the job Josh did. Some evenings, when Hannah and Eli were asleep, I would pour a glass of wine and sit up on one of the kitchen counters to watch him work, his long body tucked as close to the cabinets as he could get. He didn't mind if I nattered on, though he didn't speak much in reply. I would drink my wine and talk happily to his curved back. The intimacy of his feeling for the wood was very sexy to me. On more than one occasion I interrupted him and pulled him directly to the living room couch.

The two men worked their way along the trail of the fire, from the attic to the basement. Mott showed Josh the way fire left different types of residue that could be read for clues, white crusts left behind like the drying foam of a receding tide. He touched the crusts to his tongue to taste for traces of accelerant, gasoline or kerosene. They were standing directly above me when Mott said, "See the cracks in the windows? Your place was minutes from total destruction. Once the top windows blow and outside oxygen gets sucked in, that's it. Nothing to do but stand back and watch it burn. An old Colonial like this is lunch meat for a fire. Frankly, I'm surprised you've got anything left standing here at all."

I took a breath and steadied myself. I had already experienced this a number of times in the weeks since our fire. People spoke about our house as an object, forgetting, understandably, that to us it was so much more than wood and windows. This house was part of our sense of ourselves as a family. It held our memories and gave us a place to be ourselves completely.

Maybe it would have been easier on us if it had burned to its foundation. We could have walked away, taken the insurance money, looked for a new house in a new town. We could have turned the fire into past history, quickly and resolutely. If it had been totally destroyed, like Shelly's bakery, there would be no way to prove anything one way or the other about the possibility of arson. What if Mott's investigation did turn up evidence of arson? Or worse, what if it was suspicious but unclear?

I spotted Eli's ice hockey skates in a pile of rubble. The black leather was stiff and cracked from the heat of the fire. I ran my finger along one metal blade until the pad of my finger was covered in black soot. A century ago, Russian soldiers had set fire to my great-grandparents' village in Odessa, burning them out of their homes made of sticks and packed earth because they were Jews. I held Eli's hockey skates to my breast a moment as if I were comforting my own ancestors. A century isn't much time in human history.

I was a Jew because my parents were Jews. My parents were Jews because their parents were Jews, and their parents before them. Hannah and Eli were Jews because Josh and I were Jews. What did all this mean to me? In truth, the pseudo-Buddhism of my sixties youth had more meaning to me than my own religious background.

Josh and I did not belong to a synagogue. We did not celebrate any Jewish holidays, just as Josh's parents had not celebrated any Jewish holidays in their own home. Josh's father had turned his back on religion once he emigrated to America. What kind of God allowed the behavior Józef Waldmaski had witnessed in Lódz?

On my side there had been a California brand of atheism. My mother and father were both first-generation Americans, whose own parents had come to America as children at the turn of the century. My parents were part of the 1930s renaissance of secular Judaism, Jews who rejected religion in favor of socialism. And then they rejected socialism when, along with the rest of America, the postwar era swept them into a fervor of consumption. Once they moved from old-world New York City to new-world California, they bought Christmas trees, sports cars, swimming pools, and eventually took advantage of the American prerogative of no-fault divorce, a car crash without drivers.

Abe Fishman passed virtually nothing of the Jewish religion to his children, as nothing had been passed to him when he was growing up. In our smart, secular, left-leaning family, religion was regarded as the opiate of the masses. God was a sentimental idea, like any old mythology, useful only to those weak people who needed it. None of us knew a single Jewish prayer, and if we harbored any sort of belief in God—as I did—we knew enough to keep it to ourselves.

Not that Abe Fishman wasn't proud of being linked to Einstein, Freud, Kafka, Mendelssohn, Bernard Malamud, and Groucho Marx. He could reel off the names of a hundred Hollywood stars from Edward G. Robinson to Kirk Douglas whom the ordinary moviegoer would never suspect of being Jewish. Abe Fishman made a fine distinction: He was Jewish, but he was resolutely not *a Jew*.

There was a loud shouting from the basement. "Annie!" Josh yelled. "Come here! Come down here quick! My God, we've found it!"

The lawn was wet from a night rain, and I skidded as I rounded the house at a run to the basement door. I peered into the dark and saw the two of them glaring at something on the floor, Josh pushing the toe of his sneaker tentatively against whatever it was as if it could suddenly come alive and bite.

"Look at this," Josh instructed.

In the ashes on the basement floor was a charred tin can with holes cut in the side. It was attached to an aluminum pie plate with four neatly cut and twisted wires.

"Looks like the arsonist set it up so the accelerant would drain out slowly into that pie plate," Mott told us.

Josh shook his head. "This is unbelievable."

I stared at the contraption, trying to fathom why it looked familiar to me. Then I burst out laughing.

"It's the bird feeder! The kids' bird feeder. Don't you remember? Last summer? Hannah found a plan for it in one of her *National Geographic World* magazines. Don't you remember, Josh—how we made the thing and hung it out until we got sick of the raccoons coming up to the porch at night to eat the bird droppings?"

Josh dug his hand into his unruly tangle of soft black curls.

Ken Mott bent down to get a closer look. "Never seen a bird feeder quite like that before. Thing had us both going."

"Was there anything else you saw that looked suspicious?" I asked.

"Only this. Otherwise there was nothing here to point to anything but an ordinary electrical fire."

"We've gone through everything," Josh assured me.

"So that means we get a clean bill of health?"

"Looks that way to me." Mott unzipped his orange suit to the waist. "You guys didn't need me here after all."

Josh put his arm across my shoulders. "Believe me, it was worth it for our peace of mind."

Back by the road, Mott slipped his jumpsuit over his black shoes and folded the suit inside the cardboard box in his car trunk. My anxiety rose as he prepared to leave.

"I know nothing about electrical wiring," I said as Mott turned toward his car, "but I'm wondering, could a fire *cause* a wire to short out as well as the other way around? It seems logical. How would you know the difference?"

Mott rested his elbow against his opened car door. He had done his job, received his check, and he was impatient to get going. "It'd have to be an awfully hot fire, Mrs. Waldmas. You've got copper wire there. Copper melts at 1,083 centigrade—about twice as hot as a pizza oven. Not likely."

"But it's possible?"

"I suppose it's possible," Mott conceded. "But that's not what happened." He extended his hand to Josh and then to me, to end the conversation. Above our heads squirrels were running the Indy 500 along the high branches of the shagbark hickory, preparing their stores for winter.

Josh watched Mott's car drive out of sight. When he turned back to me, tears had filled my eyes.

"I don't get it," he said. "We just got good news."

I shrugged and lifted my eyes to the branches above.

"Huh?"

"The squirrels have their homes."

Josh pulled me to him and put his arms around me. "At least now we know it wasn't arson. I was ready to pack up and never come near this town again."

"We still have the insurance to get through. And then rebuilding."

"We'll be back in the house by spring."

"If we're lucky, by summer," I said gloomily.

"You've got to admit that was pretty funny about the bird feeder. Someday it'll make a good story. You'll see, Annie. Someday we'll be able to laugh about it."

I telephoned my father to tell him the outcome of the arson investigation, as I was in the habit of calling him with all our news.

"Now you can move ahead," he said.

"I guess I was more worried than I let on. To imagine being someone's target . . ."

"Arson's terrible, Annie. I can't tell you how terrible."

"What do you mean, Pop?" I was surprised at how adamant he was.

"Nothing."

"Then why did you say that?"

"It seems obvious, that's all."

Charles had arranged appointments with three of the most prestigious gastrointestinal-cancer experts on the East Coast, and I returned to

California to help my father make the trip back east. He brought the files Dr. Armadas had prepared for him, the history of his diagnosis, the surgical report, the pathology review, slides of cancer cells that had once been in his body. My father was an orderly man. He carried these crucial medical facts in his briefcase the same way he would have brought pertinent financial data for consideration by a potential real estate investor.

One after the other, these august doctors shook their heads. They didn't know us well enough to feel the need to lie to us as they ranked my father's as one of the most aggressive and fast-growing types of cancer. The only hope they offered was intensive radiation treatment, which would give him at best a 15 to 20 percent chance of remission.

Our last consultation was with an oncologist in Boston. As we flew back to New York, my father and I sitting side by side, and Charlie in front of us, Charlie turned in his seat and put the question to Abe.

"After all you've heard, what's your game plan? Do you want to put yourself through radiation for fifteen to twenty percent odds? Radiation is going to make you feel like shit, and there's no guarantee of anything."

"Twenty percent is better than no percent," my father pointed out, opting for the higher end of the percentages.

"There are alternative treatments we could look into, if you like."

"If this thing is growing as fast as they say, we don't have time to fool around with that peach pit crap."

"I'm not sure we should sell the alternative stuff short," Charles advised. "It's worth some investigation."

"Annie, you going to chime in here?" my father asked.

"I hate the idea of your having to cope with the side effects of radiation, but I can't stand the thought that we wouldn't try anything that holds out even the slightest hope." I turned to Charlie. "I'm not against visualization or meditation or anything like that. We should try everything. Pop, it's up to you to decide how much you can take."

"Here's what I want to do," my father decided. "I'll begin radiation in Los Angeles with Dr. Armadas. I like him. He seems to know his stuff. Charlie, you check out the alternative medicine angle. I'll start with the radiation and we'll go from there."

"How about doing the radiation treatments on the East Coast?" I suggested. "We'll get a New York oncologist to supervise it. You can stay at our apartment. I'll be able to look after you."

My father raised his chin and shook his head, the sign of something nonnegotiable. "Not with all you've got on your plate right now, Annie. The fire insurance, the construction. I'll do best back home in Los Angeles under my own steam. If you want to come out to help me get started, great, but I can handle it from there."

I turned to the window and looked out over the hills of upstate New York, a rust-colored carpet of trees. Soon there would be that cold afternoon when a strong wind would do the final job on the autumn trees and strip their limbs bare. With the specter of my fire-ravaged home and my father fighting for his life, I wasn't sure how I'd cope with that discouraging day when the last leaf was gone.

Charlie changed planes at La Guardia and headed home to Washington, and my father and I got a taxi to my apartment. We were both wiped out when we came through the door. Josh had supper waiting for us, and Hannah had a poem ready to read. When my father went into the bathroom to wash up, Hannah and Eli stood outside in the hall waiting for him.

"Remember, Grandpa's tired," I whispered.

They nodded maturely. "We know, we know."

They were used to his visits. Since they were born, he had made it his business to come to see us three or four times a year. Eli would sleep in Hannah's room in a sleeping bag on the floor and give his bed to Grandpa, but Abe and Eli often sequestered themselves in Eli's room for hours at a stretch. Seated side by side at the desk, with their heads tipped toward each other, they would pore over the directions for constructing a LEGO aircraft carrier or an Erector set electrified crane. They would barely notice when I would slide a plate of sandwiches between them. Abe and Eli shared extraordinary powers of concentration. When they worked together, I could see the boy in my father, the man in my son.

Abe emerged from the bathroom, and I realized he was working to manage his pain. All the moving around we had done in the last two days had taken a toll on him. When Hannah and Eli drew back toward me instead of rushing to him, I knew they saw it, too. Or at least they saw something that worried them. For the first time in their lives their grandfather's attention was focused inward, on his own needs. Hannah and Eli were silent as I said to Abe, "Tony called. I told him about your decision, and he agrees."

"Call Ellen, too," my father instructed, his voice dry.

"How about some supper?"

"I'll give it a try." He noticed Hannah and Eli looking up at him. "Hey, no long faces. Toys do not arrive for children with long faces."

At dinner Josh took charge of keeping the conversation going. He asked Abe's advice about how to handle our negotiations with the insurance company and encouraged Hannah and Eli to tell us about their school day. Hannah read the poem she had written. It was about the process by which a caterpillar becomes a butterfly, a subject she had been studying in school. She had written a stanza for each stage of the transformation: egg, larva, chrysalis, imago. In the final stanza she posed the question: Does a butterfly remember the stages it has been before? Does it miss them?

My father gave the answer. "Hannah, each thing it becomes uses all of what it was before. Like people. Each time we grow to something new, we build on everything we were."

I watched my father push aside his supper after barely attempting it. I talked myself through my discouragement. Not eating didn't mean dying.

At bedtime, Abe came in to kiss Hannah and Eli good night, then left me to read to them and put out the light. Barely a page into *Yertle the Turtle*, Hannah interrupted.

"How come Grandpa's so skinny?"

"Because of the operation, honey."

"Is he going to die?"

"Shut up!" Eli snarled.

"Please don't talk like that," I said to Eli.

He dug into his sleeping bag on the floor and pushed his face into his pillow.

"What's wrong?"

"She should shut up!"

"It's *my* room," Hannah insisted. "I'll say whatever I want."

I looked hard at my daughter. Her selfishness was a quality I did not admire. I went over and sat on the rug next to Eli, and threaded my fingers through his soft hair.

"The doctors are going to help Grandpa."

Eli was silent.

"Eli?"

"I heard you tell Uncle Tony about the fifteen percent."

My heart sank. Why hadn't I been more careful?

Hannah sat up in bed with her stuffed animals gathered around her. "What fifteen percent? What's Eli talking about?"

I always found the need to make split-second decisions about how to handle thorny issues one of the hardest parts of being a parent. Should I lie to my children, or should I tell some form of the truth?

"Grandpa has cancer."

"That's bad," Eli said.

"Yes, Eli."

"What are we going to do?"

"What we're going to do is pray very hard for him to make sure he gets better."

Hannah crawled out of bed and into my lap.

"Should I read the rest of the story?"

"Good idea," Hannah advised.

By the time I came into the living room, Josh was sitting alone watching TV. I settled in next to him, and he clicked off the remote. I dropped my head onto his shoulder and sighed. It had been a very long day.

"Abe said to tell you good night. We talked a little, but he could hardly keep his eyes open. I told him you'd understand if he called it a night."

"Did he say anything about the trip today, about his decision on the radiation?"

"He said you had all agreed."

"I guess that's what he wants to think."

"What do you mean?"

"Oh, you know how he is. Mr. Open-Minded, who hears the pieces he wants to hear. After listening to all these doctors, I think the truth is, they suggest radiation because they have nothing else to offer. They can't say, Go home and enjoy the remainder of your life in peace. But I bet that's what they'd like to have had the courage to say. That's certainly what Charlie took out of it. And frankly I didn't have the heart to push the point."

"Annie, your dad is a guy who needs to tackle things. Talking to him, it sounds like the radiation is a project he can take hold of."

"So you didn't question it?"

"It was clear he didn't want me to question it."

"I talked to the kids."

"What did you tell them?"

"I told them the truth."

"I thought you felt it was still too soon."

"Eli overheard me talking to Tony. I suppose it's better for them to know than to worry that there's something too scary for us to tell them."

"From the sound of Hannah's butterfly poem, she already understands he's dying."

"He is not dying," I snapped and sat up. "It doesn't help me to hear that."

Josh looked at me but chose not to respond.

The next morning while Josh walked the kids to school on his way to work, I stayed with Abe to get us both ready to fly back to Los Angeles. When the packing was done, I got out my video camera and set it up on a tripod in the living room, where my father was resting. In my profession as a documentary filmmaker I had interviewed jailed girl gang leaders, lonely pregnant teenagers, terrified young women who had been raped by their own uncles and brothers. I had sat at kitchen tables, on living room couches, in the visitors' rooms of a dozen different jails, to coax people gently into telling their stories, listening as they spoke about their anger, terror, shame. Over the years I had learned how this kind of encounter— one person finding the courage to speak, the other listening attentively— could transform a life. Battered women imagined the unimaginable, and were able to leave their abusive husbands. Victims of incest told their siblings or mothers the awful secrets that had twisted their lives. Pregnant teenagers resolved to go back to school and hang on to their futures. I liked and trusted the mystery of this process. I took pride when a defeated woman stood up and reclaimed her life.

"What's that for?" My father pointed to my video camera as he watched me set up.

"I thought we could get down some family history."

"You mean now that I'm checking out?" This was his idea of a bold joke. It was also his way of distracting me from his discomfort at the idea of the video camera pointed his way. My father had never made a practice of revealing his innermost thoughts.

"Checking out or maybe checking in. Sometimes when people get tough news like this, it gets them thinking."

"Well, you're right about that. There's something I've been thinking about that I wanted to tell you, so we might as well get it down for posterity." He pulled the ottoman close so he could prop up his feet.

"You look a lot better today. Did you sleep well?"

"Not that well. I was exhausted when I turned in last night, but an hour later I was wide-awake. To tell you the truth, I don't have much interest in sleeping these days. My mind's been going full tilt. I'll tell you what I was thinking last night. I've begun to believe my cancer might be a blessing."

I had turned the camera on in time to capture this alarming comment.

"I got your attention with that one." He smiled and then tilted his head back to make himself comfortable. "It's the truth, Annie. That's the thing I've been up with all night. See, over the last year I'd begun to say to myself that I'd done enough, that there wasn't much more for me in life. I had gotten to seventy. That was pretty damned good, considering that my own father died at forty or thereabouts. I'd done all the things I'd set out to do. A sort of 'what the hell' had taken over in my mind. It's not something I said out loud to anybody. But I was aware of it, a kind of closing down, the thought that things were nearly over, imagining the end of my life."

He looked for my reaction, but I was a professional and I knew how to remain opaque.

"I started asking myself, what am I doing anyway? God knows I didn't need to make any more money. It seemed crazy to take on another real estate project with all the pressure and demands, just for the hell of it or out of habit or to keep myself busy. But what else was there? Sure, I dated, but I knew I wasn't going to fall in love. I've been resigned to that for some time. The only things that were really important to me were you kids, the grandchildren, and skiing, I guess." He paused at this. "That's one thing I never seem to lose sight of, my love of skiing. But other than that, it was 'What's the point?' That's what I was turning over and over in my mind."

He looked around. I knew he wanted a glass of water, but I was suddenly too angry to be generous. Didn't he realize that he had told me that his love for me and my children wasn't enough to make him feel life was worth living? But how do you get angry with a man under a death sentence?

He pulled at his throat. "You got something for your old man to drink?"

Without answering him, I turned off the camera and got up to go to the kitchen.

As I let the water run, I thought of him sitting alone in the living room without a clue about the cruelty of what he'd said. I dropped ice cubes into the water, returned to the living room, and crossed over to his chair to hand the glass to him.

"Thanks, sweetheart." He smiled up at me. I smiled back stiffly.

He waited for me to turn the camera on again and settle back into my seat.

"Okay, so fast-forward to later in the year. This cancer thing becomes a possibility—my doctor tells me the news. And you know, it was no surprise to me because I expected something." He looked at me to confirm that I had heard him. "That's the truth, Annie. Sure, I was nervous. Sure, I dreaded each piece of news, and I was frightened as hell. But another part of me knew what the news would be. I had already imagined it. It was almost as if my mind had issued the invitation. When they came back with the biopsy results, it was like, all right, this is what I expected."

"You're telling me you believe you brought on your own cancer."

"Would you let me do the talking here?"

Even after all these years, his bossiness was hard for me to take. I pulled back into my chair, and he noticed.

"I want to get this out," he apologized. "I want to see if I can say the whole idea."

"Go on then."

"Planning for the surgery was the next step. The surgeon starts telling me how he's going to cut this, staple that, and I tell him, 'Spare me the details, do what you have to do.' Then I go into the hospital for the surgery, I wake up, and, surprise, I'm still here, I didn't die. And then the amazing thing. Not only didn't I die, but my four children are there. I can't tell you how that felt. You all showing up like that when I didn't ask you to come, when I didn't even imagine I needed you. I don't know if I ever felt such love before. And that's when it all made sense—of course it's worth going on, of course I want to keep on living. Don't get me wrong, I'm not saying I got cancer to get the four of you to show up. It's more like the cancer was my wake-up call. You guys show up and remind me—or maybe make me really understand for the first time—the reason for my life isn't proving myself and making business deals and more money. It's about something as simple as loving and feeling loved."

I looked at him, saw him as a vulnerable man, not my father, and I was relieved I hadn't told him how angry I had been only minutes ago.

"I know this sounds like a cliché. 'Cancer patient finds new meaning in life.' But to me—you have to understand this, Annie—it's anything but a cliché." He put his hand on his chest. "See, in spite of this thing, in spite of the fact that I can barely eat and I'm so tired I have to drag myself around all day—the sun is shining as never before. All my misgivings and self-doubt, all my acting like I'd done it all—well, there simply isn't room for that anymore."

He leaned back into his chair to rest, but his excitement wouldn't allow it, and he pushed himself forward again. "The world seems different to me today, Annie. All that shame I carried with me from my child-hood—" He flipped his hand. "I'll save that for another day." He took a breath. "See, I'm wondering if this cancer thing wasn't my way of creating a crisis that would force me to figure out why the hell I was willing for my life to be over. *That's* what was keeping my mind working all night long. That's why I say the cancer might be a blessing."

# 4

I could not have imagined how the next weeks would wear me down as I fought battles on two fronts. I still tried to keep up my daily routine of taking the kids to school each morning, putting in eight hours at my office in Tribeca, then racing uptown to be home in time to shop, make dinner, help with homework. But my life was increasingly disrupted. After I accompanied my father back to California to set up his radiation treatments, I made two more visits to check on him. At the same time I was spending hours and hours on the aftermath of the fire, getting a hard lesson in the dark side of the insurance industry, and facing the deeply upsetting prospect that we might never get enough money to rebuild.

It hadn't taken long to figure out how naive we had been in our initial dealings with Eddie Shank, the insurance adjuster. We were probably as easy for him to stalk as starving deer in winter. He had heightened our vulnerability and traded on it from his very first remark, which still gave me nightmares—that we were lucky our children hadn't been burned to death sleeping in their beds. His campaign to unnerve us continued with constant reminders, couched as help, that it was going to be nearly impossible to find a contractor to rebuild our house. "Everyone for a hundred miles is knee-deep in work, and anyway," he told me, "the top-quality guys like clean jobs. They don't take on fire construction unless they're really hard up."

One morning in mid-November, Shank telephoned me at my office. "Mrs. Waldmas, you must have someone watching out for you up there in heaven. I've got good news for you. See, I was having my coffee in town this morning, and who's there on the stool next to me but my good buddy who does construction around our area. I explained your problem, what good people you are and all. It took a little arm-twisting, but he's agreed to come up and see what he can do to help you people out. It's a bit out of his way, but he owes me a couple of favors, and I'm calling in my chits."

Eddie Shank wouldn't let me off the phone until I agreed to invite this contractor to come to our house to make his bid on the cost of rebuilding. I assumed Shank had his own agenda, maybe a kickback he'd get if we used his guy. But I didn't see any risk in letting his friend bid for the job if it meant staying on Shank's good side. We already had in mind someone we hoped would do the work, but our contractor could only do it if another scheduled job fell through. We might need Shank's contractor if things didn't work out.

Eddie Shank had let himself into our house before we arrived. In addition to the contractor, he had brought along a dough-faced man he introduced as his assistant, Mikey Johnson. Eddie handed him a clipboard. "Take good care of these fine people like I told you."

While Eddie Shank showed his contractor the work to be done, Mikey Johnson helped us prepare a list of "contents," as our destroyed belongings were now called. Mikey took notes as we climbed through the rubble trying to reconstruct what had once been there. He scratched his scalp with the eraser end of his pencil and encouraged us to be expansive. "Appears to me there must have been at least a couple of dozen towels piled there. And let's call this wooden crate a bedside table. That's what you use it for, right?"

When Josh shook his head dubiously, Mikey explained, "These insurance companies will take a pound of flesh if we don't try to beat them at their game. Eddie sticks in a little extra here, a little extra there. That's how we make you come out all right. Don't worry, this is how we do it. Eddie told me to take good care of you guys. He likes you."

Josh walked ahead. "Let's just do this fairly."

Our hearts were hardly in it as we contemplated the remains of things that had no particular monetary value but were irreplaceable—Hannah's gymnastics blue ribbons, Eli's painting of a dream in which he flew on wings over Manhattan. The awful thing, the thing Josh couldn't even bear to discuss, was the damage to his darkroom, which he had built in the small bathroom off the front hall. His printing and enlarging equipment had been destroyed, but all that could be replaced. What was unsalvageable were his boxes filled with negatives that had curled and cracked from the heat. Josh had taken a trash bag into his darkroom and methodically thrown out years of photography. He never referred to what had happened to his father's Lódz photographs, and I chose not to mention it either.

When we met back in the kitchen, Mikey Johnson handed Eddie Shank the clipboard, and Shank tore off the page that listed our contents, folded it into his shirt pocket behind the plastic sleeve of ballpoint pens, and smiled broadly. "Good job, guys."

Shank's contractor had shaggy hair and a wet nose and did not look up from his shoes. Josh began talking with him to draw him out, not for calculated motives as mine would have been, but because he clearly felt sorry for this sad sack of a guy. When he told Josh that he had been doing janitorial work at his local elementary school to make money while he was between construction jobs, Eddie Shank moved between them so fast that Josh had to step aside to avoid being knocked backward.

"Weather shut him down for a couple of weeks. That's how come he's got the time to drive all the way up here to do you guys a favor."

I nodded.

"And let's be honest about this. With you guys underinsured and all, you're going to need a contractor who'll work with you to make your dollar stretch."

"Underinsured?" Josh asked. "That's not possible. We bought full coverage on our house."

"I don't know what your agent told you, Mr. Waldmas, but I'm the one who makes the decisions here, and I can tell you the policy he sold you doesn't near cover what you should have had."

"What are you talking about?" I demanded.

"Coinsurance, Mrs. Waldmas. Go home and read your fine print. If you don't insure your house for its proper value, you lose your full insurance coverage and become responsible for part of the replacement cost yourself."

"Wait a minute," I said. "We met with the agent last June. He told us we were covered for the full value."

"I guess you'll take that up with him."

"This is craziness," I fumed.

Shank raised his hands in a gesture of conciliation. "Don't worry, I'm going to work with you here. We can offset some of the difference by putting back Sheetrock instead of plaster. No one uses plaster anymore, anyway. We'll paint where you had wallpaper, save some there. You use my guy, he'll make sure you come out okay."

"I already told you, we have our own contractor we want to work with."

"See here, Mrs. Waldmas. You can bring in whoever you want—it doesn't matter to me. You can bring in a hundred guys. I'm the one who evaluates the estimates. And once I've determined my number, that's what you've got." He cocked his thumb. "See, I've got a contractor right here— a fellow you *invited* to come in and make a bid, and he's given me his construction estimate."

My heart sank. Now I understood how we'd been set up. It didn't matter who his contractor was, whether he could hang a screen door or bang a nail. Obviously, having met this guy, we would never use him— Eddie Shank knew that. The point was that no matter what our chosen contractor's bid came in at, Eddie Shank had established the basis for an absurdly low figure he would use in negotiating down our final settlement. I felt like a patsy. I felt like prey. Mikey Johnson had been babysitting us with sympathetic discussions of our meager contents while Eddie Shank had maneuvered us into a neat corner.

We hired a lawyer and learned more bad news. Independent, small-time insurance agents like ours don't rely on commissions from insurance premiums for their living, but on the big bonuses they get if they keep the cost of claims low in their area. By insuring us for less than what we needed, he had set the stage for us to fall into the no-man's-land of coinsurance, virtually guaranteeing that we would end up paying for part of the damage out of our pockets. Our final settlement would be arrived at through a negotiation in which we had no leverage short of pursuing an expensive court case. Meanwhile, as long as our claim was in dispute, we were not allowed to touch a single clapboard or cobweb. Our house waited, as cold and dark as a stone cave.

A few weeks later, wearying of the one-day, turnaround drive we had been making to deal with the aftermath of the fire, Josh and I decided to take up our friends Nick and Elizabeth Stein on their offer to stay with them for the weekend. We had met as fellow parents in Eli's kindergarten class at P.S. 87 and discovered that they had a country house in Eastbrook, twelve miles south of Brookford. Like us, they had happened on this corner of Connecticut by accident and were delighted to find the low prices in an isolated spot that was on nobody's map of chic summer destinations. Since they were also Jewish, the coincidence of our fire and the Brookford Café fire had disturbed them. They had encouraged our decision to hire our own arson investigator and were relieved by his report. I was looking forward to the weekend with them, particularly because Nick had a talent for drawing people into his happy moods. Two months of war with the insurance company had left Josh and me irritable with the world and with each other. And I was feeling discouraged at the way the radiation treatments were melting weight off my father's already thin body, making him more frail and tired with each passing day.

When we arrived at the Steins' late on Saturday afternoon, Eli dove out of the car to play with his friend Adam, Hannah went off to find the Steins' new chocolate Lab puppy, and Nick helped Josh and me unload our things. Elizabeth led us to a bedroom at the opposite end of the house from where all the children would sleep. She had prepared for our arrival with a bowl of shiny McIntosh apples on the bureau, a candlestick on the night table, a bottle of massage oil beside it. Blushing slightly, Elizabeth pointed to the bottle. "To assist your R and R."

When Elizabeth left us alone, Josh uncapped the bottle and lifted it to his nose. "Smells like overripe tropical fruit."

"I like having friends who want to take care of me right now."

"Did you forget that Nick lost his father less than a year ago? You're not the only one who's gone through this."

"I'm not talking about my father. I'm talking about the fire, not having a place of our own to go."

"I am getting tired of your making such a tragedy out of this fire business. People deal with a lot worse things."

"I know Josh. I know I have no right to complain when there are Chinese immigrants living ninety to a room in slave barracks on the Lower

East Side. But in my spoiled, parochial mind, I miss our home, that's all. I miss the quiet times, you and me and the kids."

Josh went to look out the dormer window, where the cold sky looked gray enough to bring snow. "Our friends have their own lives. I don't know why you feel you have to take them through chapter and verse of our supposed suffering."

I caught a glimpse of myself in the bureau's oval mirror. I had tucked my frizzy hair back underneath one of Eli's baseball caps, and I was wearing a baggy sweatshirt and jeans, not even a pair of earrings. I had dressed the way I felt.

"Maybe I wouldn't have to turn to my friends for sympathy if I got a little more understanding from you. In case you haven't noticed, I've been doing most of the insurance work myself."

"And now I have to deal with your martyr trip?" Josh recapped the bottle of massage oil and put it back on the night table with a little too much force.

"You want to break that?"

He pointed to the bottle. "Did it break?"

"Can't you find some other way to express your anger?"

"My anger? Annie, we're up here in the country with the kids. It's what you wanted, right? Why can't you relax and let the rest of us relax for a change, too?"

I could feel the perverse pleasure of anticipating conflict. I couldn't do anything about my real enemies: Fire was a powerful force of nature, an insurance company was a potent force of commerce, and cancer—what more irrational force could you be up against than cells redividing relentlessly without logic? But I could take on Josh. I could convert this minor marital skirmish into a full-fledged, satisfying battle that I could escalate and win simply because my husband had no natural aptitude for argument.

"Why can't I relax?" I demanded. "You dare to ask me that, knowing the amount of shit I've been dealing with? It's one thing for you to expect me to do all this work, but then to minimize what I do on top of it—" I saw his worried look as he hunkered down in the face of my assault. If I had been wiser, that look would have been enough to slow me down. Instead it whet my appetite. "I suppose if you didn't minimize my work, you'd be stuck with feeling guilty that you weren't doing more."

I lifted one of the suitcases onto the bed to make a righteous business of unpacking it.

Josh watched me, sighed, then said, "The fact is you don't want me to do any more than I'm doing because you don't trust anybody but yourself to do it right. But you'd rather blame me than face that fact about yourself."

"Bullshit," I snapped back and flipped open the suitcase to get to work. My message was clear—he could lounge around and have this stupid argument, but I was busy with what had to be done.

Josh rubbed the tense muscles at the back of his neck. "Do you know you make people crazy with your compulsiveness?"

"And what would you have me do? Let the insurance company bring in some shitty contractor so they can get away with putting our house back together like a shack?"

"The rest of us are hapless dolts, aren't we?"

"If that's how you see yourself—"

"For God's sake, Annie—"

"Of course, it *is* true," I said, dripping with reasonableness. "There *are* areas where I simply can't rely on you."

"That's ridiculous. I'm in this as much as you."

"Maybe in your mind."

"Fuck you," he said too loudly for the thin walls.

"Nice language," I sneered.

Josh spun around, went out the door, and left me in the lurch. I could not go after him. We were houseguests. I could not shout, slam doors, push this fight to the decibels and drama that would have given me the release I sought. Josh was already down the stairs and headed for the protective custody of our hosts.

I kicked off my shoes and climbed onto the bed, pushing my back tight against the wooden headboard. I fumed, rehearsing the legitimacy of my case. Even though both Josh and I worked full-time, I was the one doing the lion's share of the phone calls and paperwork it took to challenge the insurance company. I had more of the required temperament, and I was certainly more prepared than Josh to scream and shout if that's what it took to get the insurance company's attention. But it wasn't fair, especially with everything else I was coping with—phone calls to my father's doctors all the time, trips back and forth to Los Angeles, taking care of the kids, and trying to fit a little of my own work into the cracks.

It was late in the afternoon when Hannah arrived at my bed with her arms crossed. "I'm supposed to tell you the guests are here."

"The guests?"

"For dinner."

"Shit," I said before I could censor myself. I had forgotten that Nick and Elizabeth had planned a dinner party for us. I shrugged. "Sorry. Bad language, huh?"

"You've said that word before." Hannah was never one to let me off easy.

"What have you been up to?" I patted the mattress to invite her to join me. "You like being back in the country?"

Hannah climbed onto the bed and lay back with her head against my thigh, and one leg crossed over her bent knee.

"I want a dog."

"You going to walk it?"

"Eli and me can take turns."

"And what happens when you don't want to do it one day?"

"Then you do it."

"Then we give the dog away."

"You can't do that. You can't just give a dog away. A dog has feelings. You can't just forget about it when you get bored with it."

"Exactly."

"I'm not going to get bored. It'll be my dog."

"So you'll walk it every day and never say you're too tired or have too much homework or want to go play with a friend?"

Hannah looked up at me. "How come parents always do that?"

"Do what?"

"Try to make you feel bad about something good."

"I want you to be realistic. A dog is a big responsibility."

"You just don't want me to have any fun. You want me to be as grumpy as you are these days."

"Hannah!"

"Ask anybody. Everybody says you're grumpy."

"I thought you wanted to come up to the country and have a good time."

"Yeah, right. And you're here in your room all afternoon."

"You could have come and gotten me."

"I did. And now you tell me all this stupid stuff when I tell you I want a dog."

I shook my head in frustration. When it came to wars of words, she took after me, not Josh.

"Want to help me get dressed?" I offered as a truce.

"You going to get all fancy?"

"How about I change the sweatshirt?"

Hannah sat up and looked me over doubtfully. "The guests are wearing dresses."

I sighed. This was not what I had in mind for my evening. Hannah shook her head sympathetically. Her nine-year-old world-weariness made me smile.

"All right, we'll start looking for a dog. But you're walking it," I said firmly, pointing my index finger in her direction.

I was glad to be holding my daughter's hand when I faced the abyss between my lousy mood and the lighthearted spirit of Nick and Elizabeth and the dinner guests having drinks and laughing by the living room fire. Nick was passing out slices of homemade onion tart, and Josh, who sat at Elizabeth's side with his arm along the back of the sofa behind her, gave me a frozen smile. I flushed a little, realizing that the news of our argument had surely proceeded me. Elizabeth made the necessary introductions as I found a seat and pulled Hannah to sit on my lap, my shield and comfort.

The people Nick and Elizabeth had invited were David and Susan Perlman, another New York couple with a house in the area. The Perlmans had brought along their weekend houseguests, Jerry and Martha Gornick. The Gornicks had spent the afternoon being shepherded around by a real estate agent looking at houses for sale in our area. House hunting was often an activity for weekend visitors, who could indulge a fantasy even if they didn't plan to act on it.

"We spotted a couple of terrific bargains," Jerry Gornick told us. "With the prices up here, we could afford to put in a pool and a tennis court with no problem."

"Better move fast," Nick advised. "A few more people show up here to buy weekend homes, and the local folk are going to get wise and start jacking up the prices."

"Yeah, how do we keep this place a secret?" Jerry Gornick asked proprietarily, even though he had come to the area for the first time that morning. "Some jerk will do an article for *New York* magazine. The next thing, it'll turn into a traffic jam like the Berkshires or the Hamptons."

Josh and I looked at each other and were reunited by our immediate dislike of this crude character who had been introduced as a "tax advisor to the rich and famous."

"I don't suppose there are very many Jewish families up this way?" Martha Gornick asked.

Jerry Gornick mocked his wife. "She wants to be sure there are enough women for a Hadassah chapter."

Martha ignored him. "I tried to get an idea from the real estate agent, but she didn't catch my drift, and I didn't feel comfortable asking her directly."

Elizabeth shrugged and turned to Nick. "What do you say, hon? How many Jews have we got up here?"

"I guess about as many as there are of us gate-crashing New Yorkers. None of the local folk, for sure."

"Do you mind that?" Martha Gornick asked. "I'm wondering since we're considering buying up here. I mean, do you sense any prejudice?"

"Them against us or us against them?" Jerry Gornick quipped and then took a poker to the logs in the fireplace, compelled to improve the fire even though he was a guest.

"Since there aren't a lot of Jews around here, obviously some amount of prejudice is inevitable," Josh said seriously.

I had been debating how much of this conversation I wanted Hannah to hear, and at Josh's comment I turned to Elizabeth. "What's the plan for the kids' supper? Are they eating with us, or do you want to feed them first?"

Elizabeth asked Hannah, "You guys want to eat with the grown-ups, or would you rather watch *Sleeping Beauty?*"

Hannah raised her eyebrows as if the answer was rather obvious.

"Then, how about you get the boys and meet your mom and me in the kitchen pronto? Tell Adam and Eli it's pasta and chicken nuggets."

Nick's watch alarm went off. "Time to turn the lamb."

"We'll get the kids started," Elizabeth said.

I popped up to follow Elizabeth. As soon as we were through the kitchen door I asked, "Who *are* those people?"

Josh came in behind Nick, also apparently looking to escape the Gornicks. "Do the Perlmans actually *know* these people?" Josh asked.

"David's trying to woo Jerry for some sort of business deal," Nick explained.

"Can we get hold of their real estate agent and tell her to fart in the car or something?" I suggested.

Elizabeth said to Nick, "Watch him, will you? He's already hit the scotch three times."

"Just what we need around here," Josh said, "some blowhard accountant who's made himself enough money to think the local people should treat him like royalty."

"It can't be good for the Jews," Nick teased Josh, who was famously sensitive on the subject. Nick opened the sliding glass door, and he and Josh went out to tend the grill.

Adam wanted apple juice, Eli wanted milk, and Hannah wanted water with exactly three ice cubes. As I watched Elizabeth patiently minister to each of the children's requests, I remembered how irritable I had been with Hannah and Eli that morning when they couldn't reach an agreement about what they wanted for their breakfast, waffles or pancakes. I had launched into a lecture about compromise and consideration, and now I wondered why I had made such a big deal when it would have taken only ten more minutes to give them both what they wanted. With my help their argument had escalated until I slammed down cereal boxes and bowls between them and stormed out of the kitchen. Josh had witnessed my outburst, but refrained from pointing out what a jerk I'd been, which made me feel worse. Was that what my family had begun to expect of me? Was that the kind of behavior my children were getting used to—behavior eerily like my own mother's brittle self-centeredness? Now that I was hitting some bumps in life, was I turning, like the needle on a compass, due north toward the person I was destined to become?

Josh and Nick returned to the living room to invite the guests to the dinner table. I put the children's plates in the dishwasher while Elizabeth got the children settled watching *Sleeping Beauty*. When we were all assembled, Elizabeth stood behind her seat and announced, "Seventy-six minutes of peace and quiet."

I chose the place next to Josh, and when we were seated, I took his hand. He entwined his fingers with mine, accepting my gesture of reconciliation. David Perlman made a ceremony of presenting the hundred-dollar Petite Syrah he and Susan had brought back from their summer trip to the Napa Valley. His need to impress Jerry Gornick was becoming embarrassing.

"So, the Jewish thing," David said, to pick up the conversation again as he filled our wineglasses. "The only thing that got us nervous was the Waldmases' fire."

"You had a fire?" Martha asked, eyes wide.

"About six weeks ago, right?" David looked to me.

"October fourth—a date forever branded on my brain."

"Your *house* burned? Here in town?" Martha asked again.

"We live in Brookford, the next town over," Josh explained. "That's why Nick and Elizabeth have to put up with us for the weekend. We're nomads until our house gets rebuilt."

"It was that bad?" Martha was quite disturbed. I caught Elizabeth's wink.

"It's uninhabitable," I said, "completely destroyed on the inside, a total gut job."

"Wow." Jerry Gornick was stunned into a momentary sympathy.

"But why do you say their fire made you nervous about being Jewish?" Martha pressed.

David looked to Josh to see if he wanted to recount the story, but Josh shook his head.

"There were two fires within two weeks over in Brookford. One was Annie and Josh's house. The other was the Brookford Café, a small coffee shop and bakery. It's owned—or I guess I should say, it *was* owned, because now there's nothing left of it—by a sweet older man named Shelly Weiss. He and his wife moved to Brookford from Queens to open the café about ten years ago. As far as I know he's the only Jewish store owner anywhere near here. You can imagine the coincidence of these two fires got us all a bit unnerved. The Brookford fire marshal said Josh and Annie's fire was from a short in some old wiring, but to be on the safe side they hired their own fire investigator. I'll tell you, we all breathed a lot easier when their guy confirmed the fire marshal's assessment."

"How about the bakery?" Martha asked.

"People say it might have been from one of the ovens. Also, Shelly's a heavy smoker. He was in the habit of baking through the night. Some people say he might have left a cigarette burning while he went outside for some reason. Since it burned to the ground, there's no way to know for sure."

Gornick turned to his wife. "What do you say we pass on the house hunting tomorrow morning? I doubt I'd feel so safe up here in redneck territory."

Elizabeth looked my way with a mischievous glint in her eyes.

The appreciation of David's prized Petite Syrah led to a discussion of the best vineyards to visit in California. At dessert David brought out yet another treat from the collection of wines he had left to cool in the mudroom, a port so old that the bottle was gray with mold. "The monks made this one for themselves," he said, holding out the bottle for our admiration.

I sat back in my chair to appreciate the glowing coals in the fireplace through the swirl of the port in my glass. Outside it had begun to snow. I realized, for perhaps the first time in weeks, that even though my house had burned and my father had cancer, I could allow myself to relax. I looked at Josh and thought about the end of the evening, when he and I would be alone in bed.

But this moment of peace was my undoing. In the last months I had relied on a battle-ready position, reluctant to let down my guard. I sat up in my chair, put my elbows on the table, and without even thinking, announced, "You know, it's weird about our house. At first we believed we were victims of an accident of nature, then we worried we might be victims of an anti-Semitic arsonist, but as it turns out we're the victims of capitalism. The wretched insurance company is where we're getting screwed."

The segue I made in the conversation was so abrupt that it elicited puzzled looks around the table, but it seemed to please Jerry Gornick. This was his calling—figuring out angles to protect people's assets. Here was an opportunity to show those of us around the table, whom he no doubt by now sensed disliked him, that he was not only clever, but someone they would benefit from knowing.

I explained what we had been going through, specifically Shank's determination to negotiate us down to an absurdly low settlement.

"Too bad you were so eager to bring in your own arson investigator and get a clean bill of health," Gornick assessed. "You could have made that uncertainty work for you."

"What difference would that make to our claim?" Josh asked.

Gornick sat back and crossed his arms, tucking his thick hands under his armpits. He addressed us as if he were conducting a seminar for a group of freshmen. "See, insurance negotiations are a game of football. Clever Annie here is the quarterback of the home team, and that asshole adjuster the insurance company sent to beat her down is their quarterback. Annie could have used the arson thing to start the game with a field kick deep into their half. Instead she let them take the ball on a pass and carry it all the way to her ten-yard line with their assertion that she didn't have enough insurance." He formed two fingers into a gun and took aim at me. "Tactical mistake, my dear. If you had established a reasonable suspicion of arson right off the bat, the ref would have had to call time while the insurance company pursued it. You could have taken a break on the bench with the scrimmage line jammed right up against their goalposts. If arson was even a slightly plausible explanation, the insurance company would have gone half crazy searching for the arsonist."

Since Gornick had criticized my handling of the negotiations, everyone turned toward me for my reply, some justification for the course of action we had chosen, something to put the unbearable Jerry Gornick back in his place. But I was lost in his odd metaphor.

Pleased at my confusion, Gornick went on, "Insurance companies always hope to be able to recover the money somewhere. If it's arson, they can impound the assets of the arsonist, sue the town, the alarm company, if you had one. Once arson is a question, there are lots of places the insurance company looks to get someone else to take the fall for them."

"Doesn't make sense," I countered. "If arson was any possibility at all, then Shank would have been right in there trying to find it."

"No, no, no." Gornick shook his head. "You're missing a step here. People like Shank aren't on staff at the insurance company. Maybe a couple of the very big firms like Chubb and Fireman's Fund have their own staff adjusters. The rest of them hire freelancers, fee-and-commission guys. They're brought in specially to negotiate your claim and screw you. The insurance companies can't instruct their own staffs to behave like that—too much liability. These guys are bounty hunters. Their fees are based on how low they get you. The point is, sweetheart, if your case turned out to be arson, your fellow Shank would be right out of the picture 'cause at that point they don't need him anymore—no fee, no commission, no nothing—back home with his hands in his pants."

"Don't call me sweetheart," I said. "And the fact is, we discovered our fire was electrical. So what's the point?"

Jerry Gornick reached across the table to refill my wineglass from the bottle between us. He didn't fill anyone else's. "My dear, you don't get it. Even if it didn't turn out to be arson in the end, by letting that possibility hang out there, you would have had the time you needed to strengthen your negotiating position. You should have called me. I would have walked you through it."

"It wasn't arson. That's the important thing," Elizabeth interjected. "It was an accident, something that couldn't have been helped."

"What makes you so sure of that?" Gornick pressed on. "You hire some guy who hangs out a shingle as an arson expert. Who is this person? What are his credentials?" He turned to Josh. "If you want to kid yourselves that there's no anti-Semitism in these lily-white hills, go ahead, live in the clouds. I'm not moving up here."

Nick raised his hands. "I think Josh and Annie have plenty to deal with without having the question of arson stirred up all over again."

Gornick squared off with Nick. "You guys really want to be a bunch of ostriches with your heads stuck in the sand."

"Why don't we call it a night?" Nick pushed back from the table. "I'm pretty wiped out from stacking two cords of wood this afternoon."

David took his napkin from his lap and returned it to the table. "I'm ready to head out."

Gornick turned to his wife. "Are we getting the bum's rush here?"

"It's just that we've all been exhausted by your brilliance," I told him. Gornick looked like a toad to me, hooded eyes popping, skin reflecting the candlelight in a slick of sweat.

"I think we should check on the kids," Elizabeth announced. "Come with me, Annie."

Everyone waited to see if I would come to my senses or tangle with Jerry Gornick. Josh backed away from the table to make room for Elizabeth, who had come around to take me with her to the TV room.

Elizabeth and I stood in the dark watching the good prince battle the evil queen, who had transformed into a terrifying dragon. I felt a cathartic delight each time the prince's sword punctured the dragon's undulating body. From the dining room came the sounds of the guests departing, and shortly, I heard a car starting up and driving away. Elizabeth led me back to the table, where Nick and Josh were sitting in a stunned silence.

"What a wretched human being," Elizabeth said.

"That was certainly unpleasant," Nick agreed.

"Just the kind of guy who makes you feel proud to be Jewish," Josh said.

"His being Jewish has absolutely nothing to do with it," I snapped. The three of them looked at me oddly. I was still fighting the dragon even though he was dead.

That night, despite my earlier fantasy, Josh and I settled into bed at a cool distance from each other. The fight at dinner was a cloud that did not go away.

By morning, snow had covered everything in white. I opened one eye and then the other and listened to the voices of Hannah, Eli, and Adam, who were outside at work on a snowman. I heard Adam announce he was going into the house to get a carrot for the snowman's nose, and I was reminded of the times at Mammoth when my father had supervised Hannah and Eli in the creation of snowmen, parting with his old jackets and ties to dress them up, and cigars to stick into their icy mouths. I sat up to get a view out the window. Eli and Hannah were bundled in their puffy parkas, working side by side, pushing a huge ball of snow along to begin another snowman. Coming up to the country had drawn them together; it had pulled Josh and me further apart. I lay back in bed, sinking into my own guilt. I moved toward Josh under the covers. He stirred and pulled me into the arch of his long body, teaspoon style, enclosing my waist with his arms. His skin was warm, and I felt his breath on my back. I was looking for the words to apologize for my rotten behavior, when he said into my neck, "Do you remember that I got the name of that arson investigator from Shank? Back before we figured out what a crook he is."

I undid myself from Josh's arms and faced him. "What are you saying? You think he hooked us up with someone he knew would tell us it wasn't arson?"

"Gornick's an asshole, but I suspect he does know about these things."

"What Gornick knows is how to unnerve people. I'm sure that's his real profession—unnerving his clients so they'll feel they need to depend on him. I'm not going to let him do that shit to me."

"Looks like he did a fairly good job of it," Josh commented.

"He didn't unnerve me—he made me angry. What an awful thing to stir up the question of arson as his dinner table entertainment. We all live here, for God's sake. Gornick is a sadist with a nose for people's vulnerability. We had two separate investigations that came to the same conclusion. I don't understand why we're giving this any more consideration. If you want to start down that path again, go ahead. Make it your project. But right now I have my hands full with what I've already got to cope with." I sat up abruptly and searched for my slippers on the floor.

"What's the hurry to get up? The kids are fine."

"I'm tense, Josh. I'm too tense to have sex."

"So we won't have sex, we'll just lie here together."

I turned back to him, surprised by his tenderness.

"It's a tough time, Annie. We'll get through it."

His black curls were spread out against the pillow, and his chest was bare. I considered his deep-set eyes, his beaky nose, his Adam's apple, which was the size of a goose egg. I liked the exaggerated quality of his features. He was not a handsome man by any conventional standard, but women always found him appealing. Maybe it was because he genuinely liked women, particularly the smart ones. He wasn't a great talker, but he was a good listener, at least when he wasn't faced with a barrage of his wife's criticism.

I got back under the covers. "I can't stand the way something comes along and turns our lives on end."

"It'd be a different story if your father wasn't sick, Annie. It's a lot to contend with all at once." Josh cupped his hand against my cheek. "I love you, you know, even when you're a pain in the ass. And you're right, Gornick is a sadist."

We were lying close enough that I could feel his penis stir.

"I don't see why," I said.

"Why Gornick is a sadist?"

"No, Josh. Why you love me."

He smiled. "Maybe it's best if I keep you guessing."

"I'm sorry I was such a bitch yesterday."

"I'll take the apology in services."

Josh pulled me over on top of him, and I raised my eyebrows as if I were indulging him. In fact I was deeply grateful that Josh was holding on through the roller-coaster ride of my moods. My world was shifting perilously. Too much was out of my control. And I was my father's daughter—I needed control as surely as I needed air.

# 5

The radiation treatments were so powerful that they burned a brown patch onto my father's flesh, and as his chest sunk, that dark patch looked as though his heart were pushing out from within. This guarded man, who had once seemed to have no past and no family other than the four of us, now began telling me the story of his life, most of which I had never heard before. During my visits to Los Angeles, the video conversations in which he related his history became our project and his purpose.

He started with his earliest memories, stories he'd been told as a child about how his family came to America. His mother, my grandmother Minnie Fishman, had been a young girl when they fled the onslaught of pogroms and village burnings in czarist Russia. Minnie, her mother, Getta, and her younger sister, Ofra, were rowed across the ice-packed Dnieper River in the dead of winter, leaving their dying shtetl behind them. Once again—it seemed to come in waves with the years of failed crops and famine—Russian soldiers were on a spree of persecution, kicking the bellies of pregnant Jewish women with their metal-toed boots, yanking the side curls of the old men until their cheeks ran with blood, snatching the young men and conscripting them into twenty-year service in the cruelly anti-Semitic Russian army.

It was 1898, and my grandmother, who was called Malka at that time, was twelve years old. She had already seen too many men stolen, too many dawns turned gray with the smoke of torched villages. My father told me he believed some inner current of hope had already been switched off in her. Through all her life she remained a sour soul, rooted miserably to the earth like a stubborn soup potato that would not rot but would never grow, either.

Until that trip across the icy Dnieper, young Malka's entire world had been the cluster of wind-whipped houses that sat huddled against the outside world on a muddy knoll a hundred miles west of Kiev. Their family's two-room shack had a dirt floor, and in the winter months their cow would move indoors with them. Night after night, supper was a watery beet soup. Friday nights, because of the Sabbath, there was a loaf of bread. My father remembered his mother telling him that the minutes of waiting through the prayer over the bread were excruciating for her. Bread was the softest thing in her world.

In the evenings Malka would lie in her cot beside Ofra, listening to the shtetl men chanting their prayers as they begged God's grace to light upon them in their relentless hunger. There was no Chagall fiddler floating above their rooftops. There was no kindly, bearded father to pat Malka's head and encourage her to imagine a handsome suitor. Her life was not gentle or romantic; it was cold and sullen and brutal. When Malka was eight years old, her frightened father was marched away to the army under the rifles of the Cossacks. He had not had time to leave a son growing in his young wife's womb before he was led over the hills and out of his family's life forever. Malka's last sight of her sad father was of the bare heels that showed through his broken shoes.

As she grew, Malka knew she would not have the pleasant nature or natural beauty that would enable the matchmaker to find her a tolerable husband; even as a girl, she was shaped like one of the puffball mushrooms that pushed up through the leaves on the forest floor. Her sister, Ofra, was no beauty, either. With no money, no prospects, no husband, and two daughters who were more liability than asset, Getta Peytchinov decided to make a new life in the faraway country of America. The three of them sat in the sloshing rowboat on their way to an uncertain future, but they did not touch one another or share a single comforting word.

Somehow they managed to make their way to Gdansk, where they joined Getta's sister Leah, who had long ago escaped the shtetl by running off with a traveling wine merchant. The wine merchant, whom Leah married, paid their passages on a freighter that sailed straight out into the terrifying black swells of the frigid, winter Atlantic. Leah's husband had brought along cases of fine wine to start his career in America, but he had developed too much affection for his merchandise. He was seen for the last time near midnight on the second night at sea, weaving along the railing of the middle deck. It was whispered that he had been in the company of a woman other than his wife, someone short and squat, who stood on tiptoe beside him to peer over the railing and admire the moon-flecked wake.

By noon the next day, word was out among the immigrants huddling near the steam pipes that ran through their steerage quarters: Leah's husband was nowhere to be found. By sunset Leah was wailing and davening with the slowly rocking hull. The man who was to provide for her in America was gone, and along with him the three diamonds cached in his vest pocket, their capital for the new world. The only thing left to distinguish Leah from her pitiful shtetl sister was the cargo of wine bottles, whose corks were already swelling and popping in the hot and cold extremes of the steerage compartment. Then and there Leah decided that Getta was to blame for the drowning, and she never for the rest of her life forgave her.

My father had no idea what transpired on his mother's arrival in New York City, the processing through Ellis Island—the Island of Tears—or her initial encounter with a bustling, booming America in the last year of the nineteenth century. He imagined that she and her mother and sister were terrified. They found their way to Boston, and soon after, Leah met an Irishman named Jimmy Farland, who worked on a farm in Malden, Massachusetts. Leah became Lily Farland and gave birth to two American sons. Getta and her two young daughters were on their own.

Getta Peytchinov never found an American husband for herself, but for Malka she did find a man, sleeping on a Boston streetcar. The man had arrived from Russia only months before and was coping with the new world by sleeping as much as possible. Crossing the Atlantic, Malka's husband-to-be had met a rich American Jew whose name was Fishman. He took Fishman for his own name at the desk at Ellis Island, hoping the name would make him wealthy. Malka was sixteen when she was betrothed to this man, who was nearly twice her age. On the marriage certificate, dated June 29, 1903, Isaac Fishman was listed as a mackintosh maker. Malka's name was changed to Miriam, and her age was given as twenty. So much had changed in her life. She took the opportunity to change a few other details as well.

Miriam Fishman's first disappointment in her new husband was that he had overstated his credentials. He was no tailor; he did not sew the raincoats produced by the factory in Roxbury, Massachusetts, where he had found work. Isaac's lowly job was nothing more than cutting the rubberized fabric off the bolts. He had no skill or aptitude for anything else. As the marriage progressed and Miriam Fishman grew more disgusted with her husband, she would shake her fist at him and call him "presser," the lowest of the factory castes, a rung even lower than cutter.

Isaac Fishman worked when the factory wasn't out on strike and when there were orders. When he worked, he stayed sober. When he didn't work, he began drinking on the walk from his bed to the breakfast table. Though Issac produced four children by Miriam Fishman, my father, who was the youngest, barely recalled a single detail about the man. The only clear memory he had was of his father on his deathbed.

On that day Abie—as he was called then—was summoned from his desk in a stuffy Boston schoolroom jammed with poor immigrant children. The principal was waiting for him outside in the hall, along with Abie's sixteen-year-old brother, Joey.

"You're needed at home," the principal said sternly.

Joey took long strides back up Blue Hills Avenue, and Abie had to run to keep up with him. Before they climbed to the Fishmans' two-room apartment Joey took Abie by the shoulders. "He's dying, ya know. Ya gotta kiss the bastard."

Lying in the stinking bed, Isaac Fishman looked a hundred years old. The skin had sunk around his cheekbones, and his grizzled beard was patchy on his sallow flesh. A shaft of sunlight, sliding between the closed muslin curtains, made a white streak across Isaac Fishman's stringy neck.

Abie stared at the ghastly, withered man he'd been told to kiss. He curled his fingers into fists at his sides to muster courage. He was not a timid boy. Though he was small for his age, he would dive into any fight if his status on the street required it. But this man in the bed was a stranger whom Abie knew mostly by the smell of stale alcohol and dried urine. Abie also knew the smell of more troubling things—failure, weakness, lies. The angry woman and her four children who watched Isaac Fishman die had no place in their hearts for him. He had long since become more furniture than father.

Issac drew his cramped hand from under the flannel sheet and raised it over his youngest son's head, pulling himself an inch off his pillow and narrowing his empty eyes at the only one who might still listen to him. "Abie, you must protect your mother *always*. Do you hear me?"

Abie Fishman nodded in terrified obedience as his father's eyes rolled back.

With her useless husband out of the way, Abie's mother, now a mature woman of thirty-three, began a transformation. She dyed her hair red, renamed herself Molly, and went to find herself a gentleman at the tavern on Roxbury Avenue where the Protestant life insurance salesmen stopped to drink. On the evenings when the silent man in a black suit appeared at their apartment, Abie slid off the kitchen chair and withdrew to the street as he had been instructed to do. Abie knew what women and men did together. His brother Joey had shown him how to climb out onto the roof above their apartment to spy through the window at the fat baker Tamowitz pumping away on his equally fat wife. It did not bother Abie that his mother kept company with a man who looked like an undertaker. He liked the freedom it gave him to explore the neighborhood, day or night. Abe was always first on line at Tamowitz's Bakery when the day-old bread was sold for a penny a loaf. He earned his pennies by selling admission to the roof, through his apartment, to view Tamowitz at work on his wife.

Abie's budding entrepreneurial instinct also served him in the gambling operation he ran in the alley behind Moishe's Kosher Chicken Shop, where he took bets on how long his street friends could stand at the back door viewing the chicken massacre before they had to turn away to puke. Abie never puked. He liked to stand at the door and watch the *shohet* take his razor-sharp knife to the neck of one squawking chicken after another, then pour the blood onto the sawdust-covered floor. The slaughtered chickens would be handed over to the line of women who sat by on egg crates, waiting to sear the chicken feathers with a gas flame in preparation for plucking. Soon the putrid odor of charred chicken feathers filled the shop and the street, and the smell was gut-wrenching. That's when Abie would collect his winnings.

As a boy my father was a precocious reader. He "borrowed" his reading material from the corner newsstand until he discovered the existence of the public library. To his amazement, the library loaned books for free. When his mother saw that Abie had an aptitude for reading, she put him to work reading the serialized novels from the daily newspaper to her illiterate neighbors, a penny a page. Abie was also required to read to his grandma Getta, an ancient woman with a single front tooth, who lived one week with them and the next week with her other daughter, Molly's sister, Ofra.

America had not rewarded Getta the way it had rewarded her sister, Lily, the fat and satisfied wife of Farmer Farland. Lily would not answer her sister's pleading letters or allow her to visit or set eyes on her nephews. Twenty-two years later, the transatlantic tragedy still had not been forgotten or forgiven.

Perhaps Getta was compelled to pass along this agony of rejection to her own two daughters, by pitting them against each other: Each week when she moved from one daughter's apartment to the other, she carried a locked leather trunk in which, she hinted, were riches. My father recalled the bargain Getta put forth, and how it settled like a dark cloud over their lives. The daughter who treated Getta the best would someday inherit the trunk, and the other daughter would get nothing. Though she never let anyone look inside, Getta hinted that the trunk was stuffed with the booty she had collected from the pockets of the rich families in Brighton, where she worked for years as a laundress.

Abe watched Getta fan the flames as Molly and Ofra schemed for their mother's favor. Getta would tell one daughter how much better she was treated at the other daughter's house and insinuate that the other daughter knew all about the riches inside the trunk. Then came the Sunday when Getta showed up without the trunk. When asked about its whereabouts, she wouldn't answer and never spoke again. She simply arrived every other Sunday, waited to be fed, and went to sleep. Each sister assumed the other had made a deal with their mother, and that the trunk was already stored in a secret spot. When Getta died of a cerebral hemorrhage on the trolley between her two daughters' homes, the secret of the trunk died with her, but the pain of being rejected by her own sister did not. She had passed it on to Molly and Ofra, who never saw or spoke to each other again in their lives, each furious with the other for stealing their mother's riches.

With no family ties to keep her in Boston and imagining a better life, late one night Molly Fishman emptied her Protestant boyfriend's pants pocket of the two hundred dollars he had collected that day in life insurance premiums, gathered up Abe, his sister, Fanny, and her two older sons, and fled by train to Philadelphia. There they found a cold-water flat on the edge of the railroad yards, and Abie's brothers, Joey and Philip, now in their twenties, bought fruit off railroad cars coming up from the South and carted it off to sell in the streets of the city. Molly Fishman took crates of Concord grapes and fermented them with sugar and water in ceramic crocks. When the alcohol content reached its peak, she carried her crocks to the railroad yard and ladled out the rough wine to the railroad workers. Prohibition hadn't gotten rid of liquor, but it had put the price beyond the reach of the ordinary working man. Molly became a saint in the railroad yards, and the men filled her pockets with cash.

In Philadelphia Abe went back to school. Molly gave her name to the school registrar as Minnie Fisher and introduced her son as Abraham Fisher. When he was asked his age, Abie waited for his mother to give the answer since he had learned that such details were to be adjusted as necessary. Each day, as Abie Fisher ran a terrifying gauntlet to school and back through a neighborhood filled with angry Southern blacks who hadn't found promised work in the Northern cities, he heard the calls of "kike" and felt the sting of pebbles smacking his legs. He stopped to let his tears dry before climbing the stairs to his mother, who had made it clear she was not interested in his tears. Abe was relieved the night he was awakened and made to climb onto the back of Joey and Philip's vegetable truck. He and Fanny were strapped down between the barrels of his mother's belongings. As the dawn came, they pulled onto a street on the Lower East Side of Manhattan. Joey and Philip carried their mother's barrels up the narrow stairs to a flat on the Bowery, but they did not stay. It was time for them to go off on their own in the world. Molly needed to find a new husband, and no man would keep company with a woman who lived with two grown sons. Molly Fisher became Molly Hershey, a name she had spotted on a billboard on the way out of Pennsylvania.

A new stepfather soon appeared, a fast talker with oiled hair and a wad of bills in his pocket. The bills were German marks made worthless by the war, but Jack Miner assured Molly Hershey that the League of

Nations would soon restore German pride and those marks would mean great wealth. Meanwhile, Jack Miner had a formula for hair dye. He stirred up his brew in the bathtub that sat on a raised platform in the kitchen of their Bowery flat. When his customers rubbed his hair dye into their scalps, it returned their tired gray hair to a glistening black. They didn't know that Jack Miner's secret ingredient was lead, that the dye would turn their brains to mush, and eventually, when they were too feeble-minded to notice, would finish the job and kill them. Molly's new husband peddled his hair dye to every barbershop on the Lower East Side. One morning Molly Miner woke to discover that Jack had disappeared with the gold ring he had bought her, his roll of German marks, the kitchen flatware, and all their cash. She raged for twenty-four hours and then she slept for twenty-four hours, exhausted by her fury. When she woke, she put on her apron, stirred up a new batch of black dye in the bathtub, and carried the bottles down the street herself.

Abe Miner went alone to enroll in P.S. 43. He had discovered another public library in Philadelphia and had learned enough to present himself as a thirteen-year-old, ready for eighth grade, even though he was barely eleven. He searched for a public library on the Lower East Side and set himself the task of reading the dictionary from A to Z. No matter how often his home or last name changed, words were possessions he could keep.

Abe Miner became Abe Maner when Molly's customers started coming after her with handfuls of their dead hair, and the family moved again in the middle of the night, this time across the East River to Atlantic Avenue in Brooklyn. In Brooklyn Molly Maner became Minnie Maner and set up trade as a "customer peddler," a shopping agent for her new neighbors, who had neither the Manhattan sophistication nor the knowledge of Lower East Side retailers that she did. She combined their shopping needs into one list and used the extra buying power to bargain for prices much lower than any of them could have gotten alone.

Word of Minnie Maner's skill spread quickly. The lower she drove the prices, the more customers she got. The more customers she got, the more proudly she strutted up Atlantic Avenue. Thus, in the middle of her life, Minnie Maner came into her own, and the next time she married, she married for love. Hyman Rosenoff took her all the way to Forty-seventh Street in Manhattan to pick out a diamond ring. When she showed her customers the sparkling stone on her finger, she didn't tell them that she'd paid for it herself.

The same year that Abe Maner became Abe Rosenoff was the year he discovered the Horatio Alger series in the library. He read the tales of miraculous business success and saw himself in this boy whose quick mind and willingness to work hard were rewarded by rich benefactors. At age twelve Abe was beginning to imagine his future. He wanted be a wealthy man who drove a black car and handed pennies through the rolled-down windows to poor children in the street. He knew he was smart. He knew he could reinvent himself whenever necessary. He had watched his mother do it herself half a dozen times. When junior high school wasn't challenging enough for him, Abe Rosenoff climbed the steps of Brooklyn High School of Science and told them he was fourteen. He had decided to become a chemical engineer.

As Mrs. Hyman Rosenoff, who sported a diamond ring, Minnie gained new respectability, and she used her customer peddler earnings to open a ladies' undergarments shop. But less than a year after their court-house wedding, Hyman Rosenoff disappeared, removing the diamond ring from Minnie's finger as she lay snoring. He also did a clean sweep of the cash locked in the store register and took the roll of bills Minnie believed she had kept hidden from him in a compartment under the floorboards.

Minnie's heart now hardened, not only to men but to her children Abe and Fanny, who stared at her every morning when she woke. She did show them affection in one way, though. No matter how much they had to tighten their belts as the Depression settled in around them, Minnie saw to it that her children, and particularly her youngest, Abie, wore expensive shoes. It was Minnie Rosenoff's most cherished belief that shoes were the measure of a man.

My father never forgot those tender moments of his childhood when he gazed down at new wing-tip shoes as the salesman intoned their value. He liked the heft of the thick leather, which made him feel firmly grounded to earth, like one of those life-sized punching balloons whose sand-filled bottom would make it bounce upright again whenever it was hit. Later in life, when my father no longer recalled anything of his mother's hands, lips, or eyes, what he did remember was each and every pair of the shoes she had bought him.

As if to announce that she was done with men for good, Minnie Rosenoff took back the name of the dead Isaac Fishman. When fire destroyed her Atlantic Avenue store and all the goods inside, Minnie took the insurance money and moved into a fine new location on Fulton Avenue. When the Fulton Avenue place also burned, Minnie used the insurance money to open yet another store on Flatbush Avenue. The Fishman family was moving up in the world. They no longer lived in unheated rooms upstairs above their store, but in an apartment in a building on a residential street. One Christmas, after another fire in Minnie Fishman's dry goods shop, the Italian family who lived upstairs and ran the fruit stand next door moved out. Minnie had room to expand, and installed glass-topped counters and racks for women's ready-to-wear dresses. That was the year my father began wearing vests, smoking cigarettes, and drinking vodka. He had turned fifteen.

Abe finished high school and enrolled in Brooklyn Polytech, but every afternoon after school he worked for his mother in her store, as she moved to better and better locations along the main shopping avenue in Brooklyn. Abe's job was to keep the stockroom in order and bring items out to Fanny when the customers needed a different size or color. Though Abe and Fanny worked long hours, they never received a cent of spending money from their mother, so secretly, at night, they both took small amounts of cash straight from the register. They did not consult each other on this, but each knew the other did it.

One afternoon Minnie grabbed Abe the minute he came through the door from Brooklyn Polytech. In the stockroom, out of Fanny's earshot, Minnie hissed, "She's stealing from the till! Your rotten sister. She'll steal me blind!"

Abe lit up a cigarette.

"You've got to watch over the cash register. No more going off to college. You've got to stay here all day now. You've got to protect me!"

Issac Fishman's ghost floated into the room. Abe Fishman had always been a boy without a father. He had puzzled over what it meant to be a man. He had never forgotten his father's dying words, cursing Abe with the task he himself had failed at so miserably. "Abie, you must protect your mother."

Minnie Fishman pushed her nose up to her son's chin. "*Protect me! You must protect me!*"

Abe Fishman sighed. If he was someday to become a Horatio Alger millionaire, it would have to be without a college degree in chemical engineering.

At age seventeen Abe Fishman became the man of the house, though his mother still did not give him a dime for his work. Perhaps it was the humiliation of having to steal every dollar he needed from the cash register after working twelve-hour days in his mother's store that led him, one evening as he was rushing to finish work and meet Shirley Leiberman outside the Metro Cinema, to take two dollars from the cash register right in front of his mother.

The scream that Minnie Fishman let out froze her customers in place. For one shocking moment the store was deadly silent. Then, with the audience of her sympathetic peers, Minnie strode over to her son and slapped him hard across his face.

Abe saw flecks of red floating in the yellowed whites of his mother's eyes. Her nose was a wormy crab apple. Her skin had the texture of bark. Hatred rose up like a pleasing warm tide. Abe lifted his hand. His gesture was deliberate, not impulsive. He had watched the parade of men who had come and gone from Minnie Fishman's oppressive world. He wanted at last to be one of them.

His open palm landed hard against his mother's face. When she wailed, her customers wailed with her. When she bent forward in pain and shame, they clasped their arms over their stomachs and bent forward, too. Abe remained perfectly still. So this was freedom.

A policeman came rushing into the store, and Abe listened impassively as the tale of his violence was recounted. He did not flinch when his mother instructed the officer to book him, and the policeman slapped handcuffs onto his wrists. At the police station his fingers were pressed into an ink pad and rolled from side to side on white paper. He was pushed up against a wall while mug shots were taken, front, right, and left. Abe did not offer any defense or correction to the statement given by the police magistrate to the reporter from the *Brooklyn Beacon*.

Minnie Fishman did not come to the police station to see her son, though in the end she did not press charges. After two days of sleeping in a cell, Abe Fishman was released, and he took a room in the Mayflower Hotel on Brooklyn Avenue. His mother never came to see him there, either. He never went to the store to see her. And that, according to my father, was how it came to be that he never again in his life laid eyes on his mother, Malka Miriam Molly Minnie Fishman Fisher Hershey Miner Maner Rosenoff Fishman.

# 6

Over the years my parents had told us their different versions of how they got together, part of the lore each constructed to justify their differing points of view about the failure of their marriage.

My father liked to describe the day my mother appeared at the women's lingerie counter at J. D. Barzilay and Company in Manhattan, where he had been working for the four years following his flight from his mother and Brooklyn. He had gotten used to the hard-eyed women who, even in the tenth year of the worst depression in history, came in with mink tippets draped around their shoulders and wads of bills to spend. Abe understood that these women earned their keep from wealthy men with sexual appetites, and they barely noticed him, a lingerie salesclerk trying to get ahead.

Judith Grau, waiting for Abe's attention, was something else altogether, as pale as a saltines cracker and so skinny that too much of a question would have blown her over. Abe saw that she might have been beautiful if she hadn't considered herself so ugly. She wore no makeup, hunched one shoulder forward as if she were preparing to defend herself against an assault, and her mouth twitched with worry. But she had luminescent green eyes, high cheekbones, and vibrant auburn hair tied back in a ribbon. Abe guessed she was only a few years younger than he, but light-years away from his confidence in the world.

Judith had come to Barzilay on an errand for her mother, who had been given a gift of an elegant silk slip and instead wanted the money it cost. Such a transaction was against store policy, but there was something so appealingly needy about this young woman. Abe went through a charade of arranging a return for cash. As soon as Judith left the counter, he replenished the register from his own wallet and tore up all the paperwork except the young woman's name and address. From the moment Judith Grau let her green eyes meet his in an expression of gratitude, Abe knew that this was a woman who belonged in his future.

My mother's first impression of her husband-to-be was that he was a short boy in a three-piece suit, with slicked-back hair, dark eyes, and an oily tongue, who had blackmailed her into giving him her name and address in exchange for her mother's money. Judith had been taught in the eighteen years she and her mother had humbled themselves as poor cousins in a rich family that money, its existence or lack, was the basis of all human relationships. Her mother had instructed her that their dependent financial status meant Judith must at all times be obsequious, undemanding, and ready to please. If Judith imagined a man in her future, it was a wealthy prince who would save her.

When Abe Fishman came calling that Friday night, a bouquet of red roses in his hand, Judith Grau stepped out into the hall to whisper to him, but did not invite him in. If Judith's mother, Rose Grau, got wind that a man had come to call, she would have harangued her daughter with the usual torrent of humiliating observations about her skinny body, dowdy clothes, slouching posture, and unfashionable hairstyle. Finally she would have tossed out a warning of the harm that came to women who fell into the clutches of men. The only safe place for Judith was on the couch in the Grau living room, where she would be available on a moment's notice to make tea for her mother, run her errands, read her the newspaper, or simply agree with Rose Grau's nasty view of the world. Weekly, Rose lamented out loud what a mistake it had been to give birth to her daughter, the unfortunate product of a marriage that had lasted five sorry months.

Pregnant and divorced at age twenty-two, Rose Grau had refused to touch her baby girl when the infant was brought to her after she was born. When the nurse pulled aside the receiving blanket to give the new mother a better view of her child's face, Rose scrunched her nose and turned away as if there were a bad smell. Of course she had no name ready for the birth certificate. When the nurse urged her to choose one, Rose Grau demanded, "What's *your* name?"

"Judith," the nurse had answered.

"Fine. Name her Judith."

"That's no way to give a name," the nurse protested.

"Then you give the thing a name. I don't care what you call it."

"All right," the nurse replied. "We'll name her Judith, and that will always remind you of the nurse who told you that God made a terrible mistake by giving you a child."

For several months Abe and Judith met in secret on their lunch hour, Abe from his post at Barzilay and Company, and Judith from the secretarial school she attended, since her mother insisted that a girl with no beauty and no talent needed a skill to rely on. Abe was proud to usher Judith into the Horn and Hardart on West Fifty-seventh Street and watch over her as she ate a complete lunch, at his insistence, with an extra dessert to add some flesh to her. During these lunches they discovered the thing they had in common—their mean, suffocating mothers. Abe had escaped, but Judith had not, and Abe was determined to help her. As the older man who was making his own way in the world, Abe gave Judith advice about what to say to her mother. Judith would report on her successes and failures, and Abe enjoyed his new role of protector to a young woman in unfortunate circumstances. When my mother recalled these Horn and Hardart lunches, even she acknowledged the sweetness of those months. Before Abe, no one had ever told her she was beautiful.

One Saturday evening, after six months of lunches, Abe pulled up to Judith's apartment building in a Studebaker Presidential. His superior ability to sell lingerie had earned him a raise to the incredible Depression-era salary of thirty-five dollars per week. That very morning he had used his first increased salary check to make the down payment on the car, slipped behind the wheel, and taught himself to drive.

The doorman called up and when Judith came down, Abe proudly stretched his arm across the front seat of the Studebaker and convinced her to accompany him to Battery Park, at the tip of Manhattan. Judith slid into the passenger seat, certain that when she returned, her mother would have bolted the door shut. Years later, when bitterness colored all her memories, my mother told us that the trip to Battery Park was the biggest mistake of her life. How could she say no when Abe Fishman got down on one knee, with the backdrop of New York Harbor and the Statue of Liberty, and asked her to marry him?

When Judith returned, her mother was waiting at the front door of the apartment grabbing at her chest as if she were having a heart attack.

"You disappeared! You ugly one."

Judith announced her intention to marry a man named Abraham Fishman.

Rose Grau's snarl turned into a sickly satisfied smile. Her trump card was too sweet. "I'm afraid, my dear, permission will not be granted. The law is still the law, and in the eyes of New York State, you, Judith Grau, are still a child."

When Judith reported the bad news to Abe, he came up with a plan. In Europe the campaign against Germany was going badly, and it seemed inevitable that America would enter the war. The armed forces were already putting out the call for volunteers. Rose Grau could prevent her daughter from marrying, but she could not stop her from enlisting.

Judith chose the navy, and Abe chose the air force. He was assigned to teach navigation and, even after Pearl Harbor was bombed, never left North Dakota. Judith demonstrated a talent for drawing, and spent the war years in Norfolk, Virginia, illustrating an upbeat navy newsletter shipped to WACS overseas. She created a cartoon character called Lucky Lucy, who, bumbling but endearing, managed to do everything wrong but have it come out all right. The day Judith turned twenty-one, she married Abe, but forty-eight hours later they returned to their war assignments. The realization of their error came much later. As my mother saw it, she had unwittingly married a man whose drive to escape the shame of being poor was as all-consuming as her own grasping mother's. According to my father, once freed from the narcissist who had kept her prisoner, Judith turned the tables and became as self-centered as her mother ever was, paying back Rose Grau and the rest of the world.

When the war ended and they were reunited, Abe put his entrepreneurial skills to work. For several months he crisscrossed the country by bus, buying up army surplus mattresses and shipping them to a fellow entrepreneur, who turned them into pulp for making paper. After a year of eking out a living in a dark basement apartment in Queens, Abe suggested they take his mattress earnings and move to California. In postwar America, California was nearly mythic in its promise of a new beginning. They packed their belongings into a Dodge coupe and tied what didn't fit inside onto the roof. Abe planned to come up with a business scheme by the time they saw the Pacific Ocean.

They were crossing the Mississippi River with Judith driving and Abe absorbed in a local newspaper, when Abe came across a story about three babies who had died in a St. Louis hospital because a nurse had inadvertently put salt instead of sugar into their formula. This was in a time before infant formula was mass-produced and canned, and human error and unsterile conditions often led to tragedy. Like any good entrepreneur, my father had an instinct for the critical population statistics of his time. The postwar baby boom was about to hit. The demand for infant formula would roll in like a tsunami. Why not create a business that produced baby formula in safe and sterile conditions in a specialized factory, instead of hit or miss by busy nurses? That night in a motel room west of Topeka, Abe woke out of a deep sleep with his idea fully formed. He would offer hospitals a daily delivery of freshly prepared formula made strictly according to prescription, guaranteed safe, and the hospitals would be able to shut down their formula rooms for good.

"'Healthy Formula for Healthy Babies.' That's what I'll call it," he announced out loud, but Judith only turned over in her sleep.

Abe's decision to drive south toward Los Angeles instead of north to San Francisco was also a matter of demographics. The population of Los Angeles was growing at four times the rate of San Francisco's. Judith was reluctant. She had set her sights on the rolling hills of northern California. Abe promised to find hills for her in southern California, but it was nearly a decade before they made it out of the hot, stucco ghetto of East Los Angeles.

In the early years my father worked seven days a week and often spent the nights as well sleeping on a cot in the converted army depot where he started his new formula business. He had to work out the challenges of sterilization, filling and conveying hundreds of fragile bottles, getting his pioneering service accepted. By night he invented; by day he went calling on one hospital administrator after another to try to sell them something they didn't know they needed. Within a year he had used up all the money he had made in the mattress recycling business, while my mother spent her days pregnant and alone in the stifling summer heat.

When Tony was born, Abe came to the maternity ward with news Judith had never expected. After another infant death and an expensive lawsuit, the largest hospital in Los Angeles had decided that Healthy Formula for Healthy Babies was a product they could no longer do without. It took seven more years before Abe accumulated enough cash to build his wife a house in the hills of Malibu. By that time they had three children and a fourth on the way, and Judith was resolutely exhibiting the mothering technique she had learned during her own childhood: Food and clothing were her responsibility; the rest was up to us.

During those years my father's need to control our world was awesome and exhausting. He did not like mess and would not tolerate any lack of cleanliness. Much later he explained to me that those things reminded him of being poor, a memory he detested. When I was a barefoot child running up and down the creeks of the Malibu hills, my father was always in my peripheral vision, working, building, chopping, Mount Vesuvius about to blow. It was hard to anticipate what would set him off—an empty soda can left in the driveway, a tube of toothpaste left uncapped. Our sibling battles also provoked him—what did any of us have to fight about with all that he was providing for us? We did not do it deliberately, at least not consciously, but maybe provoking his anger was the way we coped with our terror of it. My mother also seemed to relish the moment when he lost control. She would roll her eyes to call attention to his ridiculousness and to her calm superiority.

Even as he became more and more successful in business, anger or its sublimation colored my father's days, and therefore our lives, from sunup to sunset. He unleashed his rage on the natural world that encroached on our house in the hills above Malibu, hacking and sawing and splitting wood with grim determination. It took both of my ten-year-old hands to encircle one of his biceps. He burned great stacks of vines he ripped out from the undergrowth. Once, by accident, he burned a pile of poison oak branches. The oily smoke coated his skin and was sucked deep into his throat, and for a full week he lay in bed, speechless, wrapped from ears to toes in strips of torn sheets that had been soaked in cold black tea to soothe him.

My father did not soothe. He got back out of bed and built massive timber retaining walls to hold back the sliding mud of the incessant California floods. He dug culverts to divert the rushing winter rain, torrents of brown water that pulled the earth down upon us. One year the brown water created a lake that rose up to our front door and seeped in across the tiles of the inner courtyard. In a very rare moment of admiration for my father, my mother told us the story of Noah and his foresight. Abe Fishman, our Noah, proudly folded his arms across his chest: Even in the worst flooding in California history his system of retaining walls and culverts had held and had kept us from disaster.

As a child I was too innocent to make a connection between anger and shame. But I must have intuited something of its contours because increasingly, when my father's anger erupted, I felt a kind of pity for him. I sensed a well of sadness in him. I saw it in his dark eyes, his turned-down mouth. Sometimes, when I felt the early rumblings of anger building up inside him, his sadness fermenting to fury, I would try to mollify him with kisses on his rough cheeks or a performance of pirouettes and somersaults. Perhaps I did this out of fear, but perhaps it was also because I wanted to demonstrate that I could be a better friend to him than his complaining wife. My efforts must have worked often enough to keep me at it. As I grew older and saw that word play relaxed him, I would try to help him with his crossword puzzles, but I had no aptitude, and he had no patience.

There were times when my parents would go at each other like raccoons fighting to the death, with no holds barred as they adroitly attacked each other's most vulnerable spots. My father had a litany: He worked making money, making culverts, making our lives financially secure and safe. Why couldn't his wife manage to see that his children were cared for and his home was kept in order?

My mother showed little regard for his gargantuan efforts. "Maybe if you weren't so short, you wouldn't have to be such a self-important little man."

"And maybe if you weren't so terrified of being poor, I wouldn't have to work so effing hard."

"You're the one who considers it shameful to be poor, not me."

"Is that so? Not by a long shot. I'm going to end up killing myself working night and day to satisfy you."

In fact he almost did kill himself. One night, working alone in his office on plans to retool the plant in order to expand the production of baby formulas to meet a new demand for home delivery, when he couldn't stand up straight or make one foot push forward in front of the other anymore, he called a doctor. He was curled up on the cold cement of the packing bay when an ambulance arrived minutes later and two attendants slid him onto a stretcher. They delivered him directly to the operating theater at Cedars of Lebanon Hospital, since it had taken no time to diagnose his ailment as a massively infected ruptured appendix that was spreading poison throughout his body. Fifteen more minutes and he would have needed a hearse instead of an ambulance.

We weren't allowed to visit him in the hospital because we might carry germs on our shoes and under our fingernails. We waited outside in the hospital parking lot while he stood at his window, and we waved to him. I worried about the man in the window, my father in his pajamas. I did not know then that he had almost died, but I certainly knew that my mother blamed him for his own sickness.

My father emerged from his temporary postoperative cocoon of peacefulness and relapsed into his fury. Nothing provoked him more than my mother's insistent demand that he "analyze his anger." She had begun seeing a psychoanalyst. Her analyst had advised her that my father should try to reconcile with his mother, as Judith was attempting to reconcile with hers.

"You should call your mother!" Judith screamed. "You should see her! You should deal with your childhood demons. Bury the hatchet. Put all this to rest."

"I have no interest. Who even remembers what she looks like? After twenty years, all I remember is her name."

"She is your *mother*."

"So what?"

"I am a mother. What if our children refused to see me?"

"If they do, it will be because of how you failed them."

"So she failed you, is that it?"

"I have no time for this. I have work to do," he would say and stomp away from my mother and her psychologizing.

It was about then that I met my father's mother for the first and only time, the only one of his relatives whose whereabouts he still knew. My mother had brought Ellen and me back east to visit her mother as part of their reconciliation. It was our first trip to New York City, and since Grandma Minnie lived close by in Brooklyn, my mother told us that we would go to visit her, too.

One afternoon, in a sickening August heat, Ellen, my mother, and I took a Checker cab to Brooklyn. Ellen liked the collapsible seats that flipped up from the floor, and she drove my mother nuts flipping and folding from one side of the cab to the other until the cab stopped in front of a tall, brick apartment house somewhere near Sheepshead Bay.

"Go on, go on ahead." My mother edged us out of the cab.

"Aren't you coming with us?" I asked.

She pulled a scrap of paper from her purse and handed it to me. I was the older sister, the responsible one. "That's the apartment number. Go on now, she's expecting you."

"By *ourselves?*" I was incredulous.

"Go on now. I'll be down here waiting."

I took Ellen's hand, and her fingers curled tightly around mine. I was eleven, she was seven. I knew I must not scare her by revealing my own fears. My mother knew this, too. It was her trump card. I pulled Ellen away from the cab and led her into the building.

Though it was as hot and humid as a rain forest on the sidewalk, inside it was as cold as a meat locker. An old man sat on a stool, wrapped in a wool blanket, his shoulders and back curled like a top-heavy letter C that might topple forward and kill itself.

"Little girls!"

I studied the scrap of paper my mother had given me. "We're looking for 9H. We're visiting our grandmother." I said this purposefully, hoping not to reveal that the woman in 9H who was supposed to be our grandmother was someone we had never laid eyes on in our lives.

"You can walk up nine flights or take the elevator or fly, girlies. Up to you." He let out a torrent of giggles.

She must have been watching from the window because by the time we reached her apartment, the door was standing open. Ellen dug her fingernails into my palm. "We're going in *there?*" Ellen believed in the bogeyman.

"It's Grandma Minnie," I reassured her.

"Who's that?"

"It doesn't matter." I pulled her ahead.

"Grandma?" I stepped inside the open door and waited to be invited into a dark room that smelled of urine.

"Children?"

It took some moments to make out the tiny woman sitting in the chair in the dark. Her shoulders sloped as if she had no bones. Her head sat on her shoulders as if she had no neck. Her legs dangled from her chair, and her feet hung in the air almost a full foot above the floor. In the entire room the only thing that seemed alive were her shoes. They were so polished and perfect, they glowed.

"Come in, come in."

I had been taught to be polite, to respect my elders, to be courteous and kind to those less fortunate. But everything in me wanted to run from this horrid room and escape this creepy, neckless midget of a woman who was supposed to be my grandmother.

"Eat a cookie," she instructed. "Come eat a cookie, little girls."

Ellen dragged me forward to the table where the plate of cookies waited. There were six Nabisco gingersnaps arranged in a circle. Ellen stuffed one into her mouth, and I glared at her. She should say hello first. Apologizing for my sister, I said, "Hello, Grandma Minnie. I'm Annie. This is Ellen. She's only seven."

"Annie?" She considered my name as if she had never heard it before.

I was standing at a safe distance, but close enough to see her face. Her bones had given up, leaving her flesh to sink as if it were being inhaled from within. She must have been the oldest person I had ever seen. Where were her teeth and eyebrows? A thousand years ago, when she was about my age, she had crossed an icy midnight river in hopes of leaving her hunger on the muddy hills behind her. The two freckled girls standing before her were the descendants of that frightening adventure. We had never gone to bed with tears of hunger staining our cheeks. We had never been frightened, except when our parents fought. We rode horses bareback across the yellow California hills. We wore shorts to school. Our childhood was a fairy tale of comfort and wealth. We stood before this old lady with absolute confidence in our future. Her eyes slid down to our knobby knees, our skinny legs, our flowered socks. She nodded in satisfied disappointment.

She was staring at our shoes, torn red Keds, not proper leather shoes with ties. My father, the last on the long list of men who had spurned her, had failed in his most essential duty, our footwear.

"Sit."

"My mother's downstairs in the taxi," I blurted out to let her know I expected to be leaving soon.

"Your mother." She stopped to consider this notion that we had a mother. They had never met, these two women who had my father and his anger in common.

The three of us did our duty, sitting in silence, getting a look at one another. Grandma Minnie didn't ask a single question, and taking her cue, I did not offer information about my father and mother or the ferocious battles that ensued whenever my grandmother's name was spoken. In that room I gained an understanding of my father's distaste for the dreariness of poverty, and for years after I recalled the acrid smell, the fat dust balls that lurked like mice, the sticky, cracked plastic that covered the sofa where Ellen sat squeezed up tight against my thigh. For years I harbored an indescribable guilt, my grandmother sitting alone before we came, and alone again after we left. Her loneliness was a disease that I did not want to catch.

Not long after that visit our parents informed us that they were getting a divorce. They used a line I'm sure was provided for them by either a divorce manual or one of their two lawyers. "We love you all very much, but we don't love each other anymore." I wondered if they ever did. Their announcement came at the height of the postwar, family-centered fifties, and even in Malibu, California, their divorce put us on the cutting edge.

*Two*

# 7

There was an old synagogue with a high vaulted doorway on a side street two blocks north of our apartment in New York City. Looking like a leftover from another age, it was sandwiched between a brownstone that had been turned into upscale apartments and a parking garage. An oval of emerald glass pierced the wall above the arched door frame. Hebrew letters arched around the window, carved into the stone facade, but of course I had no idea what they meant. On Friday nights and Saturday mornings a small group of people filtered in through the tall wooden door.

I had never taken much notice of this synagogue, even though I had passed by it hundreds of times over the years on the walk between our apartment and the subway entrance at Ninety-sixth Street. But in January, with everything that was going on in my life, I found myself lingering on the sidewalk opposite it, at first only looking, then beginning to wonder what I might find if I had the courage to go inside.

To the left of the door a dusty, glass-enclosed bulletin board listed the times of the services and the name of the rabbi, Seymour Lowenstein. It was a name I had come across when he was interviewed in *The New York Times* about his decision to invite Palestinian activists to speak at his synagogue during the Intifada. Rabbi Lowenstein's synagogue was not one of the famous New York temples that were supported by generations of wealthy families. The *Times* had described the place as "a home for a small band of congregants who were attracted to Rabbi Lowenstein's quietly irreverent leadership." Rabbi Lowenstein had responded to the reporter in

Talmudic style, question for question: "How can our children help but doubt the value of their religion," Rabbi Lowenstein asked his interviewer, "if we do not offer them a morally sound vision of Judaism?"

I knew what he meant about having doubts about Judaism. In addition to my childhood schooling in atheism, the little exposure I'd had to synagogue life made me wary. Josh and I had been to a half dozen bar and bat mitzvahs over the years, mostly at Long Island Reform temples with stained-glass windows of rainbows and birds in flight. The carpets were thick and the prayer books thin. I did not like the stand-up-comic-style rabbis or the obvious fact that those who donated the most money had the best seats. I did not like the translations from Hebrew into English, which had all the grace of a child's first-grade reader. I did not like repeating in unison prayers that asked God to perform this or that service in exchange for our promise to be on our best behavior. If I wanted any kind of God at all—and I suppose I did, because at least privately I did believe in God—I wanted something with a little more mystery. Sometimes, sitting in those cushioned pews in the tasteful tan-and-mauve decor, an edginess would build at the base of my spine, and it was all I could do to keep from bolting.

The synagogue on Ninety-fourth Street seemed like a very different sort of place, and I was drawn to it out of an idea that, given what lay ahead, I might need some help. I was well aware that my impulse was something of a cliché, turning to religion in the face of death. But the truth was that I did feel unnerved by what I suspected was coming. So far, my experience with death and dying had been limited. My grandmother had died, a great-uncle I barely knew, a couple of Josh's relatives. But none of that was death at close range. The one thing I suspected was that close up, death, like anything else, would be made up of a hundred details, and even the most courageous, like my father, would be humiliated by the banality of half of them.

It had snowed in the night, and it was still freezing and wet on the Friday morning late in January that I finally mustered my courage, tested the synagogue door, and found it unlocked. I was a little taken aback to think that any rogue unbeliever like me could step right through. A bone-chilling cold was trapped inside the thick stone walls. I wrapped my arms across my chest and stepped through the stone arches into the sanctuary.

The domed ceiling was covered with glittering Byzantine mosaics.

Thick, wooden groins drew my eye to the very apex, where a stained-glass window glowed like a great amber eye. I dropped down onto an uncushioned wooden pew, stunned by the beauty of the place, and sat in the quiet for a long time, not sure what I wanted, or if I wanted anything.

I was about to get up and leave when I heard footsteps and looked up to see a slight man approaching me, his hands tucked into the pockets of his sweater vest, his deep-set eyes neither welcoming nor discouraging. A small, blue velvet yarmulke was perched on his wispy gray hair. He stood and studied me for a few moments, in no rush to speak.

"Are you Rabbi Lowenstein?"

"I think so."

"My father has cancer."

He nodded. "Judaism has some suggestions. Come along. We'll talk in my office. My secretary is out sick today, so there's nobody to tell me I don't have time."

As I followed down the aisle between the pews, my eyes grew accustomed to the dim light, and I saw that every inch of every wall was covered with dull bronze plaques commemorating deceased congregants. Overhead, dust-covered filigreed brass lamps hung from the ceiling on exposed wires. Up front, a worn red curtain was pulled across a walnut cabinet. I knew that was where the Torah scrolls were kept. I knew the Torah was the very heart of Jewish religious life. I had no idea at all what was written on it.

Rabbi Lowenstein led the way out of the sanctuary and proceeded down a dark hall. The hallway made a turn, and the light grew even dimmer. He didn't look back to check on me. I was alone with my second thoughts: What could I possibly have to say to a rabbi, and what interest would he have in me, a woman who knew nothing about religion?

His office was a cave of bookshelves from floor to ceiling. A round table in the center of the room and the cracked leather sofa along one wall were completely covered with papers and open books. An old Royal typewriter sat on a wooden plank that made a precarious bridge between one edge of the round table and the edge of the bookshelf. A piece of paper jutted out of the carriage, a writing project begun and waiting.

He pointed to a chair at the round table. "Sit, sit." We both stared for a moment at the pile of papers stacked on the chair he offered. Then I gathered them up and put them carefully on the table, took off my jacket and held it in my lap.

He poured two cups of coffee from a metal pot and handed one to me, pointing to a jar of Cremora on the table. "If I keep milk around it goes bad, or I give it to the cat as her reward for killing mice." On cue, a great long-haired Angora cat slunk out from underneath the couch and glided up against the rabbi's trousers.

We sat across from each other and drank our coffee without talking. I found the silence extremely awkward, but it was clear that he was quite comfortable to wait until he had something he wanted to say. Finally he encircled his chin with his thumb and forefinger. "Our scholars tell us that death is the ultimate gift we have to give God in return for His gift to us of life."

I nodded agreeably as if what he said made sense to me, which it didn't. "I thought I might need to turn to my religion now—with all that's going to happen."

"Turn to your religion? Like some twenty-four-hour fast-food chain? You don't 'turn' to religion as if it were a drive-through McDonald's."

"I once believed in God," I blurted out in my own defense. "It's just that it's been so long since I thought about it."

"Who says God wants your belief? Believe or don't believe. That's your own business. That's not what God wants. What's your name, then, Miss I-once-believed-in-God?"

"Anne. Anne Waldmas—Annie," I stumbled over my own name.

"See here, Miss Annie Waldmas—don't try to believe. Who would you be trying for, anyway?" He bent his ear forward with his cupped hand. "Try listening instead. Go back out there and listen. Listen hard. You'll hear Him."

I must have looked terribly uncomfortable because he stopped talking and shook his head. "I'm sorry. Sometimes I get a little too passionate on my subject. You didn't come here for a lecture on belief. Your father is dying. Let's talk about that."

In fact I liked his passion, and I also liked his apology. "I didn't understand what you meant before when you said death was a gift to God. If there is a God, isn't He supposed to be all-powerful? What would He need with gifts from us?"

"Good, good, Annie Waldmas. That's the question, isn't it? We need God. Does God need us?"

"What?"

"We have a relationship with the Divine. Or at least we can, if we wish. Death can be considered in the context of this relationship."

"I'm lost," I admitted, liking this man who could not rein in his intensity on any subject.

"Of course you're lost. This seemingly simple idea of a relationship with God is more complex than any of us can imagine."

"Is there something I can read to help me understand?"

"Why not?"

He pushed back from his chair to get to the bookshelf behind him and ran his index finger along the spines, examining the titles until he found the volume he was looking for. Pleased, he turned back to me. "Lowenstein's improvement on the Dewey decimal system. I put books near each other that I think might enjoy each other's company."

He searched for the page he wanted and opened the book on his desk. "Abraham Joshua Heschel," he intoned respectfully. He pressed his palm on the page and read, "'. . . this is the meaning of death: the ultimate self-dedication to the divine. Death so understood will not be distorted by the craving for immortality, for this act of giving away is reciprocity on man's part for God's gift of life. For the pious man it is a privilege to die.'" He looked up from his book. Did he see me flinch at the notion that I should consider my father's death a privilege?

"If you can help your father to understand this," Rabbi Seymour Lowenstein advised, "you will have pain, but he will not. Your pain we can deal with later."

He marked the page with a scrap of paper, closed the book, and handed it across to me. "When you're done reading, you'll have questions. We can talk some more."

"It's okay if I come back?"

He opened his hands. "Of course you can come back."

On the street, with Rabbi Lowenstein's book under my arm, I felt as if I had traveled to another planet and returned with new eyes, new ears. I made my way along the icy sidewalk to Broadway, and it seemed as if someone had gone inside my head and turned up all the dials. Instead of going into the subway at Ninety-sixth Street, I decided to keep walking. I wanted to keep examining the ordinary and strange events of a New York morning. I passed the subway entrances at Seventy-ninth Street, then Fifty-ninth Street, and Forty-second. Two hours later, when I arrived at the door to my office, my boots were soaked through to my socks, and my calves ached from the effort of negotiating the slippery sidewalks, but my mind was racing.

When I came home that night, I was so tired from my long morning walk and a full day in the edit room, that I managed to drop all our mail in front of the row of mailboxes. Lying there on the marble floor, two letters stood out from the bills and catalogs. One was a thick envelope from the insurance company, which had to contain the compromise settlement they were offering. The other was a lilac-colored envelope, addressed in green ink to "The Waldmas Family." The letter had been postmarked in Brookford, but there was no return address. For some reason the sight of it made me uneasy. When I gathered the mail off the floor, I tucked the lilac envelope into my jacket pocket, apart from the rest.

At the sound of my key in the front door Eli came running. "Mommy, Mommy, Mommy—we made the best sleds ever!" He locked on to my wrist and dragged me to the front bathroom to see the soggy cardboard boxes in the bathtub.

Hannah came to the bathroom door and folded her arms. "Bonnie took us 'cause you came home so late."

Josh joined the crowd in the bathroom. "It sounded like fun. I told the kids maybe we should all go back out."

"Now?" I asked incredulously.

"Why not?"

"Sled in the dark? Is that smart?"

"There's a full moon," Hannah informed me.

"But I'm exhausted." I handed Josh the mail, and, remembering the letter in my pocket, reaffirmed my decision to leave it there.

Josh put the mail on the bathroom shelf. He knew my tactics.

"The insurance offer came," I told him.

"It can wait."

"So are we going or what?" Hannah pressed.

"Since we can't go to the country to go sledding," Eli negotiated, softening his sister's approach.

"How about homework?"

"It's *Friday*," Hannah said impatiently. "Don't you even know what day it is?"

Eli was already dragging the wet cardboard out of the tub.

"All right. Give me a minute to change my clothes. We'll go."

In the privacy of my own bathroom, I removed the lilac envelope from my pocket and turned it over in my hands, testing my original instinct. I opened the envelope and slipped the letter out.

*Dear Mr. and Mrs. Waldmas,*

*You should talk to some people about your fire. Didn't you wonder why your house burned down right after the bakery fire? Mr. Weiss is Jewish like you, but you probably know that. Maybe it's only a coincidence, two fires like that. But maybe it isn't. You both being Jewish and all. I'm not saying I know anything. I'm writing this to help you out. Maybe you should start asking some questions around town. By the way, this isn't my real handwriting. I can't tell you who I am.*

Hannah was banging on the bathroom door to hurry me up.

"Hold on a minute!" I barked.

The letter was from a woman, I was certain of that, some bored busybody with nothing to do but stir up trouble under the guise of doing good. Wasn't it enough for her that our house had burned to an uninhabitable shell? In a cold fury I stood over the toilet bowl and frantically ripped the lilac paper to shreds. For God's sake, didn't this awful person know my father was dying of cancer? I flushed the toilet and watched the pieces disappear into the spiraling water. As the letter was sucked away, I felt my breathing calm. Maybe I had overreacted, but who wouldn't? When I saw the still, clear water in the porcelain bowl, I knew I would not be telling Josh.

Hannah was banging again.

"All right, I'm coming."

Hannah and Eli were zipped into their parkas, waiting by the elevator door, while Josh, delighted with his success at breaking my lockstep family rules, was demonstrating how to make a quarter disappear behind his ear.

I was quiet as we walked across Ninety-second Street toward Riverside Park. I held Eli's mittened hand, and Josh held Hannah's. We fought the strong winds coming off the Hudson River, holding tight to the cardboard sleds that lifted up and flopped against the mounds of sidewalk snow. Directly ahead the orange moon was rising, fat and full. Along Riverside Drive, where people had settled in for the evening, the windows of the apartments were a patchwork of yellow and white light. Eli broke away from me to climb to the top of a snowbank and beat his chest like Tarzan. Josh scrambled up to join him, and they both howled at the full moon.

Hannah and I stood apart, watching their antics. Then I caught her looking at me. She didn't really want to be as angry at me as she was. For months she had been my silent accuser when I was too distracted to remember something I had promised her or something she had told me. I went over and wrapped my arms around her from behind. Quietly, she leaned back against me, but even with the comfort of her weight, I couldn't stop the pieces of lilac stationery from swirling in my mind.

At the top of the sledding hill the four of us contemplated the steep downhill runs that had been carved out by the afternoon sledders and now gleamed in the moonlight.

"Ready for this?" Josh asked.

I made a doubtful face.

"No chickening out, Mom," Eli warned me.

I settled onto the cardboard and made a spot between my legs for Hannah. Josh did the same for Eli, and then gave the signal to push off.

We flew, two missiles, father and son, mother and daughter, bouncing off the ice bumps, spinning and turning, screeching in pure, terrified delight. When we landed, laughing, two snow-covered heaps at the bottom of the long hill, I drew Hannah close and brushed the snow off her cheeks and eyes. We wove our puffy arms around each other. It was a détente we both needed.

She wriggled free and pointed to the sky. "Let's make wishes."

I lay back in the snow beside her. "Which one is the wishing star?"

"It doesn't matter. They're all good for wishes."

Hannah closed her eyes and moved her mouth in a silent recitation of "Star light, star bright . . ." I looked over at Josh and Eli, who were also lying back and looking up at the wide sky.

"Thank you," I whispered in Josh's direction, not certain he could hear me or even if I wanted him to; he looked my way and smiled.

The next morning, after breakfast, I announced I was going out to do errands. I put on a skirt, but nobody noticed. The kids were glued to Saturday morning cartoons in the living room while Josh sat studying the insurance offer with mounting anger.

I'm not sure what drew me to the Saturday service that morning or what I expected to find there. The music that drifted out into the street had a haunting melody that contained both joy and sorrow. The man at the door handed me a prayer book and said something in Hebrew that I didn't understand. Inside the dimly lit sanctuary the few dozen people in the pews bent their heads over their books. When they sat down, I quickly slipped into a pew so I wouldn't be left standing alone. Nearby a woman held her open book toward me and pointed to the page number. I forgot that Hebrew was read from right to left and opened my prayer book backward. I glanced over to see if she had noticed my mistake, but she was already running her fingertip along the rows of Hebrew letters. I took a breath and sat back.

Rabbi Seymour Lowenstein sang out with intensity, his hands moving in the air, his eyes shut tight. From time to time he readjusted the prayer shawl that slipped off one shoulder, then the other, and then reached up and changed the position of his blue yarmulke.

At one point he spoke in English. "The opposite of disbelief is not belief, but effort. Anyone who looks to find an easy path is not a Jew. There are no absolute answers to anything—only absolute questions. Faith is a bellows. It takes in breath, it gives out breath." Of course I imagined he was speaking directly to me.

I got to my feet when the others did, sat when they sat, turned pages when I saw my neighbor turn hers. The Torah was carried in procession around the synagogue, and people moved to the ends of their pews, touched their prayer books to the Torah, then brought their books back to their lips for a kiss. I cringed. This was too ritualistic for me. What was I doing here? What on earth had possessed me to come to Saturday morning services, to stand and to sit at the bidding of a rabbi, to mumble along with Hebrew prayers I did not understand? I had never considered myself much of a Jew, but now my religious heritage was being forced upon me. I thought about our ruined house, my children's charred portraits—about Rabbi Lowenstein's claim for faith and his intensely closed eyes. I got up quickly and left the synagogue before the service was over, for fear of having to talk with anyone, or explain my presence, or face questions I would not know how to answer.

# 8

On the eve of flying back out to California to visit my father again, I had a dream that I was in a house under construction when the foundation, which had been made by filling cardboard Sonotubes with cement, began to crack, slip apart like severed Greek columns, and collapse. I was standing on the second story of the house when everything began to move, and I slid to one end along the tipping floor, grabbing at two-by-fours in the new framing to try to catch myself. Finally the movement stopped, and the half-built house was left askew, pitched into the soft dirt. I pulled myself along to a ladder, where I could climb down and out to safety. Standing back on the hillside, examining the disaster, I saw the problem clearly: I could not possibly build a new house without a more reliable foundation. The construction had to stop.

On the airplane ride I thumbed through magazines without reading. I was on edge from a converstion I had with Ellen before getting on the plane. I had called to ask her if she could plan a trip to Los Angeles soon, since my family had made it clear to me that they were getting weary of my trips away. Even Josh had pointed out that I had three siblings. Why was I the one always going out there?

On the phone Ellen had made the usual excuse about her women's center responsibilities. Though each Fishman had inherited the need to control things, we did it in different ways. Ellen dealt with me by implying that she had responsibilities beyond my understanding. To make matters worse, she had had the nerve to ask why I hadn't been down to Laguna Beach to see our mother during any of my recent trips to California.

"After all," Ellen prodded, "it's really not that much of a drive."

I made some lame excuse. The truth was I hadn't gone to visit her because I didn't want to. Maybe I didn't want to see my mother and have my loyalty to my father challenged. After all their years apart, my parents still competed over the only territory left between them, the allegiance of their children. With my father sick, I felt the need to be unequivocally on his side, as if my intense loyalty to him was some leverage against the cancer. If I wavered, if I allowed my mother to make a claim on me, I jeopardized my ability to help my father fight for his life.

I knew my mother had put Ellen on the job of finding out why I hadn't visited. I doubted it had as much to do with wanting to see me as with wanting her share of the attention. I knew I would have to telephone her and be solicitous and apologetic, and thank her for her understanding even before she gave it.

"I don't mean to pry." The hefty woman with curly blue hair, seated next to me, put down her acrostics book. She gestured toward my tightly gripped hands. "What's wrong, honey?"

"My father's ill," I explained, and quickly opened another magazine.

She put her hand on my arm. "God has His plan for each of us. Who knew He would have me flying out to California to cook up my recipes on the Johnny Carson show? Fifth time now I'm heading out to the land of sunshine."

I tried to concentrate on an article about the twelve most popular vacation destinations for families with young children.

"We have a fine time of it, Johnny and me. I'm making him my banana–peanut butter log this time around. Got ten pounds of my own bananas up top there. They've got to be oozing ripe to be equal partners with the Skippy."

When I looked alarmed, she took my arm again. "Honey, I've got eight children of my own. You can talk to me about what's troubling you."

What was troubling me was that my two-thousand-dollar video camera, the most expensive thing I owned aside from our house and car, was up there with her oozing bananas. I got up quickly, stepped over her, and opened the bin to bring the camera down safely to my lap.

"I've got two good ears." She smiled. "All the way to Cal-i-for-nigh-A."

The night before, when I telephoned my father about my flight schedule, he had reminded me not to forget my video camera.

"You have something particular on your mind for the video?" I asked him.

"I don't know. Nothing special. I'm looking forward to seeing what comes up."

Aside from the physical things, this willingness—no, this need—to talk was the biggest change in my father since his diagnosis. For as long as I could remember he had always been a person who detested scrutiny and kept a defensive moat around himself. During our years of teenage rebellion, if any of us dared question his beliefs or behavior, he became archly condescending; if we pushed him, he became cold and aggressive. As we grew into our twenties, Ellen, Charles, and I withdrew from him, both physically and emotionally. Only Tony, who had adopted many of our father's defensive habits, stayed in Los Angeles, went to UCLA, and fought with him constantly.

I had taken myself farther and farther away, first to college, then to jobs in distant cities, and finally to jobs in other countries. At twenty-four I was working as a desk assistant at the BBC in London. After two years of coping with the cynical English and their dreary food and weather, I had finally gotten my reward. I was about to be assigned to the bureau in North Africa, and I was thrilled.

A few years before that my father had pulled off a sweet deal, selling Healthy Formula for Healthy Babies to a company that was experimenting with canned formulas. At that time the commercial real estate market in Los Angeles was settling into a recession, but my father, in his entrepreneurial wisdom, decided it was the perfect moment to use his baby formula profits to launch a real estate development company. He was confident that the buildings he bought cheap would quadruple their value within a decade, and in the end he was proved right. In the beginning local investors were too nervous to subscribe to his vision, but he found investors in Europe who had a longer view. We hadn't seen each other in over two years when he telephoned late one night from California to say he was coming to London on business and to suggest we get together for dinner.

He chose the restaurant where we met because one of his potential investors told him it served the best oysters in London. I found the concept of swallowing a raw oyster to be sexually suggestive, and therefore the sight of my own father doing it was particularly repulsive. I sat across from him at the dark oak table, averting my eyes each time he tipped up a shell. He wore a sports jacket with a silvery sheen and stiff shoulder pads, and his most pressing concern was getting my advice on where to buy a gift for his new girlfriend, a real estate broker who specialized in selling the houses of dead movie stars. As a budding journalist bound for an important assignment in Tangiers, I found my father's worries about perfume versus jewelry to be painfully shallow. I drummed my fingers against the arm of my captain's chair, wishing for the obligatory meal to be over. I was anxious to return to my flat and the East Ender with dreadlocks who was waiting there. I listened with half an ear to my father's dating travails, but I certainly did not tell him mine.

Finally, my patience gave out. "Are you dyeing your own hair or are you having it done for you, because frankly, Pop, the color's awful."

Of course he hadn't imagined that anyone knew his secret, that he was coloring his hair to hide the gray. When I saw him blanch, I added, "You didn't mention how old your new girlfriend is."

My father was always ready to strike back. "Cindy's been supporting her parents since she was eighteen. Her mother has diabetes, and her father has emphysema."

"Really? You mean she has no time to run off to play journalist in the deserts of North Africa?"

"I don't know why you have to be this way." I watched the color rise in his face, and I felt satisfied.

"What way is that?"

"So goddamned judgmental. Simply because a person sells houses to make a living, you jump to the conclusion that she's not intelligent."

"Am I judgmental?" I asked, spreading my fingers across my sternum. "Or are you defensive? I didn't say anything about her being intelligent. Or not."

He began to hunt for the waiter to get the check, arching his back first in one direction and then the other, the habit of a short man who had to work harder than others to make himself noticed. "It's always this way with you," he muttered.

I glared at him. I was twenty-six years old with the first big job of my life. "Fuck you."

"Don't you dare use that language with me, young lady!"

"Don't you wish I was still fourteen and you could threaten me like that?"

Not knowing what else to do, he slammed his wallet down on the table. All eyes turned our way. He reddened again, took five twenty-pound notes from his wallet, and pushed them toward me. "Pay the bill and keep the change for yourself since you only see me as a cash register, anyway." He got up to leave. "Good luck with your life."

"I'll try to decide whether to spend it on perfume or jewelry." I sat back and watched him disappear from the restaurant, delighted that in London I had had the last word.

I hurried home, smoked a joint, and threw myself into an intense session of sweaty sex with my taciturn Rastafarian. My father evaporated from my mind. But before dawn, my eyes snapped open. Why had I been so gratified to see him squirm? Had I learned this habit from my mother?

I wrapped myself in the bedspread and went to sit by the grimy kitchen window to watch the sky grow light over the clay-tiled rooftops. London was a lonely, gray place in winter. The morning would bring more cold rain. I would spend my day in my cubicle at the BBC with my stocking feet pressed against the electric fire. My father would leave for Paris. From Paris he would go on to Rome, then fly back to Los Angeles with a briefcase full of promises. That would make him happy. He would have conquered Europe, the short, Jewish man from Brooklyn. As for me, in two weeks I would fly to Africa. It could be years before I'd see my father again.

In another mood or at another time in my life I might have thought, Good, I can't stand his defensive posturing. Why subject myself to it? He was rigid, hostile, ridiculous—all the things my mother had accused him of being during their marriage and for years after. But as the sky lightened, I didn't want to leave it like that. Perhaps I was growing old enough to feel my first discomfiting stirrings of mortality. Or perhaps it was the experience of having already lost one of my parents to the impenetrable reaches of her own defenses. It could happen. I could end up with two parents with whom formality and ritual were my own connections. Suddenly I was overcome with a powerful determination. I didn't want to let my father walk away. I couldn't.

At the desk at Brown's Hotel, I was told he had already checked out.

"Would you call up to his room?" I asked the desk clerk.

"Didn't I inform you? The gentleman's checked out."

"Call up."

A porter loading suitcases onto a cart raised his eyes. "Mr. Fishman's gone off to Marks and Spencer to get himself some undergarments. Said he'd be coming back round to collect his things. Marks and Spencer, right at the top of the road."

A morning crowd filled the sidewalks as I pushed ahead and spun through the revolving doors. As I cruised the aisles, I thought about my father's pretensions. Why did he have to buy underwear in London when the identical brands were available in Los Angeles? Then I castigated myself for my habit of thinking the worst of him. When I spotted him at a payment desk with his money extended to the shop clerk, I shouted, "Pop!"

He recoiled. Had I come to abuse him further? Did I need to track him down to the underwear department of Marks and Spencer to tell him more of what I found wrong with him? His shoulders and mouth tightened.

"I've been searching everywhere for you."

"My daughter," he felt compelled to explain to the shop clerk. "She works for the BBC."

"I was afraid I'd miss you."

My father ran his eyes over me from head to toe. I was wearing floppy bell-bottom jeans, basketball sneakers, my boyfriend's T-shirt with a picture of Bob Marley smoking a spliff. He returned his attention to the clerk and was handed his change and shopping bag. He came over to me and hissed sotto voce, "Why did you follow me here?"

"So we could talk."

"Talk about what?"

"I don't know—just talk."

"I have a plane to catch. I have a very important business meeting in Paris this afternoon."

"Maybe they wouldn't mind if you arrived a little later."

"Why should I?" he demanded.

"I don't know."

"Then forget about it, because I have business to transact."

I stopped in the narrow aisle between two counters piled high with sweaters. He moved on, his head tucked down. In twenty feet he realized I wasn't with him.

"Because I love you, and you're my father," I said loud enough for him and the rest of the store to hear.

He turned but did not speak.

"Did you hear me?"

"You followed me here to tell me *that?*"

"I'm not going to be intimidated by you," I informed him. "And I'm not going to lose my temper, either. I came to find you so we could talk. Today. Otherwise it could be years."

"Is that some sort of threat?"

I sighed, feeling enormously frustrated. "I love you, goddamnit."

He eyed me mistrustfully. He was aware of people staring at us. I walked toward him, feeling both hesitant and bold. When I came close he said, "This is ridiculous."

"Probably," I said, and hugged him, and the shoppers who had stopped to witness our small drama breathed a collective sigh of relief.

As it turned out, we hardly needed to talk through anything. It was enough that I had insisted on a reconciliation. I called in sick, and my father called Paris to tell his potential investors that he would arrive the following day. We were like two people newly in love, going around to the London sights—Trafalgar Square, the Tower of London, the British Museum. He told me the entire history and significance of the Rosetta stone and the Magna Carta, both of which he was thrilled to see. My father still loved words, and here were two of the most important collections of words in human history. Years later, when we had become close friends, he told me that the Marks and Spencer incident had been his turnaround. Never before in his life had anyone cared enough to pursue him. After that, one by one, he regained relationships with all his children, though some were closer than others. He did the pursuing, since he had learned that the risk was worth it. Each time things got a little better, he would telephone me to say, "Another Marks and Sparks."

My father took the video camera from my hand as soon as I came off the airplane. I was shocked to see how much thinner he had gotten in only three weeks. He was wearing a yellow-and-blue-plaid golf cap.

"I'm going for the Bing Crosby look, trying to act my age." When we hugged, I felt his bones. "How was the flight?"

"I sat next to a woman who's going to cook on Johnny Carson. A talker."

"Bad luck." For him the perfect flight meant getting a seat next to someone who wore headphones or was sleeping.

When we got to the airport garage, he reached into his pocket and held out the car keys. "How about you drive for a change?"

I took the keys, dumbfounded. My father had no talent for giving up control of anything, much less a two-ton moving object. The last time I remembered being behind the steering wheel with him in the car was when I was sixteen and practicing for my driving test. The lesson ended in bloodcurdling screams as I slammed out of the car and walked the two miles home.

"You're not going to kill us?" he asked as he climbed into the passenger seat.

"Not unless you change your mind and jump into my lap when we're on the freeway."

Los Angeles was too bright, even with an ochre haze of smog hanging over the horizon. On the freeway we passed the usual complement of indecently expensive cars. My father had chosen California as his escape from the dreary hand-to-mouth existence he had known as a child in New York City. I had chosen New York City in order to get away from the mindless, money-fixated culture of my teenage years in Los Angeles. Neither of us was ever very comfortable going back to where we'd come from.

"I can't wait to get through the last of these radiation treatments. They've really wiped me out." My father gestured toward the steering wheel. "I keep worrying that I'll fall asleep while I'm driving."

Again I was alarmed, not only because my father had offhandedly described a terrifying possibility, but also because he was so willing to speak of his own frailty. He had never been a man to ask for anybody's help.

"Do they say how long before you'll feel like yourself again?"

"I'm sure those nurses get special training in how to avoid answering questions like that. Right now they're obsessed with weighing me."

"And how's your appetite?"

"Everything tastes like cardboard."

"You've got to eat, you know."

Rather than engage in the argument we'd been having for weeks—my insistence that he eat, his that he had no appetite—he tilted his head toward the window, closed his eyes, and soon he had fallen asleep. I reached across him and carefully, so as not to wake him, pressed down the lock. When we got to the entrance of the gated community in which he lived, I opened the glove compartment to remove the garage door opener. He woke abruptly and pushed my hand out of the way. "I'll get that."

In my father's part of town, the exclusive upper reaches of Beverly Canyon, you never saw a human being outside a house or car unless it was one of the army of Latinos who came with the sunrise to clean, garden, and launder. My father had learned enough Spanish to hold simple conversations with the people who took care of him and his house. They were his most proximate family. He paid the tuition for his housekeeper Maria's two sons to attend a private Catholic academy so they wouldn't have to go to the hellhole of a school in their East Los Angeles neighborhood, the same neighborhood where he had lived thirty-five years before. He paid Maria's airfare home to Oaxaca whenever her mother was sick. He gave money to Arturo the gardener for the down payment on a new truck when his old one died on the Ventura Freeway. No big deal, no fanfare, no strings attached. They needed the help. He had the money. It was simple.

My arrival was always cause for excitement. Arturo stationed himself proudly by his truck, holding a long-handled shovel like a staff. Maria always put fresh-cut gardenias in my room and wouldn't let me unpack until she had seen the latest photographs of Hannah and Eli. I would use my college Spanish to tell her about their latest achievements, and she would laugh uproariously when I would inevitably confuse two Spanish words that sounded alike—like the time I mixed up the word for prostitute with the word for tiptoe when I was describing Hannah's gymnastics skills.

As we came through the door from the garage, Maria held out a glass of freshly squeezed orange juice for my father. "You drink, Señor Fish." She shook her head. "Your father, he no eat nada."

My father brushed past the offer. "You two get your gossiping done. I'm going to put my feet up in the living room."

Maria gave me her report as she fed me guacamole.

"I make his dinner. Morning, I see it in garbage. I make every favorite thing. Señor Fish, he stubborn like two oxes."

I laughed. "That's him."

"I worry, Señorita Annie. Too skinny, too much sleeping all the time."

"I'll work on him," I promised.

He had stretched out on the living room couch, his head back on a yellow silk pillow. The living room was peaceful, furnished in the spare and elegant style that my father had learned over the years from the wealthy women he dated. The celadon chenille Donghia couches had arrived during a short fling with an art dealer from New York City. The two-foot-tall jade tigers came from a trip to Japan with a woman he had met while buying endives at Gelson's Market. The Beidermeier coffee table was a gift from the ex-wife of a Chicago stockbroker. There was nothing in this living room that wasn't expensive and beautiful, and there were no tchotchkes. Abe Fishman abhorred clutter as he abhorred the memory of poverty and its dreary trappings.

With one hand tucked behind his head and the other protecting his sunken abdomen, he looked small and vulnerable. I covered him with a cashmere blanket and examined him the way a parent examines a sleeping child. It saddened me that my father, a small man, had gotten smaller. He had bared his body to repeated assaults of deadly radiation, diligently swallowed the twenty pills a day Charlie had organized for him after investigating the alternative cancer treatments, attempted to talk with good humor and respect to every nurse and medical assistant who took care of him. Would his efforts be rewarded?

Since my father was sound asleep, I went back into the kitchen to telephone Josh and let him know I had arrived. He sounded harried when he picked up the phone.

"Why do you have to call right before bedtime?"

"I'm sorry. It was the first chance I got."

"I've got Eli in the bath and Hannah finishing up homework. It's not a great time to talk."

"I didn't want to talk. I only wanted to tell you I'm here."

"How is he?"

I paused. It was one thing to notice, another to say it out loud. "He's so thin and completely exhausted. He really looks like an old man."

"It's the radiation, Annie. It's not the cancer."

I felt teary all of a sudden. "I wish I wasn't so far away from you and the kids."

"We'll manage. You'll manage. This is what we have to do right now."

"Kiss them for me. Tell them I said good night."

"Take care of yourself, too."

I went back into the living room to wait for my father to wake. The house was quiet, separated from the presence of neighbors by thick walls. Maria had folded the last of the laundry and walked down to the security gate to catch her ride home. As always she had left the house spotlessly clean, the way my father liked it. Afternoon became evening. I leaned my own head back, and soon I was sleeping, too.

When I woke the sky was dark, and my father was gone from the couch. I heard the faint sound of Japanese flutes coming from upstairs, so I knew he had gone up to his bedroom. I found him lying on his bed, propped up against pillows, listening to his music. He lifted the remote toward the stereo to lower the sound.

"Hi, sweetheart."

"Hi, Pop."

"Got dark fast, didn't it?"

"Should I make us some tea?"

"Not for me, thanks."

"How about a glass of juice?"

He shook his head and pointed me to the chair near his bed. "So tell me what's happening with the insurance settlement. Did you sign?"

"The lawyer wants to tinker with a few things. My feeling is we've pushed it as far as we can. The truth is I'm sick of the whole thing at this point. I want to get on with the project of getting the house back together."

"That's what I tried to emphasize with Josh when he telephoned to talk about it. Sometimes that extra bit of money isn't worth the hassle."

"I'm glad you said that to him. He respects your opinion on these things. I guess he hates to let them think they won."

"You can waste a lot of time in life by needing to win. I told him it was something I had to learn the hard way. The important thing is that no one was hurt and you know it wasn't arson. Josh agreed on that point. I think that was what disturbed him most of all, the possibility of arson." My father looked to me for confirmation of his assessment, but my mind had returned to the unnerving anonymous letter.

"But what if it was arson?"

He looked at me curiously. This had been settled months ago.

"It's not one hundred percent sure."

He flipped his hand. "Nothing in life is ever one hundred percent sure, Annie. You had your investigations, it's behind you. It's time to go forward now."

I wondered why I didn't tell my father about the letter. He was the one I always took my worries to. I knew the cantillations of his advice—always the two possibilities, the worst outcome, the likely one—be prepared to cope with the worst, enjoy the best. Maybe I didn't want to burden him right now. He had his own problems. Or maybe I didn't want to expose my worries to the light of day, especially to my no-nonsense father, for whom ignoring a setback and avoiding the necessary action was simply not an option.

"You wanted to do some talking with the video camera," I reminded him. "Should I set up now or do you want to wait until tomorrow?"

"We're here, aren't we? You're my date for tonight, unless you have other plans."

I brought the video camera upstairs and went to work setting up the lights, moving the ficus plant aside so that it wouldn't cast a shadow, framing the shot wide enough so that I could listen without worrying when my father shifted to one side of his bed or the other.

At the bedroom window I lingered over the sight of the patio below, remembering the night before my father's surgery, the night of the Häagen-Dazs ice cream and his first regrets.

As I put the finishing touches on my lighting arrangement, my father commented, "You sure know your stuff."

"My part's easy. You're the one who does the talking."

"That's not so hard. I've got so much on my mind these days, and there's something about the way you listen. Do people tell you that? The people you make your documentaries about?"

"You mean that I make it comfortable for them?"

"Exactly."

"Maybe I'm nosy."

"Baloney," he said. "This is a talent of yours. I'm your father. I'm allowed to say these things."

"You mean at last I've impressed you?"

"Sure, because you finally figured out the right one to interview—your old man."

I settled into the chair beside the camera and turned it on. "All right, Mr. Wisdom, let's have it."

"Have I ever told you about my notion of myself as a Manufactured Man?"

"I've heard you speak of it. I'm not sure what it means."

"It means that I constructed myself, my personality, everything, so that I would be acceptable to people." He pointed to himself. "I made this up. I manufactured it. I created an identity I could feel proud of because I believed that my real self was unacceptable. Remember how I told you I read all those Horatio Alger stories when I was a kid, how I was ashamed of my childhood, ashamed of being poor? So I invented an alternative, my own Horatio Alger myth, I guess. And then I set out to manufacture it. The Manufactured Man." He shook his head in a moment of self-mockery. "Sounds like a grade-B Hollywood movie." He got serious again. "See, with everything that's been going on lately, I've begun to wonder who the hell I am if I'm not this person I made up."

"Sometimes I feel like there's a darkness you carry in you, sadness maybe?" I touched my chest. "It feels like something you harbor, something you hide. Do you know what I'm talking about?"

"For me, it's more like an empty place, a hollowness. Maybe because I don't want to see what's in there. Maybe there's something I'm afraid to see. Ever considered that? Maybe what you call a darkness is just my shame about where I came from, being poor, all that. The shame of being poor can make a powerful impression on a child." He let his mind travel back over the years. "Your mother sends you to the butcher for a nickel's worth of soup bones. She's sending you instead of going herself because she hopes the butcher will take pity and give you more than your money's worth. She teaches you how to look down at the floor. You're not supposed to smile. You're not supposed to meet the butcher's eye. You know how I am about lying, how I hate it. It comes from those days. As a five-year-old boy I was already being sent off to con people."

"I can see how that could make you feel lousy."

"Lousy, shamed—I'm not sure. Don't most people feel unworthy in one way or another? Doesn't everyone imagine they need to be someone other than who they really are? I guess the difference here is that I've been preoccupied with it all my life, driven to create an acceptable persona. Maybe I read too much as a kid, got too many strange ideas in my head. I know I decided to construct the personality I wanted people to see. That's why I'm always careful in my relationships to make sure people don't get too close. They might see past my Manufactured Man. And that's why the thing in the hospital with you kids was such a big deal for me. I couldn't keep you at arm's length, couldn't stop you from seeing me and all my weakness. And when you did see me, you still didn't go away. I don't know how to tell you what an impact that had on me." He shrugged. "Another Marks and Sparks. See, the Manufactured Man never needed love. He didn't allow himself to need it. In fact, he fought pretty hard to reject it. That's how much he really needed it, I guess."

I was amazed at my father's candor. And what he explained made such sense. For as long as I could remember, he had been a man determined to earn people's respect but to keep them at arm's length. I was beginning to see a tenderness in him that he had never revealed before.

"I hope this won't offend you, Pop, but I've often wondered why you were always posturing and trying to look important."

He didn't bat an eye but pointed to the video camera. "I suppose that's why we're doing this, to find out." Then he leaned back into his pillows and closed his eyes.

"Tired?"

"It just comes over me."

"One more week of treatments," I encouraged.

"Yes, one more week, that's all."

The guest room where I slept was next to my father's bedroom. The sheets smelled of lemon, a gift from Maria, whose own mother in Oaxaca had placed lemon rinds beneath her children's pillows. The warm night air brought in the sweetness of the gardenias outside my window. The best part of California, the most comforting memories from my child-hood, were these luxuriant smells of the natural world.

I wondered, Could I be a Manufactured Child of a Manufactured Man? But at every season I had found true pleasures. As a child I had spent whole afternoons climbing through the hills, never feeling lonely. I sledded down slopes of dry summer grass on flattened cardboard boxes, seed pods whipping my shins. I scrambled over the camel-colored hills with my two brothers to climb oak trees and gather mistletoe to tie in red ribbons to sell door-to-door at Christmastime. In spring I gathered bouquets of fireweed, purple lupines, and wild daisies. In summer I lay in grass nests where deer had slept the night, shut my eyes, and watched the sun make paintings inside my eyelids.

With these memories I fell into a deep sleep, but sometime in the night I was wrenched awake, aware of something proximate and awful. I listened for sounds from the other side of the wall, from my father's bedroom, but the house was quiet. I knew it was not a dream, and I knew it was not the fear of physical danger that had disturbed me, but rather some inescapable piece of truth, something too disturbing to rationalize or dismiss. I knew it was not from me, or of me, but rather something I was being made to understand, some deeply felt pain. On impulse I reached out toward the wall that separated my father's room from mine, and I was overcome with feeling for the man who slept there.

In the morning my father had gray moons beneath his eyes.

"I had a shitty sleep," he announced.

I wanted to tell him about my night, to ask him. "Were you up a lot?"

"Naw. Just don't feel rested."

"They called from Dr. Armadas's office to confirm your appointment for this morning. Should we go tomorrow instead?"

"What's the difference? We'll go."

"Maybe you should go back to bed."

"I said we'll go," he growled.

"Hey, take it easy."

"I told you what I wanted."

"You eating something?" I asked tersely.

"Take care of yourself. I'm perfectly capable."

I nodded and walked past him out of the kitchen.

We waited for Dr. Armadas, my father sitting up on the examining table, and me on the rolling stool beside him, the same way I was accustomed to wait with my children for the appearance of their pediatrician. Genuine pleasure came across my father's face when his doctor came through the door.

"You remember my daughter Annie." My father was pleased to take on the role of host.

"Of course, Mr. Fishman."

We shook hands as if renewing our acquaintance, but the truth was, unbeknownst to my father, I was in regular phone contact with Mike Armadas. We would commiserate over my father's awful puns, discuss his mood, his treatments, his weight. Even from a distance, I had molded my daily life around my father's battle against cancer.

"Time to weigh in, Mr. Fishman."

My father shook his head. "You can see my bones showing without having to humiliate me in front of my daughter."

"I'd like her to see you get on the scale, Mr. Fishman. I'm going to need an ally."

Mike Armadas and I had planned this on the phone. He had hard news for my father and didn't want him to have to hear it alone. That's why I had chosen this time to come back to Los Angeles.

"Now what?"

"I'm ordering IV feeding for you, Mr. Fishman. You need to put on some weight."

I saw the flash of anger my father tried to conceal. "Dr. God should have left me more of my stomach."

Mike Armadas rested his chin in his upturned palm.

"I'm not going back into the hospital. No way."

"We can set you up at home."

"You mean I'm going to be walking around my house hooked up to an IV? How the hell am I supposed to get up and down the damned stairs?"

"Only while you're getting your drip."

"My drip? You make it sound like nasal fluid."

"Sucrose, water, and vitamins."

"No smoked salmon?"

Dr. Armadas smiled. He knew, as I did, that this effort at humor would be quickly followed by discouragement. My father dropped his chin to his chest.

"You keep doing your best to eat, and you'll be off the IV in no time."

"Sure, Doc."

My father left the examining room without saying good-bye and walked on ahead of me. This was a sign of failure, and he did not like failure. I shrugged to Dr. Armadas to convey my apology for my father's brusqueness. He raised his hands as if to say, No need.

We drove east along Wilshire Boulevard in the direction of my father's office in Beverly Hills. Our plan had been for him to go into his office for an hour or two after his doctor's appointment. He had to sign checks and discuss things with the young associate who was now taking care of much of the business. My father hadn't said a word since we'd left the medical building, and I decided to wait him out. At the next red light, he cocked his thumb north in the direction of his home. "Tomorrow," he said. "The office can wait until tomorrow."

I rarely saw my father defeated. "You'll handle this, Pop. It's not that big a deal. He's trying to make things easier on you."

He didn't answer.

"He says you're doing great, other than the eating. We have to get you back in shape again. How else are you going to ski?"

"Don't mind me, Annie. These days my moods are up and down like a yo-yo."

"You're allowed."

As we drove on in silence I could feel him doing the mental work he needed to accept the new reality of IV meals. By the time we neared the top of Beverly Canyon, the cloud had passed. Even his tone of voice had changed when he gestured to the steering wheel and said, "I'm beginning to wonder what I'd do without you."

"As your private chauffeur?"

"You know what I mean, Annie."

At home he went upstairs to change his clothes, and I took advantage of the moment to call Josh.

"I thought you'd call again last night," he said.

"I'm sorry. I don't like to leave him alone."

"Don't be too dramatic with him," Josh advised. "It's not going to help him if he's worrying about you, too."

"It's not that. I don't want to give up any of my time with him."

"Were you and Armadas able to convince him about the IV feeding?"

"Mike didn't present it as a choice. He told him that's what he was doing next, no discussion."

"And he got away with that?"

"Pop likes him. It's a setback, though. It's not what he was expecting."

"Today someone in the photo department was telling me that his loss of appetite could be from the return of the cancer as well as from the radiation treatments."

"I know. Either the radiation worked too well, or it didn't work enough. It's all depressing."

My father appeared at the kitchen door. "Want to set up the video camera?"

I told Josh I had to go.

"Why don't we set up in the atrium?" my father suggested. "It's nice in there with the sun and flowers."

The pale yellow walls of the atrium were thickly covered in bougainvillea. Purple, violet, and red flowers hung from trellises that reached nearly to the skylight. My father sat and curled his fingers around the smooth arms of a Chinese teakwood chair.

"Pop, are you afraid?" I asked when the video camera was on. He didn't flinch at the directness of my question. In fact, he seemed to appreciate it.

"Nope."

"No fear, not at all?"

"I felt more fear about dying before I found out I had cancer. Aside from the eating issue and the tiredness, I feel pretty good. I hope you don't misunderstand me, Annie—it's not that I'm looking forward to dying. What I'm looking forward to is living. In a way it feels like I'm really living for the first time in my life."

"What do you mean by that?"

"Think about it. All my life I've pushed myself to make deals, organize projects, impress this person, that person, perform, produce." He shook his head at the thought of all this. "All in the service of the Manufactured Man I told you about last night. Imagine, suddenly I don't need to do that anymore. I can ask myself, Who the hell are you trying to convince? I feel free to be myself, to *find* myself."

"I suppose that's an enviable position, except for the little detail of cancer."

He leaned toward me as if I hadn't grasped the obvious. "If it weren't for the cancer, I wouldn't be here. There's *no way* I would have gotten to this place without the cancer."

"But imagine if you had." I heard the moralizing in my own voice, but my father did not take offense.

"But I didn't. Honey, sooner or later we all die. The trick is how well you live until you die. I've spent a lot of years living without any inkling of the beauty in life. Except for the physical stuff, the truth is I've never felt better in my life."

I had seen this in him. Apart from his moments of irritation as he recognized his increasing dependence, he was calmer and gentler than I had ever known him. He combed the music stores for new CDs of Japanese flute music and let whole days go by without phoning his office. In the afternoons he lay out on the patio in the sun, pointing out the color of the sky or a flower he liked. These had never been his habits before the cancer. His life had been lists, phone calls, facing the world on full-frontal attack.

"Pop, people ask me how you are, and when I say that in a way you're happier than ever, I can see they think I'm some touchy-feely idiot, or simply crass and don't love you enough to feel sorry for your predicament. I guess I'm thinking about your state of mind, and the answer they're waiting for is how you're doing physically—if you're going to die or not. When I describe your state of mind, they assume I'm avoiding the only important question."

"And it's not the important question at all." My father was suddenly excited. "I mean, it's not that important to *me*. Not anymore. There are so many more important things on my mind. Sure, you could tell those peple, Oh, he's dying—and that would be as true now as it was twenty years ago when I was also dying. Or you could say, He's living, which is truer now than ever."

A hummingbird found its way in through the open skylight and was skittering along the bougainvillea. My father looked up and then nodded as if the hummingbird's arrival confirmed what he was trying to express. When he turned back toward the video camera, he seemed momentarily puzzled. He had gotten so carried away with what he wanted to say that he had forgotten about the camera. There it was again, exactly what he was talking about. Clinging to life was beside the point.

"It's like I've come home to myself. Unfortunately, I had to get cancer to do this, but given the choice, I'm not sure that I wouldn't deliberately choose it to make this happen." He looked at me. "I'm sorry, Annie, but it's true."

I decided to match toughness with toughness. "Last night in the middle of the night I woke with a wretched feeling. It wasn't from a dream or anything like that. It was something I felt in the pit of my stomach. I remembered our video session from the evening, and realized I was understanding what you meant when you described the shame that drove you to create your Manufactured Man. It was upsetting, Pop, really awful."

"I'm sorry, sweetheart."

"You've told me so much about your life. If there's something else you've got to tell me, I wish you'd go ahead and do it."

"Maybe there is. I don't know. Maybe if we keep talking we'll know."

I did not say what came immediately to mind, that we might not have much longer for talking.

# 9

On an unseasonably warm Saturday morning in late February, Josh suggested we take Hannah and Eli with us to Brookford when we went to meet with our contractor. Finally, after three weeks of cleanup, the work of rebuilding was under way at the house, and we felt it was safe to let the kids see it. Up until then we had left them home with Bonnie when we had to come up to Connecticut. We hadn't wanted to expose them to the images that still haunted our dreams.

Josh thought it might do us good to spend a day together at the house and be reminded of what life had been like before all the difficulties of the last four months. With the warm weather the maple sap was running. Our sap buckets had been lost in the fire, but Josh had bought new ones and hung them on the maple trees in front of our house. Each year we made a family project of collecting the sap and boiling it down on the kitchen stove. What we spent on electricity could have bought us an oil drum of maple syrup, but we treasured our annual ritual. The kitchen would fill with sweet steam, and if there was snow on the ground, we would take cups of hot syrup outside and mix it with the snow to make ice cream. Now we had no kitchen for such a project, but at least we could watch the buckets fill and be reassured of the coming spring.

The backyard was furrowed with rivulets of melting ice, and the Dumpster parked out on the road was dripping where the hanging stalactites of ice thawed. Inside, the house was a busy construction site. The roofer had fixed the gaping hole, and we had a patch of new gray shingles.

New windows were being installed, their shipping stickers still attached. Great rolls of silver-foil-covered insulation were waiting to be staple-gunned when the two-by-four framing was completed. To Hannah and Eli it must have felt like being inside the rib cage of a whale as they rushed around the open rooms shouting and listening to their voices echo.

"Please, guys," Josh implored. "We're trying to concentrate here." Over the children's heads Josh made it clear to me that he would prefer them out of the way so he could review the work with the contractor.

"Let's go for a walk," I suggested. "We can check out the sap."

Hannah led the way back out the front gate. "What's in the mailbox?"

"The mail is all forwarded, sweetie."

"Then how come something's in it?"

"We're having our mail sent to New York now," I explained.

"So how come the flag's up?"

"Are you expecting a letter?" I tried to play along with my side of a game I did not get.

"Could be something important," Hannah decided.

"Then go take a look for me."

Eli and I kicked chunks of ice off the Dumpster while we waited for Hannah to pry open the stubborn metal mailbox door. She finally extracted a single letter and held it up triumphantly. Even from where I waited with Eli, I could see that it was a lilac envelope addressed in green ink.

I rushed to her. "I'll take that."

"It says, 'The Waldmas Family,'" Hannah read. "That means *all* of us."

I was overcome with an impulse to snatch the envelope from her hand.

"The Waldmas Family," Hannah repeated, holding the letter firmly. "Which means I get to open it."

"It's not from anyone who knows us," I said, trying to contain my anxiety.

"They know our name," Hannah pointed out, turning the envelope in her hand in much the way I had examined the first lilac-colored envelope a month ago.

"That doesn't mean they know us," I argued, reaching for the letter.

Hannah squinted at me. "Does this have something to do with my birthday? Is that why you don't want me to open it?" Hannah's tenth birthday was six weeks away, and she was as focused on it as if it were an upcoming national holiday.

"I'm not telling you anything else," I said sternly, plucking the envelope from her tenacious fingers. "You don't want to ruin all your surprises, do you?"

Appeased, she ran off to check the first maple tree.

Eli ran after her. "Hey! You don't get to check all the buckets!"

I tore open the letter. Once again there was no signature and no return address.

*Dear Mr. and Mrs. Waldmas,*

*Since I haven't heard anything in town about you asking questions about your fire, I worried maybe you didn't get my other letter. What I wrote you before was that you should be asking about the fire at your house. How come you're Jewish and your house burned down right after there was the fire at Mr. Weiss's bakery? Shouldn't you start checking this out? What good does it do if you don't face facts? Better to know the truth, don't you think? Not everybody likes Jews, but I guess you know that. Didn't you hear about the fire over in Amity? They were Jews, too.*

*Sincerely yours,*

*Anonymous*

I shoved the letter into my jeans while I kept my eye on Hannah and Eli as they worked together to try to lift a heavy pail of sap from its peg on one of the maple trees. I scanned the road, the trees behind our house, the wide, brown lawn with its remaining crusts of snow. The children's swing hanging from a high branch of the shagbark hickory moved slightly with the wind. I imagined Hannah and Eli swinging there in summer. I could see the image of it as if it were a photograph of their childhood that I was looking back on. I wanted things to be perfect again. I wanted my life to be certain, manageable, secure. If I showed this letter to Josh, it would undo us all over again, unless he read it and dismissed it as the work of a crank, as I had done with the first letter. I turned toward Hannah and Eli in time to see them facing off over an empty bucket that lay on the road between them in a pool of spilled sap.

"You idiot!" Hannah yelled.

"You bumped me," Eli moaned.

"I did not!"

"You're stupid! And ugly! And *fat!*"

Hannah was hauling off to belt her brother as I screamed, *"Stop it, you two! Stop it, stop it, stop it!!!"*

They froze and stared at me with wide and worried eyes. My fury was a reaction to something much more appalling than a silly fight over spilled sap. Silently they came toward me and tucked themselves to my sides.

"It's okay," I said, comforting myself and them.

On the trip back to the city, I pretended to sleep. I didn't want Josh to be disappointed that the trip to Brookford with the kids hadn't soothed me the way he'd hoped. On Monday morning after Josh had left for work and I had dropped Hannah and Eli at school, I went back to the apartment and removed the anonymous letter from my jeans pocket where it had been since Saturday night. I sat on the edge of our bed cradling the letter in both hands as if it were a sleeping snake. I didn't want to reread it, but had to if I was going to look for clues.

The letter had no stamp. It had to have been hand delivered to our mailbox. The handwriting was carefully drawn, boxy letters with no revealing flourishes. The author was not, as I had assumed from the first letter, simply a nosy busybody. I could see that whoever wrote it had a strong sense of purpose. Did she feel obliged to do the job the fire had not done, and drive us out of Brookford? Did the coincidence of the two fires of Jewish property make her fear the trouble it might draw to her town? Small New England towns had their own way of getting rid of the things that bothered them. But what about the letter's reference to another fire? Amity was half an hour north of Brookford, on the border with Massachusetts. If there was yet another fire involving Jewish property so close to us, that was cause for real alarm. I put the letter back into its envelope and sat for a long time thinking about Josh. We were not in the habit of keeping secrets from each other. Yet I knew this information would upset him to his core. Maybe keeping it a secret was the kinder thing.

I telephoned our garage and asked them to have the car ready in fifteen minutes. Then I called my office and told my assistant I wouldn't be in. Finally I phoned Josh and told him I had to spend the day in Niantic,

Connecticut, to meet with officials at York Correctional Center to discuss my new project on women incarcerated for murdering their abusive husbands. I reminded Josh that it was a good three-hour drive each way so that he would need to be home in time for the baby-sitter. By the time I headed out, I had my reasoning well in hand: I could hold off telling Josh about the letters so long as I was taking action to discover what lay behind them.

Amity was an area of low hills and large farms. The open fields had been plowed under for the first spring planting of feed corn, and the wet, turned soil was a cold umber. I drove slowly into the town, not knowing a soul and having no clear idea of where to begin. The tiny village of Amity was too small to have its own post office or town hall. The streets were quiet, the midday sky was steel gray, and lamps were lit behind drawn curtains.

Finally I spotted the town clerk's shingle hanging below a broken sign for the Bluebird Bed and Breakfast. The house was a weather-beaten Colonial that probably hadn't seen a bed-and-breakfast guest in years. I parked on the street and went around to the side of the house, where I could hear a radio playing faintly. On the back steps an elderly woman was bent over her gardening project, poking seedlings into individual peat pots. She certainly knew I was there, but she chose not to look up. She instantly reminded me of my own mother, whose first goal in any new encounter was making it clear that things would proceed according to her needs and on her terms. The last time I had telephoned to give her my usual evasive update on Abe's condition, she had gotten me to say more than I wanted—to say how worried I was about his declining weight and energy—by implying Ellen had already told her all these things, which it turned out she hadn't.

"I'm looking for the town clerk."

"Clerk's office is open Tuesdays and Thursdays, nine to twelve."

"I drove up from New York."

"I don't make the rules." She was using her thumb to press soil around the tiny stem of each plant.

"Leeks?"

She pushed her wool cap back with her forearm to get a look at me. "Not many folks recognize a baby leek."

I sat down on a plastic-wrapped bale of peat.

"You're not from around here, then," she said, returning to her seedlings.

"New York," I repeated, deciding not to mention Brookford.

"You're looking for the town clerk?"

"I am."

"You found her. I was about to head inside for a cup of cocoa. I guess you'd like to join me."

Inside she pointed me to a chair at the kitchen table and then ignored me while she heated a pot of milk and stirred it slowly with a long wooden spoon. When she'd established that she hurried for no one, she mixed in the cocoa powder, filled two mugs, and carried them over to the checked oilcloth that covered her kitchen table. She pulled off her rubber boots and fit her feet into the furry bedroom slippers that were waiting beneath her chair.

"There," she said, satisfied. She pointed to the sugar bowl on the table. "Put in as much sugar as you like, but if you want to live as long as me, you'll keep your spoon out of it."

"I imagine you know everybody in Amity."

"Everybody that's breathing."

"You know a family that had a fire?"

"What kind of fire was that?"

"Might have been arson."

"Pretty curious, aren't you?"

"The insurance company's not quite satisfied."

"Well, how about that?"

"We like to do these investigations quietly, go right to the people we know have good information. We don't talk to just anybody with a thing as delicate as this."

"Insurance is legalized burglary, far as I'm concerned. I don't believe in insurance of any kind. This place burns down, I walk away. I get sick, they're going to have to shoot me. Anyway, I thought the Pragers got everything settled the way they liked. Since they rebuilt lickety-split."

"You know the Pragers, then?"

"Nope, never met 'em. Weekend folks come up here to pretend no one else exists in the world. Us locals are the quaint scenery. I heard he's some kind of scientist or professor or something. One of the big universities. I think it's botany. They say he's got himself quite a garden. She's one of those TV people. Nature shows. English type, fancy accent. About five years back they bought up the Rogerses' place after Arthur moved down to his sister in North Carolina. Course, I'm not surprised someone's still got questions about that fire. One says arson, another wonders how they got so much money to turn that place from a shack into a mansion overnight. Then talk goes around, doesn't it? More cocoa?" she asked.

I stood. "No, thanks. I've got to go."

"Insurance people keep busy."

When I got back in my car, I took out the reporter's notebook I kept in the glove compartment and scribbled, "Prager, prof of Botany? Mrs.— TV correspondent, English?"

It was a twenty-minute drive south to the center of Brookford. I parked in front of the post office, a converted carriage house on the village green. From my car I watched people go in and out. Most people kept post office boxes rather than take rural delivery because the trip into town gave them company, especially during the long winter. Aside from the café, which was now gone, the post office was one of the only public meeting places in Brookford.

Melinda Marks, a single mother with two young sons, had been the town postmistress for the past four years. She had the best perch in town for keeping an eye on all the doings in Brookford. People leaned on her counter, picked up old pieces of gossip, dropped off new ones. Melinda had her moods, but when work was slow, she was willing to chat. People liked her, even though she was an oddball by Brookford standards—an urban refugee with a buzz haircut.

I pushed through the glass door. Melinda looked up and stared at me. Did everyone in Brookford know more about our situation than we did?

"Mrs. Waldmas. I didn't realize you were back."

"Not yet. Three more months at least. We're hoping for Memorial Day."

She passed her hand over her half inch of ash-blonde hair, which had a slight greenish glow under the fluorescent lights. Her younger son, Melinda's spitting image right down to the haircut, was doing homework at her desk. "Mom, what's 'scintillating' mean?"

"Sparkling—something like that."

The back door slammed and Melinda's older son wove his way around the mail sacks carrying a hockey stick with his ice skates hung over his shoulder.

"Ice is breaking up. Coach says we can't play."

"Then get some homework done."

"Nope. Don't do homework until the sun goes down."

"Sort the mail. Do something." She turned to me. "Can't sit still for thirty seconds. He's as jittery as me, poor kid."

I pulled the anonymous letter out of my back pocket and dropped it onto the counter. "You don't happen to know someone in town who writes letters with green ink on lilac-colored stationery?"

Melinda folded her arms and shook her head.

"I figured it was odd enough that you might know who it was."

"No signature?"

"Anonymous."

"That's pretty weird." Melinda considered the envelope but did not touch it. "No signature, no return address. No postmark. How'd the letter get to you?"

"It was in our mailbox."

"Must have been hand delivered. Didn't come through here. Can't help you out."

"I thought you might recognize the writing."

She pushed the envelope back across to me. "No one I know."

"Mom, what's 'dissemble'?"

I didn't wait for Melinda to take a stab. "To know something without letting on that you know it," I said and left.

I considered going up to our house to check on the construction, but I couldn't do that if I didn't want to tell Josh where I'd been. I sat in my car with the lilac envelope on the seat beside me and watched a few more people go in and out of the post office. Who was it in Brookford who saw me and thought, Jew?

On the way home, I stopped for gas and telephoned Josh to tell him to expect me in time for supper. Then I called my father. I had let the entire day go by without a phone call, which was not my habit, but Ellen had finally organized her schedule to spend a week with him, and I suppose I had an impulse to play hooky from my responsibilities to my father, to spend a whole day without thinking about cancer or doctors or death.

His voice was barely audible.

"Are you okay?"

"Just tired," he whispered hoarsely.

"Where's Ellen?"

He cleared his throat, and I heard him moving in his bed, adjusting himself to a more comfortable position. "She's downstairs trying to cook up something to get me to eat. She got her kitchen talents from your mother."

At least he was well enough to try to entertain me.

"Should I have Ellen call you back?"

"I'm at a public phone."

"I'll have her call you, then."

"Pop, hang up and I'll call again. Don't pick up the phone, so she'll pick it up downstairs."

"Sure, Annie," he obliged. "I get it."

When Ellen answered, I demanded, "What's going on? He sounds awful."

"I called your office this morning. They said you were out of town for the day."

"I was in Connecticut."

"You don't call in for your messages?"

"Ellen . . ." My voice was tight.

"Dr. Armadas telephoned this morning. He wants Pop back in the hospital for tests on his liver. They want to check for something called radiation hepatitis. Armadas says it may explain the tiredness."

"That's not good news." I knew that with cancer, liver function was the canary in the coal mine.

"They're saying radiation hepatitis, Annie. Not liver cancer. They say radiation hepatitis is a pretty common thing."

"I knew things weren't going right. He's too thin and too tired. More than just from the radiation."

"He needs us to stay positive."

"Do me a favor, Ellen. Don't tell me what he needs from me."

Ellen had the presence of mind not to respond, but I knew my comment went on the tally against me.

"When are the tests scheduled?"

"Day after tomorrow. They want him to stay in the hospital for this. He hates the idea, of course."

"That's why he sounded so low."

"I called Charles and Tony. They both want to be here when he goes back in the hospital. It worked out well for Charles since he has to do some project for a regional BLM office up in Medford, Oregon."

"Things are starting to go really bad."

"Annie, calm down," Ellen said sternly.

"I'm trying to be realistic."

"Just come. You'll feel better," she suggested more kindly than I deserved.

I got back to the apartment as Josh was dishing up spaghetti. They all looked at me from the supper table, but it was Eli who asked, "You okay?"

"Grandpa has to have more tests. I've got to go take care of him." I hung my jacket on the back of a kitchen chair. "Ellen's there already. Charlie and Tony are going, too."

"This is serious," Josh said.

"They want him back as an in-patient."

"Is Grandpa going to die?" Eli asked.

I took my place at the table. "I don't know, sweetheart."

"Is God the one who decides if someone has to die?" Eli pursued.

"Yes, I guess so."

"What if God decides it's somebody's turn, but other people still need that person?"

I understood his question. Were we next in line, his parents?

"Eli, people die when they get very, very old and their bodies don't work anymore. Sometimes people die when they get a sickness and the doctors aren't able to help them. If that happens, God takes care of them in heaven."

"But God has a list of the good people and the bad people," Hannah interjected. "He doesn't take care of the bad people. He sends them back so they can try again."

Josh reached his arm across Hannah's shoulders. "Did you know there's a whole religion called Buddhism based on that very idea?"

"But I figured it out myself."

"I have no doubt." Josh turned to me. "When do you have to leave?"

"I'd like to go tomorrow morning. I don't want him to have to deal with the hospital alone."

"Can't Ellen handle it?"

"Let Aunt Ellen take care of Grandpa," Hannah urged.

Josh raised his open palms to stop Hannah and Eli from pursuing this further. "Don't make Mommy feel worse. She needs our help now."

"But you're not going to be away on my birthday," Hannah said. "Thirty-four more days, you know."

"How could I miss your birthday?"

That night I made a calendar for Josh with the kids' upcoming schedule of doctor and dentist appointments, play dates, Eli's karate tournament, Hannah's gymnastics exhibition. I paid the outstanding household bills and made Josh a reminder list of the house construction issues that needed attention. My anxiety about my father was bringing out the control freak in me. I put all this in a manila file and handed it to Josh.

"You're not going to Siberia. We can handle some of this stuff on the telephone."

"I feel better knowing everything's organized."

"No room for me to fuck up, right?"

"I'm sorry."

"You're thinking this is it, aren't you?"

"I'm hoping it isn't. I pray to God it isn't. I haven't had enough time."

The next morning, on my way to the airport, I asked the taxi to wait for me a moment outside the synagogue on Ninety-fourth Street. I wanted to wrap up loose ends before I left because I wasn't sure how long I'd be gone. It had been a month since Rabbi Lowenstein had lent me his book, and I still hadn't returned it to him.

I hurried down the dark corridor to Rabbi Lowenstein's office, but the door was closed, and a fierce, white-haired woman with eyeglasses hanging on a macramé cord regarded me suspiciously.

"Is Rabbi Lowenstein in?"

"Unavailable."

"I need to return his book." I held it out as proof that I had legitimate business. "He said I should come by when I was done with it."

"Did you read the book?" Her mission was to protect her boss from people who were superficial or insincere.

"Yes, I read it," I said, standing my ground.

"Are you a member here?"

"Rabbi Lowenstein invited me back," I repeated.

She reached out her hand for the book. "I'll give it to him."

"I want to return it myself," I insisted.

"Then you'll have to make an appointment." She returned to her project of folding and stapling newsletters.

"I have a taxi waiting out on the street. I'm on my way to the airport. I only have a minute."

At that moment the door opened and Rabbi Lowenstein peeked out, curious about the voices outside. I held the book out to him. "My father—remember—death as a gift to God. I read your book. I brought it because I'm on my way back to California. This time I might be staying awhile. He's not doing so well."

"Annie Waldmas," he tested his memory as he accepted the book. "I'm glad to see you again."

The woman looked even more irritated, now that she was faced with the evidence that Rabbi Lowenstein had made a commitment of his time that she had not monitored.

"I've got a taxi waiting. I'm on my way to the airport."

Rabbi Lowenstein nodded. "This is the time to be with him as much as you can. Don't let anyone talk you out of that. People will tell you that you are being obsessive. They will tell you to get on with your life. They will not understand. Stay with him. This time is precious. He needs you now."

# 10

I was the last to arrive in Los Angeles. Charles, Ellen, and Tony were at the dining room table digging into cartons of takeout Chinese food.

"He's sleeping." Ellen pointed her chopsticks toward the floor above. "Why didn't you call from the airport? One of us would have come to pick you up." I couldn't help but notice Ellen's phrase "one of us." She'd had her two brothers to herself, and I was horning in.

Charles tipped his chair back and reached out his hand to draw me near. "Annie, come eat."

"I rented a car. I figured with all of us here we'd need more than Pop's Porsche."

"I've gotta to be back in San Diego by tomorrow afternoon," Tony said, establishing the limits of his time commitment. "I'm signing for the money that's going to build my new shopping center."

I was still standing and taking in the picture of my grown siblings sitting around my father's table without him. Charles gave me his seat and moved to a chair next to Ellen. "Josh called to see if you'd arrived yet. He wants us to make sure you eat. He's worried you're going through some kind of sympathetic anorexia."

They examined me. I sucked in my cheeks and mimed the slouch of a runway model.

"Seriously," Charles said. "It's not going to do Pop any good if you don't take care of yourself."

"How were the kids?"

"They're going to send you a fax in the morning before school. Hannah got on the phone and did some heavy lobbying for her birthday present. She said we could all get together and go in on a trampoline for her to take to the country."

"Did they want me to call back?"

"Josh said you didn't have to. He was about to put the kids to bed. He's turning into a regular Mr. Mom, your guy."

"He likes it," I said, feeling the need to defend my marriage.

"And how about you? You able to control your urge to manage everything from three thousand miles away?" Tony asked.

"I've joined Control Freaks Anonymous. It's helping."

The intercom on the kitchen counter crackled. Abe was awake now and attempting to tune the speaker in on his end. His sleep-thickened voice came through. "You got a party going on down there? How about your old man up here? Why don't you move the festivities up a floor?"

"Want some Chinese food?" Tony called toward the intercom.

Abe's voice came back with a little more vigor. "Do me a favor, don't drag that cheap Chinese food up here. The smell would kill me."

"It wasn't cheap," Tony said. "Your children would never order cheap."

"Depends on whose credit card you're using," my father shot back.

"Let's see here." Tony got up to walk closer to the intercom. "Gold Amex. Says here, 'Abe Fishman, Big Spender.'"

"Haul your asses up here, on the double."

We filed into his bedroom, a parade of edgy Fishmans. Abe nodded approvingly. "I've got the whole gang."

Ellen and I settled on the sides of the bed. Charles and Tony pulled up chairs.

"So"—Abe folded his arms—"what's going on with everyone?"

"I've got some great news," Charles said. "Sissy's pregnant. She's due in August."

"You kept that a secret all through the Chinese food?" Tony grumbled.

"I wanted to tell everyone at once, being that it's our first."

"Congratulations, Charlie," Abe said. "That's wonderful. As soon as I get through this mess, I'm going to take a trip out to Washington and spend some time with Sissy. You made a terrific choice in that girl." He turned to Ellen. "Anything cooking with you in the romance department?"

I saw Ellen flinch at the question, but Tony did not. He leaned forward and poked her in the stomach. "Tick, tick, tick."

Ignoring them Ellen said, "I was talking to Mom the other day. She really wants to know how you're doing. Don't you think we could be a little more honest with her about your situation?"

"It's not something that concerns her," Abe said, slicing his hand through the air to indicate that this point was nonnegotiable.

"Of course it concerns her," Ellen argued. "She lived with you for sixteen years. Wouldn't you want to know how she was if she had cancer?"

He considered. "Probably not."

"Are you serious?" Ellen asked, quite hurt.

"I try my best not to think about the woman," Abe said.

"She happens to be our mother."

"And if she gets cancer, it will be important to you."

"Why can't you let bygones be bygones?"

"It's not a question of bygones," Abe explained. "I honestly don't care about her. She's not in my life, and I don't want to be in hers."

Ellen was ready to go on with this argument, but Charlie raised his hands to stop her. "Pop's got a big day tomorrow. Let's table this topic for now."

"Good idea," Abe agreed. "In fact, how about we skip the attempts at shuttle diplomacy altogether?"

Ellen wasn't giving up. She turned from Abe to us. "You know, since we're all out here, it would be nice if we made the trip down to see her. It's not like she doesn't know we've been out here visiting."

Abe folded his arms and waited to see how the rest of us would react to Ellen's proposal. It was clear that he didn't like the idea of sharing us with his ex-wife at a moment when he needed us so much.

"I'm sorry, Ellen," Charles said, "I've got to be climbing around a forest in Oregon tomorrow at ten A.M."

"And I've got to be with Pop for these tests," I added quickly.

"I'll stop in and see her on my way back down to San Diego," Tony offered.

"It's not exactly what I had in mind." Ellen flushed with anger. She had been dismissed both by her father and her siblings.

"So what's the story on these tests?" Charles asked.

"The nurses miss me."

"The blood count's off," Ellen explained.

"They want to do a CAT scan of his liver," I added.

Abe gestured around the room. "None of my genius children considered I cooked up this whole liver thing to get you out here again to spend time with your old man?"

"It worked," Charles said.

"Seriously, kids, I do have something to say since I've got the four of you together again. It's something I want you to know in case something like this ever happens to you. See, in spite of the tiredness, the worry, the endless medical procedures, when I look at the four of you and feel my love for you and your love for me, it's damned hard for me to imagine I'm anything but blessed. I want you to know that if you ever get sick like this, you stand to learn some of the most important lessons of your life. I could have dropped dead from a heart attack. I could have driven myself right up to the end and never had the chance to realize that I have four extraordinary children who love me."

Charles frowned. "You're so matter-of-fact about all this, Pop."

"Why not, Charlie? You get to my age and death is something on your mind, cancer or no. Death isn't a frightening prospect to me. Either there isn't anything there, I won't know anything, and it won't matter one way or the other, or there is something out there, which means I'll have another new experience."

"But how about the dying, the actual business of dying?"

"Look, I'd rather be up skiing. But believe me, if you feel loved, death isn't something to be afraid of."

Charlie still wasn't satisfied. "But what about facing the actual *moment* of death?"

"I don't know about that yet," Abe answered honestly.

Forty-eight hours later this rational conversation about life and death was a distant memory. Forty-eight hours later all I could concentrate on was breathing in and breathing out. I had two breaths to attend to—my own and my weary father's. We were a pair of exhausted travelers who had slipped through the looking glass and were trying to find our way home.

The medical profession had taken us over. Perhaps our hope had been too great, our trust too much. My father wanted answers, and he approached this next stage of his illness as he would have approached a business problem. He entered the hospital with his medical history in an accordion file under his arm, a cash flow statement of his physical condition, profits and losses. He was ready to put himself in the hands of experts in order to get the information he needed. Once they turned in their reports, he would retire into his own mind to decide his next steps.

At the intake interview with a young resident, Abe admitted that in addition to utter exhaustion he also had recurrent pain, both in his abdomen and in the lower part of his throat. I was sitting beside him as he described this, but I did not reveal my dismay that he had kept this to himself. My father was still a man with pride and secrets.

The young resident pressed, "Can you be more specific, Mr. Fishman?"

I could see my father found him tedious, and yet he gave more details and spoke with greater honesty about his physical condition than I had heard before.

The resident summed things up. "We're going to try to get a picture of things. Specifically we're going to look for any evidence of additional involvement." Abe nodded. This was what he wanted, facts.

When I telephoned Dr. Armadas to report on this meeting, I was told he had had to leave suddenly for Costa Rica because his father had been hospitalized with a heart attack. This information completely unnerved me, not only because he would be far away while my father was in the hospital, but because Dr. Armadas had a father of his own whom he would, legitimately, care about more than mine.

My father was to stay in the hospital for three days to complete the necessary tests. For the first day and a half I came and went, sleeping at his house and using the time to take care of household chores, and Ellen did the same. Ellen and I actually enjoyed each other's company, sharing our father's house, watching silly sitcoms together, eating takeout food. Tony had gone back to San Diego, and Charles had gone up to Oregon to work.

On the second evening, when I went to the hospital, he brightened at the sight of me, and curved his index finger to indicate that I should come near. When I was close enough so that he could whisper, he told me the news. "The kangaroos are roaming free downstairs, and the yogurt golf balls are stacked to the ceiling of the closet."

I slammed myself into an attitude of total calm and pulled a chair up close to his bed.

"The trouble is, the kangaroos can't find the golf balls."

"Oh?"

"Poor things. And everyone's been laughing at them because they're wearing purple."

"Pop?" I leaned in close. "What's going on?"

"It's been horrible, really. I wanted to get out of bed to help them, but the nurses locked me in here." He leaned toward me. "The nurses want to put me in a cage. I hear them talking. We've got to get out of here. I know the route we can take for our escape."

I sat back and took a long breath. There was nothing casual or ironic in his demeanor. He checked the door repeatedly while he ran his two forefingers over his thumbs as if he were reeling in an endless roll of paper. I was embarrassed for him, my powerful, competent father. I was also terrified.

"Pop—do you mind if I spend the night here?"

He stopped rolling and nodded. "Good thinking, good thinking."

I telephoned Ellen, and when she arrived, I stepped outside the door to describe the situation. She agreed I should sleep there in the room while she took on the job of tracking down Mike Armadas.

"Ellen, would you call Josh? Tell him what's happening. I don't want to leave Pop right now."

The nurses observed my father's agitation and judged that he needed more powerful sedatives, and the young residents on duty prescribed them. I watched the nurses push syringes into his IV and send God knows what medicines straight into his veins. They talked to him with exaggerated kindness as if he were a demented child. When they left the room, he would raise an eyebrow in my direction, wordlessly confirming our secret, his plan for our escape.

For the next twenty-four hours, I didn't leave his side. The only food I ate was off his tray. He wanted me to taste for poison, anyway.

We were off on a roller-coaster ride, climbing up slowly through hours of tense waiting, then shooting straight down into bouts of insanity. I had recently read *Jumanji* to Eli. My father's visions were much worse. The purple kangaroos were joined by a full menagerie of screeching hyenas and tigers in business suits. I considered the devastating possibility that the cancer had metastasized to my father's brain. It was the only explanation I could come up with. I longed for Charles to come. Of my three siblings, at this moment he was the one I needed. He would hold me and tell me we were doing everything we could.

As I watched over my father, the night hours passed at the snail's pace they do in hospitals. Each time he woke, it was sudden, as if an alarm had gone off in his mind to remind him of present danger. His eyes would dart in panic. His hospital pajamas, opened to his sunken belly, were soaked in sweat. Each time he had new details for me. We were under siege, but we must not reveal our suspicions until it was the right moment to act. In the worst moments I sat face-to-face with him on the hospital bed with my legs folded under me, holding his hands firmly in mine, forcing his eyes to me.

Throughout the night I focused on my job—to keep him in his bed, to keep him calm in any way I could, to keep myself from thinking or feeling too much. I worried that at any moment he could suddenly bolt. His analysis of our situation had become more elaborate. The hospital and its operatives were our enemies. I found myself eyeing the nurses suspiciously.

The ringing phone jarred me out of sleep. The sun was up. Somehow both of us had slept. I pressed the receiver to my ear, listening hard to understand what was being said.

"I've instructed the nurses to take him off everything. Can you believe they had the nerve to ask me for a written order?" The phone line echoed as it covered the distance along the ocean floor.

"Ellen found you."

"I'm sorry I had to leave. I'm the only son."

"Of course."

"They've got your father doped up on so many different kinds of pain and sleep medication, it's a wonder he isn't walking on the ceiling."

"I worried it might be brain cancer."

"Every resident has got to prescribe something on his shift or he hasn't justified his existence. I can't believe they did this to your father."

"It's not brain cancer?"

"Absolutely not. I'm flying back tomorrow. We'll check out the test results then. In the meantime, don't let them put a needle or a pill anywhere near his body."

"How are things there?"

"My father's doing fine now. They did open-heart surgery, and it went well. He's a healthy guy. He's only seventy."

"Same age as my father."

"Why, yes."

As I hung up, a nurse came through the door looking sheepish. "I'm to take your father's pulse every half hour. And no more meds."

"Why did you do this to him?" I barked.

My father's eyes shot open. Discreetly he raised a hand to caution me. It was never smart to reveal your true feelings to the enemy.

By afternoon he was getting better. By evening he was able to hold a fairly lucid conversation. I stayed in the hospital a second night, as much to keep an eye on the nurses and doctors as to watch over him. The next morning, he woke and asked with the kind of clarity left in the air after a summer storm, "Do you think God forgives, or is it our job to forgive ourselves?"

"Tell me what you mean, Pop."

"You once said to me that you sensed something dark in me, something I might be ashamed of. Do you remember that?"

"During one of our video sessions."

He turned to his window though there wasn't much to see, only a small trapezoid of blue sky framed by the angles of the hospital's puce-colored exterior walls. "There are some things we haven't gotten down on the tape yet."

"Do you want me to have Ellen bring the camera over?"

"When we get home," he said, still looking out. "There will be time enough when we get home."

"Dr. Armadas is flying back from Costa Rica today. When he arrives, we'll find out the test results and leave here."

He closed his eyes and sank back into his pillow. That was what he wanted, to go home.

When Dr. Armadas came that evening, his face was drawn. He pulled a chair up close to the bed and went straight to the bad news. The cancer was back—in three separate places. It was growing again in my father's stomach, there was an additional growth in his esophagus, and, the worst news, the news we had feared—it had reached his liver. We could try radiation again if my father wished. Dr. Armadas did not advise it. The discomfort it would cause was not worth the negligible amount of hope it held for recovery. Dr. Armadas was a direct man, perhaps too direct at this moment.

Abe Fishman studied his hands, which were folded on top of the neat hospital blanket. Was he noticing the way his flesh had shriveled, his nails had yellowed? His body, a loyal friend that had raced Italian bikes and flown down powdery mountainsides, was failing him.

The tears I shed went down the insides of my cheeks, if that is possible. I felt the muscles contract around my eyes. This news was nothing I hadn't expected—and yet . . . Perhaps it was that business again, truth finding its paths through the sedimentary rock.

"So that's it." My father pressed his lips tight. "I guess we'll have to let everybody know." I knew by "everybody" he meant his children, the four of us who had become his partners in this. "Annie, you'll have to make the calls. I'm not up to it."

"Okay."

"Just you kids for now. I'd like to make the other calls a little further down the road." The other calls would be his biking and skiing friends and his many business associates.

"Pop, this doesn't mean you're dying tomorrow."

He turned to Dr. Armadas for the definitive answer.

"It could be a few weeks, maybe a few months."

My father's face went ashen. "I'd like to be alone for a while, if you don't mind," he told us both.

Outside the room Mike Armadas said, "I'm sorry, Annie. I don't know any other way to say such things. I doubt your father would be satisfied with half-truths."

I nodded, though I was pretty sure that half-truths would have been good enough. I suspected that if Mike Armadas hadn't been so tired from traveling, he would have handled things more gently. But could there ever be a right time or a right way to give such ghastly news?

Before I made the other calls, I telephoned Josh. The kids were asleep, and he was sitting at the kitchen table reading the newspaper.

"It's as bad as we could have expected."

"Oh, Annie, I'm sorry."

"It's in his liver now, so it's a matter of weeks or months."

"Armadas told him that?"

"Yes, in just those words."

"How did he take it?"

"I don't think he expected anything so final. He talks about dying, but it's been more of an intellectual idea, an abstraction that put the rest of his life in relief. Today it was the cold facts."

Josh sighed. There wasn't much he could say.

"I hate this."

"You knew where it was going."

"I still hate it."

Dr. Armadas made two practical suggestions. He recommended renting a hospital bed for the house since it would help relieve my father's pain. He also gave me the names of some private-duty nurses. "You and Ellen can't do it all yourselves. I'm not saying now, but at some point. There's a lot to handle when someone's dying."

"How will it actually happen?"

We sat down on the arms of two catty-corner sofas in the hospital lounge. He folded his hands in his lap exactly as my father would have done when preparing to give important information. "People don't actually die of cancer. What cancer does is to weaken the body and attack the organs so they can't function anymore. At some point an infection will take hold. It will probably move into his lungs. Pneumonia is the most common thing that actually causes death. Most cancer patients go into a coma, and at that point death comes quickly. It's really not an uncomfortable way to die. The main thing is to give him enough oxygen so that he can breathe easily and to regulate his pain with morphine."

The idea of having a hospital bed in his bedroom did not bother my father the way I was afraid it might. The next morning we left the hospital, and when we helped him upstairs to where the bed was already installed, he climbed into it without a word of protest. "Home," he whispered. "God, it's good to be home."

# 11

I was sitting at my father's desk sorting through an accumulation of his medical insurance forms when the ringing phone jarred me. It was Josh. His voice was studied. He asked how I was. I said things were fine, and waited for the real reason for his call.

"I just picked up the mail."

"Oh?"

"There was a letter that was pretty upsetting."

"From whom?"

"From no one. I mean it wasn't signed. An anonymous letter from someone in Brookford."

I put aside my desk work. "What did the letter say?"

"It's disturbing, Annie. I don't know if you're in a place to handle it."

"But you called."

"Yes."

"Then maybe you'd better go ahead and tell me."

"The person who wrote it—it's looks like a woman from the hand-writing—she claims our fire was arson, anti-Semitic arson, Annie—like we were afraid in the beginning."

"Did she give any specific proof?"

"She mentioned another fire. A family in Amity. That's that town north of us up toward Massachusetts. Another Jewish family. She says their fire was definitely arson. I never heard that fire mentioned. Have you?"

"Maybe I should take a look at the letter."

"Everyone wants to jump to conclusions," Josh said to offer me comfort.

"Can you fax it to me?"

I sat watching the machine that had delivered notes and drawings from Hannah and Eli over the last months. When the telephone rang, I waited through the series of beeps that signaled the electronic connection. The page churned out, and I saw the same boxy handwriting of the other two letters. With my father listening to his Japanese music in the adjoining room, I sat alone with the copy of the letter in my lap.

> *Dear Mr. and Mrs. Waldmas,*
>
> *I'm worried about you doing all that work out there on your house. You're spending so much money. Don't you think the same person who burned it the last time will come back and burn it again? I don't know why you can't face the facts. Your fire was no accident. That business about the electrical wiring was a bunch of baloney. Your house was torched because you're Jewish, like Mr. Weiss, like that family over in Amity. Did you hear about that fire, two years ago April? Trouble is, over in Amity they let the trail grow cold. Don't let that happen to you. I'm not saying you should talk to anyone official around here. No one's going to believe we've got this kind of situation in Brookford. You're going to have to find some other way to get to the bottom of this. Mrs. Waldmas, aren't you an investigative reporter or something? Can't you look into this? Sorry to disturb you. Better to find out the truth, I always say.*
>
> *Sincerely,*
> *Anonymous*

The phone was ringing again. Not giving myself a second to chicken out from telling Josh, I picked up the receiver and said, "There were two other anonymous letters. She's written twice before—once in January, again a couple of weeks ago. I'm sorry, Josh. I didn't want to upset you."

"You didn't want to upset me? Am I a child?"

"Maybe I didn't want to have to face the truth myself."

"And we're going through with this huge construction project? Spending all this money like the letter says. Annie, for God's sake."

"Maybe because my father's sick," I said, a lame defense.

"I'm going to the state police with this. Probably the person's a crank, but all the same, I want to find out what's going on here."

"I already did a little looking into it," I said quietly.

"You did what?"

"I asked around a little. After all, like the woman said, I am an investigative reporter."

"This is not a game, Annie. This is something for the police to handle."

"What have the police done so far? Have they come up with any explanation for Shelly's fire? Have they even pursued it?"

"What kind of asking around did you do?"

"I went up to Amity."

"When?"

"Last week, when I told you I was going to the women's prison in Niantic."

"What the hell is going on here?"

"I was afraid you'd say we have to move."

"If this is true, do *you* want to stay in Brookford?"

"I knew you'd react this way."

"And you lied to me to avoid it."

"Josh, please. I found out the name of the family in Amity. Why don't we see what they say before going to the police? Let me find them."

"Aren't you busy taking care of your father?"

"Things are okay for now. He's settled in again. I've got the private nurse here helping us."

"Until we know more, I want to call a halt on the construction."

"Even if we end up leaving Brookford, we still have to finish the house to sell it."

"Find those people, then," Josh ordered, sounding very much like my authoritarian father.

As soon as I hung up, Abe called from the next room, "What's going on out there?"

He never liked the idea of things being taken care of out of his earshot. No doubt he thought the phone calls and fax had something to do with his medical care. I took a deep breath and went into the bedroom to see him.

"That was Josh. We've got some problems with the house. We might have to put the work on hold for a little while."

"Construction always has its fits and starts. Be patient." His advice sounded like an order. Or was I still bristling from the tone Josh had taken with me?

I went downstairs to the privacy of the kitchen and called New York information for the telephone number of Columbia University. I telephoned Columbia and asked for the botany department. They had no Professor Prager, but the department secretary had a database of botany monographs that she offered to check. She came back with the information that a Professor Jay Prager, chairman of the botany department at Rutgers University, had written a series of articles on serendipitous discoveries made through cross-pollination. When I called Rutgers University, the switchboard operator put me through to Professor Prager's direct line. I was unprepared and a bit unnerved when Dr. Prager picked up his own phone on the second ring.

"I'm sorry to disturb you at work. My name is Anne Waldmas. My husband and I have a house in Brookford, Connecticut, about fifteen miles south of Amity. We had a fire at our house last October. I understand you had a fire about a year and a half before ours." I paused for a moment. "I understand you're Jewish, too."

There was silence.

"Professor Prager?"

"Charlotte and I read about your fire in the newspaper. We've been wondering when you'd call. We're going to be up in Amity this weekend. Perhaps you should come over Saturday afternoon for tea."

"Can you tell me more on the telephone?"

"We're better off talking in person."

I hired a second private nurse so that Abe would be watched over twenty-four hours a day, and then explained to my father that I had to return to New York for a while. He assured me he was all right, but there was a new stoicism in him, maybe even a hint of fear.

I flew home on Friday, and on Saturday morning Josh, Hannah, Eli, and I set out for Connecticut. The day was warm and we drove with the windows down. We dropped the children off at Nick and Elizabeth's house, since the conversation with the Pragers was something we didn't want them to hear. Then we followed the directions Professor Prager had mailed to us, turning down one dirt road and another until we finally emerged at the top of a hill. The Prager house was perched above a long valley where cows huddled together, their hooves sinking into thick March mud. The rolling hills beyond were feathered with the early, pale green shoots of seed grass.

Professor Jay Prager's magnificent and eccentric garden was clearly the arena in which he made himself comfortable with strangers. He met us in the driveway in baggy, patched khaki trousers, a trowel sticking out of the back pocket, and the unbuttoned cuffs of his oxford-cloth shirt flopping at his wrists. After shaking our hands, he led us through a vine-covered wooden arch into his domain.

We followed along sod-covered paths to a garden that was chockablock with oddball statuary: a rusted unicycle planted in the ground, a marble chessboard and chess pieces on a bronzed pedestal, a polished chrome globe the size of a basketball. Most of the plants were still dormant in the early spring, but Professor Prager used his trowel to point out where his different flowers would bloom in the months ahead. Inside the green-house he showed us where rows of new shoots were getting a head start. Forgetting us for a moment, Professor Prager bent over a flat of seedlings, inspected their progress, and then delicately uprooted a few to replant them in separate peat pots.

Inside the house Charlotte Prager was organizing a British-style tea. Charlotte was a trim and tailored woman, who wore tapered woolen slacks and low-heeled pumps even on a country weekend. Before we sat down she took me on a quick tour of their house. I admired the stained glass in the skylights in their bedroom, and Charlotte looked chagrined. "Do your friends insist on telling you your fire was a blessing in disguise?"

"Yes. They know I'm not the decorating type."

"We workaholic women. We need a fire to make us domestic. I'm sure my friends would like to put a baby in a basket on my doorstep, too."

Charlotte invited us into the living room, where she poured tea and passed sandwiches. Though we all knew our purpose in meeting, none of us was in a rush to get to it. As soon as we faced it, there would be no way to return to any other subject. So we compared stories of how we came to settle in the northeastern corner of Connecticut. We talked about how we longed for Connecticut, and kept the thought of the quiet country mornings in our hearts as we went about our work Monday through Friday. "I hold my breath all week," Jay said, "and then I come here and breathe again."

Charlotte said, "I guess we need to tell you about our fire. It's two years ago this coming month, but we still live with it every day." She looked to Jay to begin the story, but he shook his head.

"You tell it."

"Are you sure?"

"This is what they came here to find out."

Charlotte set her teacup down on the table. "Every April Jay makes a pilgrimage to his favorite nursery up north in Massachusetts. Actually, it's a Mecca for gardeners from all around, they all go there, and they get talking. It wasn't anything out of the ordinary for Jay to start a conversation with this young man and invite him down to see how well our quince had weathered the winter. He came by that very afternoon, but even before he arrived, Jay told me about their meeting because there was something that struck him—he imagined that this young man's easiest relationships were with plants, which is certainly something my husband understands."

Jay kept his head bowed. This retelling was a painful ordeal.

"The two of them spent about an hour in the garden, discussing bulb depth, pruning techniques—all the things I'm afraid I don't have the patience for. And then, completely without warning, when Jay went to say good-bye, the man spit out these terrible, terrible things about Jews."

Jay raised his head. "I'll never forget what he said to me. 'It makes me sick every time I see another Jew move in around here. They dig up the ground for their fucking swimming pools and tennis courts, to show the world how much money they make, as if anybody needed reminding. That scum sucks the lifeblood out of the rest of us.'"

Reflexively Josh put his hands up to cover his ears.

Jay went on. "I ordered him off our property. I told him I was a Jew, for God's sake, one of those 'scum who sucks blood.'"

Charlotte took a breath. "The following Saturday night we went out to dinner, and when we came back our house was on fire. It was already too late to save it. All we could do was hold each other and watch it burn. We watched through the night, and I couldn't stop shivering."

I remembered my own unstoppable shivering, and I was shivering again now.

"My God," Josh whispered.

Jay bent his head again. Charlotte reached over and held her husband's hand for a moment. "We haven't told this story to anyone in quite a long time."

"How about the police? Did they find out anything?" I asked.

Charlotte shook her head and sighed. "Not much."

"Were they at least able to establish that it was a clear case of arson?"

"There was no doubt in anybody's mind that it was arson—they found the gas can. We told the police the story we told you, but we didn't have the young man's name or any idea where to find him. They say it's an open case."

Jay added, "They told us arson is one of the hardest crimes to solve because there's so little evidence to go on."

"Even if they wanted to try," Charlotte commented coldly.

"What do you mean?" I asked.

"You want the truth? The local police regard my husband as some sort of dotty scientist obsessed with flowers. And I'm a paranoid journalist with a pretentious English accent. I doubt they gave a second thought to the anti-Semitic motive."

"And what do you think?"

"Our fire was on April twentieth. Do you know what day that is?"

I looked to Josh to see if he had any more idea than I.

"I didn't know either until after our fire," Charlotte continued. "April twentieth is Hitler's birthday."

I folded one arm across my abdomen, put my fist to my mouth.

"They took pictures. They asked us a lot of questions—you know, to make sure we hadn't burned down our own house. They say they went down to Shagbark Farms to see if anyone knew the man who fit the description."

"Nothing?"

"We decided it was best to try to put it behind us. We rebuilt the house. This place means so much to us. We didn't want bitterness to spoil it."

"But what if he comes back?" I blurted out.

Josh looked at me, surprised at my insensitivity.

"It's all right," Charlotte assured him. "It's something we've had to think about. We've got alarms everywhere now. You can't see them, but this place is an armed camp. Before the fire, we never even locked our house."

"I'm ashamed to say I've dreamt about killing that man," Jay said almost inaudibly.

Charlotte took her husband's hand again.

Josh sat forward. It was our turn to tell our story. "The fire marshal said our fire was electrical, but we had some doubts because of another fire in town two weeks earlier, Shelly Weiss's bakery. The Jewish connection was hard to miss. We hired our own private investigator to examine our house from top to bottom. In the end he confirmed what the fire marshal told us, that our fire was caused by old wiring shorting out."

"One thing nagged at me, though," I interjected. "I kept wondering if a fire couldn't also cause a wire to short. It seems logical that it could go either way."

Josh went on, "The shorted wire was on the ceiling right at the foot of the basement stairs. They said that's why we had such extensive damage. Apparently the stair makes a natural chimney to draw the fire up into the rest of the house."

Charlotte rubbed her hands over her kneecaps and twisted uncomfortably.

"What is it?" Josh asked.

"The gas can. That's where they found it, where the bottom of our basement stairs would have been. They told us the same thing about the stairs making a natural draw. They said the bottom of a basement stairway is a classic spot for an arsonist to set his fire."

"I'm going to keep looking into this," I announced.

Charlotte leaned toward me. "If we can help in any way, please—anything we can do at all."

When we told Nick and Elizabeth what we had learned from the Pragers, they suggested we spend the night at their house rather than stay at our own place in Brookford, as we had planned to do for the first time since the fire. But I had ordered new mattresses, and promised Hannah and Eli a camp-out adventure in our newly constructed house.

When we arrived, I insisted we drag the new mattresses into the playroom so we could all sleep together. After the day's news, I didn't want the children out of my sight. I wanted to hear them breathing, to be able to reach out and touch them. The meeting with the Pragers had left me feeling sick and frightened. Though we couldn't speak of it with Hannah and Eli nearby, I knew Josh felt sickened, too.

In the middle of the night, when I woke to check on my sleeping family, I discovered that Josh was no longer beside me. I listened for sounds of him in the house, but there were none, so I got up, wrapped a blanket over my shoulders, and went downstairs to look.

He was sitting on the floor in the empty kitchen, peering out through the new glass sliding door, positioned like a sentinel, examining the dark. He did not turn to the sound of my footsteps, and he did not move a muscle as I crossed toward him. I sat on the floor behind him, pressed my cheek between his shoulder blades, wrapped my arms around his chest. "Josh, are you all right?"

He didn't answer.

"Maybe we're jumping to conclusions," I said softly. "Maybe it's nothing but a bunch of bizarre coincidences."

He squirmed away from me, and I felt his fury, rage against the present and against the past.

"Josh?"

"We can't stay here anymore."

I withdrew from him. "I'm not ready to assume that."

"There's no discussion. I won't come here. We're selling the house."

I folded my arms. "Now wait a minute. These are decisions we make together."

He looked at me with a mix of pity and condescension. "You're going to continue to bring your children to a place where some anti-Semitic crazy is on the loose—who knows, maybe even a group—our own little Ku Klux Klan up here? Get real, Annie. Get serious."

It always amazed me how Josh could turn from handsome to ugly in my eyes. I saw the widow's peak that made his forehead bulge, the flattened nostrils, his shoulders sloped like a drooping plant. His sourness seemed to take his body captive, make it sink and sulk.

"I'm going to figure this thing out. No matter what you say or threaten, I'm going to investigate and find out the truth."

"For chrissake, Annie, you do TV documentaries. You're not a detective. Maybe this *is* nothing but a bunch of coincidences, but the point is, I don't give a shit anymore. The whole thing stinks, and I want out."

I glanced up at the ceiling, worried his loud voice could wake the children. The one thing I was determined to do was protect my children from fear. Josh misunderstood my raised eyes and assumed I was mocking him.

"*Goddamnit, Annie!*" He slammed his palm on the floor. "I will not be milled into your psychodramas. I've put up with enough of it in the last five months. Everything is about you."

"What are you talking about? It's about everything and everyone I'm taking care of—including you."

"You're taking care of me?" Josh put his fingers to his chest. "I'm glad to know you remember I exist."

"Well, maybe I'm the one who needs a little taking care of these days."

"What the hell do you think I'm doing?"

"Then why are you talking about selling our house?"

"Because staying here is nuts, Annie! We're the victims of arson. *Anti-Semitic* arson. What do you want to do to your family? Are you that selfish? Are you that crazy?!"

I shot off the floor, threw open the sliding door, tore out of the house, fuming. It wasn't my fault that our house had burned. It wasn't my fault that my father had cancer.

As I ran out into the dark, the cold mist wet my face, and the wool blanket I held around my shoulders, one of the few things salvaged from the fire, began to throw off a nauseating soot smell. Tears streamed down my cheeks. How could Josh be so cold, so cruel? What was happening to us?

I couldn't go back to the house, but the night scared me, and I had never before felt scared in the country. I imagined Josh tracking me from behind the window, scowling, rigid. I thought the worst of him, hated the deep pessimism he had inherited from his father, from his father's father, and his father's father before him, no doubt. I hated these Jewish men who had constricted their lives rather than fight. I had married a man who withdrew from worlds that were too unpredictable or too large—a man who wanted to be a photographer but edited other people's photographs instead.

At the edge of our property, just into the woods, was the huge maple where Hannah and Eli had built their tree house with my father during his summer visits. The untreated rungs of the wooden ladder were rough in my hands, and my wet socks slipped as I climbed. I knew I was being ridiculous, running away to hide, but I didn't care. I wanted to curl up like a baby.

As I climbed up onto the tree house floor, I saw light bouncing off the branches in the forest. I looked back over my shoulder. The beam of a flashlight was loping along, and the moonlit outline of Josh's tall body followed behind it.

"Shit!" I whispered.

"Annie!" he called.

I scurried into a dark corner of the tree house and huddled there.

"Annie!" He was coming closer.

"I know you're up there." He stood at the bottom of the ladder. "I'm coming up."

The tree house shook as Josh climbed up and swung himself onto the plywood floor. The ceiling was low, and he bent from the waist, moving the flashlight beam left and right. When the light settled on my tucked body, I hid my face.

"For God's sake, Annie." The boards creaked as he moved in close.

"I don't want to talk," I muttered.

"I don't care whether you want to talk. We've got to get hold of ourselves. I'm frightened, you're frightened. It's nuts to take this out on each other."

"We want different things."

"We want the same thing."

"I don't know what you want."

"I want our family to be safe, to be happy."

I thought about this statement, its simplicity. Josh lowered himself to sit beside me and cautiously put his arm across my shoulders. "Annie, please."

"Too much is being taken away from me," I muttered.

"Annie, we have to face things."

"I'm facing things," I snapped.

"I suppose you are."

"Don't patronize me," I said testily.

"Would you please calm down?"

"You're so calm?"

"Look, I'm willing to make a deal with you. We give it three months to see what we can find out. If we can make this place safe for ourselves, we'll stay. If not, we face facts and get the hell out of here."

"And what if it takes more than that?"

"That's as far as I can go."

"This sounds like some kind of business proposition. What are we now, business partners?"

"Well, it's not like we've been great buddies lately."

"You have no sympathy for what I've been going through, do you?"

"That's bullshit."

"All right. Let's drop it. I agree to your deal. Okay? I'll take the three months, if that's all I can get."

We climbed down out of the tree house and crossed back over the lawn, walking side by side at a cool distance from each other.

On Monday morning I went to look for Rabbi Lowenstein. When I pushed through the heavy wooden doors, I was surprised to see him dragging a vacuum cleaner around the sanctuary. He looked more like the janitor than the rabbi, with a wool scarf wrapped around his neck, headphones over his ears, a Sony Walkman hooked on to his belt. Between his music and the vacuum noise he didn't notice me come in. I watched him work briskly between the pews, then stop a moment and lift the nozzle to conduct music I could not hear. When he spotted me, he seemed not the least disturbed. He tapped the button on the machine, and the synagogue went quiet.

"You do the vacuuming?"

"I thought you were out in California."

"I had some things I had to do here."

He settled down on the steps to the platform where he led services, resting the metal vacuum cleaner tube across his thighs as if it were his shepherd's crook. I slid into the pew that faced him.

"How's your father?"

"The cancer's in his liver now, which means there isn't much that can be done anymore. He's handling it pretty well. Better than me. But I came to talk to you about something else."

He leaned back against the stairs and waited.

"Last October we had a fire at our country house. It's in northeast Connecticut. At the time the local fire marshal said it was from an electrical short in the basement wiring, but there was another fire a couple of weeks before ours, the only Jewish business in our town. This past weekend we met with a Jewish couple from a neighboring town. They had a fire about a year and a half before ours. It turns out their fire was clearly arson, and they have reason to believe the arson was motivated by anti-Semitism. When we compared notes, we discovered a similarity between our two fires that suggests ours might have been arson, too, that they might have been set by the same person. My husband says we should sell and get out of there as soon as possible. But I really don't want to leave, I want to stay, to find out the truth. Our children are seven and nine. This has been a home to them all their lives. It's completely possible we're making too much out of a few coincidences. You have to believe that if there is an arsonist living in one of those towns who sets fires because he doesn't like Jews, the local authorities would know and do something about it."

Rabbi Lowenstein put aside the vacuum cleaner and walked over to a window where there was nothing to see but an air shaft. He looked out anyway. Then he turned back to me.

"I'm sorry about your house, Annie. And I'm also sorry to have to tell you that there's absolutely no evidence that people will do something about anti-Semitism in their midst even when they know about it. We have thousands of years of history to show us that people are quite capable of ignoring barbarism. But you're right about the other thing—you do have to make a choice. You can move away, as your husband wants to—or you can stay and pursue the truth, as you want to. There's no moral imperative one way or the other. No one will judge you for moving away from danger. I'm sure every Jewish thinker in the world would tell you that your duty to protect your family is as important as your duty to confront evil."

The window cast a soft corona of amber light around his wiry body.

"What would you do?"

He shook his head. "I don't have young children to protect."

"Tell me how I could be protecting my children by showing them that we run away from problems. They're young now, but someday they'd know."

"Are you prepared to accept the consequences if you choose to stay?"

"You mean that we could get hurt somehow?"

"No, no, Annie." He walked back toward me. "We may believe we understand evil, but encountering it head-on is a very different matter. If you do this—if you attempt to pursue the truth here—it will separate you from others. You may find yourself driven to do things you can't even imagine at this point."

"Maybe I don't want to feel powerless in every aspect of my life. Maybe because my father's dying. With the liver involvement, this is it, or at least the beginning of it."

"It?"

"It. Death." I shook my head. "Shit."

Pigeons were thumping and cooing outside a window high up in the stone wall. Rabbi Lowenstein sat down beside me in the pew.

"Annie, before you start looking into the truth about your fire, you've got a more pressing job in front of you."

"What's that?"

"These are important days for your father. He may need your help."

"I have been helping him," I said defensively.

Rabbi Lowenstein bent forward and folded his hands. "Annie, we Jews don't believe in original sin, and so we don't believe in confession. But there is a Jewish practice called *teshuvah*. Literally, the Hebrew word means 'turning.' It means that there's always time, always the chance to find yourself in a new way, to turn back to your true nature, to what you know to be your essential self. Because, you see, there always *is* another chance, no matter how little time is left. That's the gift God gives us with each new moment of time—the opportunity to forgive ourselves for things we feel ashamed of, to return to the self we hoped to be—a turning, *teshuvah*. But forgiving oneself can be very difficult, perhaps the greatest challenge of one's life. Most people need help to do it."

"That's how I'm supposed to help him—with his *teshuvah?*" I tried out the Hebrew word.

"Since you love him, why not? Everyone has his own valley to walk through before he can die at peace."

I fit my hands between my knees. This conversation assumed my father's death was certain, and I was not ready.

"True *teshuvah* means accepting that there are things you may have done in your life, things that may have had terrible consequences, that you cannot go back and change. The work of dying can bring regret into sharp focus. There can be very painful realizations. If you stay close and listen well, you'll know how to help him."

"But he's my father."

"Does that excuse you from having courage? Quite the contrary. Annie, remember I told you before—this is the time to be with your father as long as you can. The business with the arson will wait, believe me. I want you to go to your father and stay with him now. Even if it stretches on for months more. There is much you can accomplish. Go on. He still needs you."

# 12

That night I told Josh about my meeting with Rabbi Lowenstein and my decision to return to Los Angeles to take care of my father until he died. Things were still cool between us, so Josh didn't engage me in a discussion or question me, but he did ask, rather pointedly, how I planned to explain this to Hannah and Eli. He also wanted to know what I wanted to do about the house construction. I told him I hoped he would continue it, but the project had to be his for now.

The next morning my assistant and I reviewed all our current projects to decide which she would carry on without me and which we would put on hold. Putting so much on hold would reduce our cash flow, so next I sat with my film editor to explain the situation and suggest he look for a freelance job to tide him over. Back at my desk I telephoned both the children's teachers and described the situation so they would be sensitive to changes in Hannah and Eli. I gave Josh's work number to the teachers and assured them that he was an attentive father, but both teachers felt called upon to express their doubts about the wisdom of a mother leaving her children for such an extended period of time.

That night, before bed, I convened a family meeting. I had decided that was the best way to handle it, as a matter of family business, something we would work out together. I told Hannah and Eli that I had an important job to do and needed their help.

"Can you all look after each other while I go look after Grandpa?"

Eli took it as a matter of pride. "Of course we can." But he also wanted to clarify the potential power issues. "There's no way Hannah's telling me what to do."

"We'll work as a team," Josh told them. "And we'll send Mommy a fax every day. We'll make it our newspaper—the *Waldmas Daily Bugle*. Drawings, cartoons, letters to the editor."

"And you'll be back for my birthday," Hannah told me as a statement of fact.

As they marched off to bed with a new sense of purpose about the weeks ahead, I felt as if I had played a trick on them. Why hadn't I said that I hated to leave them, that it was a shitty situation they'd resent as soon as the truth sank in, and all the same, I was leaving them because I had to, wanted to, was driven by a complicated love for a complicated man.

The next afternoon, when I arrived in Los Angeles, my father was sitting up in bed with a yellow pad and pencil. "I'm making a list of the people I want to see. I decided it was time to start telling my friends what's going on."

I chose not to comment on how long he had postponed this. For months he had refused to see anybody but his children and his doctors, telling us he wanted to put weight back first so he wouldn't scare people, but we knew he was unwilling for his friends to see him in such a weakened state. Now that it was certain he would not regain his health, he was ready to face seeing his friends and saying good-bye. The good-byes to his family would come after. Abe liked projects. This would be his last one.

We made the phone calls, and I took charge as a stream of visitors came by. The weeks of visiting had a surreal quality. His friends came to a sleek, modern home high up in Beverly Canyon, but their purpose was primitive and tribal—to set eyes on the dying man before the Reaper took him. The doorbell would ring, and I would open it to the California sun. Healthy, tanned people would step through, doing their best to act casual. They were cordial, but also nervous, and some were clearly angry at having to face a man with terminal cancer. The visitors eagerly befriended me to establish that they now had more in common with the daughter than with the father. The dying man upstairs had become a separate species.

During the visits he often wanted me there for when he got tired and couldn't come up with a word he needed. I got used to completing his thoughts. He would look to me, certain I knew what he wanted to say, and usually I did. Over and over again he told his visitors that it wasn't the worst thing in the world to get cancer—it had helped him know himself and experience love as he had never before experienced it in his life. People were unnerved by his candor, but he didn't care. It was the gift he had to give them, this reassurance about himself and about their own futures. "Here I am, getting a chance to see my friends before I check out. It's not so bad, really."

I had to learn to know when my father had had enough of someone. He couldn't take the maudlin ones, especially the old girlfriends. I learned my cues to get rid of them politely. Saying good-bye at the front door, they would linger, hugging a little too hard the woman their own age whom one or two of them had hoped might become their stepdaughter.

One evening, as the room darkened, when he lay quietly in his bed and I sat in a nearby chair, my father broached the question of cremation versus burial. Though cremation had become popular, he wasn't comfortable with it and neither was I. Too many jokes about urns on mantels. Also, I wanted the comfort of knowing there would be a patch of grass where I could stop by and say hello. When my siblings phoned to check in, as they did each night, I did not tell them I was going to the cemetery the next day to make the burial arrangements. My father had assigned me this task, and I preferred, for now, to keep it to myself.

My "burial counselor" wore an orangish toupee that didn't match his sideburns. The two clocks in the office ticked out of synch with each other, and the word "death" was never spoken. My counselor reeled out the euphemisms: "demise," "passing on," "final rest." My father was our "loved one," "dear friend," "unfortunate soul." I was assured of the depth of the hole, that the box would be the one I had paid for, that there would be a layer of moisture-resistant plastic between the satin and the wood. They would see to it that my father would be sealed in, shipshape and comfortable. The burial counselor guided me through a list of options. The State of California had passed laws to protect the likes of me from being hoodwinked, and I was not allowed to skip over any decisions, large or small, each with a dollar amount attached. I had to review, decide, initial.

We went off to tour the floor of coffins. There was another woman there, and a young couple. It felt like Macy's mattress floor, and I wondered if I was allowed to kick off my shoes and climb into the satin-lined boxes to test them out. I tried to hang on to a sense of irony as I got my education—wood finishes, interior furnishings, handles. My counselor showed me coffins that were lacquered to a high black polish, with carved roses; others were painted baby blue and pink, like huge bassinets. "Take your time," I was advised. "These are decisions that must last a lifetime." A lifetime?

The plain cherry coffin appealed to me. It was hidden among the pine-veneered pressboard ones in a dark corner of the room. I later learned that Jewish tradition prescribes exactly such a coffin, as simple as possible and without adornments. When my burial counselor saw my choice, he sighed. I had no imagination or was simply cheap.

We drove out in a golf cart emblazoned with the cemetery insignia to inspect the choices available for my father's plot. The counselor's faith in me was restored when I dismissed the densely packed lowlands of Apple Blossom Lane—I did not want my father buried in a tract development—and pointed to the rise ahead. Wisteria Court had an arbor of lavender wisteria and a magnificent weeping willow. There was shade and a view—a bit of the freeway, the tip of a McDonald's arch, the feathery tops of faraway palm trees. There was a sense of the ocean to the west, and the sky was wide and blue.

"You've picked the most expensive real estate we've got here, Mrs. Waldmas." The jerky golf cart ride had caused his toupee to slip so that he seemed to stand at an angle to the earth. I had the impulse to set it right, for my sake, not his. I needed the earth to stay put beneath my feet right now.

"I'd like to get home to my father," I said abruptly.

"Of course, of course." He climbed into the cart and pressed the pedal.

In the cemetery parking lot I watched two Latino men unload ribboned funeral wreaths from a beat-up pickup truck. They set the wreaths on wooden easels ranged in a circle on the asphalt. The satin ribbons read, "Sympathy," "Rest in Peace," "God's Will Be Done." When the truck was empty, the two men hoisted the wreaths under their arms and carried them inside to the glass chapel like stagehands carrying props. I climbed into my car, shut the door, put the key in the ignition, and flipped on the air-conditioning. I wanted to be in a different world and fast.

Five minutes up the San Diego Freeway the car phone rang.

"So?" It was Abe Fishman, wanting a report.

"You're going to be on a hill underneath a tree."

"Sounds nice."

"You've got Jack Benny as a neighbor."

"How about that."

"Couple of other old vaudeville comedians, too. I guess it's a little hangout up there."

"Charlie arrived." Charlie had made a follow-up trip to Oregon and detoured back through Los Angeles on the way home. "We've been going through my old picture albums. He's got to head back to Washington this evening. I figured since he's here we might do some videotaping."

"You have the energy for that?" I asked, though at this moment I was the one without energy.

"I wanted to tell you a little more about my growing up, the Brooklyn part. I know I've told you a lot about it, but Charlie hasn't heard it. Anyway, there's something else. Remember I mentioned it when I was in the hospital?"

"With the kangaroos?" It had become a joke to us now.

"We talked about forgiveness."

"You talked about forgiveness," I corrected him.

"Hurry home, Annie, would you?"

When I arrived I went straight upstairs to the bedroom. My father was scowling. He wanted to manage his impatience but could not. Impatience had become synonymous with his need to control things, and in recent months he had wanted to become a man who didn't need to be in absolute control of his world.

"What took so damned long?" he barked before he could stop himself.

Charles was sitting by the hospital bed, from which my father presided over his shrunken world. I sat down opposite him. There were two empty chairs left, the seats we had brought in for visitors.

"Pop's been showing me some of his photographs. He was actually quite handsome, once upon a time."

"He's handsome now," I protested.

"Bad traffic, huh?" my father asked, to make amends.

"I was a jerk to get on the San Diego Freeway at four o'clock in the afternoon."

"That's why I told you to go down there in the morning." His agitation drew him right back into his old habits.

"Down where?" Charles asked.

"Didn't he tell you?"

"She's been down picking out my plot."

Charlie's eyes widened. "You went by yourself?"

"It wasn't so bad. The coffin showroom was the most amazing part. Liberace himself would have been pleased with some of the coffins they were selling there."

"I told you I didn't want fancy."

"Solid cherry, no frills, actually quite lovely in its simplicity," I spieled like a salesperson.

"Sounds nice."

"The guy was hugely disappointed in my choice. But I squandered our inheritance on the plot. I didn't want you jammed into some cheap subdivision. I went for a spot on a little hill—large plots, better neighbors."

"I'm next to Jack Benny," he told Charles proudly.

"I still can't believe you went by yourself." Charles flipped his jet-black hair away from his forehead. He was the handsomest of the Fishman children and the only one of us who had managed to push past the five-foot, six-inch mark.

"It didn't seem like such a big deal. Still, I wouldn't mind someone coming back with me to make sure everyone agrees on my choices."

"I'm sure you did fine," my father said. "Not everything in this family has to be done by a democratic vote. I gave you my proxy, Annie, and that's that."

"By decree of the king," Charles teased.

"So set up the video camera," my father ordered.

"King, indeed," I said.

"You got something more important?"

"I wouldn't mind taking a moment to go to the bathroom, maybe get something to drink, little slavey things like that."

In the bathroom I peered into the mirror. I had become so enmeshed in my father's needs in the last weeks that I was caught by surprise to see a separate person looking back—a forty-year-old woman in a red-striped shirt with eyelashes that my father had years ago told me were long enough to seat the fairies.

I sat on the edge of the tub. The bathroom was the one place in my father's house I could be assured of privacy. Despite my offhand report, the visit to the cemetery had left me feeling lonely. I had been in Los Angeles for three weeks straight, the longest I had ever been away from my husband and children. Their world seemed farther and farther away as my world narrowed into my preoccupation with my father's remaining days. Nearly all my time was spent inside his house, beside his bed, interpreting his wishes, speaking for him, monitoring the plastic sacks of nutrients that dripped into his veins, enough sustenance to keep him comfortable in the face of death, whenever it came. Death was on my mind, night and day. I thought of Rabbi Lowenstein, his admonition to me to stay close. I wanted to ask him, Could I fall in? Get lost in death? Find the process of dying too compelling?

While I set up the video camera, Charles told us about the trip he and Sissy were taking the following week to the Caribbean. With Sissy pregnant for the first time, Charles had not turned away from his own life the way I had. "A friend of ours has a little sailboat in Bequia. I figure it's good to start a baby off rocking in the ocean." He asked Abe, "Do you mind that I'm going, Pop? I can stay here if you'd feel more comfortable."

"Go, go. I'm fine. I've got Annie."

I bristled at my father's presumption, but it was true. He had me; I was his for as long as he wanted or needed me. That was the way I wanted it.

"You can get me by radioing through St. Vincent. I'll give Annie all the information. If you need me here, I'll be back in a flash."

"Have a good time. Don't worry about things back here. I'll tell you when I'm ready to call it quits." He turned his attention to the camera. "Is that thing on?"

"Posterity is happening as we speak," I told him.

"So how does this work?" Charles asked.

"Ask him a question."

Charles thought a moment. "Annie told me the story about your mother running away from some guy she stole money from in Boston and brewing illegal alcohol in the train yards in Philadelphia. But how did you end up in Brooklyn?"

"The point is, my mother was always trying to survive one way or the other. Did Annie tell you how we got hooked up with some guy who had a formula for a hair tonic that turned gray hair to black? The secret ingredient was lead. When the customers' hair started coming out by the handful, we had to beat it across the bridge to Brooklyn."

"What did your mother do in Brooklyn?"

"Customer peddler—ever heard that expression? She had a group of neighborhood women she shopped for. She went back to the merchants she knew on the Lower East Side and got bargains because she bought in bulk. Once she saved up enough money, she opened her own store. That's where I worked after school. We were always working, but there was never any money."

"Even when you had the store you still considered yourself poor?"

"Poor, Jewish, short, all of it. Back then being poor and being a Jew were practically synonymous, like being black, you're second-class. The places I grew up, they'd come after you—'Let's go get the kike'—and you ran like hell."

"It's amazing how different it was from how we grew up," Charles said.

"That was my ambition, Charlie. To make sure you kids didn't grow up with shame."

"Shame?" I raised my eyes from the lens. My father lowered his. "Shame?" I asked again.

"It was the way of life back then. That's how I've always explained it to myself. People did what they had to do to survive."

"Can you give us an example?"

He flipped his hand. "It's all past history. No need to burden you guys with things I'd rather forget myself."

"We're interested," Charles told him.

"What is it you want to know?" He was still ducking.

"Whatever it is you want to tell us," I said, watching his darting eyes.

"Maybe some other time."

I remembered Rabbi Lowenstein's instruction. "Pop, now is the time."

He shifted around in the bed, finding a new position against his pillows. He cleared his throat, reached for the glass of water, and looked around the room, as if checking for intruders.

"You know about bankruptcy, right? Bankruptcy, that was one scheme. You buy up all sorts of merchandise on credit and hide the stuff in storage somewhere. Then you go to court and you tell the judge, Oh,

I'm broke, I only have so much money, let me off the hook and cancel my debts to my creditors. Once the judge protects you, you get the merchandise out of storage and sell it, or maybe you've already been busy selling it and stashing away the cash."

"Clever," Charles commented.

"Clever?" Abe shook his head. "Maybe if it isn't your own mother doing it."

"What else?" I asked, watching him intently.

"Forget it, Annie. It's nothing but lousy memories for me."

Part of me wanted to pounce, but another part of me held back. He had become so frail. The joints of his shoulders and elbows stuck out with little flesh left to soften them. He received all his nutrients through the IV in his arm, and a second IV needle had been inserted in his chest to deliver infinitesimal amounts of morphine straight into his heart. His skin had become paper-thin, both physically and metaphorically. He was old and he was dying. Why push the man? But Rabbi Lowenstein had made it clear; the window would open only briefly, and this was my responsibility.

"Is there something else you were ashamed of?"

"Bankruptcies, fires—what else do you want to know?" He tried to sound casual, but there was nothing casual in his dark eyes.

"What fires?"

"The ones my mother set," he answered almost aggressively. "The first one I remember, I was fourteen. My sister was nineteen. She and my mother did it. They ran the store, they set the fire."

"How come we haven't discussed this before?"

"You didn't ask."

"I didn't *ask?*"

He closed his eyes a moment to concentrate on his breathing. Breathing was no longer something he could do well when he was concentrating on other things. He was learning to talk, breathe, talk, rest.

"I'm asking now, Pop."

He opened his eyes and considered my presence, considered Charles, then looked away to a middle distance, away from us, his children.

"I never knew how much money we had or didn't have. That was between the two of them, my older sister and my mother. I was still 'baby

Abie' to them, even though I was in high school. They didn't include me in their schemes. Maybe they figured that protecting me from what they were doing somehow made it right. They had to support me, the smart one who went to high school—I guess that was their justification. I suppose there had been other fires, maybe when I was younger. There must have been. Why else was the smell so familiar to me? But the first time I really knew what was going on was on that Christmas Eve, the fire that happened when I was fourteen. That was the night I finally understood."

"Understood what?"

"Just listen, Annie," he said gruffly.

"I asked my mother, 'Why are we going home so late?' She said, 'Oh, we've got to clean up all the Christmas stuff.' I didn't understand what they were doing, throwing paper and boxes behind the showcases and into the back of the store. They sent me out to put up the awning. That was always my job. In my usual way I'm cranking and making a racket." He smiled. "I guess that wasn't the right thing to do, wake up the whole goddamned neighborhood before you set a fire. My mother runs out and drags me back into the store. I still didn't know what they were up to. Before we lock up, she sends me back out to the street and tells me to run inside if I see anybody. After a few moments she and my sister come rushing out and hurry me home. They send me straight to bed, and my mother gets on her slippers and bed cap a moment before there's a loud banging on our door. The police are outside yelling, 'Your store is on fire! Your store is on fire!'"

Charles asked, "You really didn't realize they were going to set a fire?"

"Maybe I did, maybe I didn't. Sometimes when you don't want to know something, you don't let yourself know—when you're fourteen— old enough to be a man, old enough to do something."

"So what happened?" Charles asked.

"We put our coats on over our pajamas and ran back to the store. It had started to snow. I remember my footsteps in the snow, my sister's footsteps, my mother's footsteps. I remember the yellow streetlights, the snow coming down in the light. Funny about the details, how they all stay. Fifty-six years later, I can see it clearly. When my mother got back to the store, she put on a show of hysterics. 'My store, my store, oh, my God, my store!' She was doing a pretty good job of convincing everyone on the street until the Italian man from upstairs pushed through the crowd—"

"Upstairs?"

"The people who ran the fruit store next to us lived in an apartment above our store. You know the kind of place—there's a row of stores along the street, apartments above them." He gestured to show the configuration. "We used to live above the store ourselves, but we had moved up in the world. We lived a couple of blocks away where the buildings were exclusively residential. The Italian family had moved in after us and opened the fruit stand. This Italian man comes right up to my mother and points his finger in her face. 'It's you!' he yells at her. 'I know it's you! You set a fire in your own store. You dirty, rotten kike. I know you did it!' He pressed his face right up to hers and screamed, 'You could have killed my babies! *You could have killed my babies!*' His wife comes out of the crowd with their newborn baby in her arms. The baby is crying and crying. 'Look at her! Look at my baby! You could have killed my baby!'"

Tears were streaming down my father's face. He reached for a tissue, then looked at Charles and me. "Can you imagine? It's the middle of the night. There's smoke filling your apartment. Your family's asleep, your children. Can you imagine anything more terrifying than waking up with a fire raging through your home?"

My skin went cold, the way it had the morning nearly six months back when I had walked into our own demolished home. The fears my father described had been in my dreams ever since. It could have happened that way to us. We could have been sleeping in our house when the flames broke out. My children could have died in their beds, the very image the wretched Eddie Shank had seared into my brain. My father, whose concerns at this moment were half a century away, was not thinking about the fact that I, too, his daughter, had a fire, had feared arson, still did.

"If the fire engines hadn't come so quickly that night—and on Christmas Eve, anything is possible—it would have happened exactly the way the Italian man said. His whole family—himself, his wife, his young children—they all could have been dead. We could have killed them. We would have been murderers. Of course, no one bothered listening to this immigrant. The Italians had replaced Jews as the people everyone despised. Besides, my mother knew how to faint when things got tricky. She keeled over right on the spot. The police took her home, and the Italian family was left standing there alone. I guess they moved away. I never saw them after that night. We rebuilt the store right away, bigger and better—the next fire, that one's a complete blank. I know it happened. There may have been another fire after that. We took the money each time and made a better store. I don't remember what part I played, who else we put in danger. I suppose I made myself forget all that. Maybe I even set one of these fires. I don't know. I didn't want to know. That's what I want you to understand. *I didn't want to know.*"

He was sobbing openly. "Can you see why I had to turn myself into a Manufactured Man, Annie? I came from people who were despicable. I came from people who risked killing a child out of their own greed. I saw it. I was part of it." He shook his head violently from side to side. "I could have killed somebody. *I could have killed somebody.* You don't know what that feels like." He stared into my eyes, his mouth quivering. "I did that, Annie. I did all of that."

I moved to the bed and took his hands. "Pop, you're not like that. You're good and generous and decent."

"Oh, no, Annie. That's only what I made you believe I am. That's what I manufactured. I tried to excuse it by telling myself survival forced us to do these things. That's ridiculous. Survival? We had enough to eat. We had a place to sleep. We had our own store. To some people in the neighborhood we were the rich people. This is greed, that's all there is to it. To risk killing someone's children so you can make a fancier store? That's evil. I was part of evil. Can't you understand?"

"I understand."

"Why do you try to convince me differently, then? I let it happen. I didn't stop it. And do you know what else? Christmas morning after the fire, I climbed through the rubble scavenging for things to keep. Then I rode off on my bicycle as if everything was fine. Can you imagine? I didn't have one twinge of regret. At least I acted that way. That's why I had to make myself into somebody else. There was no way I could live with myself after I had been that callous. Being sorry now doesn't make a damned bit of difference, either. Do you understand why I got cancer—why I'm ready to die?"

Charles frowned. "I hope you're not telling us you believe you *deserve* to die."

"No, no, Charlie. It's not that I deserve to die. It's that I'm tired of living with shame. I've lived with it so long. I've held on to it all these years. I'm exhausted from the job of trying to cover up, driving and driving myself. Don't you see? Dying is the way I can let go of it at last."

No wonder he abhorred scrutiny. No wonder he had gone about presenting himself as the utterly moral man. This explained the years of battle—against the world, against us, against himself. This explained the long parade of women who were never allowed to get too close. His tremendous effort to hide now struck me as unbearably sad. Charles and I, stunned by our father's outpouring, sat in silence, full of compassion for this man, our father, a person, in our eyes, as never before.

He dropped back onto the pillows, completely spent, and closed his eyes. His eyelids were dark, the blood showing blue-violet through his paper-thin skin. And yet he looked new. There was no more need to push and plan and convince, no project through which to prove himself worthy. I remembered the word Rabbi Lowenstein had taught me—*teshuvah*. My father had made a turning, had confessed his shame, but he had not forgiven himself. Forgiveness clearly seemed impossible to him. Where could he stand so that forgiveness would be imaginable? How could he gain such a perspective? Through me, through Charles, his children, his grandchildren as well, perhaps—someday. Maybe that's why he had wanted to tell us the facts before he died. Perhaps he knew that forgiving him would be our job. Maybe someday we could make use of the lessons of his life, and in so doing, earn him the redemption he could no longer earn for himself.

# 13

When Tony drove up that Saturday to visit, I pulled him aside to tell him about the incredible experience of hearing Abe tell about the Christmas fire, his confession, and the shame that explained years of posturing and defensiveness.

"It's amazing how his cancer has changed him," I said.

"Yes and no. He's still tough as nails."

"What's this about, Tony?"

"I've been thinking about what Ellen said when we were all here before the tests. She's right, you know. Pop's attitude about Mom sucks. You'd think at this stage he could at least acknowledge her existence. I don't expect him to like her, but at least he could have a civil word with her before he dies. I think that would mean a lot to her."

"You're dreaming, Tony. I don't think either of them is interested in some sort of dramatic predeath reconciliation. It's been too many years. We may still harbor a childhood fantasy that our parents will get back together, but it isn't real. It's not them."

Tony took an envelope from his jacket. "When I stopped in last week, she gave me this for Pop." He slipped a photograph out of the envelope and handed it to me. It was a picture I had never seen before, taken when they were very young. I was stunned at how pleased they looked, concrete evidence that they had once been happy.

"Turn it over," Tony instructed.

On the back my mother had written, "May these days go gently for you. Judith."

"You're not planning on giving this to him?"

"She asked me to."

"Is this for his benefit or for hers?"

Mike Armadas appeared at the top of the stairs. He had been making house calls now that Abe had no strength to come into the office to see him.

"How's he doing?" I called up, too confidently perhaps.

Mike came down to us. "His shortness of breath might be the beginning of the pneumonia we talked about. I'm not going to order an X ray, though. I can't see any reason to put him through that since we wouldn't treat it anyway."

"What do you mean you wouldn't treat it?" Tony demanded. "That's like giving him a death sentence."

Mike was quiet, waiting for Tony to grasp the obvious, that Abe Fishman already had a death sentence. With his hand on the front doorknob, he turned back to us. "When it's my time to die, I hope I have your father's courage."

Tony and I watched the front door close.

"I'm going up to see him." Tony took the photograph back from me.

Maria was off on Saturdays so I went into the kitchen to clean up and leave them alone, which I knew my father wanted. He had begun the next stage of his good-bye project, his good-byes to us. Charles and Abe had their good-bye talk before Charles left for Washington, D.C., and his trip with Sissy to Bequia. Charlie reported that Abe had apologized for the things he believed he had done wrong as a parent. He had advised Charlie to try not to let fear govern the decisions of his life. Charles had listened with an open heart, since he had never been at odds with Abe the way Tony had, the older brother who had been left with childhood bruises, some of them quite real.

I had finished the kitchen cleanup and was turning on the dishwasher when Tony reappeared and grumbled, "I don't see how you can say this cancer has changed him. To me he's as self-righteous as ever."

I watched Tony search the refrigerator.

"Do you know what he said to me?" He turned back to face me. "Get this. The old rhino apologized for not always treating me with enough respect. What did he expect? Was I supposed to apologize back? Forgive him for things I don't really want to forgive him for? He gets a clean slate because he's dying? That's nifty." He brushed his hands against each other. "Presto, magic, my childhood was a dream."

I poured Tony a glass of juice from a pitcher on the counter. He drank it down in a single gulp, then wiped his mouth with the dish towel.

"Isn't it bad enough watching him die without having to endure all this psychodrama? I don't know how you stand it, all this *talking, talking* all the time. I swear, he's making his death some sort of theatrical event."

"In his own way he's trying to help us."

"And maybe it's a little bit late."

"I don't think so."

"Maybe not for you, his therapy buddy. Myself, I'm afraid I've got some indelible memories etched into my brain. It's kind of hard to forget your old man chasing you down the street and smacking you across the face in front of all your friends, all for the sin of leaving your bike in the driveway. You don't take a lifetime of memories like that and turn them around in a heartbeat."

"There's been good and bad, Tony. The important thing is that he's your father and he loves you."

"I wish it were that simple." He dropped his head, and I tried to hug him, but he was unbending.

"What is it, Tony?"

"I hate this fucking saying good-bye. I'm sorry. It upsets me."

"Did you give him the photograph?"

"Yeah, and what a waste of time that was."

"I told you it wasn't a good idea."

"He's allowed to try to help me, but I'm not allowed to try to help him."

"You honestly thought it would help him?"

"The divorce wasn't her fault any more than his. Wouldn't it be better if he could forgive her before he dies?"

"Probably. But hearing about how his mother set fires, I can see how he got in a habit of not forgiving. He can't even forgive himself."

That night, when I telephoned home, Eli asked once again if his grandfather was going to die. I couldn't postpone the truth any longer. "I'm sorry, Eli. It doesn't look like Grandpa is going to get better."

"Then I'm coming to see him."

Josh and I discussed the idea. I was worried about Hannah and Eli being frightened at the sight of Abe, so weak and close to death, IVs in his arms, his bedroom turned into a hospital room with nurses taking care of him. Josh thought it was important for them to see their grandfather and have the chance to say good-bye, and he wanted to say good-bye, too.

Josh also suggested, since they were coming out to California, that it might be a nice idea for us to drive down and visit my mother.

"It's not the time for that," I said quickly.

"It's been quite a while since we've seen her."

"I want to keep things simple. We'll invite her back to New York when this is all over. I'd prefer it that way, if you don't mind."

"And if the kids ask?"

"I don't know," I said, slightly exasperated. "Tell them Grandpa needs us right now."

I was pleased my family was coming, but also nervous. I had been living in the rarefied atmosphere of my father's house, where his dying gave a heightened sense of purpose to every day. This separation from the business of ordinary life also cushioned me from imminent loss. Having my family, and particularly my children, come into this realm apart felt risky, the world of living and the world of dying colliding.

When I picked them up at the airport, I was struck by Josh's youth, his glistening black hair, smooth skin, so different from the man with whom I had been spending all my days. And I was unnerved by Hannah and Eli's exuberance, as they jumped on me for hugs, climbed on the baggage cart for rides, ran up the down escalator to see if they could beat it. It was too much for me, their unquestioning embrace of life.

We stopped at the motel on Ventura Boulevard to check in and leave their suitcases. Eli was unhappy that he couldn't stay at his grandpa's house as he'd done on all his previous visits, but Hannah convinced Eli of the benefits of having the use of a pool with a water slide. As we drove up to Mulholland, I told them to expect their grandfather to be skinnier than they remembered, and I also explained that since Grandpa didn't like to stay in hospitals, we'd brought the hospital to him. He had a special bed that moved in every direction, some very beautiful nurses looking after him, food that went straight into his arm so he wouldn't have to bother with eating when he wasn't in the mood.

"Sometimes Grandpa gets very tired, so we'll keep our visits short. He's so excited to see you."

Abe's eyes were closed when Hannah and Eli tiptoed quietly into the room, taking their cue from the nurse, who brought her finger to her lips. Everyone had been primed for their arrival, and the bedroom had been spruced up, with as much of the medical paraphernalia as possible stored out of sight in the bathroom. My father had insisted on wearing the Hawaiian shirt Hannah and Eli had picked out for him during a vacation in Florida. At the sight of him lying in the hospital bed in a shirt covered with bongo drums and palm trees, his thinning hair neatly combed, his sunken cheeks newly shaved, his bed cranked up to a nearly seated angle even while he slept, I felt the thing I had feared: For the first time my father had attempted to put a mask on his dying for the benefit of the living, and the poignancy of his effort was hard for me to bear.

His eyes fluttered open at the soft sounds of our arrival, and the four of us gathered around his bed.

"Hey, kids," he whispered to Hannah and Eli.

"Hi, Grandpa," they said.

He motioned for me to hand him the glass of water that sat, as always, on the rolling cart beside his bed. He drank out of a flexible straw, which I was in the habit of putting to his lips; this time I simply handed him the glass with the straw pointed in the right direction. Once he wet his mouth, he talked more easily.

"Tell me about the airplane ride."

"They let me go inside the cockpit," Eli said.

"You're a lucky guy. They don't do that for everybody, only for kids who understand aviation." He raised his eyebrow at Hannah to include her in the adult world of white lies.

"They gave us those stupid kids' meals," Hannah told Abe. "Why do they think every kid likes hot dogs? Do they even know how they're made?"

"Why don't you order a vegetarian meal for the way back?"

"Then it's disgusting eggplant and brown rice."

Eli was quiet as he studied the details of the room. I knew he had brought Abe a present, so I prompted him. "Grandpa gets pretty bored lying in bed all day long."

"Oh, yeah?" Eli dug into his pocket and pulled out a Rubik's Cube. "I got you a present, Grandpa." He handed it out to him, keeping his distance. "'Cause you like puzzles and stuff."

"Come here, buddy."

Eli went close to the bed but stopped short of touching it.

"You're going to have to get me started with that thing," Abe told him. "Come on up," he said, indicating a spot beside him on the mattress.

Eli used the metal railing to step up, tucking the toes of his sneakers between the rungs, and then sliding into position where Abe had invited him. In a moment they had their heads bent together, hair touching. I put my arm around Josh and said softly, "You were right."

Hannah pulled a piece of paper out of her pocket and unfolded it. "I wrote a new poem for you, Grandpa."

"Will you read it to me?"

Josh went to stand with Hannah to give her encouragement, when suddenly Abe started coughing convulsively. The nurse stepped in from the hall. "Everything okay, Mr. Fishman?"

He continued coughing as he nodded. The nurse waited and watched until she was certain she wasn't needed. As I moved toward Eli, who was frozen by his grandfather's helplessness, I saw Abe's flash of anger, mistaking my concern for Eli for too much overt nursing of him in front of his son-in-law and grandchildren.

"I want to hear my poem," he said hoarsely. As I had done before, Hannah handed her grandfather his water glass with the straw turned toward him.

He smiled at her. "So many beautiful ladies looking after me."

Hannah unfolded her paper to read:

"Grandpa the Greatest"
G is for the greatest tree house builder in the world.
R is for the racing bike he loves to ride.
A is because he knows the answer to any question.
N is for the nicest grandfather in the universe.
D is for downhill skier.

P is for pun maker.

A is for all the ways I love you.

She looked up. "Do you like it?"

His eyes had filled. "Come give the downhill skier a hug."

Hannah went to the bed, and, as Eli had done, used the rungs of the metal frame to climb up. When she dropped her head against Abe's skinny chest and reached her arms around him, Eli reached over from his side of the bed and hugged his grandfather, too.

The next morning Ellen surprised us by returning unannounced from Colorado. She said she wanted to see her niece and nephew, but she also told us she had taken a temporary leave of absence from her job. When Ellen and I were alone she explained, "It was ridiculous pretending to work. I need to be with him now. Maybe to make up for lost time. Besides, I've got some news I want to tell him."

"Oh?"

"You'll probably say it's because Pop's dying."

I had no idea what she was talking about.

"The strange thing is that he actually looks a little like Pop—short, intense, handsome. Like Pop before all this, I mean. A mutual friend introduced us, said she thought we'd be perfect. She's right, except I'm no sure I would have realized it before Pop was dying."

So Ellen had a boyfriend. "What do you mean when you say it has to do with Pop dying?"

"I was always looking at what was wrong with every guy I met, instead of what was right with him. I guess because I had the habit of looking at Pop that way—always seeing him through Mom's eyes instead of my own."

"How did that change?" I asked, genuinely curious.

"Maybe watching him struggle the way he has these last months. I've seen his courage. I'm going to miss him, Annie."

For a moment we were both quiet, in our separate thoughts.

"So what's his name?"

"Ben—Ben Levy."

"Jewish."

"Can you believe it? After my string of WASP mountain climbers and Navajo jewelers."

"And does this mean we're going to get some more cousins?"

"Don't you think it's a little late for that?"

"I don't see why."

"I'm thirty-six, for God's sake."

"So what?"

"Ben wants children."

"Ellen, this is wonderful."

That afternoon we set up a card table in my father's bedroom and spent hours playing Monopoly. From his bed, Abe played partnered with Hannah, Josh and Eli teamed up, and I played with Ellen. We laughed a lot, and for a while things felt almost normal. Then, in the middle of calculating the mortgage value of the combined railroads, my father went into another coughing spasm, and this time his body convulsed so violently that Josh took Hannah and Eli out of the room. I knew the reason for the coughing: The tumor was growing up into his larynx.

After we got him settled again, I went out to my family. "He's resting now."

Eli's lips were quivering. I pulled him to me. Hannah stood apart, her arms folded, shoulders hunched, staring at me anxiously, waiting for me to fix something that she knew I couldn't.

"I think it's time for us to head back to the motel," Josh said.

"What if Grandpa wants to finish the game?" Eli asked.

"Grandpa needs some sleep now," I explained.

"I think he liked my poem," Hannah said.

Josh put his hand on Hannah's shoulder and guided her down the stairs. Eli and I followed behind.

The next morning, when Hannah, Eli, and Josh came to say good-bye to Abe before their flight back to New York, he asked for private time with each of them. I wished I could have heard what he said. I imagined he would impress on each of them what he most wanted for all of us— that we follow the prompting of our hearts and not let our fears derail us. I imagined he would remind my children of some of the things they'd done over the years that had delighted him.

When I walked them out to the van that would return them to the airport, Hannah and Eli were taken aback that I wasn't going home with them. We had never spoken of it one way or the other. I was proceeding on my reality, and they were proceeding on theirs. When I closed the front door to the house, I was overcome with guilt, yet I also felt relieved to be reentering my father's world.

Ellen was heading up the stairs. I imagined this was the moment for her announcement. I also suspected Abe might take this opportunity to say his good-bye to her, since he was moving through his good-byes now in a methodical and determined way. It was only the saying good-bye to me that he seemed to resist. Several times I had tried to get it started, but he evaded me. Maybe he believed that if there was someone still to say good-bye to, death would have to wait.

I went out to the patio to give Ellen and Abe time alone, and lay back on a lounge chair with my eyes closed against the sun. I was still resting when I heard Ellen's sandals tapping on the patio tiles. The tapping stopped. "You're sure comfortable there." She sounded annoyed.

"I'm storing up the sun. Josh said there was snow forecast for New York. Snow in April. Can you imagine?"

"Then why do you live there?" Ellen demanded.

"I guess I like adversity."

"Exactly. That's why you're the only one of us who's comfortable with all this."

"This?"

"All this *dying*." She paced back and forth in front of me so that the sun went in and out. "I told him about Ben and asked if he wanted to meet him, and you know what he said? 'If it would make you happy.' You understand him so fucking perfectly. Tell me why he says such a cruel thing."

"Why is that cruel?"

"You don't see it? God, Annie. You look at him with such rose-colored glasses. I thought Pop and I were getting along better, but it's the same old shit. 'If it would make me happy.' As if he's doing me a goddamned favor by meeting the man I intend to marry."

"He's telling you the truth, Ellen. He's dying, he knows that—it's your life now. If it would make you happy, he wants to meet him. That's all."

"Bullshit. It's his way of putting everything on everybody else. He still has to be the one in control. Not that *he* needs to meet Ben—it has to be that *I* need him to meet Ben." Ellen sat down on the patio, pulled her legs up tight to her chest, and rested her chin on her knees in an angry pout. "I could never be as good as you. You were the one he trusted. I was the little sister he never took as seriously."

"Is this what you two talked about?"

"He admitted it. He said he was sorry, but he admitted it. God knows if he ever even loved me."

"Of course he loves you, Ellen. It's just that he's always been so preoccupied with believing that no one loved *him*. We Fishmans are a bunch of edgy types going up against each other all the time to test each other's love."

"That's our legacy? Never to trust in anyone's love? Please don't tell that to Ben."

"That's one part of it. The other part is that he taught us to fight for love."

"I hate all that."

"Well, get used to it, or have a chromosome transplant."

We stared at each other a moment, contemplating our shared fate, and then both burst out laughing. I think that was the moment we knew we'd come out of this as friends.

A week later the night nurse knocked on my door at six in the morning. My father wanted me to come in and talk. I pulled the curtain aside to see the first light of another Los Angeles dawn, the only marker between the days. Then I pulled on sweatpants and a T-shirt, ran a comb through my knotted hair. As my body shrank in sympathy with my father, my hair had grown like a jungle.

I was surprised to see my father out of bed, sitting in a chair beside the glass door that led out to his balcony. The nurse had draped her own red mohair sweater across his shoulders to keep him warm. "He wanted to get up," she explained.

With effort he turned to me from the window. "I was lying there like an old man on a deck chair. All I needed was a bowl of consommé." He slowly lifted his hand and pointed out the window. "See that?" All his movements took time, even his smile. "See the hummingbirds?"

"Does it feel good to be up?"

He considered my question.

"Up, down. It's going on too long here. I've said my good-byes. What's the point of hanging on?"

He looked at me, challenging me to react. I brought a chair over to the window.

"I've said my apologies. I've asked for forgiveness. What do I have to hang around for? I can watch the flowers and the hummingbirds. So what? I'm done. What's left? To sit and wait? My bags are packed, bills paid, cash register closed. I want to check out."

He stared me down again, another challenge.

"Pop, are you asking my permission? Is that what's going on?"

"You got it, Annie. Right on." He managed to raise his arm enough to make a little fist and convey his certainty. "That's it. You're the one I need to ask."

"Pop, what's changed? How come you're impatient all of a sudden?"

"You want to know? I'll tell you. It's the hardest thing yet. I took a deep breath and said to myself, This is it. It's not that you may die, or you may sometime let go—no—it's certain. It's as certain as if I were already dead. I can look back now and say there were times of satisfaction in my life, and there were times of bitterness. There were times when I hurt very much, and there were times when I had great happiness. But all that's finished now. The excitement—whether it's another business deal, or another visit with you guys, or another ski turn in deep powder—all that's over. Remember my friend from Mammoth who came by a few days ago? Remember how he said, 'We made some good turns together'? He was right, but there are no more turns for me. That's what I understand. That's what I've *made* myself understand. I said it to myself, and now I can say it out loud to you—there are no more turns for me. And now I want to get going. I don't want to hang around any longer."

Despite himself, he got interested once more in the flitting hummingbirds.

"Pop, what you said reminds me of a dream I had about you the other night. You and I and Eli were skiing together. It was a short piece of the mountain, maybe thirty yards. You were very weak, as you are now, but you wanted to ski one more time. You were standing at the top of the hill watching Eli and enjoying him as he skied down ahead of you. Then you skied down after him. You made three wonderful turns, very slowly, and then you stopped. You were exhausted, completely spent, and yet you had utter satisfaction on your face. I felt happy because you had gotten to do exactly what you wanted to do. It took an enormous effort, but it was worth it. When I woke up the dream made me think about how you've handled things these last months, everything entailed in dying—all our talking, our video conversations, all your good-byes. You've gotten to take the last turns you wanted to before you died."

"That's the way it's been, Annie. And now I'm ready. I want to go. Yes, I'm asking your permission."

"That's not my place."

He fixed his gaze on me. He didn't want to have to say it, but he knew I understood.

"I've become your partner in this."

He nodded.

"But that doesn't give me the right to grant you permission to die."

"I need permission from somebody."

"Why?"

"I need to know I've done my work here."

Out of love for him, I tried to gather authority I didn't feel I had— and didn't want to have. "I can tell you this. You've helped each of us resolve things with you so that after you die we can go on without regrets. This has been a hardworking time, for you, for all of us. So, yes—as much as I or anyone has the right to say it, you have the right to let go." And then I looked away from him because in saying those words aloud, I realized I was resentful. "But why haven't you been willing to say good-bye to me? I need to say good-bye like everybody else. You're so involved in needing me to be your partner. Have you forgotten that I also need to be a daughter?"

He peered at me.

"I need to say that I'm going to miss watching you play with Hannah and Eli. I'm going to miss asking your advice. I'm going to miss this time we've had together, you and I. You're my father. I love you. What am I going to do without you?"

He studied his folded hands.

"Why won't you say good-bye to me?"

"I'm not ready."

"That's not fair."

"I'm sorry, Annie."

"Why?"

"Because I still need you. Maybe it's selfish, but it's the truth. Don't you see? I'm scared. I'm a man. I'm not supposed to be scared of death. And you know what scares me the most? Lying around here waiting, not knowing what's going to happen to me, when. What if one week goes by, and then another, and I'm lying in that bed, and there's nothing left of me, but still I'm lying there? Sometimes when I'm alone in the middle of the night, I lie there thinking and thinking, and my mind can't stop." He pleaded with me. "Can't you understand?"

"Are you scared because death is something you have to face alone, or is it because you're worried that the waiting will be interminable?"

"It's both. I want it to hurry up and be over with, but I also want it not to come because I'm scared of what it will be. My mind is spinning, spinning, never knowing how long this time is going to last."

"I want to be here with you when you die."

"Yes, I would like that." His thoughts went elsewhere. "I would have liked to be there for someone who was dying. But I don't know for who."

"I guess that's where I'm blessed," I said. "I do know for whom."

We sat quietly for a while, looking out the window. I reached my hand out to him, and he held it. When I saw that his breathing was becoming too labored, I suggested he move back to bed. Reluctantly, he agreed. At least he had told me why lying in the bed frightened him. I helped him until he found a comfortable position for his body, and then I put on Samuel Barber's *Adagio for Strings*. He closed his eyes, but each time he dozed off he jerked himself awake again, his eyes darting to ascertain whether or not he was still on earth. At last he slept soundly, and when he opened his eyes, he was more peaceful. He saw me and whispered, "I love you." Then he closed his eyes again and slept through the morning.

I studied the brave man who had taught me courage, the sad man who had longed for love, the determined man who had chopped and dug and hacked the wild woods to save our home from mud and floods. I remembered dancing around him once as he worked to divert a gushing river of brown water in a torrential winter rain. The rain had matted the hair on both our heads. Our clothes were soaked. I was playing. He was working. I floated boats of oak bark. He fought mud and water. His face was fierce with his task. I sang. All of a sudden, with no warning or seeming provocation, he shouted at me. He was furious that I was playing a child's game while he fought the things that threatened us. I loved him then, as I loved him now, and I managed to hold back my tears.

# 14

The clunk of the airplane's landing gear jolted me. I was three thousand miles from my father. Why had I left him?

It had seemed right and reasonable at the time. My father and I had discussed it. Hannah's birthday party was on the weekend, and even though I was worried about leaving, I knew how important it was for me and Hannah that I be with her on her birthday. My father thought it was important, too, and insisted I go. I would only be gone thirty-six hours, and Ellen would be with him. There were signs that pneumonia was developing, but the nurses were watching his vital signs, and if things took a turn, I would fly back immediately. Still, as the plane touched down, I felt as if I had left my lungs and heart at my father's house. How was I to breathe? How was my blood to pulse?

It had been nearly two weeks since I'd seen them in Los Angeles, and the sight of my family waiting for me at the gate at JFK—Josh carrying Eli on his shoulders, Hannah on tiptoe beside them—cured me instantly. Josh tenderly brushed the hair back from my forehead. "You're even thinner than when we saw you last."

Hannah and Eli each claimed one of my hands as Josh hoisted my backpack, the only luggage I had brought. At the apartment I was greeted by a "Welcome Home" sign on the front door. My family had missed me more than I had missed them. This time I did not feel guilty so much as disoriented. My children had been my undisputed priority since they were born, but the gravitational pull on my heart had altered.

Josh showed me where he had put fresh towels in our bathroom and the stack of magazines that had come since I'd been gone. He turned on the bathwater and suggested I soak in the tub and relax. He had rented a video for Hannah and Eli so we could have time to talk.

"I'll get them settled and come back to tell you the plans for Hannah's party."

I stripped down and saw myself in the mirror. Josh was right. I was embarrassed by my scrawny body, my peanut-sized nipples, my concave stomach. I hadn't gotten on a scale in months, afraid to find out how much weight I had lost. But I also did not want to eat. Eating—sustenance—could break the thin filament that held me to my father, as I held my father to the earth. I looked in the mirror and wondered if Josh would understand how fragile I felt about this physical evidence of my intense loyalty to a man who was dying.

Josh came back with two glasses of wine and placed one for me on the side of the tub, where I was already soaking, and kept the other as he sat back on the closed toilet seat and folded one long leg over the other. I saw from the preoccupation in his eyes that he was connected to the activity in the apartment in a way that I was not. I was curious to observe this, to see that I was apart from him, a visitor in his home, trying to get a sense of what was expected of me.

"So?" he asked.

"So?" I answered back, as if trying to learn his language.

"So what's it feel like to be back?"

"A little strange."

"I can understand that."

"I'm not sure I should have come."

"Why's that?"

"To show up for two minutes and then leave again."

"But Hannah and Eli were so excited that you were coming."

"Are they going to understand when I have to leave again tomorrow?"

"I've talked to them."

"I'm not sure I should have left my father. He's being very brave, but he's also frightened."

"Isn't that to be expected?"

"Even if it's expected, that doesn't make it any easier on him," I said, irritated with Josh's insensitivity.

Josh nodded but did not react. He had clearly prepared himself for the possibility that I would be snippy.

"Want to hear the party plans?"

"Not yet."

"I've got it under control. Actually, Hannah is the one who has it under control. She's planned the whole thing like a shuttle launch, from the minute the kids arrive here tomorrow morning for the zoo, right through to how we're going to manage candy at the movie."

"Chromosomes," I said, remembering the joke with Ellen. "I'm afraid Hannah's got the Fishman control freak chromosome, for better or worse."

Josh was staring at my body in the bath.

"What?" I said defensively, bracing myself for a comment about my scrawny looks.

"My own control freak has a beautiful body."

"This skinny runt is not beautiful," I said emphatically.

Josh shook his head. "Wrong."

I saw him for the first time since my arrival. I saw his long, eagle neck, the crinkled skin around his eyes, the slight tentativeness in his words and gestures that expressed his gentleness—the trait I most relied on, most envied.

"How long is the kids' video?" I asked.

Josh grinned. "Long enough. Especially for a guy as out of practice as me." He set his wineglass down on the back of the toilet, locked the bathroom door, and held a bath towel up for me. "Stand up," he said.

I stepped out of the tub, and as the water dripped down my legs, Josh wrapped the towel around me and rubbed me dry.

"I'm going to be a mess after he dies."

"I'll be here. I'll take care of you."

"It might be harder than either of us realizes."

"That's probably true."

He dropped the towel and bent to kiss my neck and nipples. I stared past him, to the blur of night outside the fogged bathroom window. I could feel his touch, but I was an observer.

"I've missed you, Annie." He took my arms and wrapped them around his back. "Hold on to me. Hold tight."

I did as I was told. His fingertips moved along my skin, across the bones of my shoulders, down the notches of my backbone, each individual vertebra.

I didn't note the precise moment when I felt the return of my desire, but I knew once it had happened. Time went away. I needed Josh, his skin, his touch, his smell. I unbuckled his belt and pushed down his pants. He stepped out of his moccasins, then slid out of his pants. I took off his T-shirt, his boxer shorts. I wanted him to be naked with me. I ran my hands down his chest, along his arms, down to his penis. I was in a rush to have him inside me. With him inside me I would be reassured of life. It was the fit I knew, needed, depended upon. When he pushed in deep, I gave a little cry, not from pain but from relief. He put his fingers below my chin and lifted my eyes to his, wiping the tears from my cheeks. My father was dying, but I was alive.

With a dozen ten-year-old girls at the Bronx Zoo, it felt as if we were our own moving exhibit. The girls groaned with shared disgust at the apes scratching their genitals. They were mesmerized by the lion pacing back and forth across his den like a street thug. They watched in bliss at the pond where the seals moved sleekly through the freezing water. Hannah was at the center of her friends.

"I wonder what they'll all be like in ten more years," I mused.

Josh put his arm around me. "Beautiful, certainly beautiful."

"I'm glad I came back. Just to be an ordinary mom for a day. It's what I needed."

"Last night Eli asked if you could stay another day."

"I wonder why he doesn't ask me?"

"I asked him that."

"What did he say?"

"He didn't want to make you feel bad. Can you stay another day?"

"No," I said. "Absolutely not."

Josh had borrowed a friend's van so we could shuttle the girls from the zoo to the pizza place on Broadway and then to the movie. As I watched the quirky immigrant mouse abruptly separated from his parents in *An*

*American Tail*, I became anxious. I checked my watch by the light of the movie screen. I was determined to make it all the way to the end of Hannah's birthday party before calling California. The parents were scheduled to meet us outside the theater at nine-thirty. Fifty-five minutes to go.

The mothers of Hannah's friends, who knew I had been away caring for my dying father, stopped to assure me that Josh had been doing a good job in my absence. I tried to be polite, but all my energy was going into managing my mounting panic. I should not have left. I knew that now. I was too far away. I could not touch him, check on him, hold his hand. When the last mother arrived twenty minutes late, Josh sensed my fury and stepped between us.

Hannah and I headed home up Broadway, while Josh went to get Eli at his friend's apartment and return the borrowed van. I was walking so fast that Hannah had to yank on my sleeve to get my attention. "Slow down, Mommy, *please*."

When I stopped I saw Hannah looking up at me, as tired and disheveled as a cat after a bath. It had been a long day of balancing allegiances among her friends. I bent to her. "You did a wonderful job, sweetheart. You were an excellent hostess." Her pink mouth started to quiver. I pulled her close as the Saturday evening Broadway crowd flowed around us. She nuzzled her wet face into my neck. "Don't go," she whimpered. "Please don't go again."

At home Hannah flattened her back against the kitchen wall as she watched me dial the phone. There was a taut wire of knowledge between us. I tried to keep my face impassive as I listened to the nurse on the other end deliver the news I dreaded. "We've been trying to reach you. Your father has a fever. His blood pressure is dropping fast. The pneumonia has definitely taken hold. With his blood pressure already this low, it's unlikely he'll make it through to morning. I'm sorry, Annie. I'm so sorry it happened this way."

"I'm coming," I announced firmly. "Please tell my father I'll be there as soon as I can."

I hung up and saw Hannah. I bit my lip hard. "I won't be gone long."

The last night flight leaving New York for Los Angeles was taking off before I could make it back to the airport. I had to wait until five-thirty in the morning to get the next flight out. I telephoned Ellen to ask her to arrange for a car to pick me up when I arrived. I didn't want to lose a minute finding a taxi. Tony was already driving up from San Diego, but Charles was still in Bequia. Ellen had called his contact number to have them radio him with the news.

"How could I have been so stupid? Why did I leave him?" I moaned to Ellen on the phone.

"He wanted you to be with Hannah on her birthday. That made him happy."

"I was shuttling a bunch of ten-year-olds around a zoo, for God's sake."

"Annie, stop it. I told him you're coming. He's waiting for you."

"The nurse said it wasn't possible he could make it through the night."

"Abe Fishman, Annie. Remember? The guy who lives for somebody telling him there's something he can't do."

Josh insisted I try to get some sleep. The alarm was set for three-thirty. He sat in the bedroom chair to watch over me.

"How can I sleep if I can't breathe?" I asked from the bed.

"Be quiet, Annie. Close your eyes."

"God's punishing me for having sex with you when I should have been taking care of my father."

"Annie, stop it."

He came to sit beside me on the bed and rubbed my back.

"When you come home, we'll all be here," he said softly.

Minutes later, it seemed, I heard Josh turn off the alarm before it rang. He put a cup of tea down on the night table, and I felt his weight settle onto the bed beside me.

"You slept," he whispered when he saw me stir.

I had woken with a single thought—was my father still alive?—but I did not want to telephone to find out the answer. There was plenty of time to hear bad news when I arrived.

In the quiet early morning I paused first at Hannah's bedroom door, then at Eli's. I had been home long enough to recall my own life. I longed for my children, my family, for myself.

On the street Josh hugged me, put me into the cab, and handed in the small suitcase I had packed with a black suit and a black dress, one outfit for me, one for Ellen.

The airplane was packed with New York businessmen and -women on their way to a day's work on the other coast. My seat was in the middle of a row in the center section, and I could only stare at the yellow eggs and brown sausages that were put before me. I doubt if I moved a muscle the entire flight. I had to take myself out of time, or I might drown in regret. Despite Rabbi Lowenstein's warning, I had left my father's side when he was dying.

As I came off the plane, I spotted a stocky Chicano carrying a square of cardboard with my name written on it.

"I have a message from your sister."

I braced myself for failure.

"Your father, he is still alive."

"What did you say?"

"Your father is living still. He did not die."

"How do you know?" I demanded.

"I have the message from your sister."

"When did you get the message?" I grilled, always the doubting journalist.

"Right now. On my car phone. Before I come in to find you."

In the car the driver telephoned the house to say that we were on the way. The nurse who opened the front door answered my question before I could ask it. "I've never seen anything like it before."

I bolted up the stairs and rushed into a room that was completely still except for the mechanical breathing of an oxygen machine. Tony and Ellen sat on either side of the bed, holding Abe's hands. He lay motionless, his legs covered with a white blanket, his chest bare. The oxygen mask that covered his mouth was clouded with the warm vapor of his breath. He stared at the ceiling, using every bit of the energy and life he still had in him for the massive effort of making his lungs work.

I put my hand on his cheek. "I'm here, Pop."

He could not move his head, but his eyes turned toward me. I knew he was deciding if I was there in the flesh or only in his imagination. When he believed in me, a tear slid down his cheek.

"Thank you for waiting for me."

He moved his eyes back toward the ceiling so he could return to his task of breathing.

Ellen pulled me out of the room. "We've been waiting for you to arrive before we increased the morphine. We didn't want to do it until you got here."

"What are you talking about?" I asked incredulously.

I had been traveling across country through the early morning, praying for the seconds to slow, trying to use whatever account I had with God to hold back death. Ellen had been up all night, watching death draw near, getting ready for it. We looked at each other, trying to muster understanding for each other across an abyss.

"We need to ease his pain."

"Is he in so much pain?"

"The nurses say it will be easier on him to fade away comfortably."

"Fade away?" Abe Fishman was not a man to fade away. "No," I said emphatically.

Ellen implored, "The nurses say it will spare him misery."

"The nurses also said he would be dead by now. Is he really in such pain? He's doing what he *needs* to do." I was remembering our last talk about death, his fear of the moment of facing the unknown. I knew this much about my father: Even if this was the last lesson of his life, he would want to have it.

"Tony says it's the kind thing."

"And how does Tony know that?"

Ellen put her hands on my shoulders, no longer the younger sister. "None of us wants to lose him, Annie, but it's over now. We have to let him go."

"Why don't we ask Pop what *he* wants?"

"He can't talk, Annie. He can't tell us what he wants anymore."

"I'll find a way to ask him."

We went back into the bedroom.

"Pop, we have to ask you an important question. We know you can't talk, so we want you to try to nod or shake your head to tell us what you want. Can you give it a try?"

He didn't move, but he seemed to be digesting the idea. Finally he nodded very slightly.

"Okay, here's the question. If we give you more pain medicine, you will fade out and sleep. That will be the end. Your death will come quickly. We turn up the morphine pump a little higher, that's all. It will be very comfortable for you, and fairly soon you'll just stop breathing. If you'd like us to do that, please try to nod to tell us so."

I could feel him settling on his decision, nearly the last one of his life. We all waited. He did not nod.

"Pop, we didn't see you nod. Let me ask you another way. Do you want to stay awake—no extra morphine? If that's what you want, try to nod to let us know."

He nodded quite quickly. I looked up at Ellen and Tony—they had seen what I had seen.

"Okay, Pop," Tony said. "We understand, and that's what we'll do."

Ellen touched my shoulder and we stepped outside the bedroom.

"What is he holding on for now?"

"For Charlie, I guess."

"But Charlie's only now coming into Miami. He has to change planes, then fly all the way here. Pop can't possibly hold on that long."

"What if we put Charlie on the phone with him? Maybe it would be enough if Pop heard his voice."

We went back to the bedroom. "Charlie's about to arrive in Miami. Would you like us to get him on the phone to talk to you?"

He nodded.

"Is that what you've been waiting for?"

He nodded again.

Ellen arranged for the Florida airport personnel to take Charlie directly off the plane and to their office. When he telephoned, Ellen explained, "As much as Pop would like to wait for you, it's beyond what's humanly possible. We're going to put you on the phone with him. He'll hear your voice. We think he needs to know he's touched base with each of us before he'll let himself go. He needs to hear you say good-bye."

We tucked the receiver onto the pillow. Tony, Ellen, and I watched as our father listened, and he seemed pleased. Then his focus changed. I lifted the receiver from the pillow, heard the dial tone, and hung up. I rested my head on the pillow beside my father's ear. Ellen went to his other side and did the same. Tony was beside her.

"You've taken care of everyone now," I said softly. "We've all had our chance to say good-bye. You've worked so hard to take care of all of us, our whole lives, and now it's time to take care of yourself. You can let go now. Your work here is done."

Incredibly, as if he had willed it, his eyes closed and his chest grew still, like a lake quieting after a passing breeze. He no longer worked for another breath. I took off the oxygen mask and put my lips to his dry cheek. Tony shut off the oxygen pump. The room was quiet. The three of us faced one another, acknowledging what we had seen, that our father had finally let go of his massive effort to stay alive, and that death had come gently.

In a few minutes Charles called back, and Tony explained that Abe had died within seconds of their good-bye. "It was the right thing," Tony assured him. "We'll see you soon."

I studied my father's face. It was serene. What an extraordinary thing this business of dying had been. Some weeks back he had told us what he wanted written on his gravestone: "He lived every day until he died." I knew now I would amend it. My father had lived every moment until he died.

*Four*

# 15

The morning after the funeral I lingered in my father's bedroom alone. The hospital bed had already been removed. The IV stand had been rolled into a corner, punishment for the job it had failed to do. There was no Japanese flute music to make this room the cocoon of peace it had been in my father's last weeks. The morning light was stark and the silence hollow.

My father's closet door was standing open, revealing the rows of clothes still arranged with uncompromising perfection—a dozen specially tailored sports jackets, the battalion of button-down shirts, and the shoes—rows of them, all fine Italian masterpieces, glinting with high polish, set out in pairs along the carpeted closet floor, more shoes than any one man could wear out in a lifetime.

I sat cross-legged on the wood floor and looked out through the glass at the darting hummingbirds. For the last two nights I had awakened over and over again to a depth of pain I had never before known in my life. I had not anticipated that the agony would be this great. It was as if my skin had been ripped away in strips, leaving me exposed, raw, and unbearably lonely. It was simple: Wherever my father was, I wanted to be there with him. In the months of preparing for his death, I had lost some outer protective layer of myself, joined his dying too willingly. I had completed his thoughts, spoken for him when he could barely speak for himself anymore, helped him with every step he took toward death. Now I was like the loyal, lovesick child watching the doors close on ET in the departing spaceship. It was a silly image, but I knew that wrenching feeling: I was ripped in half. Why wasn't I going, too?

Josh and I discussed the funeral service on the phone and decided that Hannah and Eli were too young for it, so while Josh stayed home with them, my siblings and I proceeded on autopilot and did what had to be done. We lined up as the rabbi pinned bits of torn black cloth to our collars, an indication of the torn heart inside, and our badge of warning to others—don't expect too much, don't come too close. All through the funeral service I touched my ribbon compulsively, the frayed ends satisfying my anxious fingers. Why had no one warned me? If I had known, maybe I would not have allowed myself to love my father quite so much. Rabbi Lowenstein had given me the reasons for staying close; why hadn't he explained the risks?

At the cemetery, on the breezy knoll of Wisteria Court, at the spot I had selected, I watched the newly dug grave fill with dirt, one shovelful at a time. I waited my turn to wield the shovel, and I felt my resistance grow. This was unspeakable, such finality, the rhythmic thud as the damp soil hit the wood. The Jewish custom was for each person to contribute a shovelful of dirt to help the mourners believe that this life was over. I took the shovel in my hands, and the weight of the dirt unbalanced me. Charles put his arm around my waist to help me move ahead. My eyes flooded, making a blurred world. This was my duty. I must not spill or pause. I twisted the handle in my hands, felt the smooth wood, looked into the hole in the earth, and saw my shovelful of dirt cover the last of the exposed surface of the cherry coffin. This was the worst moment. There was nothing to negotiate. My father was inside that wooden box. The dirt was fact. Someone took the shovel from my hands. I fell into Charles's arms and sobbed.

Josh picked me up at the airport without the kids. We talked very little on the ride home. The children were already asleep, so Josh settled me into our bedroom while he paid the baby-sitter. The bedroom was dark, and I didn't move to turn on a light. I sat on the edge of our bed, confused to be there, unwilling to accept the forward movement of time. When Josh returned, he had to encourage me to take off my shoes, my clothes, climb beneath the covers. He sat beside me, his hip against my back, until I fell asleep. In the morning he allowed Hannah and Eli to come in for a quick hello and good-bye before they left for school. Eli whispered, "Don't worry,

Mommy, Grandpa is already resting on a cloud in heaven." Hannah held my hand. "Maybe next time Grandpa will be born as a seal or an eagle."

Josh offered to stay home from work, but I asked him not to. I wanted to be alone in the dark behind the drawn curtains of our bedroom. Even the red light of the cable box disturbed me. I unplugged it and turned the clocks toward the walls. Then I wrapped myself in a blanket and tucked my body into the bedroom reading chair.

That evening Josh suggested I join the family in the kitchen for supper, but I declined.

"The kids need you," he told me. "You've been away from them too long."

"Not yet. Please."

"Maybe you should go see that rabbi you liked."

"Rabbi Lowenstein?"

"Isn't that what rabbis do, help people in times like this? What could it hurt?"

"I don't want to leave this room."

"I know, Annie. But eventually you will have to."

If it hadn't been for my children, I would have chosen to sit in that chair for months. The pain was its own place, another outpost. If I didn't have my father, at least I had the loss of him. Hannah came home that afternoon and stood in the doorway to my bedroom, leaning against the doorjamb, her body in silhouette, silent, staring at me. She was waiting for me to get up out of my chair and be her mother. She wanted me to go through the motions, even if we both knew that I was not fully there. The power of her need helped me see what I had to do. I would get up and carry out the idea of what it was to be a mother, external actions I could plan, while my inner life, where I truly was and wished to remain, would stay loyal to my excruciating pain.

The next morning, following the assignment I had given myself, I telephoned Rabbi Lowenstein's office and convinced his secretary to make an appointment for me. Even death didn't impress her much. Shortly before the time I was to meet Rabbi Lowenstein, and after the long hours it had taken me to move through the simple acts of choosing clothes, showering, getting dressed, I stepped onto the street and was made dizzy by the brightness of the day. Up the block a doorman was watering daffodils that had bloomed in the planters around the sycamore trees. I hadn't thought of spring. I had worn a heavy sweater, and my armpits were already damp.

The synagogue door was locked. I turned to leave, vaguely relieved.

"Hey, Annie!"

I looked back and saw Rabbi Lowenstein coming from Broadway, his shirtsleeves rolled up, hugging a takeout bag.

When he came up to the door, he handed me the bag he'd been carrying and fished for his keys. The bag gave off the rich, greasy smell of roasted chicken.

I followed him inside, still holding the bag of chicken. The synagogue was dark and cold, a comfort to me. He took back his bag and led the way around the back of the sanctuary to a fire exit, where he pushed on the bar and gave the door a sharp kick. Sunlight streamed in as he helped me step onto the fire escape and then climbed out after me and started up the wrought-iron stair. Without questioning where we were going, I climbed up after him. When we arrived at the very top, three flights up, we were above the roof of the neighboring brownstone, and it was possible to see uptown and downtown for a mile in each direction. "This is my favorite lunch spot." Two gulls flew by so close to us that we heard their squawking argument. "Like a couple of old rabbis," Rabbi Lowenstein mused as he turned over a plastic milk crate and sat on it. "Two rabbis, four opinions." He pointed to another plastic crate. "Sit, sit," he instructed.

We faced each other, milk crate to milk crate. He offered a piece of chicken, but I declined, and he took a piece for himself.

"So?"

"My father died."

"When?"

"Five days ago." My eyes filled immediately. "I had no idea how painful it would be."

"How could you?"

"You could have told me."

"There are some things you don't try to describe."

"I'm angry."

"At who?"

"I'm angry at you, for one."

"Want to tell me why?"

"You said to stay with him. I got too close. Maybe I died with him—or at least I wanted to."

"But you're lucky to have loved that much."

"I'm angry at my father, too."

"Usually that comes a little later in the mourning process. You're moving pretty fast here."

"It doesn't have anything to do with the mourning process," I said bitterly. "It has to do with the *dying* process."

"I don't understand."

"He didn't have to die—he *wanted* to die."

"He had cancer."

"Yes, he had cancer. But he believed he brought on his own cancer because he was ready to put an end to his life."

"And you believe that's possible?"

"I don't know what's possible," I answered testily.

"Why would he want to do such a thing?"

"It's what you told me about shame—how hard it is for people to forgive themselves."

"I told you about *teshuvah*."

"Yeah, that."

"Were you successful?"

"Successful? He died." I folded my arms defiantly, then looked out to the Hudson River, where a massive freighter was being pushed along by a tiny red tug. Everything was out of proportion, a world of mismatched children's toys. The skyline was two-dimensional, a stage front. I was sitting on a fire escape, talking with a rabbi who chewed a chicken leg. It was all absurd. What a fool I had been. I had helped my father accept dying. I hadn't fought against it. Why hadn't I raged then instead of now?

"Annie?"

"His mother set fire to the stores she owned in Brooklyn. My father knew about it, maybe even set some of the fires. There was one fire where they almost killed a family. He told us this shortly before he died. You know what he said? It wasn't that he believed he *deserved* to die because of what he'd done—it was because he was tired of living with the *shame* of it. That was it. That was why he wanted to die."

Rabbi Lowenstein was nodding. "Yes, yes."

"Don't you see why it would make me angry?"

"Tell me."

"Why couldn't he have faced the truth about himself instead of trying to convince everybody he was some sort of saint? If he had faced it, maybe he could have learned to forgive himself. Maybe he'd still be living."

"I'm proud of you."

"Why?"

"You helped him say what he needed to say before he died."

"So what? It didn't save his life."

"I never said *teshuvah* would save his life. It might save yours, though."

"Sometimes I hate your cryptic comments."

He pointed his chicken bone in the direction of the river. "I like to think about rivers. You can stand on the banks, or you can get in them. Either way you take a chance."

"That's supposed to be less cryptic?"

"I'm sorry," he apologized. "It seems to be my way." His attention was taken by the pigeons roosting on a ledge below. He tore off a piece of chicken meat and threw it to them.

"And now what?" I demanded. "You said spend time with him. I did that. Now I don't know where my own life is. Maybe you could give me a clue about how I'm supposed to start my life again."

"You do that by saying kaddish. Every time you come to services, for eleven months. As a Jew you have a duty. It's part of the covenant, the contract with God. When you recite kaddish, you fulfill your duty to affirm life." He leaned toward me, his hands cupping his kneecaps. "Which, you may recall from our very first talk together, is God's gift."

"I'm not signing any contracts with God."

"Your choice. And how about your other decision? What did you decide to do about that?"

In the last weeks I had been so enmeshed in my father's dying that I had forgotten that I had asked Rabbi Lowenstein's advice about investigating the possibility of anti-Semitic arson at our house in Connecticut.

"My father had a fire. I had a fire. It's an odd coincidence."

"Yes, Annie. What do you make of that?"

"Is this leading to another advertisement for the existence of God?"

"I doubt He's quite that hands-on."

"But it's odd the way these two fires do seem connected."

"Maybe when you look into it, you'll understand the connections."

That night I joined my family at the supper table. Eli and Hannah eyed me warily and were exceedingly polite, as I'm sure Josh had warned them to be.

"Who needs help with homework?" I asked as the children got up to clear their dishes.

Hannah and Eli looked to Josh for guidance.

"What? I'm not smart enough for second- and fifth-grade homework?"

"You're smart enough, Mommy," Eli assured me. "I'm supposed to practice my math facts."

"What's a math fact?" Josh asked from the kitchen sink.

"Three times four, four times eight—all that stupid stuff."

"You mean multiplication."

"They call it math facts now, Dad," Hannah informed him patiently, then added, "They've changed a few things since you were a kid and had to do your schoolwork on a coal shovel."

I laughed. Eli, Hannah, and Josh stared at me. They had not expected me to do something as normal as laugh.

"I might be pretty grumpy for a while," I apologized.

"I think we're used to that," Hannah said, then came over and climbed into my lap.

Later that night I told Josh that I was going to proceed with the fire investigation.

"I'm against this," he said flatly.

"But we made a deal. In the tree house. You said I get three months."

"You're in no shape."

"How can you say that?"

"Your father just died. You need to take it easy for a while."

"No, actually, I don't need to take it easy. I need to do this."

"There are wiser ways to deal with your grief."

"This is not about grief. It's about what I learned when my father was dying. He spent his whole life trying to avoid what he knew. He knew evil existed, yet he tried to deny it. I don't want to make the same mistake in my life."

"You believe you can earn redemption for your father by tracking down some bigot?"

"It's not a matter of earning redemption."

"Then what is it?"

"I'm not sure. That's what I have to find out—and I don't have a choice."

On Saturday morning, for the second time, I attended services at Rabbi Lowenstein's synagogue. But now I had a purpose—to stand with the other mourners to say kaddish. The prayer was in Aramaic, a language even more foreign to me than Hebrew, and yet the words were also familiar. As I recited the prayer, a memory came back from my childhood. Once a year my mother, a confirmed atheist, lit a candle for her father, my grandfather, a man she had barely known, and whom I had never met. She would close her eyes and murmur, "*Yitgadal, v'yitkadash sh'mei raba b'alma di v'ra khir'utei, v'yamlikh, malkhutei, b'hayeikhon, u-v'y-omeikhon u-v'hayei d'khol beit yisrael, ba-agala u-vi-z'man kariv, v'imru amen.*" Tears streamed down my face as I recited the mourner's prayer that Saturday and for many weeks to come. I was either unaware that others in the congregation could see me crying, or I didn't care. Several years later a woman came up to me at a social event at the synagogue and said, "Oh, yes, you were the one who cried."

# 16

I wanted to talk with our local Connecticut state trooper, Bob Lefert, away from the police barracks and his colleagues, most of whom considered it suspect to have too much sympathy for the ordinary citizen. I had experienced the state barracks once when we hit a deer on the road at night and totaled the front end of our car. We hitched a ride to the barracks to get help. The trooper on duty told us through a Plexiglas partition that we were the nineteenth deer collision so far that fall, and pointed to the public phone on the opposite wall. "Call a tow truck."

I knew the hill south of Brookford where Trooper Lefert liked to park his cruiser and catch speeders. Lefert was in his fifties and unmarried. He had the regulation crew-cut and barrel belly of a tough Connecticut state cop, but there was a gentleness about him as well. His face was soft and pink, and he had delicate, tapered fingers. When I spotted him at the turnout at the top of the hill, sitting behind the wheel of his patrol car with his elbow propped on his opened window, I pulled my car alongside his and held up the two takeout coffees I had brought along. "Can I come over and talk with you a minute?"

"Mrs. Waldmas?"

"I'd rather you call me Annie."

I tucked a bag of doughnuts under my elbow and carried one cup of coffee in each hand. He reached across his front seat to open the car door and then pushed some papers aside to clear a spot for me as I slid in and tucked my legs to the right of the computer equipment hanging from the dash.

"I was up there at your fire. I'm sorry I didn't get a chance to express my condolences to you and your family."

"Thank you. It's been pretty hard on us."

He tore a hole in the coffee lid and took a sip. "Lots of milk and sugar, the way I like it. Guess my belly here gives me up." He patted the small hill that pushed out above his belt.

"Maybe I shouldn't have brought these." I opened the doughnut bag. "Lemon filled."

"Probably shouldn't have," Lefert agreed, helping himself. "You up here seeing to the construction?"

"Yes and no. I was wondering if you ever got a look at the fire marshal's report on our fire."

Lefert's attention was taken by a car whose speed registered on his radar detector. The needle went close to, but not over, the red line that would have sent him into action. "He's a tough old geezer."

"You know him?" I asked, assuming he meant the driver.

"Old Norman Jukes is still fighting World War II."

"I called him three times this week and left messages with his wife, and he still hasn't called me back."

"Norman likes to be the one who asks the questions. I can tell you what I know about your fire, if that would help."

"Please. I'd appreciate that."

"I'm sure you know he reported your fire as electrical. But there must have been a question in his mind. About a week after the fire he sent me up to pull the fuse box and bring it down to him."

I tried to hide my shock that someone had gone into our house without our knowledge or permission, and that I was finding out about it for the first time almost seven months later.

"How come no one told us?"

He looked down at the lid of his coffee cup. "He asked me not to."

"But you're telling me now."

"You're asking now."

"Yes," I said. "I am asking now."

"I don't know what made him have second thoughts. He said he wanted to run the fuse box through some tests. A few days later he called me to come get it and put it back." He peered into the doughnut bag, began to help himself to a second one, then changed his mind. "He said he still felt pretty confident it was electrical."

"*Pretty* confident?" I asked angrily. And then I caught myself. "I'm sorry. This whole business has me pretty unnerved."

"Understandable," he said. A car sped by and the needle moved into the red zone, but Lefert ignored it.

"Did he tell you anything else?"

"Nope. Guess it was good enough for him. It's his call."

"So he didn't ask you to investigate?"

Lefert shook his head. "But seeing how it's my business to nose around, I did a little looking anyway. Went over to see those folks in Rangely with the pharmacy fire last year. You heard about that one, right?"

I put my empty coffee cup on the dashboard and tucked my arms around my chest.

"Were they Jewish?"

"Epstein?"

"Where is Rangely?"

"About an hour south of here, on the way to Providence. Small place like Brookford, nice folks. They got the fire under control before the store burned to the ground. Not like the café here in town. See, with Shelly's place, we couldn't tell what the heck happened since there was nothing left of it. Over in Rangely they found evidence of arson, a gas can, as I recall. They say there was an employee the Epsteins fired for drinking on the job. I guess they didn't want to press charges. Can't blame them for wanting to get on with their lives. There wasn't much anyone could do, anyway. The fellow had already skipped for Florida. Local law enforcement doesn't have the resources to go down and bring him back. Got to get the FBI in on a thing like that. But getting the FBI to come in—that's a whole other matter. That's the thing, isn't it? Nobody around here is ready to believe we could have that kind of problem."

"What kind of problem is that?"

"I think we both know what we're talking about, Mrs. Waldmas."

"But you said the Epstein fire was set by an employee."

Lefert turned to face me. "Mrs. Waldmas, I've been in this business long enough to know that people say a lot of different things for a lot of different reasons."

A blip showed up on the radar again, and Lefert leaned in toward his ignition key. "You'll have to excuse me. This is one of my regular offenders." I got out quickly and he sped away.

Two years back, researching a documentary on the rights of children abducted by divorced parents across state lines, I had gotten to know Julia Tucker, a civil rights investigator with the Justice Department in Washington. The day after meeting with Lefert, I checked my old files for her direct line and telephoned her at her office.

"I need some help. I'm looking for advice on how to prove a pattern of anti-Semitic arson."

"You doing a documentary?"

"Not this time, not exactly."

"How many fires?"

"Two homes, possibly two businesses."

"What's the evidence that it's a hate crime?"

"We're all Jewish."

"*We're* all Jewish?"

"One of them is our country home in Connecticut. We had a fire last October. They told us it was electrical, but I'm beginning to have my doubts."

"What makes you suspect anti-Semitism?"

"Four suspicious fires in two years in a fifty-mile radius, all Jewish property, two of them confirmed as arson—doesn't that suggest it?"

"Maybe in your line of work. In law enforcement you've got to have concrete evidence when you go after a hate crime—pamphlets, swastikas, phone threats, something like that—otherwise it's considered an ordinary arson, and it belongs to Alcohol, Tobacco and Firearms. Those guys only get interested if it's a large commercial property, or if it goes across state lines. Sounds like you've got a local police matter."

"But the local police have done nothing. Either they don't know how to pursue it, or they don't want to."

"Annie, there's something you've got to understand. An investigation like this costs a lot of time and money, which local police don't have. Even if they do pursue it, most of the time they can't put together enough evidence to get a conviction. So they aren't real motivated to get started."

"How about the FBI?"

"They're not going to come in on four fires. FBI only considers it a hate crime when there's concrete evidence and when a threshold's been established—a specific frequency of incidents versus the density of the population. They need that to prove they've got jurisdiction. No federal agency is going to put money and manpower into something if they're worried they're likely to get shut down in court for lack of jurisdiction. There are a lot of hoops here. If you really believe you're onto something, you've got to get back out there and find the tangible evidence."

"If I find it, will you hook me up?"

"It's got to be good," Julia warned. "Especially when you're personally involved."

When Josh asked me about my trip to Brookford, I was vague, and I didn't tell him about my conversation with Julia Tucker either. Josh was already reading the real estate section each Sunday and circling homes for sale. My share of the inheritance from my father meant we could afford a country house in the more traditional outposts for New York Jews—western Massachusetts, the Jersey shore, the Hamptons. He had begun making inquiries on what we could get for our house in its unfinished condition. We were trains moving on different tracks, veering farther and farther apart.

The day after talking with Julia Tucker I telephoned the *Rangely Sentinel* to see if I could get the newspaper reports on the fire at the Rangely pharmacy.

"Anything more than a year, you've got to get on microfilm," the receptionist informed me.

"How do I go about that?"

"Wednesdays only."

"Wednesdays only, what?"

"Wednesday is the day the public is allowed use of the microfilm machine."

"But I'm calling from New York."

"Self-addressed stamped envelope and a money order or personal check for two-fifty."

"I see."

"Pretty busy here. Anything else I can do for you?"

I doubted she was pretty busy. I felt fairly confident that a telephone receptionist at the *Rangely Sentinel* would rather chat with me or anybody else than return to her morning of staring at the walls.

"Have you got the beautiful weather up there that we've got in New York today?" I asked.

"It's a lovely one."

"My kids can't stand being locked up in school another minute. They're dying to get up to Brookford and get outside for the weekend."

"You come up weekends, do you?" she asked.

"To tell the truth, we consider Brookford our real home. That's certainly the way our kids see it. Everything important they ever learned—to swim, ride a bike, catch a fish—they learned up there in the country. It gets hard on them hanging around New York while we try to make a living."

"So, honey, anything else I can do for you? I'm about to close down here for lunch. I'm doing Jenny Craig. Can't seem to keep my mind off food."

"Do you remember the fire at the pharmacy last year?"

"Course I do. Place was two doors down from here."

"I'm looking for the articles on that fire."

"Why didn't you say so? No need for microfilm on that one. We made up a scrapbook. I've got it right here in my desk. We put it together for the spaghetti fund-raiser we held to get the Epsteins back on their feet again. Shirley and Harry, Jewish people, the sweetest folks you can imagine. Maybe a spaghetti dinner isn't how their own people would have done it, but we wanted to show them that this town was behind them one hundred percent."

"We had a fire in Brookford, too—the Brookford Café."

"We heard about that. Don't know if they did a spaghetti dinner like us. Guess I should have told them how good ours went. Raised two thousand dollars. So, hon, you want me to Xerox what I've got here and send it down to you?"

"Do you have a fax machine?"

"I guess I can use the one over at the library."

"Can I give you my fax number?"

"Sure, hon. Maybe this will give me something else to do on my lunch hour besides dreaming about melted cheese with ham."

The faxed newspaper accounts arrived at my office within the hour. I learned that Harry Epstein had come to Rangely from Brooklyn, New York, with his new bride right after World War II. Marching through the rubble of Dresden on his way to liberate the concentration camps, Private Harry Epstein realized he wanted a quiet life. An army buddy told him about Rangely, Connecticut, his hometown, where you could lie down and go to sleep in the town's main street at noon without worrying that a car would run you over. Harry's immigrant father had hoped his son would become a doctor. Harry went to school on the G.I. Bill and became a pharmacist instead. Small-town life suited him, and he and Shirley raised three sons, who went through Rangely schools and on to professions in law, medicine, and college teaching.

Epstein's Pharmacy had been in the same location since Harry opened in 1950. He worked twelve-hour days, seven days a week, except for the time he took off for each of his son's college graduations and the six-day Caribbean cruise the boys gave Harry and Shirley for their twenty-fifth wedding anniversary. Though the Epsteins lived three blocks from the store, Harry's real home was the pharmacy. Shirley had taken lunch to him Monday through Sunday as long as anybody could remember. In one of the scrapbook articles the townspeople reminisced about how Shirley and Harry would share their midday meal on a card table in the store's bay window. Harry said he liked looking out on his quiet hometown, where it was still possible to lie down and take a nap in the street at noon.

At 11:38 on the night of their fire, while they were watching Johnny Carson interview Bette Midler, the Epstein's TV screen went black. Within seconds there were sirens. Everyone in town, the Epsteins included, put on their coats and ran out to see what was happening.

Harry Epstein was quoted, "We watched it burn. There was nothing else to do." His wife added, "Our life burned up before our eyes."

The newspaper photos showed damage much more extensive than I had expected from Trooper Lefert's description. Only two walls of the single-story building were left standing, like false fronts on a movie set. A fire engine cherry picker hung over the rubble, and Harry Epstein was there in the foreground, tight-lipped and grim. The caption read, "Harry Epstein plans to reopen for business as soon as possible."

I had to wait till the following Thursday to make the drive to Rangely. On Thursdays Josh stayed at work late preparing photographs for the

Sunday paper. It was also the day Bonnie picked up Hannah from school and took her to gymnastics class, and Eli was shuttled by van to Randall's Island to play in the soccer league until dusk. I wouldn't be needed at home until seven.

Rangely was a town straight from the 1930s, with a Woolworth's, a drive-in movie theater, an A & W Root Beer stand. I found the lot where Epstein's Pharmacy had once been, empty now except for the tall weeds and fire debris that had apparently become part of the permanent landscape. When I drove around the corner and found the Epsteins' house, I turned off the ignition and sat. I hadn't called ahead. I hadn't wanted to frighten them.

Shirley Epstein opened the front door but not the screen. She had gray, Harpo Marx curls, and large eyeglasses that were tinted amber even for indoor wear. She held her needlepoint canvas like a shield. "Are you lost?"

I wanted to communicate somehow that I was Jewish, since my looks alone would never suggest it. I was more often taken for Irish.

"I'm Anne Waldmas. My husband and I have a house up in Brookford. You may have read about us. Our house burned last fall—right after the Jewish holidays."

Shirley Epstein considered me more closely, then called back over her shoulder. "Harry, you'd better come out here."

Harry appeared from the dark. He had a small round face, a sharp nose, and the skin around his eyes sagged like a bloodhound's.

"She had the fire in Brookford. She's Jewish."

Harry pulled open the screen door. "I guess you're coming in."

They led me into their sitting room, where shelves were crammed with books, LP records, and photographs. Below a baby grand piano was a small collection of instruments in their cases. On the mantel there was a bronze menorah and a framed Leonard Baskin print of a rabbi reading from the Torah. The curtains were drawn and the lamps were lit, even though it was the middle of the afternoon. It was evident that this was where Harry and Shirley spent their days, all of them, alone together. They returned to their accustomed seats, each surrounded by the items he or she used throughout the day—extra pairs of glasses, extra sweaters, slippers, a glass of water for each, containers of pills. Harry Epstein picked up a crossword puzzle book he'd left open on his chair, and I was reminded of my own father and missed him.

"You've been to see Shelly, too?" Harry asked in a mildly challenging tone. "Shelly Weiss. They sure put him out of business." Shirley gave her husband a cautionary look.

"My husband and I have known Shelly for quite a few years," I said.

"Then you know about his fire."

"I don't know that there's much to know," I said.

"You don't know about the swastikas he used to find on the back door of his place?"

I shook my head. Shelly and Josh had talked about many things, but Shelly had never told him this.

"He figures, and I figure, too, in small towns like these sometimes it's best to keep certain things to yourself. So I sit here in this chair. Or I get up and walk to the other room and sit there awhile. Or I walk into town and people are real nice and ask when we're going to rebuild. I say, Maybe, sometime. I don't say I'm still waiting to see if I have the heart to start all over again." He stared at me, accusing me, along with the rest of the world, of callousness. I had lost my second home; he had lost the work of a lifetime. I had an impulse to give him something, though I didn't know what. The truth, perhaps, if I could find it.

"I heard your fire was set by an angry employee who ran off to Florida."

"Sometimes all you say is yes and no. People draw their own conclusions. How are we going to pick up and move away from here? This is our home. What else do we have?"

"They told us our fire was electrical. Almost seven months later I found out that the fire marshal had reconsidered his conclusion, but no one ever told us."

Harry shrugged at his wife as if to say, And what did she expect?

"Do you have children?" Shirley asked me.

"Yes, a boy and a girl—seven and ten."

"That's what's important, then. All of this other business, it's best to forget it."

"I can't do that."

Once again Harry fixed me with his accusatory eyes. "And if you find out the truth, what are you prepared to do about it?"

I felt the loneliness of this closed-off, sad museum of a room. Shirley and Harry Epstein's faith and life had been shattered. They would grow older faster now. Would anybody notice?

"I'm not sure, Mr. Epstein. I hope I have the courage to do something."

He nodded. My honesty had satisfied him. He sat back slowly, curled his fingers over the ends of his armchair, and told me his story.

On the drive back to New York I thought about my father. Harry Epstein had reminded me of him in a number of ways. They were both short, gruff, Jewish businessmen who had fought hard for their security. Like my father, Harry Epstein didn't wish to be beholden to anyone, kept his own counsel, solved his own problems. Sitting in the Epsteins' living room, studying the sharp angle of his jaw, his compact body, his large nose, all so reminiscent of my father, I felt tenderness toward Harry Epstein, as if I had known him all my life.

That evening I arrived home in a foul mood. I went around the apartment on a rampage. I barked at Hannah for leaving her gymnastics clothes on the floor in the foyer, at Eli for leaving a trail of LEGO pieces from his bedroom to the living room, at Josh for forgetting to pay Bonnie. "What am I?" I growled. "Everybody's slave?"

I drove the kids into bed at a forced march. I had no patience for reading *If I Ran the Circus* to Eli for the four hundredth time or listening to Hannah's debate with herself about whether or not she should stop eating chicken. When the kids were asleep I went from one end of the apartment to the other straightening and obsessing, until Josh, who was sitting at the living room coffee table sorting through photographs of Eli's playoff game, snapped, "You're driving me crazy."

"So what?" I snapped back.

"I'm trying to do something here."

"Do it. I'm not stopping you."

"Can you get compulsive in some other room?"

"This is the living room, not your private office."

Josh made an elaborate business of gathering up his photographs to leave.

"Where are you going?" I demanded.

"Somewhere else."

"Then leave," I said.

Josh stopped, photographs in hand. "Do you want to tell me what happened to you today to put you in such a shitty mood?"

"Well, do you want to talk, or do you want to sort photographs?"

He sighed. "Do you want to argue, or do you want to tell me?"

"Sit back down if you're really interested in talking," I said, determined to have the last word.

Josh and I took seats opposite each other, and I thought of Harry and Shirley in their living room, their sadness as heavy as wool blankets.

"Did something go wrong at work today?"

"No."

"Was it a tough day missing your father?"

"No more than usual," I lied.

He ran his hand through his hair, the habitual gesture that accompanied the effort to maintain his patience. "I've had a long day myself. I'm not really up to a guessing game."

"There's another fire."

"What do you mean?"

"Another arson."

"Near us?"

"In a town called Rangely on the Rhode Island–Connecticut border. The pharmacy there burned last June. It belonged to a couple named Shirley and Harry Epstein—Jews, of course."

"How did you find this out?"

"Lefert told me about it. I went up there today to meet them."

"You drove up to Rangely and didn't tell me?"

"It was a last-minute decision. I didn't want to bother you at work."

Josh pushed his fingertips into his temples and began pacing back and forth across the living room. "This is getting to be a little too much."

"They know Shelly Weiss. They told me Shelly used to find swastikas painted on the back door of his store."

"*Swastikas?* How come he never said anything to me?"

"Maybe if you're the only Jewish store owner in a small New England town, you keep quiet about some things," I said, paraphrasing Harry Epstein.

Josh stopped. "It's time to bring the police into this. I'm not letting you continue with this on your own."

"I'm not so sure the Rangely police are prepared to get to the bottom of this fire any more than the Amity police were interested in investigating the Pragers'. The Rangely police already concluded that the pharmacy was torched by an employee the Epsteins fired."

"Then it's not an anti-Semitic arson."

"Harry Epstein says the employee they're talking about asked to be fired so he could collect unemployment when he left to take care of his mother."

"What did the police say to that?"

"He didn't tell them."

"Why would Epstein keep that to himself?"

"He told me that a few weeks before the fire a man came into the pharmacy early one morning before anyone else was there and screamed at him that Jewish merchants were leeches, had been leeches since the beginning of time."

"Did he describe him?"

"It's the same man, Josh."

"Why didn't he tell that to the police?"

"He says he can't—or he won't. He's lived in Rangely thirty-eight years."

"He doesn't want to face it."

"Maybe he's not so different from us. Do you remember that crass idiot Gornick? What he said about Shank getting locked out of his fee if it turned out to be arson? You know, it is possible that Ken Mott was paid by Shank to rule out arson. Or maybe it was something more benign. Maybe Mott told us what he figured we wanted to hear."

Josh's eyes grew dark. "I want to get out of there."

"You promised me three months."

"You've already had two."

"My father was dying," I protested. "I've only begun to look into it."

"Don't you see that it doesn't matter what you find out? Either you never find enough conclusive evidence to get this guy and we'll have to leave anyway. Or you find something that nails him and we'll become known as the Jews who stirred up all the trouble in the town, and then we'll want to leave. Epstein is no fool. It's a lose-lose situation."

I went to stand by the living room windows as a fire engine careened up the avenue. When the siren died away, I said, "I had a dream the other night that my father was a boy on a bicycle riding past a burning house. He was pedaling and pedaling, but his wheels had no traction. He couldn't get past the fire."

"Didn't I warn you that it's a dangerous proposition thinking you're going to absolve your father's guilt by tracking down this arsonist?"

"I told you that isn't it."

"Then what is it?"

I sat on the radiator and listened to the quiet night.

"I'm not trying to absolve my father's guilt. Quite the contrary. I'm trying to learn to accept what he couldn't accept. I'm trying to learn to be willing to see evil, to do something about it."

"And like it or not, I'm dragged into this with you."

"I guess you are," I said with irritation.

We went to bed without even a conciliatory hug, but long after we had put the light out, Josh and I lay awake until the night softened our anger.

"How do we live with this?" Josh asked into the dark. I took his hand under the covers, and he went on, "I keep thinking about my father's photographs. I keep seeing the bonfire in the street. Setting someone's most treasured belongings on fire certainly lets him know you don't want him around. Anti-Semitism and fire have a long history, don't they?"

Josh's words must have worked their way into my dreams, because by morning I knew what my next step would be. His comment that anti-Semitic arson has a long history made me focus on the fact that the Pragers' fire was set on Hitler's birthday. Maybe there would be clues in dates, in history.

Over the years I had spent countless hours at the oak tables of the Reading Room of the New York Public Library, my shoes pushed under my chair, my stocking feet tucked up under my legs. I liked the echo of clicking heels as people marched through on their private and passionate missions to track down information.

An attendant in Noncirculating Reference helped me find the volume I needed—*The Complete History of the Third Reich*. I flipped to the chronology listed in the appendix. I was already scanning the pages as I moved toward a nearby table. I had four dates to check. September 17, 1941, came up first. September 17, the date of the Brookford Café fire, was the anniversary of the decree ordering the general deportation of German Jews to concentration camps. The fire at Epstein's Pharmacy happened on June 23. On June 23, 1942, the first gassings took place at Auschwitz. Our fire was on October 4. On October 4, 1942, Himmler began shipping Jews from German concentration camps to Auschwitz for annihilation.

I rushed to the public phone in the women's bathroom to call Josh at work.

"I know you're anxious to solve this, Annie, but there's probably an anniversary of some anti-Semitic atrocity on about any day of the year."

"I need more, that's all."

"More?"

"More fires. I'm sure there are more fires, and more dates."

Back at my office I got to work organizing things the way I did when I started research for a new documentary. I set up files, made note cards, tacked a highway map to my office wall. I put colored pushpins at the locations of the four fires I knew—two in Brookford, one in Amity, one in Rangely. Using the pushpins as the centers, I drew four circles, arbitrarily marking a radius of a forty-five-minute drive from each. I underlined every town located within my overlapping circles, nine towns in all. One by one I called each town hall to get the name and telephone number of the town fire marshal. Then I started down the list.

My first answer was at the home of Jeremiah Blackstone, the fire marshal of Northbrook.

Jeremiah Blackstone was not there and was not expected back. His wife told me that he had recently had a stroke and was living at Juniper Grove, the county nursing home. When I asked her if a new fire marshal had been appointed, she said, "We don't have a lot of call for a fire marshal up here in Northbrook. The last fire Jeremiah investigated was five years back when a boy lit up a haystack for the fun of it." I scratched Northbrook off my list.

Next I reached the Quarryville fire marshal and asked if there had been any fires in the area.

"Tires in the area? If you're needing new tires, Bob's Sunoco can help you out. He's got a darned good price on 'em, and he'll balance 'em up for free."

Finally I reached Tim Brady, who doubled as the volunteer fire chief and the fire marshal of Salem, a forty-five-minute drive southwest of Brookford, a town closer to New York and therefore a more typical place for city people to escape to for the weekends.

Tim shooed his two children out of the living room so he could be alone to talk with me.

"We had a fire of suspicious origin at our house in Brookford last October. I'm trying to find out if there have been any similar fires in the neighboring towns."

"Similar in what way?"

I paused, then plunged. "We're Jewish."

He was silent long enough to make me uncomfortable.

"I've got a list," he said. "My wife says I'm crazy."

"What kind of list?"

"It could be that they're all weekenders. Here in Salem people pretty much equate it—if you're a weekender from New York that means you're Jewish. Could be whoever it is setting these fires has it in for the week-enders. Or it could be he goes after houses where people are away. I've read up a bit on arson. They say arsonists prefer uninhabited dwellings."

"How many fires do you have on your list?" I asked anxiously.

"There's been three here in Salem in the last two years. They've got two over in Carleton, about nine miles west. Down south in Grangeville they've got another two. You got the café up your way. Then there's the family in Amity, and the pharmacy over in Rangely. That'd be ten—eleven, if you include yours."

"This is incredible."

"Like I say, my wife says I'm a little nuts."

"Could you send me a copy of your list?"

"Guess I could type it up if you're interested."

"I could take down the information over the phone."

"I prefer to type it up, get the names right."

"And the dates. Could you put down the exact dates?"

"Got to borrow a typewriter. LuAnn would probably let me use hers over at the town hall."

"Handwritten's fine."

"Prefer to type it up. Especially if you're after the dates."

"I have a fax machine. Could you fax it to me?"

"Prefer to put it in the mail."

I gave him my office address and thanked him for the time he was going to put in on my account. "Mr. Brady, since you've been keeping track of these fires for quite a while, I take it you're concerned there might be a pattern here."

"Pattern, maybe. Some of them are clearly arson. Others, it's open to debate. Fire's a tricky business. The rumors fly. Everybody's an amateur detective."

"Have you tried to get an investigation going?"

"I called a trooper I went to high school with. Up here it's usually better to go to someone you know. My friend has a buddy at ATF. ATF sent a guy out to ask me a load of questions. Came by once, that was it. Guess they've got bigger fish to fry."

"But you believe there's something going on with all these fires."

"Mrs. Waldmas—was that the name you said?"

"Yes."

"Mrs. Waldmas, someday there's going to be a couple of kids playing inside of one of these houses."

This phone call and waiting for Tim Brady's list afterward put me even more on edge. A few nights later, when I went into Hannah's room to say good night, she told me, "I don't want you, I want Daddy."

"You don't want me to kiss you good night?" I asked, surprised and stung.

She didn't answer.

I sat at the end of her bed, wanting to respect her wish, but also knowing that a comment like that was meant to get my attention.

"Tell me what's wrong."

Still no answer.

I moved closer and put my hand on her back, which she had turned to me. She pulled away, tucking herself closer in to the wall and digging her arms around her pillow.

"I can't apologize unless I know what I should be sorry for."

She flipped over and glared at me, her frizzy hair a bush of fury. "You forget *everything*."

"You mean my promise to take you shopping for new fish for your tank? Didn't we say we'd do that Saturday?"

"Daddy's the only one who keeps his promises."

"Is this still about the gymnastics exhibition?" The week before, Hannah's gymnastics class had put on their final demonstration of the year, and somehow I had managed to write the wrong day in my calendar. Bonnie had taken Hannah to gymnastics class as usual, and Hannah had waited for me all through the demonstration. I felt wretched when I found out my mistake. I bought Hannah a present, apologized profusely, but I was aware that my apology fell on deaf ears.

"You always tell me how your mom was so selfish when you were growing up. I guess you two have a lot in common," Hannah said unflinchingly.

"Hannah, I've been having a tough year. Sometimes adults go through hard things. I haven't been a great mom to you. I know that. I'm sorry."

"That stuff's all over now, and you're still the same. You don't love me."

I considered whether Hannah was old enough to be told of our worries about arson, but that would be truly selfish, telling her something terrifying in order to assuage my own guilt.

"I'll get Daddy," I said, standing away from the bed. "And I do love you. I absolutely do love you."

Later that night I reported to Josh a softened version of Hannah's criticism, hoping for absolution, or at least some sympathy. He didn't oblige.

"They've both told me that you barely listen to what they say these days."

"I'm preoccupied. It's understandable."

"We're all paying a price for your obsession."

"Calling it an obsession is a little extreme."

"What would you call it?"

"I'm trying to do the right thing."

"For whom?"

"For all of us."

"Whether we want you to do it or not."

It was only the middle of May, but the days were already as hot as July and the city streets smelled of rotting garbage. I was finding it easy to look on the bleak side of things. After a week went by with no letter from Tim Brady, I began to doubt my purpose. I doubted Tim Brady as well, though

I knew I must not call to press him. Maybe the town clerk's typewriter needed a new ribbon and she couldn't get to the Kmart in Centerbrook until her car passed the emissions inspection. Or maybe Tim Brady was having second thoughts about trusting someone he had never met. Maybe his wife had warned him. They had young children. What did they need with trouble? Or maybe he had made the whole thing up, a joke on an overanxious New Yorker.

Twice a day the mail was brought around to my office by the crabby sculptor who owned the building. He considered it his prerogative to check the return addresses on his tenants' mail to be sure none of us were secret members of the NRA or had investments in South Africa. "You got a registered letter. The fire marshal of Salem, Connecticut." He held the letter out separately from the other mail, as if he expected to bargain with it. "I'm considering changing careers," I told him. "They're accepting women now."

It was shocking to be confronted with the list of fires Tim Brady had carefully typed on bright white stationery with the location of each, the date and time it occurred, the name of the property owner, all recognizably Jewish. There were twelve fires in all, the eleven we discussed on the phone and an additional one with the notation that it was a barn fire caused by a kerosene lantern falling off a hook. I flattened the letter on my desk and got out the Xerox copy I had made of the chronology from *The Complete History of the Third Reich*. Matching up the dates felt like a series of sickening blows.

April 2, 1986, Hoffman fire. April 2, 1934, Hitler declares himself fuehrer of the German state.

November 9, 1985, Leiberman fire. November 9, 1938, *Krystalnacht*, mobs attack synagogues and Jewish stores throughout Germany.

February 12, 1986, Rubenstein fire. February 12, 1940, the first deportation of Jews from German cities.

September 23, 1987, Koslow fire. September 23, 1941, the first testing of the gas showers at Auschwitz.

October 29, 1984, Greenwald fire. October 29, 1942, sixteen thousand Jewish corpses dug out of a single mass grave to be burned.

March 13, 1985, Friedman fire. March 13, 1943, the opening of the first crematorium at Auschwitz for a "more efficient disposal of Jewish corpses."

May 19, 1983, Shapiro fire. May 19, 1943, Berlin declared *Judenfrei*—cleansed of Jews.

Barely able to breathe, I picked up my telephone and dialed Julia Tucker's direct line. The call bounced to her secretary. Julia was in a meeting. From her meeting she was leaving directly for the airport to fly to Mississippi. The secretary informed me that her boss could return my call the following Friday.

"I need to talk to her right away."

"That won't be possible," I was told politely but resolutely.

"It's urgent."

"Ms. Tucker's trip to Mississippi is also urgent."

"Would you at least tell her I called? Tell her I found the evidence. Tell her it's up to eleven fires now."

"And your name?"

"Anne Waldmas."

"You're the one who did the documentary on kids and divorce. I had no idea! I was in tears for half the show. It was very powerful."

"I'm glad you liked it."

"I'll see if I can get her to call when she comes out of her meeting. I can't promise."

I sat at my desk with my hands folded in my lap, knees pressed together, back straight, waiting.

Julia called from the car that was driving her to the airport. Through static I described the eleven arsons and explained the pattern of the dates in history.

"I know it's only circumstantial," I apologized.

"It's good enough to get started," Julia assured me. "I'll call someone over at FBI before I get on my flight."

When I hung up, my eyes drifted to my favorite photograph of Hannah and Eli, which sat on my desk in a frame Eli had constructed of Popsicle sticks. The two of them are grinning, sitting on the deck in the country, arms around each other, the lush green woods behind them. I had brought my children to a place where they had been watched, targeted, hated. I had brought them there even after three anonymous letters had warned me. How would I forgive myself?

I had no idea whether I would hear from the FBI that day, that week, or never at all, so I was startled when the phone rang forty-five minutes later, the speedy response confirming my fear that I had uncovered something serious. The caller identified himself as the director of operations of the Connecticut regional office. I'm certain he realized as he listened to my story that I was having trouble breathing.

"It will be all right, Mrs. Waldmas. We're going to help you now."

# 17

The first thing I saw sliding out of the fax machine was the seal of the Federal Bureau of Investigation. Jack McCall, the Connecticut special agent assigned to our case, had sent a map with directions to the place where we were to meet him, an unmarked office building that belonged to the FBI an hour from New York City.

The previous night I had been up past midnight organizing my research into a coherent presentation. I made a color-coded chart with the dates of the fires and the related dates in history. I took the road map off my office wall and marked the locations of the eleven fires. I wrote up a list of contacts and telephone numbers: the Epsteins, the Pragers, the Weisses, Tim Brady. When I finished preparing these things, I felt satisfied and even proud, but now, as Josh and I drove north on Route 95 to our appointed meeting, I began to worry that I would come off as an overzealous journalist with an ax to grind or, worse, be taken for a crank. Why had I highlighted the dates in Magic Marker?

There was a hard rain, and the tires of the tractor trailer in front of us tore strips of water from the highway. I watched our windshield wipers rhythmically scrape away two clean half-moons. With the windows closed, the air inside the car was sticky. I had worn a suit for our meeting with the FBI agent. I wanted to look like a respectable, mature woman— not the anti–Vietnam War, SDS rebel that I fantasized had turned up on the FBI computer when they checked to see if Josh and I were people they could trust. Back in the days of marches and demonstrations I would not, in my wildest dreams, have imagined I would someday look to an FBI agent to rescue me.

"It's a little weird, isn't it?"

Josh was concentrating on the driving as trucks passed on both sides of us in the pounding rain.

"What's that?"

"You and I were such troublemakers in the sixties, and here we are meeting with an FBI agent."

"I doubt this guy is going to give a damn about our position on the bombing of Cambodia."

"I'm not going to show him my chart."

"I like your chart."

"It's too play school. He's going to think I'm over-the-top."

"You've got a right to be over-the-top, if what you've uncovered is true."

"You believe me, then?"

"Why wouldn't I believe you?"

I gave him a moment to get out of the sandwich of speeding trucks.

"Because all you've ever said was that I did this to get over my father's death."

Josh took a hand off the steering wheel and moved it over to my bare knee. "We're here together. I'm proud of what you've done."

"Then you won't start singing the Mr. Rogers theme song when I pull out my color-coded chart?"

We followed the precise directions that instructed us where to park and how to buzz through to an unmarked door on the fourth floor of an office building in an industrial park. Dressed in a yellow button-down shirt, blue-and-red tie, and navy-blue slacks, Agent McCall apologized for the secrecy as he let us in. It was not that our case needed such precautions, he explained, but this office, which gave us a convenient meeting point halfway between his base in Connecticut and our home in New York, was used in undercover operations and its location had to be kept secret.

We followed him through a maze of empty desks to a nondescript conference room where a pot of coffee was brewing for us. There was a long table surrounded by too many folding chairs for our small meeting.

McCall's briefcase was already open on the table, and squared up beside it was a fresh legal pad and a ballpoint pen. McCall stood while Josh and I helped ourselves to coffee in styrofoam cups.

Jack McCall was older than I expected from our brief phone call, probably in his late thirties. His blond hair was cut short, but it was a soft cut, more like a high school English teacher than a law enforcement officer. He had perfect features—piercing blue eyes, thick eyelashes, a chiseled chin—a grown-up version of the guy who had been voted the handsomest member of the senior class.

"It must have been tough going in that rain," he said as he invited us to sit down. "I was lucky enough to miss it since I started out early to be sure to be here first."

"We must be pretty important if you didn't want to leave us hanging out in the parking lot," I said.

McCall answered soberly, "Mrs. Waldmas, let me assure you: The FBI takes hate crimes very, very seriously."

He sat across from us, his spine as straight as an arrow, and I examined him for clues to whether or not he was smart enough for me to trust. I was still my father's daughter. My mind went to the collection of children's school pictures he certainly had in his wallet, the Little League coach's uniform hanging in his closet. One thing was certain—he didn't fit my knee-jerk assumption that anyone who chose a life of law enforcement was either stupid, authoritarian, or a tissue slice away from criminality himself.

"Before we get started, I'd like to give you a telephone number where you can reach me anytime." He withdrew his card from his briefcase, wrote a number on the back, then pushed the card across the table. "If you don't get me directly, tell the agent who answers the phone that it's urgent. I'll call you back day or night, no matter what the time."

"Why would we need that?" I asked.

"I want you to know that I'm available to you. Something may come up. You may feel frightened. There could be any number of things."

Josh put the card in his shirt pocket, which annoyed me. I wanted the card for myself.

"From what I understand, you've been researching the possibility of a pattern of anti-Semitic arsons that includes your home and others."

"Homes and businesses," I corrected.

McCall pulled his pad toward him. "Why don't we take things in chronological order."

I told our story with a compulsive amount of detail. I felt I had to make it interesting, the way I would have done if I were pitching a documentary proposal to a potential financial backer. I had to make it clear that there were good guys and bad guys, that there was a story that would hold an audience's attention to the end of the program.

I described the phone call the morning of the fire, the fire marshal's assessment, the fused copper wire theory, how we had hired our own investigator because of the Brookford Café fire only two weeks before ours. I recounted what we had learned from the Pragers, the connection with Hitler's birthday, Josh's comment about the history of anti-Semitic arson, how that set me on a hunt for dates. I introduced the cast of characters—brokenhearted Shelly Weiss, disconsolate Harry Epstein, earnest Trooper Lefert, curious Tim Brady.

When I was done, McCall put down his pen. "You've done an impressive job of investigating, Mrs. Waldmas."

I knew, from years of experience, that this was the moment to reveal the weakness in my argument, and then to answer it. I brought out my chart and map and spread them on the table.

"I know the FBI has to have clear evidence of anti-Semitism in order to meet the threshold that justifies an investigation. I have no swastikas to show you, no burned crosses, nothing like that. Whoever set these fires left his signature in a more sophisticated way—he gave us history, he used his brain. He wants us to know that his hatred for Jews isn't based on envy for our intelligence or success. He wants us to see that he's as smart as any Jew and that his hatred for Jews is an informed opinion."

Jack McCall turned to Josh. "Do you think your wife would like to come to work for the FBI?"

"I was worried that my arts-and-crafts project would seem a little strange," I confessed.

"It would have been my next step. We look for patterns. But there's one thing I'm not following. You said your own fire investigator ruled out arson. What changed your mind?"

"Meeting with the Pragers convinced us that we had reason to pursue this."

"Yes, but what led you to make contact with the Pragers after you were assured that your fire was electrical?"

Josh slapped his forehead and turned to me. "Annie, you left out the *letters*." He turned back to McCall. "We got three anonymous letters from someone telling us we should investigate our fire further. The letters suggested anti-Semitism."

"It was just some town busybody trying to stir up trouble."

Josh looked at me quizzically. "Those letters are what got us thinking."

"Can I take a look at them?" McCall asked.

"I didn't bring them."

I saw the two men exchange a quick look. I had brought everything else imaginable.

"I flushed the first one down the toilet the same day that it arrived. It upset me. I wanted to get rid of it."

"That's certainly understandable," McCall acknowledged. "The other two?"

"They're locked in my desk at my office."

He nodded. "Sometimes people aren't comfortable parting with evidence, Mrs. Waldmas. Those letters are the one concrete thing you have to hold on to, to touch. After all, those letters are what's made it real, this unimaginable thing that's happened to your family. Could you send me copies?"

I took a fresh look at our FBI agent, who had spoken with such consideration. Our eyes caught for a moment.

"I'll send them to you tomorrow."

"Can you tell me what particularly struck you about the letters?" McCall was now addressing himself exclusively to me.

"My first reaction was that the person was trying to get us to leave Brookford."

"Why would anyone want to do that?"

"I'm guessing that before the fire, the local people didn't think much about our being Jewish. But after two fires in such a short time, maybe they worried that our being Jewish could bring trouble to their town."

"You'd never experienced any prejudice there before? No one ever said anything to you before the fire?"

Josh and I shook our heads.

"I did try to see if I could find out who wrote the letters. I went by the Brookford post office to see if the postmistress recognized the handwriting. I had the feeling she knew more than she was willing to say. But that's the way it is in small towns like Brookford. People don't necessarily say what they know, even if they have no real reason to hide it from you. Especially someone like Melinda Marks, being a bit of an oddball, a single mother, and fairly new to Brookford herself."

"Melinda Marks?" McCall wrote down the name on his pad.

"The postmistress."

"But that sounds like a Jewish name."

I turned to Josh for his opinion.

"Not in Brookford."

"Tell me, Mrs. Waldmas. Does anyone in Brookford know you've been in touch with us?"

"When I first talked to Trooper Lefert, he hinted that the only way to get this thing solved was to get the FBI involved, but we didn't talk about it specifically, and I haven't talked with him since. Other than that it's only Josh and me."

"I suggest we keep it that way for now."

Josh said, "I'd prefer if people in town never found out we were the ones who brought you into this thing. But how will you explain your presence?"

"You said Tim Brady spoke with an ATF agent. It's simple enough to suggest that ATF asked us to take this on."

As we said good-bye at the unmarked door, Jack McCall assured us that he would start work immediately and would be careful to guard our privacy—but he wanted something in return.

"We're in the same business, you and I," he said to me. "I know how hard it is to leave an investigation to someone else once you've put in your time and energy. However, for your safety and for the safety of your family, I'd like you to let us handle it from here."

"I'm happy to turn it over to you," I lied.

McCall telephoned a few days later to thank me for sending him the copies of the letters and to tell me that he had been in contact with Alcohol, Tobacco and Firearms to submit the papers necessary to take over the investigation. This essential formality could take a week or two.

"But ATF already dropped it," I protested, knowing that government red tape might actually drag on for months.

"We have to proceed carefully with this step. If we don't properly establish our jurisdiction, the case will be thrown out in court."

"But you can get around that with ATF," I pressed.

"Annie, law enforcement is not the same as making documentary films."

I bridled at this comment. I also noted that he had called me Annie for the first time. I knew this technique. I had employed it often myself as a reporter, using the telephone to establish a friendship that would have been presumptuous in person. The next time he phoned, a week later, I was feeling a little less cordial.

"There's good news and bad. ATF has formally handed over the investigation."

"The bad news?"

"I'd like you to stay away from Brookford for the time being."

"Why?"

"Annie, you've got to understand as we go along that I won't be able to tell you everything."

"Memorial Day's coming up. Our house is finally livable again. I wanted to move us back in by the holiday weekend."

"This is your decision. I can't stop you. I can only tell you that if it were my family, I wouldn't take the risk."

"Don't I deserve a *little* more information than that?"

"Perhaps you should think about how much you really want to know—considering your family is involved."

"Don't be ridiculous."

He paused. "The person in question has guns."

"Guns?"

"I'm afraid so."

"That means you've located him."

"I can't respond to that, but I would like to feel certain that you won't make use of your home for now."

"I'm sure there are plenty of people up there who have guns, for hunting, if nothing else."

"Perhaps this will make it clearer to you. This individual cuts photographs of Jewish people from newspapers and nails them to trees behind his house to use for target practice."

"My God." I folded one arm across my stomach and pressed in hard.

"I'm sorry to have to tell you this."

Looking for a shred of comfort, I asked, "It's definitely an individual, not a group?"

"So far it appears that way."

"Can you tell me one thing? How did you find this out?"

"We've established a source in the area."

"Really?" I was amazed at the swift reach of the FBI.

"That's usually the best way to work, especially in a town as small as Brookford."

"Is it someone I know?"

"All I can say at this point is that there's a local person who's aware of what's been going on. I can't tell you more than that."

"But I'm the one who got the investigation started."

"We had an agreement on this."

"What was that?"

"That you would step aside and let us take over."

"But I can help."

"Your family's involved here. It's not wise."

"Surgeons operating on their own children."

"That sort of thing, yes."

"So I have to put my trust in the FBI."

"How about putting your trust in me?"

"He really uses photographs of Jews for target practice?"

"Yes. I'm afraid he does."

I hung up and curled into a fetal position on my office couch. Someone passed by in the outside hall, whistling. I tried to imagine whistling, but my mind was stuck on the vision of photographs with bullet holes. It took quite a while before I was able to telephone Josh to tell him that we were not to use our house.

"I'm going to get my own goddamned gun. If that bastard comes anywhere near our house again, I'll kill him. I'm not joking, Annie. I'll kill him if I see him."

"There is some good news in this, Josh. They know who set the fires. It's only a matter of time until he goes to jail."

"I'm glad you have such confidence in our legal system."

"What's our choice? You're not going to get a gun. That's preposterous. You'll be the one who ends up in jail."

"I'll tell you what I'd really like to do. I'd like to take this guy to face Shelly Weiss and that other couple in Rangely, make him see how he's wrecked their lives." A week ago we'd heard that Shelly Weiss had had a heart attack. His wife had taken him to her mother's house in Arizona to recuperate far away from the tragedy that had literally broken his heart.

"But isn't that exactly what he wants to do, wreck all of our lives?"

We needed to make a last trip to Brookford to meet with the building inspector to have him sign off on the completed construction and then close up the house. On Saturday morning we left the children with friends in New York, since we had no intention of letting them anywhere near Brookford. As we went around the rebuilt house locking up, my fear mounted. I kept peering out the windows, imagining a rifle leveled at our heads.

When Josh piled the car with the last of the construction debris to take to the dump, I asked him to drop me in town so I could tell Melinda Marks to keep forwarding our mail to New York. The bells on the post office door made her look up, but she did not come forward from her desk.

"Beautiful day," I called out, but she stayed focused on her work. She was dressed for the warm weather in cutoff shorts and a T-shirt. Her buzz-cut hair had grown out, a topiary in need of trimming.

The bells hanging on the door sounded again, and Caroline Willis came through. Caroline was a widow who supported herself growing herbs and selling them at her roadside stand. I was one of her steady customers.

"Hi, Caroline. Can you believe this day?" I asked.

"My babies love it. This is when they're happiest, before the hot weather sets in." She considered me. "I haven't seen you lately."

"The fire."

"Of course, I forgot." Caroline turned to Melinda. "She had that awful fire."

"How can I help you?" Melinda stepped up to the counter, all business.

"I filled out a change-of-address request to last until the end of May. Looks like we've got to extend it."

Melinda examined her shelf of forms, handed one to me, then asked Caroline, "You looking for your mail?"

"All that weeding I do. I'm getting that carpal tunnel thing. Can't turn that postbox lock for the life of me. Would you mind?"

As Melinda went to retrieve Caroline's mail, Caroline watched me fill in the forwarding form and asked, "Hear about poor Shelly Weiss?"

"His heart attack?"

"Yes, and that wretched insurance company still hasn't paid him a dime. Can you imagine? Shelly loses everything he's worked for, and they have the gall to suggest he did this to himself. You didn't go through any of that with your insurance, did you?"

"We had a battle, but it's settled now."

Melinda handed Caroline her mail. Caroline went for the door. "So long, ladies. Happy spring."

Melinda pointed to the form I was filling out. "You can leave that on the counter when you're done."

I pushed it across to her. "Is my writing clear? Sometimes people have a hard time with our name. I guess because it's Jewish. Your name sounds Jewish. People ever say that?"

"Nope."

"Have you given any further thought to who might have sent that letter I showed you?"

She shook her head again.

"I see. And people never figure you're Jewish because of your name?"

She frowned. "What's with you?"

"Now that Shelly and his wife have gone to Arizona, I guess Josh and I are the only Jews left in Brookford."

"I'm the postmistress, not the census taker," Melinda said coldly.

I gave the change-of-address card another push in her direction.

She examined the form. "You didn't put down a date you want your delivery resumed."

"It's indefinite," I said and turned on my heel.

Before Josh came by to get me, I dialed Jack McCall's beeper from the public phone outside the town hall. He called back within minutes.

"The postmistress knows something," I told him. "I'm positive. And remember how you asked whether she was Jewish when you heard her name? I've got a hunch you might be right."

"Where are you, Annie?"

"Outside the town hall."

"In Brookford? Didn't we agree you'd stay away from there?"

"We had to meet with the building inspector and close up the house. While we were here, I figured I'd fill in the form to keep forwarding our mail."

"I see."

"I suppose I could have done it by phone."

"Did you have something else to tell me?"

"Only that when she saw me walk in, she got incredibly uptight."

"Are you certain you want me to proceed with this investigation?"

"What do you mean?"

"We can't both do it."

"I thought you'd want to know this."

"Know what?"

"That the postmistress is aware of something."

"You're going to create problems for yourself *and* for the investigation if you don't stay out of it," he said impatiently. "As I've already made clear to you a number of times."

When Josh pulled up, I climbed into the car but did not tell him what I'd done. I knew he would pounce on it as more evidence that I was too deeply involved in this thing, and for all the wrong reasons. The following morning I telephoned McCall to apologize.

"I'm sure this is extremely hard on you and your family."

"I don't know what's so hard about having your home burned down by an anti-Semitic psycho."

He was silent.

"I'm sorry. It's my control-freak personality. I guess I'm not the type to sit back."

"Your unwillingness to sit back is a good quality. It's what got us here. Don't get me wrong—I admire it."

"I figured you for someone who preferred the soccer-mom type."

He laughed, the first spontaneous response I had gotten out of him.

"Look, you have my promise again. This time I'll try to keep it."

"I'll tell you as much as I can as we go along. I hope you understand, there are some things I can't say—for your own safety as much as anything."

"One thing. The person who's giving you information in Brookford—does whoever it is know it was me who got in touch with you?"

"I told you I'd protect you."

"That's not a direct answer."

"It will have to be enough."

"How about Lefert? I assume you've been in touch with him."

"We always work through local law enforcement."

"Another indirect answer."

"But you keep pushing, don't you?"

Through June and July our Brookford home waited, newly constructed and echoingly empty. We tried to make it up to Hannah and Eli with a few weekend trips, but inevitably, as we reached Sunday afternoon, Josh and I found ourselves bickering, tired of pretending to be having fun when we weren't. I knew I had no right to complain about not being able to go to our second home when half the world didn't have a first one. But all the same, being banished by an anonymous hatred began to depress us deeply. We were at odds with the lighthearted summer world we tried to join, and we grew impatient with our friends, who were both fascinated and not quite convinced that we were victims of anti-Semitism. Some argued that the fire had to be the work of a disturbed teenager in need of counseling. Others brought us theories of a northward incursion of the Ku Klux Klan.

Jack McCall continued to telephone on a regular basis to give me updates, and in these phone calls we began to develop something of a friendship. We even joked about my compulsive need to know everything and his careful parceling out of enough information to keep me at bay. I wasn't surprised when he began to break his rules and tell me more than he should. I had done documentaries that involved detectives, and I knew there was always a moment when they began to say too much. They were like psychiatrists who reveal intimate details of their patients' disorders, or priests who tell their housekeepers the sins they hear in confession. Professionals who deal with aberrant behavior day in and day out need to gossip about what they hear or it begins to overwhelm them.

Without ever revealing the arsonist's name or where he lived, little by little Jack McCall drew me a picture of him. He was in his late twenties, the brilliant son of wealthy parents who had repeatedly bailed him out as his obsession with anti-Semitism led to expulsion from one prestigious college after another. At Yale he had climbed on a table during a final exam in history and shouted anti-Semitic slogans. At Amherst he sent copies of *Mein Kampf* to every Jewish professor on the faculty. His last college, Boston University, accepted him only because his family offered a hefty donation and the assurance that their son would enter counseling. But at BU he carried on a campaign to try to stop the school from providing office space to the Hillel Society, the Jewish student organization, and eventually he was asked to leave there, too. But even with all this background on their suspect, they still didn't have the concrete evidence needed to arrest him, for our fire or for any of the others.

"It's more sit and wait, then," I said dispiritedly when Jack and I were talking on the phone one hot afternoon in August.

"To get a conviction, it has to be done right."

I was interrupted by my assistant, who announced that my brother was on the phone. "It's the big news."

"The baby?"

"Let him tell you."

"I'm an aunt again," I explained to Jack McCall before I took the call.

"Now, that's something nice," he said.

"I need something nice," I admitted.

Charles was calling from the maternity floor, where he was holding his new son in his arms. "He's perfect, Annie. Better than perfect." Sissy was forty-two, four years older than Charles, and in the last few weeks they had been worried about the pregnancy.

"Have you given him a name?"

"Abe—of course."

"I like that. And when do I get to meet my nephew?"

"Tonight, tomorrow, as soon as you can get down here."

"Sissy deserves a little rest before people start descending on her. How about I come down first thing in the morning?"

"Make it as soon as you can."

Charles gave Sissy the telephone, and we had the coded talk about childbirth, the excruciating pain and the temporary insanity it causes. Sissy was exhausted but very happy.

"I'm coming down tomorrow, if that's okay."

"Absolutely. He needs to meet his godmother."

"His godmother?"

"What do you say?"

"What do I say? I'm thrilled."

We Fishman siblings hadn't seen one another at all in the four months since our father's death. I suppose we needed to get back to our own lives. There was my father's estate to settle, but Tony took charge of that. Ben and Ellen had announced their engagement, although no wedding date had yet been set. I guess we all assumed that our next gathering would be at their wedding. That provided some security that we wouldn't unthinkingly drift apart now that we didn't have my father to bring us together. But I'm sure each of us had some ambivalence. Did we really want the expectations and irritations that came with extended-family life?

I knew the answer to that question without a doubt as I rode in from Washington National Airport and found myself talking a blue streak to the Jamaican cabby, telling him about my new nephew, that I was to be the godmother, that the baby had been named Abraham after my deceased father. Charles was holding Abe in a bundle against his chest when I came into the hospital room. Morning sunlight streamed through windows, and Sissy sat up against the pillows, a picture of contentment, her thick, black hair pulled back in a ribbon, her heavy breasts filling one of Charlie's button-down shirts.

"Aunt Annie," my brother introduced his son, "meet the prince."

I peeked into the hospital blanket and saw the red, wrinkled flesh of my new godson. His chin quivered as he pressed his lips together, discovering an interest in sucking. "Hey, fella," I said softly. He opened his eyes to the new voice, and I saw the same intensity of his namesake as he busily examined the blur that was me.

"Pop would be so proud."

When the baby let out a squeak, Charles asked Sissy, "Should we try the breast again?"

Sissy unbuttoned her shirt and her breasts came free. With her fingers she lifted her nipple to a ready angle as Charles settled baby Abe against her. He rooted around and Sissy whispered encouragement. "Here you go, little guy." In only a moment it seemed to make sense to him. He opened his tiny red mouth, and his lips took hold as his small cheeks bellowed in and out.

"A genius," Charles pronounced.

The baby lifted his hand into the air as if feeling for the embryonic fluid he knew. He sucked diligently, and we all watched little Abe Fishman's accomplishment. Then his eyes closed as he rested his head against Sissy's breast. Charles touched my shoulder and pointed to Sissy, whose eyelids had also drifted closed. Charles took the baby from her arms to lay him on his stomach in the bassinet beside the bed. He tucked the receiving blanket smartly around his son and admired his handiwork. He whispered to me, "I'm starving."

We went through the hospital cafeteria line and set our plastic trays opposite each other at a round Formica table by a window that looked out over the hospital parking lot. Charles ate his yogurt and banana and told me every detail of the birth. He told me that Sissy was the most courageous and perfect woman on earth, evidently forgetting that the less-than-perfect sister who sat opposite him had survived the same ordeal twice. "I am indebted forever," he announced seriously.

"You know, part of the deal if you bring one child into the world is that you have to give the kid a sibling."

"So that years later his sister can tell him how to run his life?"

"Maybe he won't be lucky enough to get a sister."

"Speaking of running your life, what's going on with your arson investigation? It seems to be taking forever."

Charles had scraped his yogurt container clean. He yawned and sat back, stretching his arms along the backs of the adjacent chairs. He had been up all night.

"It's the way the law is written. A citizen of this country can carry out outrageous acts of anti-Semitism, but unless you've got concrete evidence of a specific hate crime, there's not a damned thing anyone can do about it. Have I told you what this guy does to amuse himself? He uses newspaper clippings of Jews for target practice."

"You've got to be kidding."

"I wish I were. And yet they say there's not enough evidence for a search warrant. You start to feel quite differently about the holy First Amendment when you're on the victim's side of things."

"Isn't the FBI famous for ignoring people's rights?"

"Not our FBI agent. He's a straight shooter."

"So go around him. You're a journalist. Dig up something on this lunatic. You're the one who uncovered this in the first place. Keep working at it."

"I gave my word I'd hold back."

"Who is this FBI agent who's got you cowed?"

"He's a good guy. I like him. Actually, I like him a lot."

Charles gazed out over the parking lot. I knew he was trying to decide how to help me, what course of action to suggest. It was both his nature and his profession to preserve things of value—forests, homes. He was still pondering as we rode the elevator back to the maternity floor. Before we got back to Sissy's room, he put his hand on my shoulder. "Maybe you could use your media contacts to bring some pressure. In situations like this sometimes the press has more power than law enforcement."

"I'll consider it," I said to put him off.

"I don't understand why you're being so passive. It's not like you."

I brushed past him. "Sissy's probably woken up and wondering where we disappeared to."

That night, back in New York, I telephoned Charles. "It's not that I'm being passive."

"Then what is it? Because something's stopping you."

"I thought about it on the way home. To this creep we're vermin corrupting his world. We're not even human to him. Maybe that's why I've been willing to back off and let somebody else deal with it—maybe it's too upsetting for me to handle directly."

"This doesn't sound like my sister the investigative reporter. I've never known you to sit back and do nothing."

"I've done plenty," I bridled. "I got the FBI to come in. That was no easy feat."

"Apparently you've got to do more."

During the summer months Hannah and Eli were ferried by bus to camp in New Jersey every day, so my days were free from eight in the morning until five in the evening. As long as I asked my assistant to cover for me if Josh called, I could skip out of work and make the drive to Brookford and back without my family even knowing I was gone.

When I drove around town looking for him, Lefert wasn't in any of the usual spots on either end of town where he parked and trolled for speeders. At last I found him sitting in his car on the one street in the center of Brookford that had a clear view of the whole village green. This time I came bearing goodies from my favorite Italian bakery. As I approached his car, I held the bakery bag high so he could see it through the windshield.

"Imported from New York," I said as I opened the passenger door and handed my treat across to him.

He peeked inside. "Good choice." He plucked a cannoli out of the bag.

"How come you're parked up here?"

"Sometimes I like to sit and keep an eye on things."

"Anybody special you're watching for?"

"What kind of question is that?"

"A direct one."

"Direct questions. That's sometimes a good approach."

Lefert studied the cannoli at eye level, bit off half of it, then closed his eyes to savor the taste.

"I guess you're aware that I know about the FBI investigation," I said.

He didn't respond.

"Too direct?" I asked.

"I assumed as much." He cradled the remaining half of the cannoli in his open palm, putting off for a moment his inevitable surrender to it. "Course, I had my suspicions about this guy all along."

"I guess I never would have suspected a guy like that from such a wealthy family," I said, laying out a line and hook.

"With *that* father? Old man Lewis has never exactly made a secret of how he feels about Jews. They say Lewis hasn't allowed a Jew to work at his banks in over fifty years."

Even though I was a seasoned journalist, my heart quickened. After all these months, I had finally heard the arsonist's family name.

I stared ahead through the windshield and, along with Trooper Lefert, surveyed the perfect New England town. "Not hiring Jews is one thing, but burning people's homes—you'd think they'd get him help."

"The parents probably like it fine the way they've got it. The kid stays holed up in their cabin on James Lake, and they never have to deal with him showing up unexpected at one of their fancy Boston dinner parties."

Now that I had learned the information Jack McCall had carefully kept from me through all our phone conversations, I had to restrain myself from pouncing on Lefert for more.

"I wanted to thank you for everything you've been doing to help us." I reached for the car door.

"You rest assured, Mrs. Waldmas. I'm not sleeping till I see that snot-nose Colin Lewis run out of this town."

Colin Lewis, on James Lake. I had everything I had come for.

"How about your goodies?" Lefert pointed to the bag I had left on the front seat.

"For you."

That night I waited impatiently for Hannah and Eli's bedtime, anxious to tell Josh what I had found out, to show him there was progress, that the arsonist had a name, an address, and would eventually be caught. I let Josh assume I had learned all this from Jack McCall, since I did not want to tell him I had driven up to Brookford.

Josh was grim. We were in the kitchen, waiting for tea water to boil. The kettle sang. Josh turned off the flame but didn't pour the water.

"I thought I was telling you good news."

"You're telling me they know who the asshole is, they know where he lives, they know his family—and they still haven't done a goddamned thing to put the guy where he belongs. I'm supposed to construe that as good news? What am I, a child you're humoring while you rub shoulders with the FBI?"

"You know they can't do anything until they have more than circumstantial evidence. Jack's doing everything he can."

"This is your buddy *Jack*, now?"

"I'm not allowed to call him by his first name?"

"Call him whatever you want. The point is that you're losing sight of what we're doing here."

"What *we're* doing? Tell me, please—what exactly have *you* been doing to solve this thing?"

"I'm not doing anything because I've accepted that it can't be solved, at least not to the point where I'd want to go back there. Maybe it's time you came back down to earth and accepted that, too."

"And then what?" I poured water into my own mug but not into Josh's.

"Like I've said all along—we sell the damned house."

"The *damned* house?"

"Don't you see what this is doing to us, Annie?" He raised his hands like a traffic cop, as much to calm himself down as to stop me from taking this argument any further. "Look, play detective. Take on the whole world's problems. Try to absolve your father of his lifelong guilt. Whatever your mysterious motivations are. Keep ignoring your children for a few more months. They've gotten used to it anyway." He raised his finger between us. "We've already gone way past the time limit I set five months ago. And frankly, I can't bear to have a discussion about anti-Semitism every goddamned day of my life. By September first, if this idiot's not caught, we're putting the house up for sale."

# 18

Early the next morning, while Hannah and Eli watched cartoons and waited for the camp bus, I called Jack McCall's beeper number. He phoned right back as always, keeping his original promise to me to be available whenever I wanted to talk.

"Tell me again why you can't arrest this guy if you know for sure that he's the one who burned our house."

"I've told you, Annie. We have an evidence problem. Either we find a way to get a confession out of him, or we have to wait for him to do something to incriminate himself."

"Tell me the truth—are we ever going back there?"

"I've told you the truth all along. An arson conviction is very, very hard."

"You're avoiding my question."

"Ask me again."

"What's the point of all this? If it's such a long shot, why are we even bothering?"

"Didn't you once tell me you did a documentary on how hard it is to convict a rapist? Does that mean you stop trying? If nothing else, you're setting the stage to get him on the next incident. We may not get a conviction in your case, but somewhere along the line—"

I was standing at our kitchen window, staring vacantly into the dreary alley between apartment buildings. There was nothing in my view that lifted my spirits. Jack's voice was disembodied and far away.

"That's why you're raising our hopes? So sometime in the future he'll get arrested? You're putting us through all this when you know we're going to have to move out in the end anyway?"

"Annie, would it help if we got together and talked?"

I sat at the kitchen table. My eyes had filled at his offer. I pushed around some daisies that were wilting in a vase. There were smashed Cheerios on the table, spilled milk, a single sock that had no twin—all the dreary details of slogging through life. From the living room I could hear the screeching chase of a stupid cat-and-mouse cartoon. I was losing my perspective, my good humor, even my reliable sarcasm.

"I'm coming into New York City next Tuesday morning to attend a seminar on new rules for evidence collection. What do you say we get together afterwards for lunch?"

"Where's the seminar?"

"In an office building near Grand Central Station."

"The Oyster Bar's right there. Do you like fish? I mean, I don't eat oysters. I prefer my food dead. What time is your seminar over?"

"I should be free by one-thirty. Is that too late for lunch?"

"It doesn't matter. I don't usually eat lunch."

The following Tuesday, riding the subway up from my office to Grand Central, I tried to remember what Jack McCall looked like. Though we had talked many times on the telephone, and often at length, we had met only once in person, the day I presented my research. I recalled that he was vaguely boyish looking, had blond hair, blue eyes, and that I figured he probably coached Little League.

I was at the restaurant in time to have a glass of white wine before I spotted Jack threading his way between the lunch tables packed too closely together. He looked more sophisticated than I expected—Italian-cut suit, dark tie loosened at his neck, blond hair brushed back behind his ears—not boyish at all; in fact, very much a man and quite attractive. I wondered how I had missed that.

"You're on time." I felt like a girl out on her first date with the football captain.

"I skipped out early. I couldn't take any more. Four hours of beating around the bush, and it finally adds up to them telling us our hands are tied even tighter than before." He pulled out the chair across from me and dropped into it like a boxer exhausted from a fight. "Maybe I should become a journalist like you. You guys get away with murder." He turned to the waiter. "Dewar's on the rocks." He asked me, "Do you mind? It's the middle of the day, I know."

"Do they tell you when to drink, as well?"

"Dewar's," he repeated to the waiter. He pointed to my glass. "And another white wine as well."

He took off his jacket and rolled his shirtsleeves up above his elbows, revealing forearms thickly covered with sun-bleached hair.

"Do you coach Little League?" I asked.

"I know, I'm a cliché."

"Earnest, yes. But not a cliché."

"Thank God. I would have had to kill myself."

"Over Little League?"

"Over not being clever enough to impress a New York woman."

Our drinks came while Jack was describing one of the cases in his morning seminar. The Supreme Court had reversed the conviction of a serial killer because of a problem with how the FBI had obtained the evidence.

"The agent went into the killer's house to get crucial evidence—a videotaped description of the killings—without the search warrant in his physical possession. The judge had guaranteed the warrant by phone, and the agent knew the guy's girlfriend was on her way to destroy the tape. So the guy gets off on appeal when the videotape is ruled inadmissible. God bless the Supreme Court for keeping America safe for sadistic criminals."

"There's the little matter of the Bill of Rights."

"I wonder how many serial murderers were out roaming the streets of Philadelphia when Jefferson and his buddies were figuring out how to protect people's privacy rights?"

"Your reactionary side."

"And proud of it."

Jack ordered the fried calamari special, and I ordered an appetizer of fish cakes. To our left a literary contract was being negotiated on a napkin. On our right the financials of a real estate deal were being discussed. No one seemed in much of a hurry to conclude lunch and leave. Outside on the street the humidity and the temperature were both heading toward a hundred.

By the time our plates were cleared, I had gone through three glasses of wine and Jack had finished two scotches. I began to feel self-conscious about my choice of a low-necked, sleeveless summer dress. The air-conditioning was chilly on my bare skin.

"Jack, I really need to know the truth from you. How long is the FBI going to keep you on our case if you can't turn up enough evidence for a conviction?"

He shook his head ruefully. "And here I was hoping I would get away with a social lunch."

"Then you wouldn't be able to submit the bill on your expense account."

"Believe me, I have no intention of doing that."

"Josh wants to sell the house. I'm losing ground in the argument every day. He says this is all a waste of time, that the guy's never going to jail anyway."

"He may be right, Annie."

"I didn't want to hear that."

"Look, at this point I'd be happy if we could run him out of Brook-ford so you and your family could go back there. He'd go somewhere else to make trouble, but sooner or later we'd get him. I'd see to that."

"Do you know that this is the first time you've acknowledged to me that he lives in Brookford?"

"I figured by now you assumed it."

"But you never said it before in so many words. Have you finally begun to trust me?"

"I've trusted you all along. You know very well I've told you more than I should."

"You never told me his name or where he lives."

"Because part of my job is to protect you."

"Tell me how knowing his name puts me in danger."

He sat back, appraising me. Was he also noticing that I was someone different from whom he remembered? He moved the salt and pepper shakers to a new spot on the table, looked at them, then moved them back. The waiter started toward us, then slid away when he realized we weren't ready for him to collect the check.

"I've been concerned that if you knew his whereabouts, you might be inclined to look in on him."

"Citizen's arrest?"

"You once told me you're not the type to sit back."

"But I'm not the cavalry either."

"You have to remember he has guns. He drinks, he gets wasted, he sits in his lawn chair in his Nazi helmet and shoots off his twenty-two rifle."

"You think I'd be nuts enough to go near this guy?"

"Maybe nuts, maybe impatient. I know you want your home back."

"I guess I shouldn't take your concern for my welfare too personally."

"I don't know why not."

If he was flirting with me in order to keep me under control, it was working. The wine had filled my head. For the moment the thought of Josh and our endless, boring argument about whether or not to sell the house was pleasantly at bay. The unrelenting pain of losing my father was also temporarily shelved. I was having lunch with a man who was not my husband. I allowed my mind to slide into the realm of possibility, and that scared me straight.

I downed a long drink of water to dilute the wine pumping through my veins, and then took cover in a question.

"How do you explain someone like him? Does he fit some typical profile?"

"He's a classic. For starters, the father is a rabid anti-Semite. That alone wouldn't mean the son was going to become an anti-Semite, much less an arsonist, but the father also has a notorious mean streak. He bullied his son from a very young age—did all the sadistic things fathers like that do to turn their sons into 'real men,' since with all that money his son will never have to prove himself in any legitimate pursuit. My guess is that this guy hates his father as much as he reveres him, a dangerous combination. Sons of sadistic fathers—they need their own special subsection of the FBI."

"Why can't you confront the parents with what's been going on? Couldn't they be persuaded to get their son into some sort of treatment?"

"We tried that. The minute we approached the family, the father brought in a battalion of lawyers to threaten a defamation suit against the FBI and damned near shut the case down. I had to go into my boss and present the case all over again, point by point. He's still not completely convinced it's anything but a bunch of coincidences."

"You never told me that."

"It's not your battle."

"And how come you're still in business?"

"I begged."

"You begged?"

"Annie, this guy marches around his backyard doing the goose step with his rifle on his shoulder. How long before shooting at a photograph isn't enough?"

"I wish I knew how you get all this information."

"You know I can't tell you that."

"It's Lefert, isn't it? Bob Lefert, the state trooper."

"Bob's helping us. But he's not close enough to dig up this kind of stuff." Jack scowled. "Dammit, I don't know what it is about you. How do you always manage to get me to say more than I want to? Why is it so important for you to know every step I take?"

I drew back into my chair. This was the first time he had lost his temper with me.

"Jack, the person helping you—whoever the hell he or she is—that person knows that I'm a Jew and that I'm despised because of it. It's hard to explain to you how that feels—how it makes me feel small, powerless, pitied. When you feel frightened as a Jew, you begin to believe there must be a legitimate reason people detest you. Why else would someone hate you without even knowing who you are?"

He reached toward me, then stopped. "It's Melinda Marks. And she's Jewish, like you suspected. So forget the idea of being pitied."

"Melinda Marks?"

"Don't you dare talk to her, Annie. Don't you dare go near her. She's been seeing this guy. He doesn't know she's Jewish. God knows what he'd do if he knew."

"Jewish women did that in the concentration camps, too."

He recoiled from me. "Don't you trust *anybody*?" He reached for the check and pushed back his chair. "I've got to make a four o'clock train."

"Little League practice?"

"It's my kid's swim meet," he said coolly, "but you were close." He pulled out cash to leave with the bill. "I'm doing my best, Annie. I'm doing everything I can." With his jacket hooked over his shoulder on his thumb, he stood a minute looking at me, then put his hand on my bare shoulder. "I'm sorry. I'm sorry for barking at you."

As soon as I got back to my office, I telephoned Charles. I needed to distance myself from Jack McCall.

"I did what you told me to. I did some more checking on my own."

"And?"

"The arsonist's name is Colin Lewis. He's from a Boston Brahmin family. They own banks. The father's a renowned anti-Semite with a blanket policy against hiring Jews."

"And why does this Colin Lewis terrorize your neck of the woods?"

"His family owns a cabin on James Lake. It's a private lake in town. I guess they stash him there to keep him out of trouble."

"What does your FBI buddy say to this?"

"He doesn't know I know."

"Oh?"

"I don't want him thinking I'm going behind his back."

"This is your home, Annie. You have a right to keep fighting for it. Wouldn't Pop tell you that?"

"Because Pop never thought anybody could do anything as well as he could."

"Yes, but also because he had courage. You fight until you get to the truth. Isn't that what he wanted to teach us, Annie? Isn't that what he proved to you and me at the end of his life?"

"It could be one of my stupider moves."

"Then don't be stupid, be careful."

For a few months during my senior year in college I had dated a brilliant student from Boston named Henry Draycott. I knew from the alumni magazine that Henry had become a journalist and covered city politics for *The Boston Globe*. When I telephoned, he was pleased to hear from me.

"I wish I was calling to say hello."

"Something's up?"

"It's got to stay between us for now."

"You're leaving your husband and marrying me."

"I'm serious, Henry. You're a reporter. I need to know I can trust you to keep this to yourself for now."

"Of course, Annie."

I told him about our fire and the connection to the Lewis family of Boston. "I thought you might have come across the Lewises in your work."

"Who hasn't come across them. The Lewises are one of the biggest families in this city—you know, donors to everyone who will give them a plaque or put their name on a building. This family's the real item— old-line WASPs with a nastiness gene. The great-grandfather, Endicott Lewis, not only was in business with Andrew Carnegie but they fished together. It was a toss-up who was the bigger son of a bitch."

"Don't the Lewises own banks?"

"It was textile mills first, then banks. You've got a top-drawer arsonist, Annie."

Henry did a microfilm search at *The Globe* and turned up one article that specifically mentioned Colin Lewis. He had been implicated in a suspicious fire at the Hillel Society of Boston University. At Boston police headquarters, Henry called in a chit from a records department desk sergeant, who produced a file on the Hillel Society arson. The file had been stamped closed on orders from the Boston DA's office.

"I told you they're a powerful family," Henry said when he called back. "I don't know if Elliot Lewis is someone you want to tangle with, but I can give you one thing you might be able to use—the old man is phobic about bad press. He doesn't like any press, for that matter. But wouldn't it be sweet? Can you see him with his linen napkin in his lap, opening his morning paper? 'Lewis Family Legacy—Boston Blueblood Implicated in Anti-Semitic Arson.'"

"Slow down, Henry. I don't know if we're quite ready for that. But, look, thanks for the help."

"Glad to be of service. By the way, have you seen what this guy looks like? I made myself a present of his booking photo."

"No kidding?"

"I'll fax it to you."

The photograph fed out from my fax machine within minutes, first a polo shirt, then a narrow neck, raised chin, unshaven cheeks, aquiline nose, sunken eyes. Colin Lewis had posed for his booking photo with a sneer that said he considered himself untouchable. Money was no object. Lawyers were on call. Privilege would protect him. It always had, it always would.

On the morning of August 28, standing back-to-back in the kitchen as we took care of the kids' breakfasts and exchanged the necessary information about the day's schedule, Josh reminded me that my September 1 deadline was four days away. I said I was aware of that, and reminded him that I had to drive up to Wethersfield later that day to meet with the Connecticut commissioner of corrections. It was possible that I would have to spend the night in a nearby motel and come back the following morning.

The heat and humidity were oppressive by midmorning when I picked up our station wagon and drove downtown to Tribeca to pack my video equipment. In my office I ran the camera through its checks and put in a new cassette. I took a freshly charged battery as well as a backup battery and packed the leather strap that attached to the camera so I could hang it off my shoulder while walking. I could have taken a much lighter still camera, but with the video camera I could shoot continuously until I was sure I had a frame that could be singled out and made into a photograph. That was my goal—a single, printable photograph. Josh knew the power of photographs. When he learned what I had chosen to do, he would understand. Two and a half hours later, I passed the Wethersfield exit and continued north. At Hartford I turned onto Route 84, northwest to Brookford.

James Lake was on the northeastern border of Brookford, within the town limits but more than five miles from the village center. The families who came there from Boston could go directly to their lake homes without ever passing through town. They preferred privacy, their own secure enclave. Most of the families who owned this private lake had held their sections of shoreline for two and three generations. If a family fell on hard times and needed to raise cash, its property was quietly bid out among the other lake families. Outsiders were severely discouraged from trying to settle, but the residents allowed the townsfolk to enjoy the nature footpath around the lake.

I had walked this path in all seasons. My favorite time was the fall, when the reflection of the changing leaves made a shimmering orange-and-red carpet. Hannah and Eli liked to walk the path in summer, when the blueberry bushes that dipped from the banks into the water were full of fruit. In winter, when the Boston families were long gone, the four of us

would troop out onto the middle of the lake to listen to the seismic crack-
ing of the thick black ice.

It was getting on into the afternoon by the time I set out on the path
wearing the shorts, T-shirt, and hiking Tevas I had packed and changed
into at a rest stop on Route 91. I wanted to appear to be an ordinary
August hiker as I alternately gazed out at the lake as a walker would and
then peered into the woods to consider each house I passed.

I felt certain I would know the Lewis cabin when I saw it, and I had
not wanted to arouse curiosity by asking anyone in town where it was.
Once I found the place, I would return to my car and drive back on the
road that circled the lake, parking as close as I could before proceeding on
foot through the woods with my video camera strapped across my shoulder. It would be nearing dusk by the time I returned. I would find a safe
spot to watch and wait for Colin Lewis to appear in his Nazi helmet with
his rifle in his hands. If I was lucky he would be doing the goose step the
way Jack McCall had described. Then I would use my own weapon, my
video camera, to capture a photograph of the armed anti-Semite.

I walked steadily for half an hour. Each time the path emerged into a
clearing in front of a house or cabin, I paused to decide if it was the place
I was looking for. Most of the houses had beach towels draped over porch
railings, canoes tipped on their sides, hammocks tied between pines. And
there were the smells of summer, barbecues being fired up, corn boiling. It
was a lazy afternoon, but I was feeling anything but lazy. I was charged up.
At last I was taking action. I would not be stumped or stopped by a priv-
ileged brat whose father had intimidated the FBI. I would get my house
back.

On the shaded end of the lake, when I came out of a thicket of undergrowth, my attention was caught by a single shaft of sunlight hitting a
patch of open ground. I saw that a stand of trees had been topped to allow
light through. Then I followed the sunlight down from the trees to a garden enclosed by a rail fence.

This late in August even the most devoted Brookford gardeners were
letting their flowers have their head and forgiving the encroaching weeds.
Not so in this sunlit garden, alive with asters, monkshoods, hollyhocks in
full bloom, all carefully weeded and dressed with freshly turned soil. I
fought against my impulse to appreciate the beauty of this garden, the

dedication of its gardener. I forced myself instead to recall Jay Prager's stricken eyes as he recounted the epithets that Colin Lewis spat at him.

The wooden cabin was a dingy contrast to the flowers, a graceless hovel. The back porch was stacked with old newspapers that spilled down the broken stairs. Shopping bags overflowed with beer bottles, and an old mattress leaned against one wall. Green paint peeled from the porch posts. Clapboards were broken off, revealing the tar paper underneath. The window shutters hung askew, and the torn window shades were drawn tight. This cabin did not belong on James Lake. I felt the chill of it. There was no summer here.

I stayed behind the protective cover of the brush, gnats buzzing around my head. The ripe earth, the fume of mushrooms, the sweet pine, the dank composting leaves, filled my nostrils. Close by, the wake of a passing canoe lapped against the lakeshore and slapped the underbellies of fallen logs. Voices of children came across the water like bells.

There was no sign of life around the cabin, not a sound. Only the half-opened screen door and the pickup truck parked close to the porch suggested that Colin Lewis was there. Was he sleeping away the afternoon? Or was he awake, scissors in hand, cutting out photographs of Jews for target practice? I considered the beautiful flowers in the garden and remembered that the Nazis who ran the concentration camps had organized Jewish orchestras to perform Mozart for them. Sensitivity to beauty did not rule out evil.

The porch door opened inward. I froze. Nobody emerged. Was he standing inside? Had he seen me?

I stepped back, my heart slamming in my chest. I wanted to run, but I wanted to see him.

He appeared, stood a moment, then eased himself down the broken stairs, a shadowy night animal slowed by the brightness of the day. He wore a sleeveless T-shirt, khaki pants, army boots. He was slim and unshaven, and as he stepped into the light, I saw the vulnerable quality that had enticed Jay Prager to befriend him, Melinda Marks to want him, that could easily have intrigued me in another set of clothes and circumstances. His appeal set alarms off in my heart, and as he turned into the woods behind his garden, the hundred feet between us suddenly felt like no distance at all.

I wheeled and tore back in the direction I had come. I jumped fallen logs, pounding ahead to put distance between us. When I dove into the front seat of my car and locked the doors, I was breathing hard. I folded my arms over the steering wheel and dropped my head against them, smelling my own fear. I could go on with my plan, or I could retreat. Only I would know that I had failed.

I turned the key in the ignition and backed out onto the road. I drove into town, circled the town green, drove slowly past the post office, where Melinda Marks would be sorting mail, followed the road out toward our house. I drove along under the arc of maples in their fullness, succumbing to a memory, a longing, an ache for the sweetness of summer. Slowly I passed my home but could not bear to stop.

On the other side of town I filled the tank at the gas station and dialed Josh's work number from the public telephone. I was going to tell him I'd be back in time for supper, that I wasn't staying overnight in Wethersfield after all. But the sound of his voice on the answering machine reminded me: I did not want to give up. I wanted our home back.

"Things are going slowly, but I'm getting somewhere. It looks like I'll have do more convincing in the morning. Kiss the kids and please don't let them stay up too late. I love you, Josh. I really do."

On the James Lake Road I found a turnout to park my car. I checked the camera battery again, then hoisted the camera across my back. I set out, stepping over the dry culvert and into the woods.

A century ago these woods had all been cleared for farmland. Lengths of stone wall remained as vestigial markers of where one field had been separated from the next. The few grand old maples amid the new pines had shaded the simple farmhouses. I cut around the trees and low brush, and the damp coolness began to calm me. My determination had been rekindled. After about twenty minutes of hiking, I made out the blue horizon of James Lake and spotted the dark outline of Colin Lewis's cabin.

I decided to give myself a moment to rest and prepare my mind, choosing an ancient maple up ahead, pushing toward it, anticipating the relief of leaning back against its trunk. I slid my back down the rough bark, put my camera carefully on the dry pine needles beside me, hugged my knees to my chest, closed my eyes.

As I drifted, I coached myself for the job ahead. I had directed a hun-

dred camera shoots. I knew how to stay focused and calm. I would carefully choose a secure spot from which to watch and wait with my camera.
It might take hours, but eventually, with patience, I would get my shot.
Then it would be a simple proposition to have a photograph delivered to
Elliot Lewis. An anonymous note attached? A warning of the bad publicity
to come? I had not yet worked through all the details, but I did know that
if Elliot Lewis didn't do something about his son when he saw my photograph of him wearing his Nazi helmet, doing the goose step with a rifle on
his shoulder, I would ask Henry Draycott to write the story. If Henry
Draycott was stonewalled by an editor with ties to the Lewis family, I would
take the picture to one of the alternative newspapers in Boston. Some
irreverent journalist would salivate at the prospect of skewering Elliot
Lewis. The story would eventually get to Brookford residents who read the
Boston papers. When they learned about the vicious and dangerous man
who lived among them, they would find a way to send him packing. My
scheme was reasonable. It could be done. I leaned my head against the tree
and allowed myself to doze. Soon I would be ready to go on.

The touch on my shoulder sent me flying to the forest floor. I scrambled away, clawing the dirt to escape the man grabbing me. When I tried
to scream, a powerful hand pressed over my mouth, fingers pushing
against my bared teeth. I opened my mouth and bit down hard. The man
yelped and then released me. I bolted to a safe distance and then looked
back over my shoulder to see how much damage I had inflicted.

"What are you doing here?" I hissed, incredulous.

Jack McCall shook his hand in the air to relieve the pain.

There was a sharp tapping nearby. We both snapped our heads
toward the sound.

"A woodpecker," Jack McCall said.

"A woodpecker," I repeated.

I looked around for my video camera, which had toppled off into a
tangle of tree roots. I reached for it and pulled it into my lap.

"What's that for?" he demanded.

I hugged the camera closer. "To take pictures of him."

He stared at me, hamstrung between fury and compassion. I knew I
could crawl toward him, reach across the distance between us, pick the
pine needles from his hair, run fingers along the tense furrow above his

eyebrows, apologize. I imagined this, saw him imagine his version of it, saw him withdraw from the possibility of what could happen between us.

"How did you know where I was?"

"Lefert saw you drive into town this afternoon. I drove up here with my siren going all the way. I had a hunch what you'd be up to." He got to his feet. "Annie, I don't know what you're trying to do. This is not a game."

That was too much for me.

*"How dare you! How dare you say I think this is a game? It was my house that burned! It's my family that was in danger! You're not Jewish. You don't have a clue. You have a goddamned nerve telling me I think this is a game!"*

My shouting echoed across the lake. Jack whipped around toward the Lewis cabin, on guard. He grabbed my camera, dug his fingers into my forearm, yanked me up and away from the lake and back through the woods, running hard and forcing me to keep up.

His sedan was parked in a small, open field well off the road. We did not exchange a word as he put my video camera on the roof and took out his car keys. I looked down at myself, my shorts, my Tevas, my scratched legs.

"I'm driving you back to where you parked," he said flatly. "Get in the car."

He slid my camera across the backseat. As I climbed into the passenger's side, I had to push aside a pile of books. I picked one up and read the spine. *Hitler's Germany.* I picked up another. *A History of Anti-Semitism.* I waited for an explanation, but Jack ignored me and got behind the wheel.

The tires spun in the dry summer grass as he played the gas and brake pedals, rocking the car forward and back until it gained enough traction to move. He maneuvered the car out of its hiding place in the meadow and gunned the engine once he got back on the dirt road.

We rode in tense silence. After a while I asked, "Why the library?"

He seemed to be considering what he wanted to do. He had been too open with me all along, had dropped his professional guard, and it had put us both in danger.

"Getting into the mind of your villain?"

He kept his eyes on the road.

"Jack?"

He still did not look at me.

"I'm sorry."

"Didn't you remember I told you he has guns?"

"I was trying to help."

"Don't try to help anymore."

My car wasn't much farther down the road. I wanted to make the seconds slow, to make the ride last longer. I needed more time.

He braked behind my car but left his motor running.

"What have you learned from your books?"

"Quite a lot," he said tersely.

"Please tell me. I'm interested."

"All right, I'll tell you. I'll tell you because maybe that will convince you that I do have some sympathy and understanding for you as a Jew. I thought I knew a lot about the Nazis, but until I started reading, I had no idea of the extent of their systematic plan to exterminate each and every one of you."

I tucked myself against the passenger door waiting for him to say more, but also not wanting to hear it. The encounter in the woods had changed something between us. He didn't feel obliged to be kind anymore.

"The Germans went after Jews like it was a public works project. They took away the jobs of every Jewish professor, every Jewish museum director, factory manager, doctor—virtually every professional Jew in Germany. They made them train their Aryan replacements, and then they sent these same Jews out to sweep streets and collect garbage. Long before any talk of concentration camps." He turned to me. "I'm sure you already know this."

"Some of it."

"I had no idea of the long history of anti-Semitism in Europe, well before the Nazis."

"We were the wretched moneylenders, the Shylocks."

"I read about that, too. Christians needed Jews to make their commerce work since Christianity made it a sin to lend money. And then Christians accused the Jews of doing the work of the devil. When Hitler came along, he capitalized on centuries of hate. Did you know that before Hitler began the slaughter, there was a world population of eighteen million Jews? When the Nazis killed six million, they destroyed a third of the entire Jewish population on earth."

Should I tell him that a Jew, religious or not, never takes a breath without some awareness of this history?

"Jack, I came to get pictures of Colin Lewis because I thought his parents might finally do something if they were afraid a photograph of their Nazi son might show up in a Boston newspaper. A friend of mine who's a reporter for *The Boston Globe* told me that Colin Lewis's father is phobic about bad press. Without any concrete evidence to convict him, I thought that the only possibility for getting him put away was confronting his parents with the threat of bad publicity. I wanted to help you by doing something you're not allowed to do."

"Can I trust you not to come back here, or should I call Josh?"

"Don't you dare call Josh."

"Annie, what if Colin Lewis had found you before I did?"

"He'd have no idea who I was."

Jack looked at me but did not speak.

"What?" I demanded.

"Of course he knows who you are. He has photographs of your family—you and Josh and the children. He took pictures of you—I don't know how, I don't know when. He uses them the way he uses all the others."

I brought my hands to my mouth and whimpered. He reached across the front seat and drew me to him. I was shaking uncontrollably.

"I shouldn't have told you, Annie," he whispered into my neck.

"No, you shouldn't have told me. You shouldn't have told me." I pulled away from him. "*Fucking Colin Lewis! Fucking FBI! Fucking Melinda Marks! This is about my family, for God's sake. This is about my family!*"

I reached into the backseat for my video camera and threw open the door to leave.

"Will you be able to drive?"

"Of course I can drive!" I slammed out of the car with my camera under my arm. "What are you talking about? Of course I can drive!"

Jack tailed me all the way to the main highway. For six miles I watched him watch me, but I never slowed or let myself imagine what could have happened if I'd stayed. When I turned onto the highway heading south, he pulled over and watched until I was out of sight. Slowly my fury left me, and in its wake came a trembling that did make it hard to drive. The idea of my family's photographs being shot at was unbearable. My chest tightened with the memory of seeing Colin Lewis, his disconcerting vulnerability, his wretched self-assurance. I had assumed the protection of the role I was used to—reporter, documentarian. But I had gone beyond that role. I remembered Rabbi Lowenstein's warning—in the face of evil I might be driven to do things I didn't understand.

South of Hartford I checked into a roadside motel. I could have continued on to New York. I could have made up a story for Josh about my morning appointments being canceled. But, for this one night, I wanted to be alone.

I took a shower in a tin stall with a skimpy spray and lukewarm water. The spareness of it appealed to me, as did the hard bed—a thin mattress supported by a plywood board—and the cheap mirror that gave me back a distorted, flattened reflection. I studied my nude body. A little bit of a tummy had come back in the months since my father's death. I had a tan, and my face had broken out in freckles as it did each summer. My frizzy hair was beaded with water from the shower. My breasts were so small they made the top half of me look like an adolescent girl.

Still nude, I sat on the edge of the bed. No one knew where I was. This ten-by-twenty-foot room was all the world I needed. For this night I was not a daughter to a father, or a wife to a husband, or a mother to a child. I was a pebble on a beach, a small, gray one, easily passed by. My thighs, my knees, my knobby ankles, stretched out in front of me. I was a forty-year-old woman with a past behind me, a future in front, and here, alone, I would think.

I crawled under the thin covers and relished the feel of the cool sheets against my bare flesh. I was pleased to be alone, to feel the limits and presence of my self. It had been ten months since the morning I received the phone call about our fire; the fire and all that followed—my father's diagnosis of cancer, his telling me he was ready to die, his confession about his own fire—all this had stopped me like some unseen, massive underwater rock, my hull torn asunder, ship's siren suddenly going off, no time to stop and consider, only the urgent necessity to act, make things safe, make my ship seaworthy. This had been my fortieth year, as it had been my father's seventieth. What had I learned? What had I seen by the light of our two fires? Certainly I had witnessed the potency of denial. My father had not wanted to admit or acknowledge his part in evil, and so the denial of it had drained his life away. Maybe that had carried over to me; my own denial had allowed me to spend too many months ignoring a very real threat to my family. I thought back over all the Saturday afternoons in late spring when we had visited our house to check on the construction progress. Eli and Hannah had played happily on the lawn out back. They had taken turns pushing each other on the swing that hung from the shagbark hickory. They had collected pinecones at the edge of the woods. What if during all the time they were playing, Colin Lewis had them in his rifle sights? How could I have stood by and allowed my children to be in mortal danger? Why had I been unwilling to know? This was the question that demanded an answer as I lay there alone. Was I living out the legacy my father had put in place—dealing with the existence of evil by denying it? And was I compelled to find the truth now in order to break that cycle, to free us both from the legacy of his fire?

In the hours before dawn I slid in and out of a fitful sleep as my mind worked to thread together the things it knew. At last, waking into clarity, Jack McCall's reading project came back to me, his description of the Nazis' coolheaded, systematic plan to rid Germany of Jews—a public works project, as Jack described it. That's what gave me the clue. I had understood from the start that Colin Lewis was intelligent, deliberate, calculated. Of course he would have a plan. Now I was sure I knew what it was.

I drove through the dark morning and arrived in New York City before the sun was up. I continued down the West Side Highway past the Ninety-sixth Street turnoff, straight on to my office in Tribeca. I hadn't studied my arson investigation file since handing the information over to Jack in May. Now I spread it open on my desk, took a deep breath, and read through the Xerox of the chronology of the Third Reich. I considered every single date from the birth of Adolf Hitler in Braunau on April 20, 1889, to October 16, 1946, the execution of Nazi war criminals at Nuremberg. As the sun came up, I dialed Jack's beeper and waited for his call. I imagined him sleeping in his bed, the beeper on his night table, his wife by his side. I wondered what she was like, and I was glad that I had not made a mistake I would have had to regret.

Standing by my office window I watched the morning light transform the opaque gray Hudson to a gleaming silver. I felt newly peaceful, uncharacteristically patient. It was only a matter of time. Life would become normal again. I would have my home back.

When the phone rang, I let my hand rest on the receiver a moment before picking it up.

"Are you all right?"

"I'm fine," I said. "I'm sorry to bother you so early."

"I'm glad you called. I'm glad to know you got home safe."

"I know how to get him, Jack. I know what to do."

"Annie—"

"Please, Jack. It was your reading that gave me the idea. Colin Lewis has his own public works project—like the Nazis. Think about it. Except for the fire on Hitler's birthday, every one of the dates he chose for a fire coincides with a specific step taken by Hitler to rid Germany of Jews. Colin Lewis is conducting his own campaign—cleansing the northeast corner of Connecticut, house by house, store by store. He's using the Nazi dates as his schedule."

Jack was quiet as he considered this.

"I went over the chronology again this morning, that list I copied from the library. September first, 1941, comes up next. That's the day Hitler decreed that all Jews had to wear the yellow star. It fits right in. The yellow stars identified Jews to be rounded up. Talk to Jews who survived Hitler and they'll tell you that the day of the yellow stars was one of the worst days in their lives. It was the day they understood Hitler had targeted every one of them. September first, Jack. That's in three days."

"It makes a lot of sense."

"I think so, Jack. I really think so."

"We'll watch him around the clock."

"Thank you."

"For what?"

"For listening to me. After all I've put you through. I'm sorry about yesterday."

"It's a good thing Lefert spotted you."

"Yes."

We were both silent. I wasn't ready to hang up, and it seemed he wasn't either.

"Where are you calling from?" I asked. "It's so quiet on your end."

"I'm out in my garage."

"At home?"

"I was in bed when I got your call."

"But why the garage?"

"I wanted to be alone."

For the next three days I couldn't concentrate on anything. I didn't hear from Jack about the plans he was making, but I didn't expect to. And I didn't talk to Josh about any of this, either. I wondered if I would ever tell him about what had happened at James Lake.

On August 31, I sat by myself in the living room and read late into the night, and even when I finally climbed into bed next to Josh, I couldn't calm my mind enough to fall asleep. When the phone rang at four-thirty on the morning of September first, I grabbed the receiver.

"Annie, is that you?"

"Jack, what's happened?"

"We've got him. We're at the barracks. Lefert's booking Lewis right now."

"You've actually arrested him?"

"It was just like you called it. Lefert and I waited at the end of the road to his cabin. About three in the morning, his truck pulls out driving real slow, no headlights. I called for back-up, and we were on him all the way down to Rangely. Finally, he pulls up at a house that belongs to a Jewish family that comes up from Providence on weekends. We got a Polaroid of him pulling a gas can from his truck. He was still blinking from the flash when we put the handcuffs on him. Lefert checked out the cab of his truck—matches, newspapers, and guess what else?"

Josh was awake now. He came around to sit next to me on my side of the bed. I tilted the receiver away from my ear so he could listen, too.

"He had a book buried under all his junk, a book like the one you found at the library, a Nazi history with a chronology of dates. He had drawn a line through the date of every fire we know about. It was exactly as you imagined, Annie. This is the piece of circumstantial evidence that will convict him without a doubt."

"I can't believe it."

"Believe it, Annie. Believe it, my love. You can go back there now. You have your house back. You made it safe for your family."

"Thank you, Jack. Thank you so much."

Josh took the receiver from my hand and hung it up. He put his arms around me and we held on to each other for a long time. Josh did not comment on Jack's indiscretion, though I knew he had heard it. I wasn't the only one who had drawn away from our marriage in the last months. Josh and I had work to do, trust to rebuild, love to repair.

"It's September first," I whispered. "I made the deadline."

"Indeed you did," Josh whispered back. "Indeed you did."

Five

# 19

Eli and I handed the new boards up to Josh and Hannah, who fit them together along the floor of the tree house. It had been Josh's idea to give the tree house a face-lift, a project for the two weeks we were spending in Brookford before the start of school. Perhaps he remembered how the floor shook when he climbed onto it the night of our fight, or perhaps it was his way of apologizing for having taken the position that we should give up and leave Brookford, or maybe it was simply his intuition that we needed to do something very concrete, working together as a family.

Hannah, Eli, Josh, and I spent many days at it, talking through and drawing up our plans, going to the lumberyard to select the wood we wanted, the hardware store for nails and hinges, tag sales for rugs, a rocking chair, a table. When we were finished, we were sure it was the best tree house in Brookford. Josh set up his camera on a tripod and used the self-timer to take a photograph of the four of us in the "living room" of our new tree house, a photograph I will always treasure. Hannah and Eli are tucked between Josh and me, and Hannah has her arm up over her head so that her hand can reach around my neck. She has me back, she has me—and she wants the camera to record it.

On the day before we were to return to the city, I was hurrying to get the last bulbs dug into the flower beds when I spotted Melinda Marks driving up the road. On Saturday afternoons, after the post office closed, Melinda sometimes made the Brookford rural deliveries herself, steering her beat-up Subaru from the middle of the front seat so she could lean over to open the mailboxes. I watched her car out of the corner of my eye. She had been the lover of the man who had torched our house. Even though she had helped the FBI, I did not want to face her.

I continued stabbing my trowel into the damp soil. The sight of Melinda Marks had rekindled the fear that could still well up in me, unheralded and unstoppable, at any time of day or night. The worst of it was the awful image of photographs of my family tacked to trees. How long before I would feel safe in my own house? How long before the night was just the night, noises only benign reminders of the splendid natural world?

Colin Lewis's parents were trying to negotiate psychiatric treatment for their son so a public trial wouldn't unleash further bad publicity for the Lewis family. Meanwhile Colin was out on bail, theoretically restricted to the Boston area by order of the court. Jack McCall had organized an FBI detail to keep track of his movements, so that if he did make a move out of Boston, he would be picked up immediately. Jack promised me that whatever happened to Colin Lewis, wherever he eventually ended up, they would watch him. He advised us for the time being to change to unlisted telephone numbers both in New York and Connecticut, and warned that no matter how securely Colin Lewis was locked up, whether it was in a jail or a mental hospital, it would be some time before we would recover from the fear.

I knew Melinda Marks could put the mail into the box without coming to a full stop, but when she arrived at our mailbox, she did not drive on. She had seen me, and she knew that I had seen her. If I wanted to feel comfortable in Brookford, I was going to have to face her.

Melinda had her elbow on the opened passenger window and continued to stare ahead through the windshield when I came up to her car. I looked down at my muddy blue jeans and dirt-caked hands, aware of the differences between us. A single mother raising two kids on postmistress pay would not waste her money on daffodils.

"So, we've moved back in."

She nodded but kept her eyes trained on some invisible thing up the road. She dragged her hand back over her newly sheared hair. Then she reached for the cigarette pack on the dash, lit one, and took a deep drag.

"I hope you're planning to keep this to yourself. It's a small town. I've got two kids to raise."

"What is it that I'm supposed to keep to myself?" I asked coldly. "That you're Jewish?"

She shot me a hard look.

I took pleasure in her discomfort. "I wasn't supposed to know that?"

She stubbed her cigarette in an ashtray already stuffed with half-smoked butts.

"You think I care about that?"

"But you do keep it a secret."

Melinda sighed. "New York City and Brookford are very different places."

"I'll try to keep that in mind," I said and stepped away from the car.

"About Colin Lewis. That's what I'm talking about. No one knows we had a thing. I'd like to keep it that way."

"Of course you would."

"It's not what you imagine, Mrs. Waldmas."

"Oh?"

"He was nice at first—handsome and smart and from a good family with buckets of money. Sure, he was a little odd, a little lost. I guess I figured I could fix that. The winters get real long up here."

She was looking up at me, asking for my understanding. She gestured to the seat beside her. "Can you come in and sit a moment?"

I went around to the passenger door as she lifted her carton of mail into the backseat.

"When did you know?"

"Know what?"

"That he was the one who set my house on fire?"

"About a month before I sent you the first letter."

"Wait a minute. *You* sent those letters?"

"He got drunk one night—drunker than usual—started bragging about the fires, saying awful things about Jews—he's the real thing, a Nazi, he really hates us. He scared the hell out of me. I tried to stay away after that, but I was afraid he'd turn on me, he may even find out I was Jewish. So I forced myself to focus on his flowers and slowly tried to break it off. Then I figured out the idea of sending you the letters."

She stared ahead as she spoke, and I considered her delicate profile, her sheared head, the tiny silver studs that pierced the edge of her ear.

"Why didn't you go to the police and tell them what was going on and get them to protect you?"

She turned abruptly. "Do you know who that family is? Do you really believe I could have gone to the police and woken up the next morning still employed? A post office job has benefits, a government pension. This is the most security I ever had in my life. Do you have any idea what it's like to have two boys to raise on your own and nothing to fall back on? I don't have a dime in a savings account. I don't have parents to bail me out. It's just me and me," she said, pushing her thumb to her chest.

"So you wrote anonymous letters instead?"

She smiled with a hint of pride. "I knew you did TV shows. I figured you could pull the right strings and get somebody from the outside to come in here. Bob Lefert's sweet, but no local cop can go up against this kind of thing on his own."

"But when I came in to ask about the letters, why didn't you say something to me?"

Melinda pulled herself up. "I barely knew you, Mrs. Waldmas. I had no idea if you'd understand the problems of a single mother who can't afford to lose her job." She paused a moment, then plunged ahead. "Besides, it took three letters to get your attention. Frankly, I wasn't even sure you *wanted* to know the truth."

It was my turn to stare through the windshield, and hers to consider the revealing aspects of my profile, to study the person who had preferred to be dumb and numb and allow her children to play in the rifle sights of a madman.

"I guess it was too awful to believe."

"Yes."

I turned back to her. "Then how come you agreed to give information to the FBI?"

"I felt terrible that I had waited so long to tell anybody. When they asked my help, I was glad I could do something."

"What if he had found out you're Jewish?"

"I didn't think he'd hurt me, but I did worry that something could happen by accident, all his marching around with that stupid rifle, drinking himself into oblivion. Believe me, I thought about your kids. The guy is really sick. He's really crazy."

"My God, I had you all wrong. I owe you an apology."

"I'm the one who needs to apologize—for not just telling you."

"But you helped the FBI. That took incredible courage."

She shrugged. "My courage. Your brains. I guess we made a pretty good team."

"What can I do to thank you?"

"All I need is that we keep this to ourselves. I like it here in Brookford. My boys watched their father overdose on heroin. I want them to have a different kind of life."

I reached across the front seat to put my arms around Melinda. She let me hug her, and she hugged me back.

The low angle of the afternoon sun sheeted the car's rear window with radiant light as Melinda Marks drove on to finish her Saturday mail run. A battalion of Canada geese passed overhead in a cacophony of flapping and honking. I looked up. I liked these birds, their noise, their awkwardness, their dogged perseverance. Melinda's car grew small before it crested the hill and dropped out of sight. I went back to finish planting my daffodils. As I turned the dark soil and threaded it through my fingers to remove the rocks and roots, I thought how very much I had yet to learn about people and the human spirit.

On Monday before I went to work, I stopped by the synagogue to tell Rabbi Lowenstein about the successful outcome of the arson investigation. His secretary didn't try to talk me out of seeing him, since she recognized me, but she warned me he was busy and could only spare a minute. She knocked on his door and opened it a crack to tell him I was there to see him. He nodded, accepting my presence, bent over his books, a world away.

"That's good news," he said, after I had given him a brief rendition of the story. It was clear he was preoccupied.

"I guess you're busy."

"It's the season," he explained.

It was the middle of the High Holidays, the ten-day period that stretches from Rosh Hashanah, the Jewish New Year, to Yom Kippur, the Day of Atonement, the most important period of the Jewish calendar. Josh and I had never observed the High Holidays, but now that I had been attending services on a regular basis to say kaddish, for the first time in my life it seemed odd to let this time pass without acknowledgment.

"I guess I'm not such a good Jew," I apologized.

"You've still got a chance at Yom Kippur, if you like."

"Atonement?" I made a face.

"This Wednesday. All day, if you're going to do it right."

That night I told Josh I was considering attending Yom Kippur services.

"Don't let me stop you."

"No chance of your coming with me?"

"Annie, I know this religious thing is becoming important to you, but you have to understand, it's not me."

"It's odd the way it stays with me from one week's service to the next, the melodies of the prayers, the beauty of the place."

"Are you planning to light a memorial candle for your father before Yom Kippur?"

"Am I supposed to do that?"

"That's what Jews do."

The next afternoon I found a store on Broadway that sold Jewish religious items. The man behind the cash register didn't look up at my arrival, so I spoke to the yarmulke on his bent head.

"I need a candle."

"So?"

"Do you sell candles?"

"Does a Judaica store sell candles?" He raised his head only slightly. He had dealt with my kind before.

"I need a memorial candle for my father, who died this year."

He flapped his hand at me as he emerged from behind his cash register. "Come, come."

The narrow aisle was crammed with boxes full of the various items required for religious observance—prayer shawls, yarmulkes, mezuzahs, menorahs. The memorial candles were stored in the cardboard box they'd been shipped in. He touched his pink finger to the edge of one box and lifted his chin. I considered my choices. Some of the candles were in amber or blue glass jars, others were set in tin. All had Hebrew lettering on the sides. I did not dare ask what any of it meant or why I should choose one over another. I picked a candle in amber glass, and he led me back to the front of the store.

At the cash register, perhaps taking pity on me, the shopkeeper launched into a lecture on the rules for lighting a memorial candle on the eve of Yom Kippur. He pointed his finger at me. "Proscriptions, rules—*kav-vanah*—the holy contract with God! Strike the match eighteen minutes before sunset, no more, no less! Cover your eyes when you say the prayer. A must! Then do not touch! You women are always touching! Leave the poor candle be, for the sake of your departed father. *Sit, pray, do not touch!*"

I carried my purchase away in its humble brown bag, feeling equally humbled. At home I set the candle on the living room mantel and stared at it awhile. How could it be that so many months after my father's death, at the very thought of him, my temples ached with the tears still to shed?

When Hannah and Eli came home from school, I showed them the candle and explained that this was the beginning of a Jewish holiday called Yom Kippur, and that I would light the candle before sunset, in memory of Grandpa Abe.

"Yawn kipper?" Eli scrunched his face.

I tweaked his cheek. "Yom Kippur is the day we're supposed to look at ourselves and decide what we could have done better in the past year. It's the day we ask God to help us become better people."

Eli leaned against me. "I miss Grandpa."

Each Friday and on Jewish holidays, an Orthodox religious group placed a tiny ad at the bottom of the front page of the *Times*, announcing the precise time for lighting candles that day. I checked the ad, watched the clock, and lit my candle. I covered my eyes and made up my own prayer. I prayed to miss my father less someday. And then I decided instead to pray never to miss him less, never to lose his memory.

The next morning I put on a dress and set out alone. The sidewalks along West End Avenue were full of people on their way to the dozen different synagogues in the neighborhood. Hasidic men in long black coats, side curls, and black fedoras walked ahead of their wives and children. Young families on their way to the liberal Reconstructionist synagogue carried the dolls and books that would keep their children busy through the family-friendly service. Twenty-something couples in matching business suits walked along, part of the Yuppie return to religion. The Upper West

Side had the largest collection of Jews outside Israel, Jews of every stripe, and this morning I actually felt a part of it. When I turned into Ninety-fourth Street, people were coming from both avenues toward Rabbi Lowenstein's small synagogue, where the wooden doors stood open.

The sanctuary held many more people than usually came for the weekly services, so I had to climb to the balcony to find a seat. I took the prayer book from its holder, a special *siddur* for Rosh Hashanah and Yom Kippur, which was different from the one I had grown used to in my five months of saying kaddish. In those months I had followed the transliterations of the Hebrew prayers until now I could sing along comfortably. And I had begun to understand the structure of the service as it unfolded through a series of blessings, repetitions of certain prayers, times of silence, the reading aloud from the Torah. I looked forward to Rabbi Lowenstein's discussions of the week's Torah selection. He drew on references from Shakespeare to Freud as he led us through a study of the complexities of human nature, and the idea of a compassionate but demanding God. Mostly I looked forward to the peacefulness that I discovered there, a deepened sense of all things, the certainty that there was meaning beyond what I could know, touch, explain. All this did not lend itself to language and analysis—my usual tools—but rather to what Rabbi Lowenstein had first offered—to a special kind of listening.

With a single powerful chord the organist called to attention all those still settling in their pews. A few more chords and Rabbi Lowenstein appeared from a side door, spectacularly dressed for this service in a long white robe that covered him to his shoes. He lifted his yarmulke and recapped his head, his habitual gesture. Then he stepped up to the bimah, opened the prayer book, and with the cantor, a young woman, at his side, began the opening prayer.

The two of them sang out urgently, their voices matching, note for note, passionate and unrestrained, leaving no doubt that this was to be a different kind of day. They did not look out at the congregation but kept their eyes tightly shut. Rabbi Lowenstein made his hands into fists and punched the air, punctuating the prayer, demanding involvement. Yom Kippur did not allow bystanders. This day would have its way with you, whoever you were, whatever you believed, however hardened your heart had become in the intervening twelve months.

As the Yom Kippur service unfolded, the prayers reserved for this day were returned to again and again, each recitation taking on deeper meaning. Like a driving wind, we came back to the *Vidui*, a haunting recitation of our collective confession of sins. We called out an alphabetical list from A, "We abuse," to Z, "We are zealots for bad causes." I did not think of myself as a sinner, but repeating the list a second, third, fourth time, I understood a different meaning of sin. "We betray, we are cruel, we destroy, we embitter, we falsify, we gossip, we hate, we insult . . ." The list was altogether human. I had failed in all these ways.

As the melody of the Vidui became familiar, I filled my lungs with it. I was newly aware of my companions in the pew. J, K, L, M . . . "We jeer, we kill, we lie. We mock, we neglect, we oppress. We pervert, we quarrel, we rebel. We steal, we transgress, we are unkind . . ." When we came back to the Vidui prayer for the fourth and fifth time in the day, I no longer heard my own voice apart. I had joined the river of voices, a river of sound, a collective hope, our common history, an ache for forgiveness. "We are violent, we are wicked, we are xenophobic. We yield to evil . . ."

Rabbi Lowenstein spoke to us. "Shame is the heaviest of the burdens that we carry. It weighs us down like bricks. The soul can't breathe with the burden of it. Examine, repent, renew. The gate is open to you today, this day of days. Tomorrow it may be closed. Tomorrow may never come. You have this moment, God's gift to you. Remember yourself. This is the act of *teshuvah*. This is the work of turning." I thought of the morning Rabbi Lowenstein sent me off to Los Angeles with my lesson in *teshuvah*. It was true, as Rabbi Lowenstein said. I had seen shame weigh down my father to his death.

Rabbi Lowenstein announced that we would take a break from the service for two hours. He invited congregants to stay in the sanctuary if they liked, to sit in the quiet and rest. I decided to go outside, imagining I would take a peaceful walk along the Hudson River, but the sharp light of the day, and the noise and activity on the street, were too disturbing. It was as if the long hours of prayer had removed layers of my skin. I hurried back inside to wait for the service to resume. As I waited, I dozed, and in a half-sleep, revisited the year I'd been through.

When the sanctuary filled again and Rabbi Lowenstein returned, he announced *Yizkor*, the time set aside for prayers in memory of the dead.

"If this is a day of atonement, why do we pray for the dead? Hasn't their chance for atonement passed?" He opened his arms to the congregation, an invitation. "Your ancestors have not lost their chance because they have you. Through you they come into this day. You have the opportunity to repent and renew on their behalf. You can do this through your work and your prayers. They loved you. Through you they can be forgiven."

I do not know which blocked ventricle of my heart was opened by those words—all of a sudden I was sobbing. My neighbor in the pew, a young woman to whom I had not spoken in all the hours we sat side by side, offered me her shoulder. At last, when my sobbing stopped, I recalled the moment when my father and I finally managed our much-postponed good-bye. I was about to fly back to New York for Hannah's birthday. It seemed the right moment to confess to him that I felt guilty that I would go on living while he would die. Frail and greatly weakened, he had pulled himself up in bed and spoken to me with more tenderness than ever before in my life.

"But this is as it should be," he told me. "This is in the nature of things. I am Abraham David Fishman. My father was Fishman before me. You are Anne Fishman Waldmas. Your children are Eli and Hannah Waldmas. They will have their children. Eli and Hannah will go on without you someday as you must go on without me. This is what we're here for. Your job is to be Anne Fishman Waldmas. It's as simple as that. I am ready to die now, and you are ready to go on living. We each have our part along the way."

The afternoon waned, and the light coming through the stained-glass windows slowly deepened from amber to rust. We sang the *Neilah* prayers into the half-light of dusk, and even when that light was gone, no one moved to turn on lamps in the sanctuary. It was a sad time. The precious day was nearly over.

Then, suddenly, Rabbi Lowenstein lifted his arms and announced, "Open the doors for the children."

A procession of children started down the center aisle, each child holding a lit candle. The organ played "Hatikvah," the Israeli national anthem, and as the congregation rose to its feet and sang, the children advanced toward the bimah and gathered around Rabbi Lowenstein. The yellow flames of their candles danced in the dark. I had no idea who these children were, where they had come from, or how they had been organized for this extraordinary moment. What I did know was that next year I wanted Hannah and Eli to be among them.

# 20

The fall and winter passed, and we settled back into the normal routine of our family life. I continued to go to synagogue for my weekly recitation of kaddish, though I went on Friday nights instead of Saturdays so we could spend our weekends in Brookford. I went even though I had begun to find saying kaddish tedious, words I could now recite in my sleep, standing there with my thoughts elsewhere. Sometimes new people got up to say the mourner's prayer, while others who had been standing up with me as long as I could recall no longer rose, his or her eleven months of reciting kaddish finally over. My time would soon be up, too, and I wondered if I would make it all the way. I prided myself on a certain level of self-awareness, but I managed to miss the fact that the boredom I now fought was a vain effort to anesthetize myself to the pain right up ahead.

Close on the heels of the tedium, a yoke of depression fell over my life. Moving through the day took more energy, and things that should have been pleasurable felt meaningless. I took longer to get out of bed. I sat longer with my coffee before dressing. I wanted no forward movement, no expectations. When I finally began to feel the pain itself, I reverted to old habits to try to avoid it, attacking goals and requiring my family to attack with me. Josh did not take my regression well. The memory of our months of estrangement was still too raw. He retreated from me, going to work early and staying late, but I was after him the minute he came through the door, presenting lists and complaining about the household chores he had not done. Hannah and Eli would rush to meet him, latching onto him physically even before he shed his coat, looking for an ally in the face of my unrelieved foul temper.

Late one Friday night, after yet another recitation of kaddish, I lay in bed, edgy, attempting to read a book that did not hold my interest. Josh came into the bedroom, unbuttoning his shirt.

"This synagogue thing is starting to feel stale to me."

He sat to untie his shoes. "Maybe you've outgrown it."

"Are you saying it was a crutch?"

I saw Josh sizing me up, evaluating my mood, wanting to avoid being drawn into another meaningless conflict. "Maybe you should go see your rabbi."

I folded my arms. "Would you stop patronizing me, Josh?"

He shook his head. "What's going on with you? You've been acting premenstrual for a month."

"What's going on with *you*?" I growled back.

Without another word Josh went over to his night table, took his book, and left the room. I knew he would read in the living room until he was sure I was asleep. I considered pursuing him to provoke a satisfying argument. The impulse to get up and pick a fight was so strong that I had to grab the pillow from behind my back and grip it hard to keep myself from doing what I knew was wrong.

I put out the light, burrowed under the quilt, and fought for sleep. My mind drifted back to a disconcerting thing that had happened to me that afternoon. I was at my desk trying to figure out how to collateralize a short-term bank loan for part of a film budget, and I reached for the phone to dial my father's number. It was an ordinary reflex—asking his advice had once been a regular feature of my life. Then I remembered he was dead.

I put on my bathrobe and padded through the dark apartment to the living room.

"Josh?" I waited in the doorway for him to acknowledge me. "It's almost a year."

Josh kept his eyes focused on his book, but I knew he wasn't reading.

"It feels like nothing has any meaning."

The couch breathed as Josh got up. He stood for a moment, considering the wisdom of attempting to console me, came a little closer, but stopped at a careful distance.

"Annie, it really might be a good idea for you to go back and talk to your rabbi friend. He was able to help you before."

"I guess I could give it a try."

He came up and put his fingers below my chin to make me look him in the eye.

"Is that a promise?"

I pouted, then nodded glumly.

He sighed. My ambivalence discouraged him. I shrugged, the best I could offer for an apology.

"You'll get through this," he said. "You got through all the rest."

The secretary was out, and Rabbi Lowenstein wasn't in his office when I knocked. I had a hunch where I could find him. Sure enough, the emergency exit door was propped open. I climbed onto the fire escape, into the bright sun, and looked up to see the soles of Rabbi Lowenstein's shoes on the metal grating three stories up as he moved about watering his plants.

"Rabbi Lowenstein!" I called up to him.

He peered down. "Annie! Come up, come up!"

He gave me a hug and I burst into tears. He had a trowel in one hand, and I could smell the tang of fresh potting soil. I started to pull back, but he held me tighter.

"Time for a talk?" He turned over the plastic milk crates so we could sit.

"I was going along fine, and now I feel awful again. I have to force myself through each day. The anniversary of my father's death is coming up."

"You know what I like about you? Some people try to snooze through life. Not you. If there's a lesson to be learned, you're going to get in there and learn it—like your father, right?"

"What's my lesson here?" I picked loose chips of paint off the metal railing.

"Is it a lesson if I tell you?"

"I hate that shit."

"What shit is that?"

"Rabbis and therapists—answering questions with questions." I pointed to the courtyard below, a cemetery of broken appliances. "I risked my life to climb up here to ask for help. Can't I get at least a little bit of an answer?"

He folded his arms and studied me, as usual in no rush for words. "How do you like my little garden up here? The hardy ones will make it. Crocuses, daffodils, tulips. Bulbs have the stuff of new life within them."

I grimaced. "If I don't get a question, I get a metaphor."

"You and your father had a spectacular friendship, Annie, but a year is all you get for mourning. Sorry, those are the rules."

"What rules? Judaism is not going to dictate a timetable for my feelings."

Rabbi Lowenstein put his soil-stained hands on his knees and narrowed his eyes at me. "Let me tell you something, my little rebel. Judaism is the collected wisdom of five thousand years of human experience."

I felt the metal bars of the fire escape press into my spine as I shrank back.

"Got it?"

"Got what?" I asked petulantly.

His hands flew up. "Time to move on. Life is about living. That's your job!"

The following week when Tony called from San Diego, his voice sounded so much like our father's that I had to stop a moment before I could talk with him. Tony lived closest to the cemetery, so he had been taking care of the arrangements for the gravestone. Jewish tradition required that the gravestone be placed and unveiled on the first anniversary of a person's death, and the cemetery people had asked if we wanted to hold the traditional service at the gravesite. Now that I was attending services on a regular basis, I had a reputation in the family as the "Jewish one," and Tony wanted to know what I thought we should do.

I recalled my fire escape session with Rabbi Lowenstein. "Let's get together and do it the way it's supposed to be done."

"What way is that?"

"The unveiling is a ritual to end the year of mourning. We'll get to see each other. We could bring our kids. If I take Hannah and Eli out of school, could you bring your guys, too? It'd be great to get the cousins together. We need to show them that we're still going to be a family, even without Grandpa to drag us together."

"Assuming Sally will let me have them when it's not one of my official days."

"Tell her they need to meet their new cousin. I'm sure Charles and Sissy will bring the baby."

"Then it's a done deal," Tony said.

"That's what Pop would have said—a done deal."

The idea of a family reunion for the unveiling took hold fast. Ellen said she was going to have an announcement for us, but then couldn't hold back. "We got married!"

"When?" I asked, slightly hurt.

"Last week. We got a friend of Ben's, a judge from Denver, and we convinced him to drive up to Bear Lake with us. We stood there by the lake and exchanged our vows. It didn't make sense to wait any longer, and neither of us wanted a big wedding anyway. Maybe because it feels like we've already been married forever."

"Congratulations, then. Pop would have been very happy."

"It was like he was there watching us."

"I know what you mean, Ellen. I know what you mean."

Josh, Hannah, Eli, and I flew cross-country the day before the unveiling, and for a long, lazy afternoon hung out at the pool of our hotel on the beach in Santa Monica. A little of my inheritance was paying for the sort of luxuries I was sure Abe would have approved. I imagined him smiling down at the sight of us relaxing, the sun baking us brown, Josh and I taking turns napping and watching Hannah and Eli flop around on an inflatable giraffe. It had been a long time since we'd spent an afternoon doing absolutely nothing.

The plan was to gather at the cemetery early the next morning and then have a family picnic afterward on the beach in front of our hotel. Tony had the assignment of bringing beach chairs since he was driving up from San Diego and could stash them in his trunk. Ellen volunteered to organize the food. Josh and I picked up wine and juice. Charles and Sissy, traveling three thousand miles with a seven-month-old baby, were exempt from all other duties.

The next morning, when I stepped out onto the balcony of our hotel room, the sky was gray. Josh had the television on inside and called out, "They're saying rain." He came to stand by the open glass door. "Is it supposed to rain in California?"

"I like it gray."

He reached his arm around my waist inside my T-shirt. "My melancholy Annie."

"Today I'm allowed."

"We can move the picnic up here to the room if we have to," Josh suggested.

The reunions happened at a curb stenciled with Pop's cemetery address, Wisteria Court. We arrived in four separate cars, three of them rentals. Whatever uncertainty any of us felt about this gathering was quickly eclipsed by the genuine pleasure of seeing one another. For a few moments the reunion, not the unveiling, was the main event. We examined our new family member, Abraham David Fishman, and met our new in-law, Ben Levy, and Hannah and Eli were quickly in a huddle with their California cousins.

Rabbi Lowenstein had helped me find a local rabbi to do the service for us. Rabbi Sarah Baum pulled up to the curb in a white Jetta. She was barely five feet tall, wore her blonde hair in a pixie cut, and was probably pushing twenty-seven. She was clearly accustomed to making her way through first meetings, and her handshake was confident. "Hope the rain holds off for you."

Rabbi Baum led the way down the cement path to the plot where we had gathered a year ago to bury our father. I was impressed that she had done her homework and knew exactly where to go. Before we reached our destination she stopped and offered yarmulkes from her shoulder bag. She had brought bobby pins to secure the children's yarmulkes, which she distributed to all five of them without regard to gender. Then she took out a prayer book and left her shoulder bag of supplies on a stone bench on the path.

"Before we begin, I'd like to say a few things about what today is all about." She spoke to all of us, but addressed herself especially to the children. "Do any of you know why you waited a whole year before putting a marker on your grandfather's grave?"

The children shook their heads, interested but cautious.

"Any ideas?"

"It's like a birthday," Eli offered.

Rabbi Baum smiled. "Yes, exactly. It's the anniversary of your grandfather's death. Which also means that each one of you is a year older than you were when he died. You've had a year to get used to living without him. That can be pretty hard when you loved someone as much as I know you all loved your grandfather."

I saw the tears start down Ellen's cheeks.

"You're going to say some prayers for your grandfather, and you're going to say some prayers for yourselves as well. You're going to ask God to help you go on with your own lives now."

Rabbi Baum returned to Eli. "You know how it is when you have your first birthday—you don't even know how to walk yet. But pretty soon you start walking on your own, and by your second birthday you're already talking. At the end of the service here today you're going to have to start walking ahead on your own without your grandfather."

Eli was clearly confused. "I know you can walk and talk," she reassured him. "It's only a way of saying how strange it can feel to go on in life when someone you loved isn't here to go on with you. It can feel a little like having to learn to walk all over again." Her gaze moved above the children's heads to the adults. "I'm sure your parents know what I mean." She pointed the way down the path. "Everybody ready?"

In preparation for the unveiling a cloth had been placed over the stone that recorded my father's name and years on earth. With the cloth still in place, Rabbi Baum said prayers of blessing in Hebrew, mentioned Abraham Fishman's children and grandchildren, and then read the traditional graveside prayer from Ecclesiastes, "To everything there is a season, a time for every experience under heaven . . ." As she softly intoned the comforting words of the prayer, I thought again about my father's powerful words of comfort: I was Anne Fishman Waldmas, daughter of Abraham Fishman, who was the son of Minnie and Isaac Fishman of Russia. Standing at my side were my children, Hannah and Eli Waldmas, and someday, God willing, they would have children, and their children would have children, too.

Rabbi Baum knelt to remove the cloth and read aloud: "Abraham David Fishman, Beloved Father and Grandfather, 1918 to 1988. He lived every moment until he died."

I knew that walking away would be the hard part. As we lingered by the grave, our silence was full of a thousand unspoken things. Slowly we moved back up the cement path. We walked in our family groups, Josh and I with Hannah and Eli, Charles and Sissy with baby Abe, Tony with his three children, and Ellen and Ben. We walked separately as siblings, and yet we were together as never before.

By the time our caravan drove into the beach parking lot in Santa Monica, the cloud cover, both in the sky and in our hearts, had passed. The kids tumbled out of the cars and tore straight for the water, pulling off their shoes and socks as they ran. Ellen and Ben picked a spot on the sand and laid out a banquet of everyone's favorite foods—sesame noodles for Charles, cold duck with plum sauce for Tony, fresh mozzarella with tomato and basil for me.

The sun dropped slowly toward the ocean as we lay about on blankets, ate, drank wine, played Frisbee, took walks up and down the beach. Charles and Sissy had brought a small beach tent for the baby, and throughout the warm afternoon one or another of the children crawled inside to nap alongside the new cousin. Tony, Charles, Ellen, and I compared notes about the past year, the difficulties we had each encountered in getting over our father's death, the return to our own lives. Josh, Sissy, and Ben listened, understanding that for this afternoon the four of us needed to be siblings more than spouses.

At last Tony stood up and brushed sand from his pants. "My kids have school tomorrow, and Sally was adamant that I get them back in time for dinner."

"We've got to get going, too," Ben said. Ben and Ellen had a six o'clock flight to Denver and then the long drive up to Boulder.

As we went to work cleaning up our section of the beach, Ellen remarked, "I guess this was our wedding party."

Ben put his arms around Ellen's waist and kissed her.

Charles picked up the tablecloth I had dropped onto the pile of damp towels, shook it out, and handed two of the corners to Tony. They raised their arms so that the tablecloth made a *chuppah*—a wedding canopy— above Ben and Ellen. I gathered the cousins, who were playing nearby, and drew them into a circle around the newly married couple. Charlie sang, "When I get older, losing my hair, many years from now . . ." Ben took Ellen in his arms and danced beneath the chuppah.

As we sang and danced, some of the other groups leaving the beach with their chairs and towels paused to enjoy our antics. We spun faster and faster around the wedding couple, our bare feet kicking up sand, the day's powerful mixture of memory, sadness, reunion, lifting us off.

Charles and Sissy were the last to leave, on their way to catch a flight back to Washington so Sissy could teach the next day. Josh, Hannah, Eli, and I were staying over to drive down to Laguna Beach and spend time with my mother. After over a year's estrangement, I was ready to take up my relationship with her again. The unveiling seemed the right moment, an ending to some things and a beginning for others.

Sissy was crouched in the backseat of the rental car, giving baby Abe a fresh diaper for the trip. Charlie watched her, his arm propped on the open door. I drew back, wishing they didn't have to go.

"Come visit us in New York as soon as you can," I said. "Little Abe needs to hang out with his cousins."

Sissy turned. "And his godmother."

We waved them off down the street that ran between the beach and our hotel. Standing barefoot, our calves caked with sand, Josh, Hannah, Eli, and I were alone again. I rested against Josh, and he put his arms around me. Hannah and Eli leaned into us. We were quiet. We were a family.

That night, past midnight, I woke and I went outside to watch the ocean where the moon threw a bright path on the water all the way back to land. On the street below, Rollerbladers skated by. Inside my family slept.

I went back into the room, took hotel stationery from a desk drawer, and found two blankets in the armoire near the pull-out sofa where Hannah and Eli were curled into two tight balls. I slipped back through the balcony door, pulled it shut behind me, and settled down at the patio table with one blanket around my legs and the other across my shoulders like a shawl. There was a chill in the air, but I was tucked in and warm.

I sat for a while with my hands folded in my lap and let my mind drift. Then I opened the leather folder of stationery and withdrew the pen from its loop. I flattened out a single sheet of paper, put the date in the right-hand corner, and wrote by the moonlight above.

*April 5, 1989*

*Dear Pop,*
 *Today we gathered at your grave to bless your stone. Your family, with new members. Sissy and Charles had their baby, a boy, and of course*

they named him Abe. Ellen married Ben, and they're talking about children, too. All good news that I know would make you happy.

Pop, things were pretty tough for me after you died. Maybe I took on
too much of your dying for my own good. I began to share a part of my
skin with you. I don't know if it was the right thing or the wrong thing to
grow so close, but I do know that the pain afterwards was tremendous,
and I had a hard time finding a way to go on. I had to sort out parts of
you to take into myself and keep, and parts of you to let go of forever. To
do that I had to give a lot of thought to the shame you harbored in your
life, your belief that you had been associated with something evil.

I realized that your belief led you both to deny the existence of evil and
at the same time be obsessed with exposing it. Somehow, growing up as
your daughter, I absorbed this conflict from you. On the one hand I chose
a career in which I try to expose bad deeds, and yet it took me a shocking
amount of time to face the awful thing plainly in front of me when my
own house was burned down by a vicious anti-Semite. I'm amazed by the
thread between your fire and my fire, fifty-six years apart.

There's one more thing that strikes me in all this. You were so determined to confess the truth before you died. To do that, you had to find the
courage to face up to what you had tried to deny your whole life, the evil
you believed you harbored inside. Your courage in doing that changed me
for life. I am now less frightened of evil, more willing to see it, and therefore more able to fight it. Because of that, because of what I learned from
you as you were dying, I have my home back.

So, thank you, Pop, for this part of my inheritance. I suppose we all
need courage to look at the truth of the story we carry forward, a story
always seeking a beginning and an end.

I love you, Pop. I miss you. I always will.

# ACKNOWLEDGMENTS

The daily work of writing can feel like repeatedly walking off the end of a pier. Keeping at it would be impossible without the help of family and friends. I am deeply and happily indebted to Jane Rosenman, my editor at Scribner's, a writer's dream with her incisive but gentle touch; Susan Moldow, publisher extraordinaire; Lorraine Bodger, whose loving dedication to making words do their work is indefatigable; Elizabeth Kaplan, the most optimistic and energetic agent a writer could hope for; Susan Dalsimer, who helped every single step of the way; Michael Dorris, who dogged me until I gave him pages; Amy Entelis, the sanest person on the face of the earth; Jonathan Galassi, who kindly built confidence in a novice; Gates Gill, who has an uncanny gift for knowing what other people need to do and the generosity to risk telling them; Elizabeth Leiman Kraiem, for her wisdom in the ways of Jewish liturgy; Rabbi Roly Matalon, who spoke plainly to me about anti-Semitism; Rabbi Marshall Meyer, of blessed memory, my first teacher of Judaism; Julie Michaels, for her unflappable good sense; Faith Sale, my first writing teacher, who touched hundreds of millions of words in her too-short life; Martha Saxton, whose way of being a friend is synonymous with the word "trust"; Meredith White, an angel on earth, who sent me home to write; Ed Wenner, who loved me enough to tell the truth of his life; Sim Wenner, who gave me my first typewriter and first model of the writer's life; Jann Wenner, sweet and generous brother, great reader, constant friend; Merlyn Ruddell, my cherished sister and partner in so many things; and above all, my funny, loving, encouraging, magnificent husband, Gil Eisner, who gives everything meaning; and our two glorious children, Jake and Sophie, who bring treasures home to us at the end of each working day.

# ABOUT THE AUTHOR

Before turning to fiction, Kate Wenner was a print and television journalist, who won many professional awards in her fourteen years as a producer for ABC's *20/20*. She has traveled extensively as a journalist, student, and volunteer. Ms. Wenner worked for a year in a communal village in Tanzania and described that experience in her book *Shamba Letu*. As the recipient of a Michael Rockefeller Memorial Fellowship, she spent a year in a small village in the Andes in Peru, and traveled throughout Central and South America. Ms. Wenner was awarded a CAPS Grant for Fiction. She now lives in New York City with her husband, a painter and freelance illustrator, and their two teenage children.

Printed in the United States
By Bookmasters